Other Titles by Cheryl Brooks

Echoes From the Deep
Dreams From the Deep
Justice From the Deep
Cowboy Delight
Cowboy Heaven
Must Love Cowboys
Unbridled: Unlikely Lovers Book 1
Uninhibited: Unlikely Lovers Book 2
Undeniable: Unlikely Lovers Book 3
Unrivaled: Unlikely Lovers Book 4
The Cat Star Chronicles: Rebel
The Cat Star Chronicles: Wildcat
The Cat Star Chronicles: Stud
The Cat Star Chronicles: Virgin
The Cat Star Chronicles: Hero
The Cat Star Chronicles: Fugitive
The Cat Star Chronicles: Outcast
The Cat Star Chronicles: Rogue
The Cat Star Chronicles: Warrior
The Cat Star Chronicles: Slave
The Cat Star Chronicles Bundle: Slave, Warrior & Rogue
Sharing (Sextet Anthology)
Entanglements (Sextet Anthology)
Occupational Hazards (Sextet Anthology)
Mistletoe & Ménage (Sextet Anthology)
Dirty Dancing (Sextet Anthology)
Small, Medium, & Large (Sextet Presents)
The Lady Takes a Pair (Sextet Presents)
A Tale of Two Knights (Sextet Presents)
Midnight in Reno
If You Could Read My Mind (writing as Samantha R. Michaels

Soul Survivors Book 3

Justice From the Deep

CHERYL BROOKS

DERRYMANE PRESS

Derrymane
Press

Justice From the Deep
Soul Survivors Book 3
by Cheryl Brooks
Published by Derrymane Press
Copyright © 2017 Cheryl Brooks.
Cover design by Dragonfly Press Design
Cover images by Adobe Stock
ISBN-13: 978-0-9864274-7-3

www.cherylbrooksonline.com

For Jacques, Carl, and Neil

ACKNOWLEDGEMENTS

My heartfelt thanks go out to:
My terrific critique partners, Nan Reinhardt, T.C. Winters, and Sandy James.
My keen-eyed beta reader, Mellanie Szereto.
My buddies in IRWA for their support and encouragement.
My friends and family for their love and understanding.
And Google Earth for helping me find my way around County Clare.
I couldn't have done this without you!

Without her, the next generation of humankind could be the last.

Chapter 1

THE DRIVE FROM THE CLIFFS OF MOHER TO LISCANNOR TOOK ONLY A few minutes, but to Susan Maxwell, the trip might as well have taken a week. Her feet dragged as she walked down to the docks when her step should have been springy and light. She should have been pleased to see the boat and its crew. They had, after all, plucked her and two other women from a life raft after their plane crashed into the sea off the west coast of Ireland.

"And there she is," Susan muttered as she approached the dock. The *Branwyn Eostre* rocked gently at her moorings, her blue and white hull reflecting off the waves. The two crewmen were busy on deck, undoubtedly tucking their craft in for the night.

Seamus Quinn and Ian… Had she ever heard Ian's surname? She didn't think so. If she had, it didn't register. Not like the name of the boat itself, which, according to her captain, was derived from Branwyn, the goddess of love, sexuality, and the sea and Eostre, the goddess of spring, rebirth, fertility, and new beginnings.

New beginnings, hell.

"Every ending is a new beginning."

"Shut up," Susan said absently. She hadn't quite gotten the hang of ignoring the voices that had taken up residence in her head in the wake of the crash. Cleona Mahoney, one of her fellow survivors, had told her they would help her to—Susan couldn't help but chuckle—save the world.

Yeah, right. How can I save the world when I couldn't even save the man I love?

"Forget that," she whispered aloud. "He isn't in the group."

That omission had been the unkindest cut of all. When she might have drawn comfort from hearing Chuck's voice, it had been denied her, save for those few frantic moments before the plane went down.

One of the first flights she'd been on as an attendant had been with him.

"You're who?" she'd asked. "Chuck Yeager? Seriously?"

It had seemed like such a joke at the time, one Chuck had used to his advantage on frequent occasions, although he'd only been named after the famous aviator. His last name was actually Travers, the "Charles Yeager" having its source in his parents' expectations of him—not that he'd ever had the chance to be anything but a pilot, given the number of them in his family.

She and Chuck had enjoyed an intense, passionate affair that ended shortly before he met his future wife. Although he and Susan had remained good friends, he had moved on to find love with another, whereas Susan never had. Chuck and his wife lived with their two children in a big old house in southern Maryland. Susan still lived alone in the same Newark apartment, partly because she'd never met anyone who measured up to Chuck, but mostly because she'd never really stopped loving him.

She'd never met any of Chuck's family, but at least they were still alive to mourn him. Entire families had been aboard that plane, all of them lost along with the 747's full complement of passengers and crew—with three exceptions. Four, if you included the dog.

Susan still wished she'd been among the dead. Twice now, she'd stood on the edge of the cliffs gazing down at the rocks while mentally calling out to Chuck's spirit. Refusing to accept the ensuing silence on her first visit, she'd gone back there again. Redoubling her efforts, she concentrated on him so hard she could almost see his face, but if he was there, he wasn't talking.

How could she have received a telepathic communication from him when he was alive and he not be among the others after his death? Both times, Cleona had interrupted Susan's attempts to contact him, although whether her intervention was fortunate or unfortunate remained to be seen.

And now, instead of airplanes, she'd been told to seek out a boat.

Great.

Seamus, the younger of the two men, glanced up from his task and swept off his cap, revealing a thatch of dark brown curls. "Well, now… I wouldn't have thought we'd be seeing you again."

"Me either," Susan replied. "But here I am." She drew in a fortifying breath. "I was told to hire your boat."

An eyebrow rose as he strolled over to the port side. "And who would've told you that?"

Another sigh. "Cleona. She said I was supposed to find you and hire your boat."

"Did she happen to say why?"

"No, she didn't." Saving the world wasn't going to cut it as an excuse. Not with this guy—especially since she didn't fully grasp the need herself. "I think…" She straightened as an explanation suddenly occurred to her. "I think she thought it would help me to, um…recover."

With a slow nod, he rubbed his chin in a contemplative manner. "I see. Would you be wanting it tomorrow? We've an hour or so free in the afternoon."

"Whenever," she said with a shrug. "I'm not really sure it matters."

He glanced toward the horizon. "Or would now be a better time?"

She was still staring at him when she realized her mouth had dropped open. "N–no. I don't think so." The mere thought of being out to sea at night set off a shiver.

"Just as well," he said. "It'll be getting dark soon, and there's some weather moving in." He cocked his head. "You said you needed to recover. You look fine to me—a bit pale, perhaps, but—"

"Please don't start that again."

A smile tugged the corner of his mouth. "Start what?"

"That crap about redheaded women being fierce."

"Ah, but it's true, isn't it?" His eyes narrowed to a squint. "You were plenty fierce before." His gaze shifted toward the top of her head. "And you're still a ginger."

"Hmm…" She pressed her lips into a firm line. This was a

conversation she truly didn't want to have. "How do you know the color didn't come from a bottle?"

The boat rocked as he took a step closer and peered up at her. "It's been almost two weeks since that plane went down, and the roots of your hair look to be the same shade as the ends. Something tells me you wouldn't have been in any mood to dye your hair."

He was right, of course. As adrift as she'd felt, she barely had the inclination to wash and comb it.

"Adrift, hell. You're clinically depressed. And rightly so."

The shrink was talking to her again. She had to bite her lip to keep from retorting aloud. She took a moment to regroup before saying, "You're probably right."

"So tomorrow, then? At about three?"

She nodded. "That should work." Deeming the conversation over, she turned to go.

"Hold on." Within seconds, he'd climbed nimbly up the ladder and hopped onto the quay. "Can I get a phone number in case we need to call you?"

She stood there for a long moment. *I'm gaping again.*

"You have a mobile phone, don't you?"

Actually, she had two. One that worked, and one that didn't. Oddly enough, she didn't know the correct number for dialing either of them. Nevertheless, she fished through her purse for the phone the airline had given her. The other one was back at her hotel in a bag of rice. She didn't know what she'd hoped to accomplish by trying to dry out some stranger's phone, but it had given her something to focus on at a time when her life had lost any semblance of order.

"Nice purse," he commented.

She glanced up at him in surprise. Granted, it was a Gucci, but why a fisherman would notice such a thing defied logic. "The airline people gave it to me in London." Her fingers touched on the smooth plastic of her phone. "Here it is. Hold on while I look up the number." Something as simple as a phone number should've been easy to remember, but for some strange reason, she hadn't been able to commit it to memory.

"Why don't you just call mine?" he suggested.

Deeming it easier than delving into the settings on her own device, she tapped in the numbers as he rattled them off, then pressed the Send icon. Within moments, his phone rang—playing an ordinary ringtone, as opposed to something more distinctively Irish.

"We're connected," he said, checking his phone. "All we have to do is look under Recent Calls."

So simple... Unlike Cleona's talents. She'd been using Ireland's stone towers to communicate with Susan, which was weird as all get-out, but was, thus far, their only mode of contact, if somewhat inconvenient. Not only did Susan have to climb to the top of O'Brien's Tower, she had to pay the two-euro admission fee every time they needed to talk. Still, as a means of proving that something spooky was going on, such "calls" were unsurpassed. At least it proved she wasn't losing her mind.

Or did it? Perhaps their peculiar abilities were a sign of mutual insanity. She waited a moment for the shrink to chime in—which, of course, he didn't. None of her ghostly cohorts ever answered questions on demand. They only made random comments whenever the spirit—her choice of words elicited a mental eye roll—moved them. They hadn't said anything when she'd stood at the edge of the cliff. She'd told Cleona that the cliffs were the only place she could find peace, when what she'd really meant was that the voices ceased as she approached the edge. Maybe it was their way of trying *not* to goad her into jumping—or holding their collective breath to see whether she would.

"Um...where are you staying?"

"I'm at the Cliffs of Moher Hotel." The description had intrigued her—*Unassuming lodging with restaurant and bar*. You couldn't go wrong with a place like that—aside from the fact that it was the only hotel in Liscannor that wasn't booked solid when she arrived.

"So you decided not to stay on in London?"

She shook her head. "I was there for about a week. I tried to avoid this place, but it kept calling to me."

If he thought her reasoning was strange, he was at least tactful enough hold his tongue. "It's a nice enough hotel," he said. "And

I'm not a bit surprised you came back here."

Susan waited for the obvious quip about being anxious to see him again. But once more, he didn't comment. "Oh? Why is that?'

His gaze swept the bay and the surrounding village. "There's a kind of magic to this place. I've lived here all my life and I still can't explain it—although the proximity of St. Brigid's well might have something to do with it." His eyes met hers once again. "Have you been to the well?"

"No—at least, not yet." She had passed by the site a number of times. Even without a sign to point the way, the statue of St. Brigid standing in her glass case by the roadside was hard to miss. Thus far, however, Susan's only comfort had been walking along the cliffs rather than visiting the local holy places. She wondered why. In the wake of such a terrifying disaster, she ought to have sought solace in every shrine in Ireland.

"You should go," he urged. "It's not far from here. People visit from all over. Even without the religious aspect, it's an interesting spot. Very soothing to the soul."

She nodded. "I'll do that."

Ireland itself had provided a measure of healing. The sweeping vistas of County Clare contrasted with neat, whitewashed buildings, and a pub sat right beside the site of the holy well, the perfect mix of magic, practicality, and natural beauty. The air was clear and fresh, carrying with it the faint tang of the sea, which was the only clue that the ocean was so near. No lawns sloped down to a sandy beach; the land was well above sea level, as the height of the cliffs demonstrated so vividly.

"I could take you there now if you like," Seamus said after glancing at the horizon once again.

Susan smiled to herself, thinking that perhaps it was a seaman's habit to consult the sky rather than his watch to mark the time of day. "That's very kind of you, but I know the way. And I have a car." Truth be told, one of her excursions to the cliffs had been accomplished on foot. Walking exercised the body and calmed the mind—except when her hitchhiking ghosts decided to chime in. Would they be as quiet at the well as they were on the cliffs? Either way, she'd have bet money that her resident shrink would tell her that visiting the well was good therapy.

"It is."

Figured that would get you going again.

Seamus shifted from one foot to the other as his smile slowly broadened. "You misunderstand me."

Deliberately, perhaps. Cleona had seemed to think Seamus could aid them in their quest to save the world; no doubt she would read Susan the riot act for pushing him away. "Okay, then. If you really want to take me there, I have no objection to allowing you to do so."

"Your enthusiasm is bowling me over," he said with a mocking grin. "But I'll take that as a yes."

"See now… That wasn't so hard, was it?"

Oh, hush up.

He offered her his arm. "Shall we?"

"Don't you have to do more, er…boat maintenance before you go?"

"Ian will take care of the rest. We were nearly done anyway." Turning toward the boat, he waved at his shipmate. "Oy, Ian! We'll be heading out now. I got us a three o'clock for tomorrow."

Ian waved back. "Is that the ginger Yank, then?"

"Aye, it is. Told you she'd be back, didn't I?"

"That you did." Ian nodded toward Susan. "Good to see you, lass. You look a mite better than you did the last time we saw you."

"I'm doing okay," she said. "At least, as well as I can be."

With a wag of his head, he went on, "A terrible business, that. Still amazed anyone survived. The investigators talked to us the other day. Said it was a miracle, and I didn't argue with them."

"Investigators? Really?"

"Aye. Asked us to tell them everything we remember—not that our story would be any different from what any other witnesses could've told them. Just checking the facts, I'll wager."

"I suppose so." Susan shouldn't have been surprised. She'd been interviewed at length in the aftermath, although "interrogated" would have been a more apt description.

No. That was too harsh. "Debriefed" was closer to the truth.

"We're going up to St. Brigid's well," Seamus said, filling the gap in the conversation. "She hasn't seen it yet."

Ian nodded. "An excellent notion. We could all stand a bit of spiritual guidance after such a tragedy."

Susan nearly laughed out loud at Ian's choice of words. Somehow she doubted either man suspected she was already carrying around her own private pack of spiritual guides, none of whom had seemed particularly religious. Thus far, the shrink had been the most vocal, leading her to assume he'd been charged with the task of keeping her from offing herself long enough to—she cringed at the thought—save the world.

Perhaps the other spirits would help her with the actual planet-saving.

Chapter 2

SEAMUS GLANCED AT SUSAN BEFORE ADDING, "OR SPIRITUAL comfort" to Ian's comment. He would've given a lot to have spent the past several days comforting her rather than carrying on with business as usual. Not when meeting her meant that nothing would ever be the same.

No one ever told him what it would be like to finally find the right woman. He'd never known what to expect—what signals to watch out for or how he would feel, let alone that it would occur as the result of one of the all-time most improbable chance encounters. He'd known she was the one from the moment he laid eyes on her. Stripping off his sweater to wrap it around her shivering shoulders on the day of the crash had seemed perfectly natural—to the point that he'd all but ignored the other two women's needs. He'd only been recalled to his senses when the blond woman—Jillian Dulaine, her name was—had asked if he had any blankets.

Their time together had been brief, not allowing for much conversation. Even so, he could scarcely mind what he was doing while she was aboard, and she hadn't been far from his thoughts ever since. He'd read every scrap of information about the crash in the press and online, all the while hoping that someday, somehow, he might reconnect with her.

And now, here she was, asking to charter his boat.

What are the odds?

The offer to take her to the well had been prompted by his needs rather than hers. She intrigued him in a way he couldn't begin to explain. He wasn't about to let her out of his sight now.

He gestured toward the car park. "Shall we?"

Susan replied with a somewhat absent nod and turned away from the dock with a vague wave of farewell at Ian. Despite his attraction to her, she obviously wasn't feeling it on her end. At least, not yet. Push her too hard and she never would.

He led the way to his car, an aging Vauxhall Astra that was even less conducive to picking up women than the *Branwyn Eostre*. He opened the door for her and waited until she fastened her safety belt before closing the door.

She shifted in her seat, seeming hesitant and perhaps a bit uncomfortable before aiming a brittle smile at him as he climbed in on the driver's side. "Who's the captain? You or Ian?"

"The boat was my dad's. Ian used to work the boat with him, and I kept him on after Dad died, so I guess you could say I'm the captain now." He grinned as he started the engine. "Ian is captain in practice, though. More experience."

She nodded, her gaze drifting from his face as her smile faded. "I don't know if I ever thanked you guys for rescuing us. I'm sorry if I didn't, but thank you. We really appreciated you coming so quickly."

"No need to thank us," he said as he pulled out of the parking space. "It's all a part of life at sea. You help whenever you can, knowing it might be you that needs help the next time."

"I suppose so." Her voice still sounded rather faint, lacking the firm diction that had characterized her tone on the day of the crash. "It's a shame everyone doesn't live by that code."

"I can't argue with that." He fished around for a topic of conversation that wouldn't be too personal or too prying. "I'm assuming the airline gave you some time off. How long will you be in Liscannor?"

"Maybe forever—although I'll have to find someplace else to stay if I do. I don't know. I'd like to go home—and I probably will. Just not yet."

Perhaps there was hope for him after all. "Why the delay? Not wanting to get on another plane?"

Her derisive snort surprised him. "If that were the only issue, I'd have left already."

"How so?"

"I–I lost someone on that plane. I'm not over it yet. I may never be, even though Cleona said we were—" She stopped abruptly, catching her lower lip between her teeth.

"She said you were what?"

Her laugh was sharp and mirthless. "I'd better not say. You probably already think I'm about to go off the deep end or else you wouldn't be taking me to a shrine."

"I don't think anything of the kind, although healing *is* St. Brigid's specialty."

With another absent nod, she turned toward the side window. "I finally figured out why this place looks so strange to me."

After the mention of insanity, Seamus thought it best to humor her abrupt change of topic. "How so?"

"The houses and barns are distinctively Irish, but it's the lack of trees that makes it seem so odd—almost like driving through Kansas or Colorado. A vast, treeless expanse of gently rolling hills."

"I've never thought about it, myself. That's just the way it is around here."

She was right, though. Except for the tree-covered hillside across the road from the well and the small grove behind the well itself, there were no woods or forests to speak of, only the occasional isolated tree scattered amid green pastures and the ever-present gorse. Funny how he'd never considered it strange until now.

"There's the well." He turned left onto the road that ran past the cemetery behind the well and pulled into the tiny parking space by the steps. Continuing to play the gentleman—his mum would've fussed if he'd been anything less—he got out and went round the car to open the door for her. She took his hand without comment, although considering the graceful manner in which she rose to her feet, she hadn't needed his help. Two weeks prior, she would've declined his offer with a disdainful glance. She'd been angry back then, perhaps because of the loss of the person she'd mentioned. Who was it? A lover? A friend? A family member? She hadn't said, and he debated the wisdom of asking her to explain.

Deeming it best to avoid the cemetery for now, he steered her toward the gate in the stone wall that encircled the well. St. Brigid stood in her glass case atop a dais of stone with shrubs and flowers massed near her feet. He'd always thought of the statue as being the saint herself, perhaps because of the serenity he felt whenever he gazed up at her face.

Susan walked around the statue, studying it from every angle and taking pictures as any dutiful tourist would have done. When she followed him into the cave-like entrance to the well, she seemed properly awed by the hundreds of tokens left there by visitors and worshipers alike, but it was the water pouring into the well from the niche in the stone wall that held her transfixed.

He knew the feeling. The sunlight glinting on the water from the opening above and the trickling sound echoing on the walls of the cave combined for an effect that was as mesmerizing as it was soothing. He'd stood there for what had to have been hours after his father's funeral, and he wasn't the least bit surprised when Susan knelt down and cupped her hand to scoop up some of the water. As she stood and held out her hand, allowing the water to sieve through her fingers, the snapshot of his father that Seamus and his mother had placed on the wall caught his eye. The photo had already begun to fade, but his father's smile and twinkling eyes were as warm and genuine as ever.

It wasn't until he felt Susan standing beside him that he realized he'd been staring at the picture almost as long as she'd been captivated by the water.

With a smile and a bit of a blush, he nodded toward the photo. "That's my dad. Died about four years ago. That was taken not long before he passed."

Susan peered at the photo. "Died fairly young, then?"

"Aye. He was only fifty-four. Lung cancer—most likely from smoking, they said. Never picked up the habit myself."

"Neither did I." She laughed again, a self-deprecating, ironic sort of laugh. "Always tried to live a healthy lifestyle and then nearly got myself killed in a plane crash."

"But you didn't die," he pointed out. "Must be your reward for all that healthy living."

This time, her laugh was more of a snort. "If you can call it a reward. I'm not so sure it doesn't qualify as a punishment."

"Mum felt the same way. Always hoped she would pass before my dad. Said she didn't want to face living without him."

"And how is she now?"

"Well enough," he replied. "Hasn't found a new man yet, mainly because she hasn't bothered to look."

Seamus had a similar problem himself. One severely broken heart had put him off the idea of taking a wife. He might have dated and flirted a bit since then, but never once had he felt the need to take the first step in a more serious direction. Susan, however, had reawakened the inclination. He could scarcely believe his luck in her actually seeking him out, especially since he'd already begun the process of relegating her to the status of the one that got away.

"Four years, you said. I wonder…how long does it take?"

"Before your heart mends, you mean?" With her nod, he thought for a moment before replying. "Sometimes never, I suppose. But hopefully sooner rather than later."

"That sounds pretty vague." Her wry smile gave him a tiny ray of hope. "You're not much help, are you?"

"None at all," he declared, while at the same time marking her slight change of attitude with approval. *More like the fierce ginger I remember.* "Would you like to see the rest of the grounds? It's quite pretty up on the hill." Until you came to the cemetery, although as cemeteries went, St. Brigid's was more serene than spooky.

"I'd like that," she said, her voice whisper-soft once again.

Not missing another opportunity to take her by the hand, he led her out into the sunlight and up the steps, which were flanked by beds filled with more shrubs and flowers.

"It's very beautiful here," she said. "Someone obviously tends the grounds with lots of loving care."

"Aye, they do. I've been known to lend a hand myself, although I've had less time of late." He should make that time, though. Simply being near the well had always improved his sense of well-being.

On the other hand, being near Susan had done something very similar.

* * * *

Seamus was a decent sort, really. Susan had to admit she'd misjudged him. He wasn't an obnoxious flirt. He was a man who tended shrines and drew his livelihood from the sea.

The sea…

Susan's body had flooded with warmth the moment she touched the water. Not the cross or the stones or the statues or the flowering plants… No. The water was what had brought the voices in her head back to the fore.

"Do you feel it?" one of them asked. *"The oneness with our water planet?"*

Go away, she admonished. *I feel happier here, that's all.*

"You feel the heat, though. Don't you?"

Yes, I do. But I don't think it means what you think it means. She'd nearly laughed aloud when that quote from *The Princess Bride* resurfaced in her mind, particularly since she never dreamed she would ever be amused by anything again.

"You might be surprised," said one.

"Let it flow," said another.

She'd stood and turned abruptly away from the well only to find Seamus staring at one of the many photographs adorning the wall of the grotto. His response to her presence had given her an easy means to escape the nagging voices.

Now, as she and Seamus strolled across the grassy hill above the well, she felt at peace, a feeling similar the way she felt while standing at the edge of the cliffs. Except that at the cliffs, the voices had let her be.

Cleona had advised her to embrace the madness of hearing voices. Susan wanted to reject it completely. She was being selfish, which was the only way she could view the matter now that she knew she was supposed to help save the world.

Ridiculous.

Yet the supernatural aspects of the crash and its aftermath continued to haunt her. She'd heard Chuck's voice as though he'd been standing right beside her, urging her to do what she could to save herself and as many of the passengers as possible. It didn't seem fair that all she could have of him was his last ditch attempt to save her when he seemed bent on destroying everyone else aboard that plane—that and some stranger's cell phone. She'd completely forgotten about the phone until finding it in her pocket when they reached Inisheer. She probably should've given it to the airline officials, but it was one of the last things Chuck had touched, and she was reluctant to part with it. Being doused with seawater had probably rendered it inoperable anyway—worthless to anyone except her.

He'd succeeded, though. She was alive and well, walking the green hills of Ireland. Too bad she hadn't been able to save any of the others, although she suspected Cleona might have been in her section. She still wasn't sure about that. Perhaps she never would be.

Seamus was an excellent guide, providing a running commentary on the saint and various aspects of the shrine and the grounds. Unfortunately, Susan doubted she would retain even half of the information. Crossing the small lawn, she laid a hand on the tall, lichen-covered cross and felt nothing. No spiritual messages, no supernatural powers. Clearly, water had to be involved for anything of that nature. Had Cleona known how important water would be when she told Susan to charter a boat? Perhaps she did, especially since she claimed to have her own set of voices to tell her such things.

In a way, Susan was envious of Cleona. Her voices had at least been helpful. Susan's had been annoying enough to make her consider jumping off a cliff.

Seamus had also irritated her at first. Now his accent and cheerful demeanor seemed mildly therapeutic. He was good company, and she had no need to wonder what his wife or girlfriend might think about them being out together. At least, she didn't think he was involved with anyone. Had he told her he was single? She couldn't remember.

Spending time with Chuck had been completely different. Although neither of them had been attached at the time, they'd been discreet to the point that very few people knew they were seeing each other. Even if it *had* been common knowledge, with the plethora of clandestine affairs going on around them, their romance probably wouldn't have raised any eyebrows, and it was ancient history now. Nevertheless, she did her best to avoid drawing attention to the number of his flights she bid on each month. She might only get one of her choices, but simply being on the same plane with Chuck made her feel whole again. Either way, they were still good friends—friends with a closeness of spirit that had culminated in his last desperate plea.

Had he known he was going to crash the plane before they boarded? Why hadn't he warned her? For that matter, why hadn't he warned the airline or called the police? He could've refused to fly, or at least delayed the flight in some way. All she'd gotten from him was that he had to do it or more people would die, including his family. How had he known that? For the thousandth time since the crash, she wished his voice were among the others. He could've told her something useful, or at least comforting. Her onboard shrink had been analytical and his advice was probably sound, but for pity's sake, why couldn't he have been Chuck?

Seamus cleared his throat in a you-really-aren't-paying-attention-to-me-are-you manner.

"Sorry. Woolgathering." Did anyone ever use that term anymore? Sheep shearers, perhaps? Maybe Cleona's boyfriend the sheep farmer used it. Or—heaven forbid—one of her resident voices.

"I asked if you were hungry. I thought we might stop in at a pub."

Jesus. First the excursion to the well and now dinner. Wasn't it enough that she'd hired his boat for the morrow?

The morrow? Yet another archaic phrase. One of her voice buddies must be positively ancient. Or Irish, which would make as much sense. An incredibly old Irishman. Or woman. Their genders weren't always easy to identify at first. In the beginning, she'd only assumed the shrink was male because he tended to be somewhat condescending. She made herself a promise to call Cleona as soon as she got back to her hotel. She needed more particulars if she was going to be of any help at all in the "saving the world" scheme.

"Hungry…"

A tiny grin quirked his lips. "You know… For food?"

Truth be told, she wasn't hungry for much of anything. Food had lost most of its appeal, and she'd picked at every meal since the crash, whether it was served in a fancy London eatery or one of Liscannor's excellent pubs. However, a glance at her watch at least proved it was dinnertime.

"I should probably eat something," she conceded, frowning. "Now that you mention it, I'm not sure I ever had lunch." Breakfast was a bit of a blur—along with most recent events. She blamed the extra souls she'd acquired, whether they were truly responsible or not.

"Such enthusiasm," Seamus murmured as he steered her toward his car. "Good thing my company isn't responsible for your lack of interest."

"And how would you know that?"

"I'm fairly certain I wasn't on your mind at lunchtime."

"Mmm… You're wrong about that. I *was* thinking about you— and how much I dreaded seeing you again."

He drew back, pressing a fist to his chest in dramatic protest. "You wound me, lass. You truly do."

"Yeah, right," she drawled. "Like my opinion really matters."

Astonishingly, he took her hand and raised it to his lips. "You'd be surprised how much."

Chapter 3

THERE. HE'D SAID IT. THE BALL, AS THE SAYING WENT, WAS NOW IN her court. Even though it was the very last thing he wanted to do, he released her hand and started toward the car park.

The weather he'd mentioned earlier picked up speed and met them at the car. Occasional raindrops quickly became a torrent as they hurried inside and slammed the doors against the downpour.

What was it about a closed vehicle in a rainstorm? Isolating them from the weather and the rest of the world, creating a sense of intimacy where there had previously been none. "Didn't get too wet, did you?"

"Not enough to matter." She punctuated her sentence with a short laugh before adding, "Nothing like being dunked in the Atlantic."

"Been dumped in the drink a few times myself. Not pleasant in any weather."

A frown creased her brow. "Guess you know what that's like, then."

"Aye. A big swell took me over once—that was the worst. Another time or two was due to my own carelessness." Seamus would have preferred to have more in common with her than a dip in the sea, but it was a start.

"Who saved you?"

"My dad once, Ian another, and the third, well, I suppose you could say I saved myself."

"Sounds like you're getting better at it. Saving yourself, I mean."

He shrugged. "Dunno about that. Experience doesn't always guarantee a good outcome." With a flash of lightning and a deep roll of thunder, the storm intensified. "There's a great place to get out of the rain not far from here, and I know the fish is fresh because I caught it myself. D'you like fish?"

"Not especially. Although I'd rather eat them than have them eat me—as long as they don't taste fishy."

"Freshness makes all the difference in the world," he said. "You'll see." He reminded himself that Susan had been in England or Ireland long enough to have sampled the local fare, much of which had its origins in the sea. If she preferred lamb or pork, being a fisherman would be a much harder sell, even though his living was supplemented by hauling tourists around. He shuddered to think what he'd have missed if he'd been out on an extended fishing trip instead of doing the Cliffs of Moher run.

Fate must have taken a hand in the matter. Granted, connecting with Susan Maxwell might take him to a few places he'd just as soon not go, but it was every bit as likely that his life had taken a serious turn for the better.

He started the car and headed south toward Liscannor. Although there were several good restaurants in the area, this first dinner needed to be special, and he was guaranteed a table—as well as a catch of the day he'd caught himself—at one particular pub, no matter how busy the place might be.

Sometimes, it paid to have an in with the chef—and the owner.

"We'll head for my mum's place, then," he said. "Best fish in County Clare."

Her expression was even more aghast than her subsequent tone. "Your mother's house? I don't think—"

"Relax. It's her pub, not her house. Mum tends the bar and my sister is the cook—or chef, as she prefers to be called—and I've a cousin who's a waitress."

"You mean Quinn's on the main street?"

"The very one."

"Funny, I've had lunch there twice and never made the connection."

"No reason you should have," he said. "Quinn is a fairly common surname in these parts." He grinned. "Got lots of aunts and uncles and cousins."

"Must be nice. I don't have a lot of...family." Her halting speech hinted that this was a bit of a sore spot for her. Having a large family could be awkward at times—it was difficult to go anywhere without running into one relative or other who knew his history and was quite willing to add another chapter to the saga—but it was also comforting to know that in times of trouble, Mother Mary wasn't the only one he had to call on for words of wisdom.

"Aye, it is. Wouldn't know what to do without them. So...no brothers or sisters?"

"One brother," she replied. "He lives in Seattle now—we were originally from Miami—and he's married with a young son. Given my line of work, it's no wonder we don't see each other very often. My father died when I was seventeen. Mom never remarried, although she's had a few boyfriends. I have an aunt and some cousins, but again, we don't see each other much. I can't remember the exact date of our last family reunion—if you could call it that— but it had to have been when I was in grade school."

Seamus couldn't conceive of being that separated from family and friends, but then, the lifestyle in Liscannor was a far cry from life in the States. Even relatives living on the east coast of Ireland wouldn't have been too distant to visit.

"Strange, I'd have thought working for an airline would help you get around more than that," he said as he turned the car onto Main Street.

"Not when you're mostly flying the overseas routes. I haven't flown out of Miami in ages, and I never *have* worked a flight to Seattle."

"But you can choose, can't you?"

"Yes, but the bidding goes by seniority. I'm not all that 'senior,' so I mostly get the leftovers."

He nodded and pulled into the parking space near the pub's entrance. "We're here," he announced. "And from the looks of it, we shouldn't have any trouble getting a table."

For a Friday evening, Quinn's wasn't too crowded. However, business would pick up once the music started. Would she stick around long enough to hear him play? Maybe, although the question first and foremost in his mind was whether she would stay through dinner. Granted, her car was still parked at the dock, but because everything in Liscannor was within walking distance—her hotel was just down the street—not having transportation wouldn't necessarily prevent her from leaving. And if she left during the show, he couldn't exactly hop down from the bandstand and run after her.

Well, he *could.* Unfortunately, nearly everyone in the pub, save for a few tourists, had known him from birth, which meant the good-natured harassment would be instantaneous and prolonged. Simply walking in with a gorgeous ginger was enough to garner unwanted attention. Too bad he didn't have the time to take her someplace where he was completely unknown—although even in those places, someone might recognize her from the news. The stories about the crash hadn't even begun to die down as the names of the deceased were released and the reactions of their loved ones were reported.

He hadn't lost anyone in the crash, although he knew others who had. Local memorial services had been held even though none of the dead that had been identified were connected to Liscannor's residents, and the likelihood of any being found decreased with each passing day. According to reports, the plane had been so badly broken up that parts of it were strewn across a vast area of the ocean floor. Several crash victims had washed up at the base of the cliffs, most of them so battered by the rocks that they were as yet unidentified. Seamus, for one, was very glad that the people he and Ian had picked up were alive. Dealing with those bodies could only remind him of the one he'd thankfully never seen.

Christina had fallen to her death from the Cliffs of Moher. No one knew whether it had been deliberate or accidental, but Seamus had known her well enough to suspect that her death might have been a suicide. Her fits of depression had been so profound that even the best of his love wasn't enough to overcome them.

Had he fallen for another like her in Susan? Possibly—although as much as he feared the possibility, he also had some assurance that those deeper similarities were unlikely. Susan had grit and courage. Despite her having have been bruised by her ordeal, he had faith that she would bounce back eventually. And he had every intention of being there when she did.

Fate hadn't brought them together twice for nothing. He planned to make the most of the opportunity.

* * * *

The atmosphere of Quinn's pub was cozy rather than stylish, triggering a wave of warm contentment that washed over Susan as she crossed the threshold. Along with the usual pub grub, the chef served up some gourmet delights that Susan knew from firsthand experience were significantly more upscale than the décor. Too bad she hadn't had the appetite to truly appreciate any of it.

Seamus led her to a booth, and she sank into the seat with a grateful sigh. "I wish I weren't so tired and sleepy all the time." Once again, exhaustion had struck without warning, robbing her of the strength to do anything beyond melting into the woodwork. Normally, she had more than enough energy to go all day and a good portion of the night. Not anymore.

"You aren't over the crash yet," Seamus said. "Give it time."

"I'm beginning to wonder if I ever will—get over it, I mean."

The crash wasn't the only thing from which she had to recover. Losing Chuck would extend the recuperative period for a good deal longer than mere physical trauma.

She glanced at Seamus. Why did he bother? She'd sensed a flirtatious nature when they'd first met. Now, she wasn't so sure flirtation was what he had in mind. Friendship, possibly. Yes, that was it. Perhaps he'd lost someone on the plane. Perhaps he was grieving too.

"Did any of your friends or family die in the crash?"

"The parents of one of my school chums and another couple from London whose mum and dad live here," he replied. "We held a joint memorial service at the local church."

"So many? How awful." One would have been bad enough, but four people with connections to such a close knit village? That was as devastating to a community as a flood or a tornado, minus the property damage.

"Yes, it was. Makes me want to go after whoever was

responsible and—"

"It wasn't his fault." Her protest burst from her lips without warning.

"Excuse me?" he asked. "It wasn't *whose* fault?"

She closed her eyes. Her inner cheering section should have something to say. Then again, that sudden outburst might have been it. Should she tell him about Chuck? For that matter, *could* she?

"I, uh, knew one of the pilots. He was...a good friend." Understatement of the year, yet could she truly claim him as anything else? She was the one still carrying a torch for him. From every other perspective, at the most they were friends, and at the least, coworkers.

"And he crashed the plane?"

"You don't know that," she snapped. "No one does."

"Ah, so he was more than a friend."

"What makes you say that?" Her affair with Chuck was ancient history. Seamus couldn't possibly know anything about it, and most of the people who knew about it at the time had probably forgotten.

"He must've meant something to you or you wouldn't have reacted so strongly."

"He did mean more. I—" No. She was not going to admit she was still mooning over an old boyfriend, especially one who was now a married man. Not only that, he had fathered two children since then. She should've given up on him long ago. "I just hate that he's being blamed for the crash. Chuck wasn't the only pilot, you know. There were two people in the cockpit. He might've had nothing to do with it."

He did, of course. His last thoughts—she couldn't truly call them words—proved it.

"The plane is going down. We have to do it or even more people will die, including my family. Save yourself and as many passengers as you can."

A bit cryptic, but clear enough on two counts.

One, the crash was deliberate. And two, he'd been coerced by a threat to his family.

A threat from whom? And why? The other pilot must've also

been threatened, hence the "we." There was no way that plane would've gone down unless both pilots cooperated or one was incapacitated in some way. That sort of altercation would show up on the recordings in the black box, although nose-diving a 747 into the ocean floor would make recovery of the box difficult, if not impossible.

The answers to those questions had yet to be discovered. There was one other question, though. How did any of that relate to what Cleona had said about saving the world?

"I see. Well, I doubt we'll ever know why things happened the way they did." He rose from his seat. "Don't go away. Are you okay with Guinness?"

Susan nodded, although she wasn't perfectly clear on what she was agreeing to—the beer or staying put.

Jillian had wanted a pint of Guinness while they were en route to the Galway hospital. Susan had been the one to quash the notion by repeating the airline official's admonition for the ladies to be fasting and sober when they arrived for their medical exams. She'd hated being such a killjoy, and to date, she had yet to drink that pint, or even a shot of Jameson. Although Susan had come through the disaster with virtually no injuries—not even the mild concussion that Cleona had sustained—the doctors had advised against imbibing any alcohol for a few weeks so as not to mask any behavioral changes.

Like energy-sapping depression.

Seamus returned from the tap with two foaming glasses of dark beer and set one in front of her.

"Drink it slowly," her inner shrink advised. *"You don't know what alcohol will do to you."*

With any luck, it'll knock me flat on my ass. As empty as her stomach was, that response was practically guaranteed.

"What is it they say about Guinness?" she said after the first taste. "That it's like drinking a loaf of bread?"

"I've heard that. Never tried drinking bread, so I can't honestly say I know how it compares."

To Susan's surprise, she actually laughed. *And I'm not even drunk.* "Good answer."

"There now, that wasn't so hard, was it?"

Arching a brow, she gave him "The Look" over the brim of her glass. Chuck had once said she could destroy a man with that same glance. She'd already given it to Seamus at least twice—perhaps even more—and he was still breathing. Maybe Chuck was too sensitive. Either that or Seamus was oblivious.

No. If anything, he was too perceptive.

Could he tell that she'd been hearing voices? And if so, would he care? Then again, if she ever decided she wanted him to leave her be, all she had to do was report what they'd said to her and he'd probably take off running. If that didn't work, the story about talking to Cleona via Ireland's stone towers would do the trick in a heartbeat.

Clearly unperturbed, Seamus wiped the beer foam from his upper lip. "I remember that look." He paused to take another drink. "Didn't scare me then and it doesn't scare me now. But I'm glad to know you're still capable of delivering it."

She raised her glass in a mock salute. "Another pint and I'll be back to my old, bitchy self."

"I wouldn't say you were bitchy." A hint of a smile threatened. "Just your typical fierce ginger."

"You won't let that drop, will you?"

He shook his head. "Not until it fails to get a rise out of you."

"Mmm… Guess I need to practice better self-control."

"Ah, but then you wouldn't be yourself. And if you can't be yourself, who would you be?"

Susan could think of several personalities that would vie for dominance given the chance, although her money was on the shrink. "So what you're saying is that I can be as fierce as I like and it won't bother you. Right?"

His eyes narrowed. "Up to a point. No need to overdo beyond what's normal."

Normal. What on earth did that mean? "I gave up being normal the day you pulled me off of that raft."

"Same here."

Another shot of "The Look" was imminent, but she held it in

check. Was he serious? Had the tragedy affected him that much? Or was he referring to something else entirely?

"How so?"

"I met you."

His prompt reply nearly drew a scathing retort, which, given his role in her rescue, was uncalled for.

He saved my life. I at least owe him civility.

"Can't say meeting me has ever affected anyone so profoundly before," she drawled. "At least, not to my knowledge. Why you?"

He glanced at his glass of Guinness as though seeking its advice before his brown-eyed gaze sought hers. "I think you know. You just aren't ready to admit it yet."

"In that case, forget I asked."

"Will do." The threatened grin finally materialized. "For now."

The waitress strolled up to the table, a pair of menus and a pad of paper in hand. "Hey, Seamus. Would you like to look at a menu or are you ready to order?"

"Ready as I'll ever be, Iris," Seamus replied. "I'll have the catch of the day—grilled—and the seafood chowder."

Susan smiled at the pretty, dark-haired girl. Was this his niece? Or was she a cousin? She couldn't remember.

"Cousin."

Thanks.

"Don't mention it."

Now all she needed was for one of the voices to tell her what to order. However, when an eager voice chimed in with *"seafood platter,"* she chose to ignore the suggestion. If Seamus was responsible for supplying the catch of the day, she might as well give it a try.

"I'll have the same."

Chapter 4

IT'S HARD TO KEEP GOING WHEN ALL I WANT TO DO IS SLEEP.

Susan had almost forgotten what it was like to sleep through the night. Terrifying scenes from the crash invaded her dreams, rendering any further attempts at slumber futile. The nights then melted into days that were equally murky and bleak.

For the moment, however, the dregs of her dreams had ceased to trouble her, and she was actually able to appreciate Seamus's company as well as the meal. She'd barely had time to blink before their soup arrived. Hot, creamy, and thick with chunks of crab and lobster, the chowder combined with the beer to calm her overwrought nerves in a way that made her wish she'd tried the combination sooner.

She'd nearly finished the soup when Seamus asked, "Feeling better?"

"Is it that obvious?"

"Aye," he replied. "Your shoulders relaxed after the third spoonful." He peered at her face. "That pinched look around your eyes is gone as well."

Definitely perceptive.

"Guinness and chowder," she mused. "Who knew they were such great cures for stress?"

He chuckled. "If you've ever met up with a stressed-out Irishman, he's probably one who hasn't seen the inside of a pub for a while."

"Considering the plethora of pubs around here, that probably doesn't happen very often."

"Probably not." His unabashed grin and twinkling eyes were starting to grow on her, and she especially liked the way the corners of his eyes crinkled when he smiled.

My hero…

Not really. He'd simply been in the right place at the right time. Susan and her fellow survivors had been safely aboard the life raft long before the boat reached them. Essentially, they'd saved themselves.

So why did she feel as though he'd saved *her*?

Perhaps his effect on her had nothing to do with boats and life rafts. Perhaps it went deeper than that. Perhaps her change of mood had more to do with him than the beer or the soup.

She glanced up as their waitress approached with their dinner, threading her way through an increasingly crowded room.

"Good thing you got here when you did," Iris said as she set the plates on the table. "Otherwise we might've had to feed you at the bar. The place is startin' ta fill up."

"Like sitting at the bar would be such a hardship, what with the tap being so close," Seamus teased. "Nor would it be the first time."

"I can certainly vouch for that." With a laugh, Iris trotted off.

Susan picked up her fork and inhaled deeply. For the first time in what seemed like years, food actually smelled good to her. The grilled fish was flanked with crisply fried potatoes and a salad of fresh peas, watercress, and a vegetable that she'd recently learned was called samphire. At first glance, she'd thought it was asparagus. However, one taste had proved her wrong; the flavor and inherent saltiness of the seaside plant were entirely different.

While the jury was still out on her opinion of samphire, Susan's first bite of the fish was like an explosion to her taste buds. "You weren't kidding about the fish. It's fabulous."

"Have I ever steered you wrong?"

"Not yet," she admitted. "Although the total number of hours we've spent together probably add up to less than a day. You still have time."

"True, but I have every intention of keeping my track record clean."

She couldn't help smiling at him. He really was sweet, and on top of that, he seemed sincere.

"See? It's all a matter of perspective."

Oh, hush up. When I need your help I'll ask for it. Not that asking questions ever works with you people.

The chuckle that resonated through her mind had her hoping her band of hitchhiking souls weren't planning to live vicariously through her.

Talk about weird...

Susan spotted another young woman making her way toward their table. Someone wearing an apron and possessing the same brown eyes and curly hair as Susan's dinner companion.

"Don't look now, but I think the chef is coming to check up on us."

Ignoring her advice, Seamus twisted around in his chair. "Aye, that's Enid, all right. Iris must've ratted us out."

Susan giggled.

"Oh, God. Was that—? That really was a giggle. Gotta be a first."

If you guys don't shut up...

"You'll what? Sic the Ghostbusters on us?"

Maybe.

"Well, now... You're here early." Enid surveyed her brother with critical eyes. "And still in the sweater and jeans you've probably been wearing all day."

"So what if I am? Haven't had the chance to go home and change."

"Never mind. What with all the fish I've cooked in here today, no one will care if you smell like them." Susan hadn't noticed any problems with the way Seamus smelled, and she was about to say so when Enid's gaze landed on her. "I'm guessing this lady is the reason for your lack of proper grooming?"

"I–I suppose I am," Susan stammered, unsure as to whether Seamus was being ribbed or ridiculed. "He was kind enough to show me St. Brigid's Well and invite me to dinner."

An arched brow suggested this wasn't the type of response Enid was expecting. With a roll of her eyes, she rounded on Seamus. "A date? Seriously?"

Heat prickled Susan's cheeks. "Not exactly—"

Seamus held up a hand. "Enid, I'd like you to meet Susan Maxwell, one of the survivors of that big plane crash."

Enid took a step back, her expression going from incredulous to blank in less than a heartbeat. "Oh. For a moment there I thought—"

"Thought what?" Seamus leaned back in his chair, eyeing his sister with a glimmer of amusement.

Despite the repentant sag of her shoulders, Enid's words came out in a rush. "That you'd finally gotten over Christina." Without waiting for her brother's reaction, she turned to face Susan. "Sorry if I sounded rude. It's just that seeing him with a woman—I mean, it's great, of course—but I never expected..."

"Let it go, Enid." Seamus was smiling and his tone was gentle, but his eyes glittered with warning. Clearly, this was a topic he would just as soon she hadn't brought up.

Nodding, Enid drew in a shaky breath. "H–how's the fish?"

"Perfect," Susan replied.

"Ah, well...nice to meet you, then. I'm glad you made it, although after seeing the video, I can't imagine how anyone could've survived such a catastrophe." Enid waved a vague hand toward the rear of the dining room. "Must get back to the kitchen."

Susan summoned up what she hoped was a pleasant, disarming smile. "Nice to meet you too."

"Give a yell if you need anything." With a quick nod, Enid hurried off.

"My, that was awkward," Susan said when Enid was out of earshot. "I take it Christina is an old flame of yours?"

"Aye, she was. But that was long ago."

Although Susan suspected there was more to the story, she hadn't forgotten the look Seamus had aimed at his sister. It wasn't the sort of look she ever wanted to receive. Nonetheless, there was an additional question that had been plaguing her for some time.

"There's been no one since?"

He shook his head. "Not like that." He went on with his meal, once again leading her to believe that his love life wasn't something he felt comfortable discussing.

Good. That makes two of us.

Her gang of "hitchhikers" wasn't saying anything either.

* * * *

To say that his relationship with Christina wasn't Seamus's favorite topic was a gross understatement. Despite knowing that he wasn't responsible for her actions, he had never completely forgiven himself for her apparent suicide. When she was on the upswing of her mood disorder, she'd been so brilliantly alive, expounding on concepts that were decades ahead of her time. But when she was down, she was lower than the Mariana Trench.

She'd been a frequent visitor to the cliffs, insisting they spoke to her of possibilities no one else could even begin to imagine. Many had thought her mad. Seamus knew better. The only form of madness she could claim was her genius, and she'd had that in spades.

He seldom discussed Christina with anyone, but given her recent loss, he thought Susan might at least have a comparable perspective.

"Christina was different," he said after a bit. "Completely unique. Most folks around here didn't understand her the way I did—not that I can claim to have fully grasped her theories—but I understood *her*, if you take my meaning."

Susan only nodded, leaving him to wonder if she'd had a similar connection of her own or if she was merely being polite.

"She had some wild ideas," he went on. "And even though they didn't always make sense to me, I could appreciate the intelligence behind them."

"What sort of ideas?"

He chuckled. "She said she knew how to save the world."

Susan froze with her fork somewhere between her plate and her lips, and a blush rose up her neck to stain her cheeks. "Really? How?"

"Oh, lots of ways. Conversion from fossil fuels for one. She had this vision of energy transfer from the sun—more directly than anyone had ever imagined it. Something about a conductive paint or coating to go on surfaces of cars and buildings—even roads—that would convert the sun's rays to energy to power the lights and move vehicles without ever having to start an engine or string a wire." He glanced at her face, which was now completely devoid of color. "Do those theories frighten you?"

She stared at him for a long moment. "N–no," she replied. "It's just that… No. Never mind." With a slight shudder, she drew in a breath. "She sounds fascinating."

"She was that, and no mistake." His mind's eye drifted back to the first time he'd seen Christina, standing on the quay, her auburn hair flying about her face and the skirt of her gauzy yellow sundress billowing in the wind. Barefoot and beautiful. "Totally one with earth, sea, and sky, like Mother Nature's favorite child." He blinked as he became aware that his gaze had shifted into the nothingness of space. He glanced up, the contact with Susan's moss-green eyes smiting him like a hammer on an anvil. "Forgive me. I don't normally talk about her. She died a long time ago."

In the next instant, he knew exactly why he'd felt free to say what he had, and he also realized something about the woman who sat across the table from him. She and Christina were connected somehow. A connection that went far beyond an affinity with the Cliffs of Moher.

They had the same eyes.

A tingle of awareness crawled up his back to tighten his scalp. He had to say something—anything. "You put me in mind of her." Even as he spoke, he regretted the comparison. "Not that you look anything alike, really. The similarity goes deeper than that." His subsequent shrug wasn't the slightest bit feigned. "Can't explain it any other way."

Her befuddled expression cleared so quickly, he could almost see the light bulb shining above her head. "So *that's* why you were hitting on me. I wondered."

"Hitting?" For a second or two, his jaw threatened to drop. "Oh, chatting you up, you mean?"

"I suppose so." Her gaze swept his face. "Except for your sister, you don't remind me of anyone—old boyfriend or otherwise."

Relief loosened the knot of tension gripping the back of his neck. "That's just as well. Both of us having déjà vu moments would be a bit much. And Enid and I do look a lot alike."

"You certainly do." With a brief smile, she returned her attention to her dinner. Clearly, the subject was closed.

Seamus wondered what the devil he should talk about next. Should he tell her about the band? Some women were impressed by that sort of thing. Others couldn't care less. Christina had seen it as a natural extension of his personality—his love of music intertwining with his life at sea.

One thing for sure, a musician's life was far less dangerous than that of a fisherman. Like most of the locals who derived their living from the sea, he respected the vast power and unpredictable nature of the North Atlantic. Those who refused did so at their peril.

After a sip of Guinness for courage, he plunged ahead. "If you've no plans for the evening, my mates and I will be playing from about nine until they chuck us out."

"Here, you mean?" With his nod, she continued, "The only *plans* I have are for tomorrow at three o'clock. Can't vouch for whether I'll still be here when they chuck you out, but I might stick around for a few songs. Should be interesting. What instrument do you play?"

"Banjo and guitar, mostly. Been known to pick up an accordion on occasion, and I sing a little harmony, as well."

"Really? I'm impressed. I never could sing harmony unless someone was singing it with me—I wound up on the lead every time—and my clarinet playing was so horrible the music teacher begged me to quit."

"I'll not believe that," he scoffed. "No music teacher would ever say such a thing."

"Yeah, well, you've never heard me play. My mother toughed it out, but my dad would always find some excuse to leave the house whenever I practiced." Her eyes took on a mischievous glint. "He started several home improvement projects that semester, and the garage has never been quite as clean again."

"That's the way it was when I first started, except that my dad just went fishing. Mum was busy at the pub so I had the house to myself."

"What about Enid?"

"She was off with her girlfriends." He grinned. "By the time she moved on to having boyfriends, I was getting pretty good."

"I bet they thought you were cool."

"Not really. Musicians aren't exactly a rarity around here." Unlike women who intrigued him. Susan was striking rather than beautiful; sonnets might not be written about her face, but it wasn't one you'd soon forget. He certainly hadn't forgotten it, nor had he forgotten her voice. So soft that if you closed your eyes, you might think she was a young girl. Until her temper flared. Then there was no mistaking her for a child.

"So tell me again," he began. "Why did you want to hire the boat?"

"Because Cleona told me to."

"You do everything Cleona tells you?"

"Well...no. But she *was* rather insistent."

"I see." He didn't, of course. "And where is it you want me to take you?"

"I don't know that either." With a slight shudder, she added, "I certainly don't want to sail over the crash site."

"Just as well," he said. "The Coast Guard would warn us off if we did. We've been told to give the area a wide berth while they're diving on the wreck." He cleared his throat. "If it's scenery you're after, there are miles of coastline that are worth a look, even some nice beaches if you fancy a walk along the shore at some point. Lahinch Beach is just across the bay and Spanish Point isn't far. Or would you be wanting to do some fishing?"

"I'm not sure," she replied. "There's something about water, though. Something important..." She looked down at her plate and began pushing a few stray chips around with her fork. "Honestly, this story gets more bizarre every day." Squeezing her eyes shut, she blurted out, "It's the voices. We've all been hearing voices."

"Voices? We? You mean all three of you?" Seamus somehow managed to dial back the incredulity in his response. He'd heard of mass insanity before, but this was different.

She nodded. "Me, Jillian, Cleona..." After one furtive glance at his face—even if she hadn't heard it in his tone, his skepticism was surely plain to see—her expression became shuttered, secretive. But only for a moment. With a resigned sigh, she went on, "Guess I might as well tell you, no matter how crazy it sounds. We've each picked up a collection of souls from the plane, and they talk to us. I don't know how exactly, but they're supposed to help us save the world."

The back of his neck prickled, setting off a sense of déjà vu he could have easily done without. "How? From what?"

"From mankind. We're destroying ourselves bit by bit. Unless we stop, the next generation could very well be the last."

Disbelief gave way to macabre fascination as his voice dropped to a whisper. "How could you possibly know that?"

"I don't." With a smile, she added, "I'm making this up as I go along. Can't you tell?"

Despite her offhand remark, Seamus suspected there was more to it than that—although exactly what, he couldn't have said. "It doesn't seem that way to me. You say it like you actually *know*."

She shrugged. "Maybe I do. Maybe I don't. All I did was open my mouth and the words came out. It's like I'm—"

"Possessed?"

"Yeah. Just like that."

Seamus leaned back in his chair and stared at her, wondering what the devil he'd gotten himself into. Christina might've been a bit mental, but she had nothing on this bird. Susan didn't need a boat. She needed a psychiatrist—and the sooner the better.

Chapter 5

THAT WAS A MISTAKE.

"No shit. We aren't possessing you. You still have free will."

Thanks, but I'm not sure that's the only thing bothering him.

Susan slumped in her chair. "You think I'm crazy, don't you?"

"The thought *has* crossed my mind," Seamus replied. "Although the more I think about it, the less likely it is that the three of you would have the same sort of symptoms."

"Auditory hallucinations, you mean?" With his nod, she smiled grimly. "The worst part of it is I was having them even before the plane went down. Guess that makes me the craziest of all."

Judging from his expression, which had undergone more changes in the past few minutes than most people's went through in an hour, he was inclined to agree.

Snatching up her napkin, she gave her fingers a quick wipe before tossing the napkin onto her plate. "I should go." She fumbled for her purse—the snazzy Gucci she still wasn't used to thinking of as her own—and pulled out a wad of euros. "This should cover it." Dropping the bills on the table, she stood so abruptly the chair legs screeched across the floor. Turning on her heel, she'd taken two steps before remembering she'd chartered his boat for the next day. Leaving in a huff would make the excursion awkward to say the least. "See you tomorrow afternoon."

Seamus stood even faster than she had, knocking over his chair in his haste. "Wait—"

She put up a hand. "I'm okay, Seamus. Not crazy—at least I don't think I am—just tired." *Carrying the weight of the world will do that to a girl.*

"Let me walk you back to your hotel."

She shook her head. "I think I need to be alone for a bit. This is the most interaction I've had with a human being since the crash. Maybe I'm not ready for this kind of—" This kind of what? Intimacy? Familiarity? Camaraderie? "—closeness." It had felt good, though. An unburdening of the soul followed by a lightening of the spirit. Lighter, yes, but still not quite…normal.

What would it take to feel normal again? Saving the world or saving herself from herself?

"Now, there's a dilemma if I've ever heard one. You should've been a psychologist—or a philosopher."

Clearly, her hitchhiking shrink was still on board.

Why can't I get rid of you?

"Because you need me."

If only everything were that straightforward. Seamus wasn't smiling anymore, no doubt realizing he was facing a lunatic who should've been locked up weeks ago.

She pressed her fingertips to her temples. Perhaps if she squeezed hard enough, the voices might vamoose, although she would undoubtedly lose some brain cells in the process. Then she really *would* need a shrink—or a surgeon.

"Look. I appreciate everything you've done, Seamus. Dinner was lovely and visiting the well was…spiritual. But right now, I need to clear my head a little."

He nodded as though he understood—either that or he was simply humoring the basket case who'd hired his boat. "Aye. Best if you sort things out a bit." A tiny smile dimpled his cheek. She hadn't noticed the dimple before. Was there another one on the other side? "But if you change your mind and think you'd enjoy a bit of music and fun, come on over any time before twelve. We'll be here."

"Thank you. I–I'll see how I feel later on, but I doubt I'll be back."

"I'll say good night, then. Pleasant dreams."

"If they are, they'll be the first since the crash."

"Give it time," he advised. "Who knows? This may be the night."

That was the trouble with him; he was so damned optimistic. Anyone who fished for a living would have to be, although fishing didn't appear to be his only job. Not that local bands earned much. He probably earned more by dabbling in the tourist trade. "Good night, Seamus. Have fun."

His hint of a smile stretched into a full-fledged, two-dimpled grin. "Generally do."

Oh, God. What would it be like to have that kind of attitude? It certainly couldn't have been evident in the weak smile she gave him in parting. He deserved better than that. Considering all he'd done for her, she should've at least paid for his dinner. Perhaps she had. She hadn't bothered to count the cash she'd tossed on the table. It might've been enough. She still owed him, though. Owed him her life and possibly her sanity.

I can't think about that right now.

She made her way from the pub, walking the short distance to her hotel. Once inside her room, she remembered her intention to call Cleona—on a phone this time—only to dismiss it as yet another thing that could wait. She turned the deadbolt on the door, dropped her purse on the desk, and nosedived onto the bed, thanking heaven for self-catered hotel rooms. If she'd had to turn down the covers, she probably wouldn't have bothered. Toeing off her shoes, she dragged the comforter up over herself and closed her eyes.

Her head was spinning like a Tilt-A-Whirl, and for a moment it seemed that her dinner, delicious though it had been, was about to make a comeback. Deep breathing forced down the nausea, but the dizziness persisted. The vision of waves breaking against a rocky shore found its way into her mind's eye as her head seemed to melt through the pillow.

A walk along the cliffs would have cleared her head better than anything. Unfortunately, darkness had already fallen, making such an excursion too dangerous to contemplate.

Not now. Not yet. But soon…

* * * *

As Susan left the pub, Seamus hoped no one else had noticed her precipitous departure. But, of course, they had. Every eye in the place was on him as he picked up his chair and resumed his seat. As small as the dining room was, the whole story was bound to have made its way to the taproom by now. He was a little surprised his mother hadn't already pounced on him for details.

Replaying their conversation didn't help very much. He hadn't actually said she was mental, had he? No. She'd beat him to it by saying the words herself, which was a good sign, really. Most mental cases didn't admit to being more than a bit off-kilter. At least, he didn't think they did. She'd claimed to be tired rather than crazy, whereas Christina had only confessed to having "moods."

Moods that eventually led her to her death.

Downing the last of his beer, he stood and pocketed the money Susan had left behind. He would count it later and deduct it from the boat rental. No way was he letting her pay for dinner when he was the one who'd done the inviting. Paying for the meal was a matter of principle, not to mention the gentlemanly thing to do. Mum would snatch him baldheaded if she ever got wind of the tale. Unfortunately, anyone in the pub could fill her in.

With a sigh, he headed into the taproom and took a seat at the bar, which gleamed with wax and the smooth patina of age. He didn't know who was responsible for the task now, but he'd put a considerable amount of elbow grease into it as a boy.

His mother looked up from the tap with a wry smile. "Shall I pull you a Guinness, or does this call for a shot of Redbreast?"

"I'll stick with beer," he replied. "Let's hear it, then."

"What, I'm a mind-reader now?" As if there was nothing Lorna Quinn didn't know about the goings-on in her pub. She pulled a foamy pint and slid it across the bar.

"Thought it best to get the lecture over with sooner rather than later."

"Ah, that." She swept a lock of straight, graying blond hair from her forehead. "I'm sure there's nothing I could say that would change anything. Enid told me about the woman. Pretty lass, she said. But then, you always were partial to ginger hair."

"Got nothing to do with it," he insisted. With a frown, he realized what he'd all but admitted to. *No going back now.* "Her hair color isn't the only thing I like about her."

"I'm sure it isn't. And I'm just as sure you're about to regale me with the rest of her sterling qualities."

Now that he'd been put on the spot, Seamus was hard-pressed to describe his attraction to Susan, let alone enumerate her "sterling qualities."

"She strikes me as the strong, independent type," he finally said. "At least, she was at first. At present, she's a bit—"

Addled? Mental? Depressed?

"—troubled."

"That's understandable given all she's been through lately." Clearly, Enid hadn't omitted any of the details of his dinner companion's history. "What d'you make of her?"

Seamus exhaled sharply. "Beats the devil out of me. One minute she seems perfectly normal and pleasant, and the next, she's lost in a fog."

Her eyes widened with a hint of alarm. "Not another Christina, I hope."

"I don't believe so. She wasn't like that on the day of the crash. Something's happened to her since then." He wasn't about to tell his mother about the voices—whether real or hallucinatory. "She hired the boat for tomorrow. I'm hoping to learn more."

A gaze that seldom missed a trick met his own with a piercing stare. "And why is that so important? She's a Yank, right? She'll be heading home eventually. Nothing there for you to get involved with."

On the surface, Seamus agreed. A relationship with a foreign national, not to mention one that was somewhat unstable, was inadvisable to say the least. The world might be getting smaller in many ways, but the actual distances hadn't changed one iota. On the other hand, his dear mum had been rather protective in the wake of Christina's death. He knew of at least three women she'd warned off when they expressed an interest in her only son. There were times when he'd considered that intervention to be fortuitous.

This was not one of those times.

"I'll figure that out on my own. It's well past time that I did."

"I suppose you're right," Lorna said, although her expression was even more doubtful than her tone. "But be careful. I don't want you getting hurt again. If she makes you happy, I'll be glad of it—although I honestly can't see that happening. I just don't ever want to see you the way you were after Christina died."

"Neither does anyone else, myself included," Seamus said. As morose as he'd been back then, the only person who could stand to be around him was Ian. The ladies in his life didn't have a monopoly on melancholia. He'd endured his fair share and then some.

Danny Ryan slid onto the barstool to Seamus's immediate right. After calling out his order, he rounded on Seamus. "Charmed another one into walking out on you, I see."

Seamus aimed a withering glance at his band's drummer and lead singer. "It's what I do best." Arguing with Danny was pointless. Best to simply agree and move on.

Lorna pulled another pint and pushed it toward Danny. "Thought that was your specialty, Danny."

"Aye, it is," Danny took a long drink of his beer, swallowing several times before taking a breath. "That was a rare fine woman, though. Wouldn't have let her walk away, meself."

Despite being inclined to agree, Seamus waved a hand toward the door. "If you hurry, you might catch her."

"Might do that," Danny said. "But I'm guessing she'd take a swing at me if I did."

"Possibly." If it he hadn't been feeling so protective toward Susan, Seamus would've enjoyed watching the altercation. "I didn't want to provoke her, which is why I let her go."

"You're a wiser man than me." Danny drained his glass, then clapped Seamus on the back. "What do you say we get set up?"

"Be there in a bit," Seamus replied, raising his glass. "I prefer to savor a pint instead of guzzling it." He saw no need to hurry. Fine-tuning his banjo and guitar took far less time and effort than putting up a drum set.

"No point in that," Danny declared. "The first five swallows are the best. Prefer to quaff them all at once and enjoy the burn. The rest is just to empty the glass."

"Suit yourself, mate." Seamus took another sip, wondering whether he should've gone after Susan. This might've been one of those make-or-break moments, and he'd missed the opportunity. For the first time in longer than he'd care to admit, he regretted his commitment to the band. If she'd stayed, that would've been different. He could've watched her, played for her, even sang for her. Then again, perhaps her abrupt departure was what came of trying to cram a month's worth of "dates" into a single day. Perhaps she could only tolerate him in small doses.

Cheery thought.

"You're awfully quiet," Danny observed. "Hope this means you'll be playing better than usual and not be wasting time chatting up the audience."

Seamus rolled his eyes. "That's your job, not mine."

As the band's leader, Danny did most of the talking, and because he fancied himself as an Irish version of Phil Collins, he nearly always tossed in a cover of "In the Air Tonight" amid the standard Irish tunes. Seamus would've preferred to play a few Mumford & Sons songs, but Danny had resisted—possibly because he couldn't be bothered to learn new material. Danny was rarely up before noon, claimed to run five miles a day, and tended to stay out until after the pubs closed. How he managed to earn a living the rest of the time was a mystery.

On any given day, Seamus was up before dawn and was done in by midnight. However, he would have made an exception if Susan had been the sort to stay out until the wee hours. As a flight attendant on transatlantic flights, she probably worked a more bizarre schedule than a hospital worker on rotating shifts. Adjusting to different time zones was nothing new to her; it was her dreams that disturbed her sleep, making her seem so…fragile. If he'd been though a similar ordeal, he probably would have nightmares for a month, perhaps longer. Post traumatic stress, they called it.

Danny shoved himself away from the bar and stood. "I'll leave you to your thoughts, then. See you at nine."

Seamus didn't bother to look up, merely nodding his reply. A glance at his watch proved he had time to run home for a shower and shave. Susan had already spent part of the evening with him smelling of the sea, but it couldn't hurt to put forth a bit more effort in case she chose to put in an appearance later on.

He'd already had two chances to make a good impression on her.

He saw no point in botching the third.

* * * *

The dreams had been bad enough before. This one was horrible.

Her stroll along the cliffs seemed pleasant enough, until a vaguely familiar runner dashed past her. In the next instant, she was flying out over the cliff wall, her screams snatched away by the rushing wind. The rocks below gnashed at her like giant, bone-crushing teeth. Within moments, she was swimming away, her soul cutting through the ocean waves with the ease and artistry of an otter before bursting forth into the light of an azure sky.

Susan awoke, drenched in sweat—or was it seawater? A numbing chill permeated her limbs, obliterating every other sensation.

I'm...dead?

"Not you," a strange, lilting voice replied. *"Only me. You're still alive and we must keep you that way."*

Susan forgot why. Then the knowledge resurfaced in her mind. "Oh, yeah. Gotta save the world."

"No. The world will endure whether humans thrive or perish. Your task is to save the people. And to do that you must avoid the cliffs."

Susan's protest burst from her lips. "But it's the only place that I—"

"Feel safe?" A musical laugh followed. *"I was warned to stay away from the cliffs, but there are other perils. The cliffs are simply the most obvious. You must beware. I'll give you the link if you'll plant roses on my grave."*

"The link? To what?"

"Does it matter?"

She frowned. "No, I don't suppose it does." *Who are you?* She hated to ask anything more or even say it aloud for fear that something worse might occur as a result. "Please. I just want to sleep. I'm so very, very tired..."

"You're not tired. You're afraid of what they want you to talk about."

"I'm not afraid. I just wish they wouldn't keep asking me the same damn questions. 'What does it feel like to nearly drown? When did you first realize the plane was going to crash? Did you know you were going to make it? Were you afraid of dying?' All of those and more. I'm sick of it."

"Suit yourself, then. But you must answer me one question. Will you be kind to Seamus? Will you love him? He needs you."

Susan counted two questions but ignored that minor detail for the more pressing need to know— "Who *are* you?"

Once again, melodic laughter reverberated through her mind. *"You should've figured that out by now. Promise me you'll be good to him."*

"How could I not be? I mean, I barely know the man, even if he did help save my life."

"You know him far better than you think you do. Enjoy discovering the rest of what makes him so wonderfully unique."

"Unique? You're kidding me, right?" Having met thousands of people during the course of her career, Susan knew that "unique" was a description that fit every last being that walked the earth. Even identical twins weren't indistinguishable from one another.

"Wonderful, then," the voice amended, sounding more distant than before. *"He truly is, you know. But don't worry. You'll see."* With each word, the voice faded even further.

"Wait," Susan exclaimed. "You never told me who—"

"Doesn't matter. Just trust me."

"Yeah, right," Susan drawled. "That's what you all say."

"We say it because it's true." A tiny giggle rippled by like a scent on the wind. *"And because no one ever listens to us—not at first anyway."*

"You say that like you're part of some sort of organization." Susan couldn't believe she was actually encouraging this conversation rather than trying to end it. Something was different about this one.

"I am, although I'm not necessarily in contact with everyone.

Just those that are the most...relevant."

A light dawned. "You're Christina, aren't you?"

"Ah, that would be telling."

"But it's true. Besides, if you don't tell me who you are, how will I ever know where to plant the roses?"

Silence followed. Didn't matter. Susan was already convinced. Rolling over, she peered at the clock. She'd only been asleep for an hour or so and she was wide awake now. The band was probably still playing down at the pub. She could slip in unnoticed and listen for a while. God knew she wouldn't fall asleep again for hours.

She sat up and stepped into her shoes.

It couldn't hurt to find out if the band was any good.

Not to mention discovering whether Seamus was as wonderfully unique as the voice claimed.

Chapter 6

BY THE SECOND SET, SEAMUS WAS FORCED TO ADMIT THAT SUSAN had no intention of returning to the pub that evening, which was probably for the best. She needed rest, and he needed time to mull over the day's events. Concentrating on each song had been difficult early on, especially since he kept checking the door anytime anyone wandered in. So far, however, he hadn't seen any ginger-haired Yanks.

By this time, his playing ceased to require much conscious effort, freeing him to indulge in any thoughts he wished—thoughts that never strayed from the woman he'd helped rescue. Was there something special about Susan? Or would he have felt the same if he'd rescued anyone else?

Probably not. His feelings for Susan were undeniable. Seamus and Susan. Their names even sounded good together. And Susan Quinn? Why, that was even better.

Dream on, man. She's not only a Yank, she's a bit of a looney.

No. That wasn't it. The more he pondered the notion, the more convinced he became that she wasn't insane. She was part of some sort of cosmic, spiritual event.

Seamus was Catholic enough to believe in the occasional miracle, and her survival certainly qualified. He'd watched that jet plunge into the sea like a platform diver with perfect form, disappearing beneath the surface in seconds. For a moment or two, he almost believed he'd imagined the entire scene. That is, until the *Branwyn Eostre* rolled with the massive wake and wreckage began to surface.

Then he'd spotted the raft. He'd assumed its deployment was either an automatic activation or a malfunction of some kind because no one could have survived such an impact. No one.

The three people climbing onto it proved him wrong on both counts.

No doubt about it, he had witnessed a miracle. But why had three women been the only ones spared? Why those three in particular? And why were they hearing voices? He had so many questions he wanted to ask Susan, he didn't even know where to begin. Three possessed women who were supposed to save the world…

Except she hadn't said they were possessed, only that it was *like* being possessed. They'd each been hearing the voices of the dead. Once he acknowledged that possibility, he could dismiss the insanity issue once and for all. There was nothing insane about being involved in a miracle. The greater purpose would be revealed in time. He only had to accept the idea and wait for the outcome.

Why couldn't he do that?

Because he'd met Susan, and she'd come back to hire his boat. He was caught up in the chain of events now, although his role was uncertain. Perhaps his task was as simple as providing the boat. First for the rescue, and now for the…

Resolution?

Preposterous. Nothing was going to simply float up from the depths and explain the whys and wherefores of what happened to that plane. Divers might eventually discover cockpit recordings that would prove that the jet was under someone else's control or that one or both of the pilots had deliberately crashed the plane. Their motivations might even be explained. God knew there'd been enough speculation in the press, especially after several terrorist groups claimed responsibility.

The funny thing was, none of the survivors had reported any evidence of a hijacking, nor had there been any hint of trouble in the radio transmissions prior to the crash. The general consensus now was that the pilots had either been coerced into taking the plane down or one of them had been a terrorist on a suicide mission.

He and Susan certainly weren't going to find anything from the deck of the *Branwyn Eostre,* and he was damned if he'd go for a swim in the North Atlantic.

Going to a beach would've made more sense, and he was a little surprised she hadn't jumped at the suggestion. Wreckage would be washing up along the coast for months, perhaps even years. Would she make it her life's work to find it all? Even if she did, how was that going to help her save the world?

After the last song in the set, he was reaching for his drink when Danny got his attention with a quick tap on the snare. "Would you take a look at that?" he said and nodded toward the door.

Seamus was definitely seeing things now. A ginger-haired apparition stood just inside the door, keeping to the shadows like a movie star hoping to avoid recognition. However, if the eye roll she aimed at him was any indication, she knew she'd been spotted.

"I'd never have believed she'd come back," Danny said. "She must like you after all."

Seamus snorted. "More like she couldn't sleep."

"Maybe," Danny said. "Either way, you'd best go talk to her before someone gets the jump on you."

"Meaning yourself?"

"I'll give you to the count of three before I make a move." Danny leaned toward the microphone and announced, "We'll be taking a short break now." He waved down the ensuing chorus of groans. "Or would you prefer we stopped for the night?"

Seamus stole a glance at Susan as yet another round of protests began. Thankfully, she was smiling. Needing no further encouragement, he put down his banjo and stepped off the bandstand.

Susan was still smiling as he approached. "You guys are really good."

"Some nights are better than others," he said. "This was one of them. I'm glad you decided to come back. I really didn't think you would."

"Neither did I." She grimaced. "You might say the decision was made for me."

"Seriously?" Perhaps she was more *possessed* than she realized. "They *made* you come here?"

"No. Nothing like that." She hesitated for a moment, then

shrugged as though resigned to tell all. "I had a dream."

"Good or bad?"

"Let's just say your wish for pleasant dreams wasn't very helpful."

"Ah. So it was more of a nightmare, then?"

She nodded. "Seemed that way at first. Then it changed into something else. Or maybe I should say some*one* else."

"Any idea who?"

"I have my suspicions," she replied. "But I'd rather not say just yet."

"I take it they don't always identify themselves?"

"None of mine have. Cleona knew the name of one of hers, the rest were lumped into what she called the Array. Jillian only had three, and she knew exactly who they were. Mine are like a gang of hitchhiking strangers. Except for the one in that last dream. I'm not sure about her—or how I picked her up."

"Not someone from the crash?"

"I don't think so. She was different. Different way of speaking, different agenda."

"Not interested in saving the world?"

"Ultimately, yes. The rest of the time, I can barely keep up with everything. Death benefits and certificates… It's a mess." She stopped as though his baffled expression must have registered. "That didn't make a bit of sense. Did it?"

"Um…yeah—I mean no. Not a bit."

"The officer reached inside the car and took out his gun, brandishing it about like some nut from—" She paused again. "Where do they keep the nutters locked up? Not in the facility in that magazine article. What a stupid idea. Not sure why anyone would want to preserve their body after death. I mean, why? Chances are, by the time they learn how to do any of that waking up and curing you stuff, everyone you know will have died. All your friends. Your family. Sure there may be some descendants, but—"

"Susan." He put up a hand to stop her. "You really aren't making any sense at all." Thankfully, the din of conversation was loud enough to keep them from being overheard. "D'you think you should…"

"See a shrink? No need. One of my hitchhikers is either a psychologist or a psychiatrist. Not sure which—or even if he's legit. Maybe I shouldn't do this while I'm half asleep. You never know what I might say."

Truth be told, he thought she'd gone far enough already. On any other occasion, he'd have offered her a drink. This time, however, alcohol in any form seemed like a really bad idea.

She pressed her fingertips to her temples and shook her head. "I think…I think maybe their random thoughts are getting through. Probably because I'm so tired. I can't control them and keep them in the background where they belong."

"So you're saying none of what you just said is relevant?"

"Probably not. I should just shut up and go home. You don't need a nutter like me to deal with. Especially after Christina."

"I'll be the judge of that." Placing a hand on her elbow, he steered her toward an empty chair in the corner. "Take a seat. I'll have to start playing again in about fifteen minutes. Might give us enough time to sort this out."

She was laughing as she sat down. "I always said you were an incurable optimist."

"Always?"

She frowned. "No. Although I was thinking that earlier. Maybe someone else here knows you."

As unlikely as it seemed, he was inclined to agree. Reminding himself once again that suspension of disbelief was vital when taking part in a miracle, he pulled a chair up beside her and sat down, doing his best to keep an open mind.

"Pages were mixed up," Susan said suddenly. "Copies of this, that, or the other book were stashed in a locker somewhere." She fidgeted with the strap on her purse before tapping her chin. "No. I got all of those out a long time ago."

He simply stared at her, completely aghast at what was happening. He was sitting in his mother's pub with a woman who was clearly having a mental meltdown. He hadn't spoken with Jillian or Cleona since the day of the crash, which meant he only had

Susan's word for it that they'd had similar experiences. Everything Susan had told him could be the workings of her own deranged mind. He wanted to believe her, but it was getting tougher by the second.

"Don't mind me," she said. For a moment, she sounded perfectly normal until she added, "He's the one who should be worried. The grass hasn't been mowed in ages. Aren't you using the tape anymore? It worked well enough the last time."

Was there any way to stop this madness?

She tilted her head and smiled. "You're really cute. Christina said you were wonderfully unique. She should know."

His throat tightened in a way that should've prevented him from ever speaking again. As it was, his words came out in a harsh whisper. "You've been talking to Christina? How could you possibly—"

"Test for that?" She nodded. "The test was done just now. Leaving it for too long made the difference. There's something in the attic. I can hear it scrambling around up there. Probably a chipmunk. There are gobs of them around here."

He had to do something to bring her to her senses, and he had to do it fast. In such a public place, slapping or shaking her was out of the question. Not only would he never forgive himself, no one else would ever let him forget it.

Despite its effectiveness, his ultimate choice was almost as bad, aside from being something he'd longed to do since he first laid eyes on her.

A good, long kiss shut her up quite nicely.

He half expected her to knock him senseless—she'd already proved she had no qualms about walking out on him—but returning the kiss? He never expected *that*.

If he hadn't known better, he'd have said she'd planned it, teasing him until he simply had no options left.

At the moment, however, he truly didn't care. Her lips were petal-soft and yielding, their flavor a heady mix of mint and her own unique essence. His body, which had been on full-scale alert from the moment he'd spotted her, responded instantly, making him wish they'd been somewhere—*anywhere*—else. Granted, they weren't exactly onstage, but it was only a matter of time before someone noticed. His money was on Danny.

Or his mother.

A loud sniff from Susan broke his concentration, and she drew back slightly. "I think I'm okay now," she whispered against his lips. "You can stop whenever you like."

"Better not put it that way or we'll still be here when the pub opens tomorrow morning." They wouldn't be *sitting*, of course, but they would definitely be in the same general area.

"Mmmhmm... You're such a flirt. I was right about you to begin with."

"Not true. Ask anyone in the pub if you don't believe me."

She leaned back in her chair and glanced around the room. "Believe it or not, no one is acting like they saw that."

"Probably didn't spot us, then." A peek over his shoulder verified her claim. "Trust me, this crowd doesn't turn a blind eye to anything." He arched a brow. "I wouldn't have thought it of you either. I'm amazed you didn't throw a punch."

"No point in that. Especially since it had the desired effect. At least, I *think* you were trying to stop me from raving like a lunatic." A tiny smile curved her lips—lips whose lusciousness he'd finally enjoyed firsthand. "Or was there another reason?"

"And here I thought you were smarter than that," he drawled. "Of course I had another reason. A man doesn't kiss a woman unless he wants to, even if she's stark, raving mad."

For the record, he wanted to drive her madder still. Wanted to make her to cry out in ecstasy. Wanted to feel her hands roaming over his body. Wanted to hear her beg him for more.

He swallowed hard, shaking his head in an effort to banish a mental image that threatened to consume him.

"Aha..." Her soft voice combined with a slow, secretive smile to bewitch him even further. "So you took advantage of my lunacy to further your own nefarious intentions?"

"Wouldn't call them nefarious, exactly. Passionate, yes," he admitted. "But honorable on the whole."

* * * *

Susan didn't question Seamus's honor. However, she had her suspicions about her gang of hitchhikers. They'd started cheering the moment she responded to the kiss and were now congratulating one another on their ingenuity.

I'll be so glad when you're gone.

"You'll be wishing we'd stayed longer if we don't get you laid before we go," came the reply.

I thought you were supposed to help me save the world, not get laid, she chided. *Besides, I think I can manage a bit of nookie without any assistance from you. Seamus seems more than willing.*

"Yeah, well, you needed us to help break the ice."

And you did that, so now you can just BACK OFF.

She hoped she'd put enough emphasis on that directive to make it stick. Unfortunately, the fact that her hitchhikers were already dead limited the number of dire consequences with which she could threaten them. When it came to coercion, they probably had the upper hand anyway. After all, *she* was the one being haunted.

"Honorable and passionate sounds good," she told Seamus after shushing her onboard cheering section. "Certainly better than dishonorable and passionless." She cleared her throat and forged ahead. "Believe it or not, all that crazy talk was my gang of hitchhikers trying to goad you into kissing me. Sorry about that. "

"No need to be sorry, although I must admit I'd be much happier if you'd been the instigator."

"Better a devious plot of my own than the schemes of a third party?" She nodded. "Yes...I can see how that would make a difference. Although, for the record, there was at least one part of that kiss they didn't control."

"I'm glad to hear it." His self-satisfied smile proved he understood her perfectly. "Speaking of your hitchhikers, they strike me as being more like stowaways. I mean, you have to voluntarily pick up a hitchhiker. Seems to me they climbed aboard without your consent. Splitting hairs, I realize, but there it is."

"Hmm... You're right. Stowaways *is* a more apt term."

Hear that, gang? You're nothing but a bunch of stowaways.

Not surprisingly, this new designation drew a somewhat mixed response. What *did* amaze her was the casual nature of Seamus's suggestion. Then again, perhaps he was only humoring her until the Garda arrived to cart her off to the nearest mental institution.

"You have to stop thinking that. No one has locked up Cleona or Jillian. You need to call them in the morning."

I'm surprised you guys can't connect us directly.

"Their 'stowaways' have moved on. Only Earth can connect you now."

Or the sea…

Seamus nodded toward the bandstand. "Time to get back at it." Grasping her hand, he gave it a gentle squeeze. "Thanks for coming, and please don't feel obligated to stick around for the next set. I know you must be tired."

Not only was the warmth of his touch a balm to her soul, it also drew an appreciative sigh from the stowaways. Who knew ghosts were such hopeless romantics?

"I might actually be able to sleep now," she said. "And if I do, I'm not leaving my bed before noon. After all, I don't have an appointment until three."

He smiled. "I'll be waiting."

Chapter 7

SUSAN SLEPT THROUGH THE NIGHT AND INTO THE MORNING, no drugs or alcohol required—unless she counted the Guinness she'd had with dinner. Her visit with Christina or the kiss she'd shared with Seamus might have been responsible, but there was no clear evidence to support either possibility.

On closer analysis, however, she was forced to admit that the kiss with Seamus had done the trick. Everything else had happened prior to or during her aborted "nap" earlier in the evening.

Before opening her eyes, she subjected herself to a thorough head-to-toe assessment. No headache. No dizziness or nausea. No pain. Her vision was clear when she opened her eyes. She felt rested and refreshed.

She sat up, amazed at how normal she felt. Had the worst passed? Were the voices gone?

"Nope. We're still here."

"I should've known it was too good to be true."

She got up and headed for the bathroom only to discover that the shower had been magically transformed into a little piece of heaven overnight. The soap smelled sweet and fresh. The towels were thick and soft against her skin. None of those things had registered before. Her dulled senses had finally returned to their customary sharpness.

Thank God.

She had two tasks for the day. First, she had to find Christina's grave and determine the feasibility of planting roses there. And second, she needed to call Jillian and Cleona.

Her stomach interrupted her plans with a loud snarl.

"Okay. You win. Breakfast first." Susan had no qualms about listening to her body and providing its basic needs. What she *didn't* want was any further meddling in her relationship with Seamus by the stowaways.

"No more making me talk out of my head either," she said firmly. "We can work together without you guys making everyone think I'm nuts."

"Understood."

"Good."

"The kiss helped, though. Didn't it?"

"Probably. Thanks for that, but enough's enough. Got it?"

"Okay, okay, okaaayyy."

Susan pressed her lips together to keep from smiling but immediately abandoned the attempt. Hiding her feelings from the stowaways was impossible. They might not be able to *see* her expressions, but they were certainly privy to her emotions.

Normally a rather private person, Susan had always found it difficult to share her feelings. Now she had no choice. Her emotions were laid bare to the scrutiny of a group of total strangers. Nothing could compare to that. Certainly no living person could accomplish such a complete invasion of privacy. Theirs was a mind-to-mind connection, an exchange of thoughts that couldn't be turned off or ignored.

"Sorry. We'll try not to intrude so much."

Whether they planned to intrude didn't matter because they'd obviously read her previous thoughts.

"We can keep quiet, but we can't avoid hearing what you're thinking. There's nowhere else to go."

Susan hadn't considered that aspect. They were probably just as anxious to get out of her head as she was for them to leave. They hadn't asked for what happened to them any more than she had.

Working together in harmony would move things along much quicker. All they had to do was save the world, then the stowaways could move on and she could get back to some semblance of normalcy. Both Cleona and Jillian had made it through a similar period of weirdness. Their voices were gone. Their lives had undoubtedly changed as a result, but they were over it now.

Except for their connection with Earth, which might turn out to be permanent. Susan had already felt it three times: twice at O'Brien's Tower and once at St. Brigid's Well. Being one with the planet forever wouldn't be so bad. She would get used to it. Eventually.

Right now, however, the sun was shining brightly with the promise of a lovely day. The temperature hadn't been out of the upper sixties during her entire stay thus far, so she dressed warmly, choosing a pair of tan slacks, rubber-soled shoes, and a wool sweater over a knit turtleneck top. She could always change again if that attire wasn't appropriate for boating. She'd been freezing cold the last time, but she'd also been wet and mildly hypothermic to begin with. On this trip, she had every intention of staying dry.

She headed down to the hotel restaurant and took a seat at a table by the window. Her appetite now completely restored, she ordered the full Irish breakfast and was finally able to do the gargantuan meal some semblance of justice. While sipping the last of her tea, she considered asking her waitress where the nearest cemetery was located when she realized the only thing she knew about Christina was her first name.

Undaunted, she pulled her phone from her purse and began a search of nearby cemeteries. Kilmacrehy turned out to be the closest, in addition to the one she had already seen at St. Brigid's Well. Seamus hadn't pointed out any particular graves at St. Brigid's, but that didn't necessarily mean Christina wasn't buried there. Nevertheless, as she scrolled through the list of names on the survey of each cemetery, she found lots of Catherines and Kathleens, but not a single Christina.

Seamus did say she was unique.

She scrolled back to the top of the Kilmacrehy listing and noted that the survey hadn't been updated in fourteen years. Seamus hadn't said how old Christina was when she died, but given their romantic connection, she figured they had been fairly close to one another in age. Seamus couldn't have been much over thirty, therefore Susan felt safe in assuming that Christina had probably died within the last ten or twelve years, perhaps even more recently than that.

The directions provided on the website were simple enough—

the cemetery was located about a mile from Lahinch on the road to Liscannor near the end of the golf course. Reversing those directions meant that Kilmacrehy was even closer to Susan's hotel than the Cliffs of Moher—definitely within walking distance.

Setting out at a brisk pace, she soon left the town behind. She passed no other pedestrians, and because traffic was light, the only sounds she heard were the wind whistling through the tall grass growing alongside the road, the gulls crying overhead, and the distant rumble of the sea. She might have been any tourist on holiday, enjoying a morning stroll with no agenda beyond exploring yet another of Ireland's many historic sites. When she reached the turnoff to the church, she stopped to take stock of her surroundings.

For anyone wanting a burial site with an ocean view, Kilmacrehy was tough to beat. The church itself was a huge, ivy-covered ruin crowning a slope facing the bay. Stone crosses dotted the graveyard, most of their ancient inscriptions impossible to decipher. Farther down the slope, a rocky terrace separated the older graves from a newer section where the land dipped and flattened before stretching out toward the beach. Susan picked her way through the thick tufts of grass between the markers, but upon reaching the terrace, she surveyed the neat rows below with dismay. In addition to being marked with headstones, the newer graves all had stone slabs covering the full length of each plot, presumably placed there to prevent the coffins from being unearthed by the surf. Planting roses there was out of the question.

Had Christina known what an impossible request she'd made? Susan stared at the unyielding stones in disbelief until a lone, grass-covered grave off to the right caught her eye. The headstone showed no sign of weathering, and as she approached, she found its inscriptions sharp and readable. A single rose had been carved above the name Christina Marie Dunleavy. According to the dates, six years had passed since her death at the age of twenty-two.

Susan looked about her. The view of the bay was breathtaking, of course, but even the grass looked a bit worse for wear. Whether roses could live there was anyone's guess. She might plant one only to have it die and be mowed down by the caretakers.

Then again, Christina hadn't said she expected the roses to live. All Susan had to do was plant them.

"Why couldn't she have asked for a gorse bush?"

"Not nearly as pretty," the stowaways replied.

"Thanks, guys," she drawled. "That's *so* helpful."

"The ground-cover type of rose is very tough and relatively carefree," said a confident, female voice. *"You might try one of those. They call them Flower Carpet Roses around here."*

Susan exhaled sharply. "Finally, something useful! I'm glad at least one of you knows a thing or two about gardening."

"Happy to be of service."

"Now all I have to do is find a plant nursery." She hadn't seen one in Liscannor. Hopefully, there was one in Lahinch. If not, Ennis and Doolin were within easy driving distance. Surely someone, somewhere, would have roses for sale.

Susan drew in a deep, cleansing breath of the crisp sea air. Saving the world was a laudable goal, but the job was as daunting as it was abstract. Planting roses, on the other hand, was specific, doable, and far more constructive than traipsing back and forth to the cliffs hoping to commune with Chuck's spirit.

"Not gonna happen. He's gone, and as far as you're concerned, he was gone a long time ago. You need to let go and move on." This time, the voice was similar to that of a wise, if somewhat exasperated, friend.

"I know. Believe me, I know." That being said, Christina had been dead for nearly six years. In all that time, Seamus hadn't let go, much less moved on.

Or had he?

A resounding snort ripped through her mind. *"I'd say he has now. He's definitely exhibiting indicative behaviors."*

Susan closed her eyes and counted to three. The shrink was back.

"I was never gone."

Fine. Although right now, the gardener would be more useful. I've never planted a rosebush in my life.

"Nothing to it," the gardener said. *"I'll coach you."*

Am I going to remember all this stuff when you're gone?
"Maybe. Dunno for sure. I've never done this before."
That makes two—or should I say several—of us.

The one other voice Susan thought she should have been hearing from was conspicuously silent. Perhaps Christina was only allowed to visit her dreams. Susan had been joking when she told Seamus she was making everything up as she went along. However, the joke would've been a lot funnier if she hadn't suspected someone else of using the same method to establish the rules.

To what link had Christina been referring? Did it relate to her death or something else entirely? Was it a link to her suicide note? Seamus hadn't used the actual term, but if his description was accurate, Christina had displayed symptoms of a bipolar disorder. He obviously suspected her death was a suicide, which made sense in a way. After all, she wouldn't have been the first person to jump off a cliff in a fit of depression. No doubt Susan's resident shrink would agree.

Still, if Christina had wanted anyone to know she was planning to kill herself, she could've left a note or sent out an email or a text beforehand. She could even have done it from the edge of the cliff if she'd had a cell phone handy. She didn't need to give someone the link in exchange for planting roses on her grave.

Actually, the more Susan thought about it, the more convinced she became that Christina's death *hadn't* been a suicide. She had no proof, of course, but that explanation simply didn't feel right; it was too pat, too convenient, too *easy*. The woman in Susan's dream had sounded more mischievous than morose. She'd also seemed genuinely concerned about Seamus and his future happiness. If his happiness was that important to her, she wouldn't have wanted him to suffer the aftereffects of her tragic suicide.

Ruling out suicide left two other possibilities. Accidental death or murder.

Seamus had mentioned that Christina spent a lot of time at the cliffs, which could have made her complacent enough to cause a fatal lapse in judgment or predictable enough to allow anyone observing her habits to plan her murder.

If her death had been an accident, the link might be completely unrelated. However, if she'd been murdered, it might reveal a possible motive. What better reason could there be for Christina's "visit" than an attempt to solve her own murder? But if so, why trade roses for that information?

I really have to stop thinking about this.

Mulling over the possibilities was pointless. Susan would get the link after she planted those roses and not before. The only catch was that she had to be dreaming in order to be contacted again, and sleep wasn't always easy to come by.

She glanced at her watch. If she wanted to get the roses planted and make the calls to Jillian and Cleona before three o'clock, she'd best get moving. Walking on to Lahinch was an option, but after calculating the weight and bulk of the necessary items, she figured driving there would be best.

During her walk back to Liscannor, Susan came to terms with yet another aspect of the airline tragedy. All those senseless, meaningless deaths… Something worthwhile had to be derived from the carnage—some meaning, some hope. In recent weeks, she'd almost lost the ability to see that there was good in the world, scattered as it was amid so much hatred, violence, and greed.

There'd been times when the destruction of humankind might've seemed like a wise choice on the part of whatever entity was responsible for man's cosmic destiny. Was this one of those times? Or was the moment ripe for a sweeping change for the better?

Susan had never been a believer in the supernatural. Never gave the possibility of ghosts or mental telepathy a second thought. That is, until the connection with Chuck in the moments prior to the crash. Everything that had occurred since then could only be explained as the work of some powerful, supernatural force.

If the crash had been accidental, she could've dealt with that. She would have directed her anger at whatever person or glitch was responsible. But the crash of Oceana Airways Flight 2324 was no accident. She'd known from the very beginning that it was murder on a massive scale, a crime the man she loved had been forced to commit in order to prevent even more deaths.

Saddled with that knowledge and not a single shred of proof, she'd had to shove her anger aside in a desperate attempt to continue functioning. That anger now resurfaced, strengthening her resolve to see to it that none of those deaths had been in vain. She didn't know how or when, but she would do everything in her power to ensure that justice was done.

Seamus and Christina were part of the solution. The threads tying everything together were hazy and indistinct, but she could still see them. She'd been trying so hard to reconnect with Chuck she'd missed the one pathway she should've been searching for all along: The trail that led from Seamus to Christina and what Cleona had said about scientists, politicians, alternative energy, and saving the world.

Seamus had been the link from the very beginning. Instead of dismissing him, she should've teamed up with him from the moment the airline had released her.

No wonder Cleona had told her to find him.

His boat wasn't the most important factor.

He was.

Chapter 8

As Seamus could've predicted, by morning, Ian had already heard about the result of his "date" with Susan.

"So tell me, Seamus," Ian said as he fired up the boat's engine. "What did you say to make her walk out on you?"

Seamus arched a weary brow. "I told her she was a stupid Yank and I never wanted to lay eyes on her ugly mug again."

Ian's response was equally fictitious. "Sounds like something you would say."

"It does indeed." Seamus cast off the moorings before joining Ian at the helm. "Shall we leave it at that?"

"Not until you tell me the real story."

"I wish I could," Seamus replied. "To be honest, I'm not sure her departure had anything to do with me. She said she wasn't used to being around people yet and that she needed to clear her head. She's also been having bad dreams."

"Not surprising," Ian said. "Poor lass, she's probably exhausted."

"That's partly my fault. I took her to the well and then straight on to dinner. I tried to talk her into staying for the music, but by then she'd had enough of me, although she *did* come back later on."

"Of course she did." With a broad wink, Ian added, "What woman could resist your brand of Gaelic charm?"

Seamus chuckled. "I dunno, but I'm guessing they number in the millions."

"That's as may be, but perhaps it's good that she'll have most of today to herself. By this afternoon, she may be ready for more company—yours especially."

"We'll see."

"Aye, that we will." Ian steered the *Branwyn Eostre* toward the open water. Once they'd cleared the harbor, he nodded toward the group of passengers gathered at the bow. "Best you be getting up there for your tour guide performance. I declare, we've had more feckin' tourists to contend with since that plane went down. Ghouls, the lot of 'em. Curious, thrill-seeking ghouls."

"But they do pay extra to get within spitting distance of the Coast Guard ships."

Ian sighed. "There is that. Even so, I'm looking forward to going out with just the one passenger this afternoon. If you were to ask me, which of course you didn't, I'd say she was the only one with any business going anywhere near that wreck."

"I don't believe that's what she plans to do, although she wasn't terribly specific about where she wanted to go. I'm thinking she might enjoy a cruise to Spanish Point, but we'll leave that up to her."

"Makes me wonder if she only chartered the boat with an eye toward spending time with you again."

"Yeah, right."

With a roll of his eyes, Seamus headed off to begin his stint as tour guide. He wasn't about to tell Ian the real reason Susan had come looking for them. If she wanted Ian to know she'd been hearing voices, she could tell him herself. As for a possible itinerary, once they put out to sea, all she had to do was pick a direction. She couldn't very well change her mind and walk away like she'd done at the pub, nor would he give her the opportunity to do anything rash.

He'd already rescued her once.

He had no desire to have to do it again.

* * * *

By the time Susan reached Liscannor, isolated rain clouds were rolling in from the sea like a flotilla of battleships, bringing gentle showers interspersed with periods of sunshine. Granted, she was in Ireland, and if she'd been so inclined, she probably could've spotted a rainbow—perhaps even the requisite pot of gold at the end of it. But she was on a mission.

"A mission from God."

Judging from the inflection, she suspected there was a *Blues*

Brothers fan among her stowaways.

"You meant that as a joke, right?"

"I did, indeed. Might be true, though."

Susan certainly couldn't argue with that. "Wait. What do you mean it 'might be true?' Don't you guys *know*?"

"Um... No, we don't."

"Do you mean to tell me that you still don't know whether God exists even *after* you're dead?"

"We haven't exactly made it to heaven or hell yet, so we don't know any more than you do."

"Great. Juuussst great."

The sky unleashed yet another shower as Susan reached the parking lot where she'd left her rental car. A mad dash for the door kept her from getting drenched, but her clothes were already rather damp from the previous sprinkles. "So much for intending to stay dry today."

"You might want to change into your jeans anyway. Those pants you're wearing aren't sturdy enough for gardening."

"Right."

After a quick stop at the hotel to change into dry clothes and look up the nearby plant nurseries, she set out for Lahinch, thanking the technology gods and Oceana Airlines for a phone with a search engine. They'd given her one of the newer models, which was supposedly waterproof. Too bad the phone Chuck had found wasn't a similar type or she'd have figured out who it belonged to by now. How long did it take to dry out a phone? Surely two weeks was long enough. Maybe even too long, given the corrosive nature of sea water.

Of course, if she ever *did* find the owner, she would have to return the phone. She wasn't ready to do that yet.

She found the nursery in short order, bought a spade and two rose bushes—one a buttery yellow and the other a deep coral pink—and then stopped at a convenience store for a large jug of water. Thus equipped, she headed back to the cemetery.

The sun was shining again when she arrived. Locking her purse in the trunk, she dropped her keys in her pocket and set out for

Christina's grave, somehow managing to carry everything in one trip. A handful of tourists were taking pictures in and around the church, but the graveyard itself was empty.

Except for the caretaker, who was mowing the grass near the shore.

She hadn't expected that. She might have gone to all this trouble only to be told that permanent plantings weren't allowed.

The man must have seen what she was carrying because he stopped his mower and started up the slope toward her. Dressed in the ubiquitous Aran sweater and twill trousers, he was tall and thin with a slight curvature to his upper back. Wisps of gray hair peeked from beneath a green and black woolen cap—the traditional sort that usually looked ridiculous on tourists, but suited him perfectly.

Susan set the roses down beside the grave and greeted him with a smile. "There was no one here to ask earlier, so I'll ask you now. Is there any rule against planting roses here?"

"None that I'm aware of," the man replied. He gestured toward the headstone. "Did you know the lass, then?"

"Well enough to know she wanted roses planted on her grave."

He nodded as though he understood. "'Twas a sad thing when she died. Lovely girl. Such a tragedy. They say she jumped, you know."

"They actually *proved* her death was a suicide?"

His expression hardened, his lips forming a moue of distaste. "That was the coroner's ruling, but I'll not believe it. Not for a second. Why, I'd watched her out playing in the surf since she was a child. Moody, they said she was, but never to me. She was always so full of life and had so many grand ideas."

"She told you about them?"

"Oh, aye. She was a great talker, was Christina. Gave me all manner of pictures she'd drawn, as well."

Susan's scalp tightened. "What sort of pictures?"

"More like diagrams, you might say. Some were very detailed, but each one as pretty as any painting you'd see in a museum."

"Do you still have them?"

"Aye. Wouldn't want to part with them. Perhaps it was wrong of me, but her family never asked to see them." A frown furrowed his brow. "I suppose I should do something with them before I end up here among the rest of me tenants. Write a will or some such thing."

"Could I see the drawings sometime?"

"I'd be very pleased to show them to you." He pointed up the hill beyond the church. "See that yellow house across the road on the left? If I'm not here in the churchyard, I'm there most anytime you'd care to stop by." He jerked his head toward the mower. "I'd best be getting back at it before the rain decides to pop in for another visit."

"Same here," Susan said. "I've already gotten wet once this morning."

"Well then, I'll leave you to your planting, and I promise to do my best to keep the roses blooming."

"Thank you," Susan said. "I'll be staying in Liscannor for a while. Not sure for how long, but I'll water them whenever I can."

"That'll be nice." His gaze swept over the graveyard. "This place has always been rather drab. We could use a bit of color."

Susan had seen cemeteries back in the States that rivaled some botanical gardens. Kilmacrehy was stark and windswept, but with a beauty all its own. "It's very interesting, though."

"Christina loved this place. Said it was special—even more so than the cliffs or the holy well." He paused, searching Susan's face with eyes that were surprisingly clear when, given his apparent age, she might have expected the milky film of cataracts. "Said she could hear voices speaking to her from the waves out there on the shore."

The tightness in Susan's scalp spread to her shoulders before escalating into a shiver.

"Aye, you might well shudder," he said. "She could do that to you. Tell you things, wondrous things that would make you stare in awe. She had the gift, you see." He shook his head sadly. "Death took her too soon. She wasn't nearly finished yet." He paused, once again fixing his piercing gaze with Susan's own. "But you knew that about her, didn't you?"

"I believe I did," Susan replied, even though she hadn't heard this much about Christina from Seamus. Was this man the link Christina had promised her? Not an electronic link to a specific website or cache of information, but another person? "Mr..."

"McKenna," he said, holding out a hand. "Robert McKenna. Been the sexton here for nearly fifty years."

Susan introduced herself as she shook his calloused hand. "Nice to meet you, Mr. McKenna. I look forward to seeing Christina's work. I have plans for the rest of the day, but I should be able to come back tomorrow."

"Anytime." With a wave of farewell, he headed back to his mower.

Was this her task? To discover more about Christina's ideas and bring them to the forefront of whatever field they represented? Possibly. But how could those ideas—which, if Seamus was correct, were a bit on the radical side—bring about justice for those who'd lost their lives in the plane crash? Would they even enable her to find justice for Christina?

She stared after Robert as he made his way down the grassy slope. So Christina could hear the voices in the waves down there, could she? Or was it merely the murmurings of the sea she'd heard? Given Susan's strange experiences with the ocean and other water sources, she wouldn't have been surprised if her morning shower had been as spiritual as her previous encounters. Perhaps it had been.

She glanced at the potted roses sitting at her feet. "First things first."

Picking up the spade, she cut through the turf, removing two circular sections slightly larger than the diameter of the pots. The soil was loose and sandy, making it easier to dig than she'd expected, and she heaped the dirt onto a sheet of plastic the folks at the nursery had thoughtfully given her to protect the carpet in the car's trunk. Her stowaway gardener had recommended that she bring it along to keep things neat at the gravesite, a suggestion that had proven to be truly excellent advice.

Absorbed in her work, she hadn't noticed the darkening sky until the thunder began just as she was lowering the second rose into its bed. She quickly filled in the gaps around the root ball with the loose dirt and then got to her feet. Robert was nowhere in sight, but one look at the sky was enough to prove this would be no gentle shower.

"I might not have needed that jug of water after all."

Nevertheless, she uncapped the container and watered the newly planted roses, adding more soil as the dirt settled. She wasn't far from the shore, so she gathered up the edges of the plastic sheeting and dragged the whole mess down to the sea.

The air was heavy with the smell of fish and rotting seaweed. Beyond the high tide mark, the sand lay smooth as glass, despite the tempestuous waves that were now battering the coastline. The rumble of thunder was continuous, repeating over and over until Susan thought she'd go mad from the monotony of it. Then the rain began, the first drops splattering her face and arms as she heaved the dirt and turf onto a pile of dead seaweed.

Raindrops beat a staccato rhythm on the firm sand, and she stood transfixed, the plastic sheet hanging limply from her fist as she gazed out over the frothy waves. She hadn't been this close to the ocean since the day of the crash. Standing at sea level rather than on the dock or the cliffs, she was awed by the power and majesty of the stormy surf. The thunder rolled on, maintaining the same pitch and volume until a jagged bolt of lightning struck the water less than fifty yards in front of her. A horrendous clap of thunder followed, and the torrential rain began.

Susan draped the sheet of plastic over her head and ran back to the grave. Gathering up the empty containers and the spade, she started up the slope, keeping to the open lawn rather than threading her way through the forest of ancient markers. The church offered little or no shelter, its roof having caved in centuries before, so she sprinted around it and headed for the parking lot.

Reaching her car, she dropped everything, unlocked the door, and jumped inside, allowing her makeshift umbrella to slide to the ground before yanking the door shut. Moments later, she screamed as lightning struck again, this time so close it nearly blinded her before setting off a thunderous explosion that shook the car and rattled her teeth.

If this was how Earth planned to talk to her, she wasn't sure she was brave enough to listen.

Memories of the conversations she'd had with Cleona resurfaced. The connection between the stone towers had been supernatural in the extreme, but it had also been relatively peaceful. This was terrifying.

"And sometimes a thunderstorm is just a thunderstorm," the shrink chimed in, misquoting Sigmund Freud.

"Yeah, right. Although the timing sure makes me wonder."

"I'd say you already have enough to go on for one day. Meeting Robert was…fortuitous."

"If you want to call it that," Susan said with a derisive snort. "Do you suppose Christina knew he'd be cutting the grass today?"

"Possibly. If her soul is tied to the cemetery, she would probably know a great deal about what goes on there."

"That makes sense. I'm guessing he's the link she promised me. If so, I doubt I'll ever hear from her again."

"Is that a problem?"

"Not really. Just an observation."

She blew out a long breath. Here she was sitting in a rental car in a thunderstorm after planting roses on the grave of a woman who'd been dead for six years—one she'd spoken with in a dream but had never actually met—and she was discussing the matter with a dead psychologist.

Too weird.

"It is, isn't it?"

"After all this, I need to talk to some real live people on an honest-to-God telephone." A dash of normalcy never hurt anyone.

She waited until the rain finally slowed to a sprinkle, then got out to pick up her trash. After shaking off as much water and dirt as she could, she stowed everything in the trunk. If Christina knew everything that went on in her graveyard, Susan certainly didn't want to annoy her ghost by leaving a mess. She was already being haunted enough as it was.

She drove back to Liscannor and picked up an order of fish and chips before heading on to her hotel. She ate a leisurely lunch, telling herself she deserved the break even though she knew she was stalling. However, after Googling how to make a conference call from a cell phone, she decided she'd put it off long enough.

Susan didn't know why she was so hesitant, especially when out of all the people in the world, those two women were the only ones who could possibly understand her dilemma. How could she tell the truth about the crash without incriminating herself in the process? After all, once the supernatural element was eliminated, the only way Susan could've known the plane was going down was if she'd been part of the conspiracy. She'd be lucky not to wind up on death row.

There had to be another way to prove that Chuck had been an innocent pawn. All she had to do was find it. Unfortunately, while evidence of that nature might ensure justice for him, she doubted it would be enough to identify the actual perpetrators and put them behind bars. Making those guys pay for their crimes was going to take a group effort.

With a firm nod, she picked up her phone and began tapping in the numbers.

Chapter 9

SUSAN CONNECTED WITH JILLIAN DULAINE FIRST, THEN PUT HER ON hold before dialing Cleona's number.

Who knew a conference call would be so easy?

The three women had barely gotten past the exchange of greetings when Jillian said abruptly, "You know, it just occurred to me... The airline gave us these damn phones. They might be bugged."

"I hadn't thought of that," Susan said. "But I suppose it's possible." During the course of their rescue and its immediate aftermath, Susan had developed considerable respect for the tall, blond assistant bank manager from Memphis. Although initially shaken by the disaster, she'd held up remarkably well after that, and showed no signs of belonging to the dumb blonde category.

"I actually prefer the stone-tower method myself," Cleona confided in her soft, Texas drawl. "Less technology and more magic means little or no chance our transmissions might be intercepted." A petite, fair-skinned brunette, Cleona hadn't fared as well in the wake of the crash, requiring sedation to get her aboard the flight from Inisheer to Connemara. However, the tone she'd taken with Susan during their previous "communications" demonstrated the return of an intelligent, decisive nature—one that had undoubtedly made her a valuable asset to the marketing department of the university where she worked.

"You'll have to bring me up to speed on this stone-tower thing," Jillian said. "Unless I can get the same effect from Stonehenge."

"No idea about Stonehenge," Cleona said. "But what we did was pretty cool. I was up on a watchtower on Garnish Island, and I actually talked to Susan at O'Brien's Tower, which was miles away near the Cliffs of Moher. Later on, I contacted her from the

Cahergall stone fort."

"Cool, yes, but not terribly portable or convenient," Susan reminded her. "If you're really worried about the phones being bugged, Jillian, we could each get one of those untraceable 'burner' phones. You know…the kind the criminals use on all the detective TV shows?"

"Not a bad idea," Jillian said. "I might look into that, especially after Ranjiv writes that article about us—did I tell you he's a reporter for *The London Times*? Anyway, something tells me lots of people will start hounding us after that goes public."

"You don't really think the airline would monitor us, do you?" Cleona asked. "I can't imagine they'd be involved in this scheme. That crash cost them a bundle, not to mention the number of people who canceled their flights because they were too scared to fly."

Clearly, Susan should have been communicating with these two in the traditional sense every day since they'd left the hospital in Galway. She'd anticipated having trouble telling them apart on the phone—that is, until she heard Jillian's Tennessee accent again—but she hadn't expected to feel quite so far out of the loop. "Speaking of the 'scheme,' would you mind explaining exactly what you think the scheme is and who's behind it?"

"I'm guessing the oil producers are responsible, along with all the politicians they've paid off to keep the world dependent on oil," Cleona replied. "In addition to the hundreds of tourists and business travelers who died in the crash, there were also several delegates en route to an energy summit in Paris. When you combine that with the murder Jillian and Ranjiv solved, plus the assassination plot that Kevan and I uncovered, everything points to that scenario. Too bad we can't prove it."

"Proving who committed those murders took some doing," Jillian added. "Especially when you consider that most of our clues were provided by ghosts."

Susan faced a similar problem. "I'm not sure how much proof I can dig up, but I ran across something today that backs up your theory. Six years ago, a local woman by the name of Christina Dunleavy was killed in a fall from the Cliffs of Moher. Her death was ruled a suicide, but—and I really hope you can believe this—she spoke to me in a dream and told me that if I planted roses on her grave, she'd give me the link to something. While I was planting the roses this morning, I met a man named Robert McKenna. He's the caretaker of the cemetery, and I'm convinced he's the link Christina was talking about. Christina was Seamus's girlfriend at the time of her death, and according to him, she had some amazing ideas on alternative energy. Robert said almost the same thing, plus he scoffed at the suicide ruling. He has some of her stuff—diagrams and such—and he said he'd show them to me tomorrow."

"That sounds interesting," Jillian said. "Anything else?"

Susan swallowed her nerves and plunged ahead. "Remember when I said that the crash wasn't an accident? It wasn't. The pilots deliberately ditched the plane."

"And you know that *how*?" Jillian prompted.

"One of the pilots was Chuck Travers, a guy I dated several years ago. We broke up after a few months—he has a wife and kids now—but I never really got over him, and we were still friends. I know this sounds crazy, but right before the crash, he told me the plane was going down, and he wasn't using the intercom. It was like his voice was inside my head. He claimed they had to do it or more people would die. He urged me to save myself and as many of the passengers as I could. That's why I put on a life jacket and released that raft. I'm still not sure how I ever got out of the wreck alive, but I did, and so did the two of you."

"Ranjiv's mother told me to unbuckle my seat belt and said that I was going to make it," Jillian said slowly. "Not only were we underwater at the time, she had already died. So, no, your story doesn't sound crazy at all."

"The man sitting next to me handed me a life jacket," Cleona said. "But even that wouldn't have been enough to save me without the help of the sea. I'll swear it reached down, pulled me out of the wreck, and shoved me toward the surface."

"A huge bubble of air pushed me out of the plane," Jillian said. "But I never would've made it if a swimmer hadn't told me how to orient myself and swim to the surface. She was also already dead when she told me that, and so was Katie's owner when she urged me to save her dog. Those were my three extra 'entities.' Cleona had an entire array of them. I'm guessing you acquired several yourself, right?"

"Yes, I did," Susan admitted. "They've been talking to me ever since—although aside from a psychologist and a gardener, I have no idea who the others are or how many I picked up. I'm not even sure they know themselves."

"Hmm...well, at least you know part of the truth about the crash. Solid evidence would be helpful, though."

Susan snorted out a laugh. "Just wish I knew where to look for it."

"That's why I told you to charter the boat," Cleona said. "Do you think you'll be able to communicate with Chuck if you're on a boat near the crash site?"

"God only knows," Susan replied. "I can't say it worked terribly well with Christina. I spent half the morning planting roses on her grave and didn't hear a peep from her. I decided Robert was the link without her input. I dunno...maybe she can only reach out to me in dreams. Up until last night, I hadn't been sleeping very well." No doubt those near-miss lightning strikes would trigger an inconvenient relapse of her insomnia.

"I hear you on that," Cleona declared. "That buzz in my ears nearly drove me nuts." She paused for a moment. "By the way, do you still have everyone you started off with?"

Beyond the shrink insisting that he'd never left, Susan had no clue. She hadn't exactly been able to call the roll. "How the hell would I know?"

"I always got a headache when one or more of them left," Cleona replied. "At first, there were so many voices that all I heard was a buzzing sound. After they thinned out, I could understand them better. They knew lots of stuff too—sort of like having a search engine in my head—and they each had different reasons for moving on. Some of them stuck around long enough to help us catch an assassin, but others left after my first home-cooked Irish meal." She giggled. "Quite a few of them took off after I kissed Kevan for the first time."

The kiss Susan had shared with Seamus hadn't triggered any headaches, which led her to suspect that *her* stowaways were holding out for sex. She didn't see that happening anytime soon, although after reviewing the possibilities, she considered going for it just to cull the herd a bit. Plenty of people had sex for stranger reasons.

Well, no, they probably don't...

She drew in a fortifying breath. "I haven't had any headaches so far. My stowaways seem intent on sticking with me for the duration."

"Well, if you feel a pain near your temple, that's probably what it is."

Unless someone were to hit her upside the head, which was entirely possible given the number of murders tied up in this tangled web.

"That's why we're here. To help you and keep you safe."

Susan had just mentally thanked her stowaways when another unexplained detail occurred to her. "But what about Christina? She wasn't on the plane. She died six years ago."

"Ballycarbery's ghost has been dead a lot longer than that," Cleona said. "Kevan picked that one up. No idea how. His take on it was that Earth could toss in any spirits it liked."

"And you're sure Earth is doing all of this?" If Earth was indeed a sentient being, it hadn't bothered to introduce itself to Susan. Not yet.

"Absolutely," Cleona replied. "I mean, it makes sense, doesn't it? After all the damage we've done to the planet as a species, Earth has finally had enough and is using the three of us to fight back."

Susan couldn't argue that mankind hadn't exactly been considerate when it came to exploiting planetary resources. But considering all the controversy concerning climate change and mass extinctions, she had her doubts about what three women could achieve. "Nothing against us, but I can't say we were the only ones I would've chosen for the job."

"That's the beauty of it," Cleona exclaimed. "No one expects us to do anything of the kind—or to have the knowledge to pull it off. You see, I had this…experience in the Black Valley. I felt like I was a tree growing deeply into the ground, and Earth's spirit told me I was the Carrier of Life's Preservation. Sounds weird, I'll grant you, but I'm guessing it's because I know the key to a formula that we suspect will make solar power more efficient and affordable."

"I had a spiritual connection with Earth at Stonehenge," Jillian added. "We now know lots of things we couldn't possibly have learned on our own. Things that other people were killed for knowing."

"There *is* some logic to that," Susan admitted. "But along with saving the world, I'd like to clear Chuck's name without incriminating myself. If either of you can figure that one out, be sure to let me know."

"Hey, I identified a murder suspect based on what I *allegedly* overheard on the plane without ever telling anyone that I got the firsthand info from a ghost," Jillian said. "I'm sure we can come up with something."

Cleona laughed again. "Kevan and I did practically the same thing. We had a Garda sergeant believing that Kevan was an undercover agent with access to all sorts of secret intelligence. Worked fairly well at the time, although we did come clean eventually—sort of." She hesitated briefly before continuing in a more serious tone. "Listen, Susan. There are people who can be trusted with the real story. People who can help us. You just have to find out who they are."

Susan was fairly certain that Seamus and his family could be trusted, and she felt the same way about Ian. Robert was an unknown, but Christina had obviously trusted him enough to tell him about the voices she'd heard coming from the waves. Not only had he seemed accepting of this ability, he'd even referred to it as a "gift." That same story would've triggered a totally different response from just about anyone else. Two weeks ago, she would have dubbed it madness herself.

Not anymore.

"You said something about an interview?" Susan prompted.

"Right," Jillian replied. "I want you both to talk to Ranjiv and tell him your story—the real story, not the politically correct one. After that, we can decide how to explain everything, and then he can edit the account to make it seem less…ghostly."

"Gotcha," Cleona said. "I was a little worried about that. Not that the true story wouldn't be interesting, but we want people to actually believe us."

Susan chuckled. "What? You think they won't buy the original version?"

"Come on now," Jillian said grimly. "Do you really think anyone would take us seriously if they knew the truth?"

"I can think of several people who would," Cleona replied. "But you're right. They're probably in the minority."

"Yeah. I'm guessing there aren't many practicing Earth-worshipers nowadays," Susan said. After a moment's reflection, she added, "I'm not sure there ever were."

A brief glance out her window at the green hills of Ireland had her revising that opinion. Earth was at least tangible, providing a sense of realism to the older, nature-based religions. Whereas gods, angels, and demons were abstract entities that required faith.

The Earth goddess… Mother Nature… Demeter…

"The sacredness of all things."

Those words echoed through her mind, bringing to light beliefs and notions she'd rarely considered before. The sea, the sky, the earth—all sacred, all inextricably entwined with mankind. Not possessions or wealth, but wind, rain, and the tectonic plate movements that caused earthquakes and tsunamis. Having experienced such disasters firsthand, any Earth-worshipper might pray for mercy and seek to appease that particular entity—whether conscious or not.

The supreme goddess, the lesser deities, the mountains, the wind, the weather, and, most important of all, water. Without it, life on Earth would not exist.

Bombarded with these new thoughts and ideas, any conversation between Jillian and Cleona faded into the background.

"You get it now, don't you?"

I believe I do.

Susan glanced at her watch. "Sorry to break up the party, but I gotta go see a man about a boat."

"Sure thing," Cleona said. "Let us know what happens."

"Even if nothing seems significant," Jillian added. "You never know about these things. Stuff that appears trivial at first may turn out to be really important."

"Will do," Susan promised. "Talk to you later."

As Susan switched off her phone, another such device came to mind. What to do with that waterlogged cell phone? Surely it was dry enough by now. Should she try turning it on and charging it up? She'd already checked the connection port and knew it used the same type of charger as the one she had. The power was different in Ireland, though. She might end up blowing a fuse or tripping a breaker. Perhaps she needed an adapter.

Seamus would be able to help her with that. Plus, as a seaman, he'd probably dealt with phones that had gone for a dip in the ocean, although his best advice would probably be to pitch the damn thing and forget about it.

"No matter how trivial..." she mused aloud.

After freshening herself up a bit, she dropped both phones in her purse and headed out.

* * * *

Seamus was helping the last of the afternoon's passengers disembark when he spotted Susan strolling along the quay.

Now the real fun begins.

Her first words surprised him a little. "I just realized I never asked about the fee for the boat."

Recovering quickly, he grinned. "I should charge you double since you never paid me for the last trip."

A shy smile curved her lips as she flicked a stray lock of hair from her face. "You probably should. You might even tack on an extra charge for an unscheduled cruise."

Shy or no, she was as stunning as he remembered, the mere sight of her momentarily tying his tongue into a tangle of knots. He wet his lips, recalling the intoxicating flavor of her kiss and how delightful she'd felt in his embrace—a recollection that triggered an impulse to sweep her off her feet and carry her aboard that required considerable self-restraint to suppress. He'd never considered himself to be the swashbuckling-pirate type, but there was a first time for everything.

Fortunately, Ian came to the rescue. "Come aboard, lass," he called out. "It'll be lovely having only the one passenger for a change."

"I take it that doesn't happen often," she said as she moved closer to the ladder that clung to the wall of the quay.

"Not very," Ian replied. "Although if anyone knew about you being on this trip, we'd have had a clamoring horde to contend with. You're quite the celebrity, you know."

Susan's luscious lips formed a moue of distaste. "I could do without any more of that, thank you. Although I haven't exactly been hounded for autographs."

Seamus was of the opinion that she should've been hounded for her beauty alone, although he was pleased that not everyone shared his fascination. He could handle competition. However, he saw no need to wish for it.

Susan's eyes took on a steely glint as her lips formed a firm line. "You still haven't answered my question."

"And what question would that be?" Seamus asked.

Her eyes narrowed even further. "The fee for the boat."

"Aye, well, that's negotiable, you see."

That drew a smirk. "Another dinner?"

She'd paid for the last meal they'd shared. Seamus wasn't about to let her get away with another. "Perhaps."

Arching a brow, she glanced toward Ian. "Is he always this manipulative?"

"When it suits him," Ian replied. "How about we just say the price won't break your bank account?"

"What bank account?" she said with disgust. "Right now, I haven't the slightest idea how much money I have beyond the cash the airline gave me. I mean, I have a credit card, but I haven't accessed my bank statement since before I left Newark. Don't know whether I got paid or not."

"Might be worth looking into," Ian suggested. "Although I'm guessing you not only got paid, but your paycheck was probably a bit larger this time."

Her brow rose in surprise. "I hadn't thought of that. Hush money?"

Ian shook his head. "More like hazard pay."

"You have a point, although they never mentioned anything of the sort." She frowned. "But then, I *have* been somewhat out of touch lately."

"Been keeping your phone turned off?" Ian asked.

She nodded. "I've barely spoken to anyone since the crash."

"Isolating yourself when you should have been seeing a counselor," Ian said with a sage nod. "It's time you stopped doing that."

"That's part of why I'm here."

Pausing, she directed a searching gaze toward the horizon. What did she see out there? Was she seeking permission? Reassurance?

Her firm nod seemed to corroborate his suspicions. "There's something I have to do, and I need help to do it. I've already told Seamus part of what's been happening, but I need to tell you both everything." She drew in a deep breath. "Can I trust you?"

Chapter 10

SEAMUS HAD HEARD SOME STRANGE TALES IN HIS TIME—NO DOUBT Ian had heard even more—but Susan's account of recent events blew past the rest of those stories and left them choking in the dust. Her telepathic connection with the pilot followed by her miraculous survival. The souls she and her fellow survivors had acquired and the mysteries the other two women had been instrumental in solving. Their suspicions about who was behind the overall plot based on the people who'd been targeted, as well as those who had the most to gain. Proposed strategies for exposing the responsible parties. The story was wild enough even without the supernatural elements. "I can't honestly say it doesn't make sense, but—"

"I'm not crazy," Susan insisted. "None of us are. You should know that by now."

"I wasn't going to say that." From the moment she'd come aboard, she'd impressed him with her calm demeanor and straightforward recital of the facts. This was the Susan he remembered from the day of the crash. Her take-charge attitude alone would've made a believer out of anyone. "But what can we do to help?"

Supporting her would be easy enough, but actual contributions? He and Ian weren't the ones hearing voices. According to Susan, Cleona and Jillian had each acquired a love interest to help them in their quest, and for the chance to become a permanent part of Susan's life, Seamus was perfectly willing to swallow the whole unbelievable yarn. But he still would've liked to have some idea of what his role would be.

Ian tipped his cap to one side, scratching his scalp. "Can't imagine what we could do meself. Although I'd dearly love to knock a few billionaires off their high horses."

"Sounds like fun, doesn't it?" Susan said eagerly. "Imagine the looks on their faces when they get hauled off to jail."

"Seems like we'd be up against some pretty insurmountable odds, though," Ian went on. "I'm guessing this wouldn't be the first time the oil barons have gotten away with murder."

"You think that's what Christina's death was?" Seamus prompted. "A murder?"

"I'm convinced of it," Susan replied in a tone that brooked no argument. "She didn't tell me so directly, but the dream I had just before she spoke to me... I don't see how it could be interpreted any other way."

Seamus wasn't sure how that news affected him. On one hand, he could console himself with the knowledge that Christina hadn't been despondent enough to commit suicide. He might have been able to help her with that. But murder? He couldn't have protected her from that fate unless he'd found a way to keep her from spending so much time near the cliffs. No one had ever been able to break her of that habit—one that had provided her killer with a golden opportunity. The trick would have been staging her "suicide" at a time when there were no witnesses.

Of course, this was all assuming that Susan's dream had been a true one. Either way, Christina was dead, and there still wasn't enough evidence to locate and identify her murderer, much less successfully prosecute him.

"You said she was killed by a runner?"

"Seemed that way to me," Susan replied. "The runner ran past, and then Christina went flying over the cliff."

He grimaced at the thought of both women experiencing such a horrific event. Susan had already been through a plane crash, which was terrifying enough. But now, she knew what it felt like to die. He shook off the subsequent shudder. "Don't suppose you saw his face in your, um, *dream*, did you?"

A ragged breath escaped her. "Yes, I did. And so did she."

"Who—?"

"Someone she'd seen before, but had never actually met," Susan replied. "I'm sure of that."

"Not a local, then," Ian said. "She'd have known anyone living within ten miles of the cliffs, possibly more."

"So...familiar enough that she might've seen him before, but no one she actually knew," Seamus mused. "Plenty of tourists around and plenty of them runners. Some staying long enough—" He stopped as yet another bone-chilling thought occurred to him. "Think you could identify him?"

Her smile was grim. "What makes you think Christina's killer was a man?"

Seamus nearly choked on his own spit. "You're not serious."

"Oh, but I am. Definitely a woman." She closed her eyes. "Long brown hair pulled back in a ponytail. Exotic-looking eyes. High cheekbones. Tanned and fit, like most runners. Standard running clothes and shoes." She opened her eyes and shrugged. "That's all I can tell you about her."

"I can't think of anyone I know who fits that description," Ian said. "And I know most everyone in County Clare."

Susan shifted her weight against the gunwale. "Cleona and Kevan helped the police catch one assassin—a Middle Eastern man who'd been responsible for the bombing that killed Kevan's parents. They haven't found out much about him yet, but this woman could've belonged to the same organization."

"A terrorist cell?" Seamus suggested.

"Sort of," Susan replied. "Except they appear to be paid assassins rather than actual terrorists. A few known terrorist groups have claimed responsibility, but that might simply be a matter of convenience."

Seamus nodded. "Letting someone else do their dirty work and then taking the credit."

Ian cleared his throat. "I'm thinking we should put out to sea before continuing this conversation." As if to illustrate his point, he aimed a glance toward the assortment of people were strolling along the wharf, a few of them taking photos.

"I believe you're right." Seamus looked at Susan. "Where would you like to go?"

She shrugged again. "I'm not sure it matters. Your choice."

"Then we'll head for Spanish Point," he said, a little surprised at his own decisive tone. "If anyone is watching you, they might expect you to visit the crash site. Going the opposite direction should throw them off."

Ian started the engine and adjusted the throttle. "I reckon we should get used to these cloak-and-dagger tactics, although I'm not sure anyone would ever guess what we were up to—or what *you* were up to, I should say."

"I think that's the reason I've managed to keep a low profile for so long," Susan said. "No one could ever guess how much I know, much less how I know it."

"Not unless they're into ghost stories," Seamus said. After casting off the moorings, he returned to where Susan stood with her hip resting against the railing, her brow knit in a frown. "Better give us a smile, darlin'," he advised. "We're off on a sightseeing trip, remember? Don't want anyone watching to think you aren't enjoying yourself."

Her reply consisted of a wry grin and a barely perceptible shake of her head.

"Guess that's the best we're gonna get."

As Ian piloted the boat through the tiny harbor and out into the open sea, Seamus tried to imagine other possible explanations for both the dream and Christina's death.

Obviously Ian was doing the same thing. "You're sure Christina saw her killer?" the older man asked once the boat was under way. "I mean, someone could've been coming up behind her rather than running toward her."

"Possibly," Susan conceded. "But wouldn't the woman she saw have seen whoever actually pushed her over the cliff?"

Ian scowled. "I hadn't thought of that."

Seamus joined in. "He could've been close enough behind her that the woman who ran past wouldn't have seen what he did— although she might be able to identify the perp."

"The perp?" Susan echoed with a roll of her eyes. "You've obviously been watching too many cop shows."

"Doesn't everyone?" Seamus retorted. "I wouldn't go telling

this story to the guards, though. Not without some serious editing."

"That's what Cleona and Jillian had to do," Susan said. "This is one case where the lie is a whole lot more believable than the truth." After a few moments, she added, "I don't think it could've been anyone behind her. That woman would've heard her scream and would probably have come forward as a witness."

A gasp escaped him before he could temper his response. Of course Christina would've screamed; even if her death had been a suicide, the fall would've been frightening enough to make anyone cry out.

"Sorry," Susan said. "That was careless of me."

"No need for apologies," Seamus said. "I just hadn't considered her screaming before. Don't know why."

"Might've made the situation easier to bear," Ian suggested. "Although with most violent deaths—"

Seamus put up a hand. "Deciding whether Christina screamed won't help us solve her murder." Her death was already heartbreaking enough. Further discussion certainly wouldn't ease the pain.

* * * *

Susan kept forgetting that Seamus had an emotional stake in the dilemma she now faced. He hadn't lost any loved ones in the plane crash, but he'd been in love with the girl who'd spoken to her in the wake of a dream. Yes, Christina had screamed. Susan knew that as if she'd suffered the same fate. In a way, she had. She just hadn't died as a result.

Yet.

"Right." Susan said. "How long until we get to Spanish Point?"

With the change to a more neutral topic, the lines of strain around Seamus's mouth faded slightly. "About an hour and a half, depending on the wind and current."

"Sounds good." Susan still had no idea what she would do when they arrived or whether their destination even mattered. Simply being out on the water might be enough. Although enough for what, she didn't know.

Truth be told, she was hoping for some sort of startling

revelation because seeing the face of the murderer might not be such a hot clue after all. Christina had been dead for six years. Unless she'd been killed by a local, which seemed unlikely, anyone responsible for her death would have left the vicinity long ago.

Besides, Christina hadn't said anything about solving her murder. She'd only wanted roses planted on her grave and for Susan to be kind to Seamus.

"She didn't only want you to be kind to him. She wanted you to love him."

The voices had been silent for some time now. Clearly, she'd only been allotted a brief respite. This one had a different tone from those she'd heard before. Grandmotherly, almost, and distinctively Irish.

"We're not so bad," the voice went on. *"We can be very helpful if you'll let us. And Christina was right; Seamus really does need you."*

Yeah, right. Like he needs a hole in his head.

"I'm sure that's not true. He's already very fond of you. Can't you tell?"

I suppose so, Susan conceded with an inward sigh. One nice thing about a ride in an open boat, no one expected her to talk much. The wind, the waves, and the engine conspired to drown out most conversation. Except for the conversation only she could hear. *Tell me, why are you here?*

"I was old and tired, and I hurt all the time. All I wanted was to see the old country once more before I died. Didn't even get that. Not really. Your eyes see it differently—unbiased and unaffected by the patina of memories."

Is there some place you need to go before you can move on?

"Aye. You're already heading in the right direction. Perhaps my time has finally come."

How much longer that would take was unclear. The coastline seemed unchanged from one minute to the next. Perhaps the current was against them as Seamus had suggested. Either way, the boat seemed to move so slowly through the sea. Almost as though searching for something it had lost.

"Where are we now?" she asked aloud.

"About half a mile north of Spanish Point," Seamus replied. "We can get in fairly close there if you'd like to see the beach."

Susan didn't need the inner voice to tell her that this was precisely what she needed to do, exactly where she needed to go. The gentle sigh of relief was all she needed to hear. "I'm good with that." Her own inner voice, however, had a slightly different take on the matter. "Wait a minute. 'Get in close?' You mean we can't dock there?"

"Unfortunately, no. Not quite what you'd call a harbor there, which leads me to the reason why it's called Spanish Point. A good bit of the Armada was wrecked on those rocks."

"But there's a beach, right?"

"Aye, but unless you were wanting to swim to shore, you'll have to drive over there some other time."

"Great," Susan grumbled. She needed to get her feet in the surf. That much, she knew. But today was obviously not the day for that.

"You could take the dingy in," Ian suggested. "It's the getting back past the surf that's the hard part. I could come round to pick you up, but—"

"No need," Susan said. "I can see it from out here." She studied the rugged coastline. "The Spanish Armada, you say? I'd always heard the English fleet was responsible for the Armada's defeat. Sounds like Mother Nature did it for them."

"In a manner of speaking," Seamus replied. "The Armada was badly weakened by the battles with the English. The gales and the rocks did the rest, along with disease and starvation."

Susan smiled to herself. Perhaps that was one other time when Earth had fought back, although she doubted that mankind during the reign of the first Queen Elizabeth had been quite as hard on their planet as modern man.

"I think I do need to go there," she said. "Tomorrow, maybe. After I see Mr. McKenna."

"Might want to go to the beach first," Ian advised. "A sexton would likely be in church on a Sunday morning."

Susan closed her eyes, shaking her head. "Sorry. I should've realized that. I can't seem to keep track of the days anymore."

"Could be you need to take some time off," Seamus suggested. "A day's rest would do you good."

"Maybe." She looked up as the boat approached the tip of a rocky peninsula. "Is that it?"

Seamus nodded, pointing toward the northeast. "Spanish Point is up that way beyond those rocks. The beach should be coming into view shortly."

This was information Susan didn't need. As they rounded the point, the wide expanse of sandy beach with foamy waves breaking along the shore was as familiar to her as her own reflection. Memory stacked upon memory like books in a box. Strolling hand in hand with the most handsome boy she'd ever seen. Chasing one another through the pounding surf. Laughter and kisses shared beneath a sky the color and clarity of the sapphire he gave her when he asked her to marry him. The sensuous warmth of his embrace. The breathless joy of falling in love.

"Oh, my... What a wonderful summer that was. Thank you, dear."

And with the briefest of twinges near the tip of Susan's left eyebrow, she was gone.

Pain had no part in the tears that filled Susan's eyes, save for the ache she felt at never having experienced such heady emotions herself. Previously, she'd worried that her stowaways might try to live vicariously through her. Now it seemed that the opposite was true. Even when her affair with Chuck was at its zenith, she'd never felt the feverish delight of young love.

But she knew now. Knew what she'd been denied—mainly through her own fears and inhibitions. Susan had never allowed herself to let go. She'd been the serious one. The responsible one. The one who'd seen love as an inconvenient complication in an orderly life.

My God, what I've missed. The boat surged on through the waves, rocking the deck beneath her feet. She looked down at her hands, white-knuckled on the railing.

"Susan..." Suddenly, Seamus was behind her, his arms wrapped around her waist. "What is it, luv?"

The endearment seemed too natural, too casual to mean anything. But had anyone ever called her that? No. Not even Chuck. Nor the staid fellow who'd escorted her to the prom. What an awful night that was. He'd tried so hard to be friendly, but she was too stiff, mainly because she didn't want him to get the wrong idea.

Seamus stroked the side of her face, his fingertip unerringly finding the source of her most recent discomfort—and loss.

"One of my stowaways left me," she whispered. "I didn't want her to leave—or wasn't ready for her to leave. She'd only just begun to speak to me—like she was my long-lost grandmother or something. I know it sounds crazy, but I–I'll miss her."

Susan gazed out over the beach as the after-images of her elderly stowaway's most cherished memories faded into nothingness.

Seamus held her in his arms, his silence allowing her to finish her story at her own pace. No prompting. No pressure. Only support.

"Her name was Emma," she finally said. "She fell in love right here on this beach sixty years ago. All she wanted was to see Ireland one last time."

He pressed his lips to the spot he'd touched. "And some greedy bastard decided not to let her live long enough to do it."

Susan started to protest that Chuck was no such thing until she realized that he wasn't the one to whom Seamus was referring. Seamus was right, though. Chuck had only been a pawn in a much larger game. Someone else had instigated that crash. Someone who'd decided the lives of the passengers and crew weren't important. None of their hopes and dreams were significant in any way. Only their deaths mattered. Only their senseless, irrevocable deaths.

"Yeah. We need to find that bastard. And when we do, we need to make him pay."

And pay, and pay, and pay...

Chapter 11

Silence reigned as the boat slid past the beach. Seamus had known this trip would be an emotional one. He just hadn't expected those emotions to have one of Susan's stowaways as their source. As it was, he thanked God that Ian was in the know. Otherwise, he'd have had to come up with some plausible explanation for Susan's reaction to seeing Spanish Point beach, presumably for the first time.

Now all he had to do was decide where to go next. They were almost to the rocky headland north of Quilty, which was as good a spot to turn around as any. Or should they keep going? Still holding Susan in his arms, he aimed a questioning glance at his crewmate, hoping for suggestions.

Ian didn't disappoint. "If you still fancy a walk on a beach, Susan, we could go on down to Baile An Tsagart. It's not far, and there's a wee harbor there."

That was Ian for you, always the calm voice of reason. Seamus had enjoyed the opportunity to hold Susan in his arms. A stroll on the beach sounded even better. With a gentle fingertip beneath her chin, he tilted Susan's face up toward his. Despite the tears in her eyes that tore at his heart, he managed a smile. "What do you say to that?"

"Sounds perfect," she replied. "I really need to walk on the sand—maybe even get my feet wet." Her voice had lost the quaver that had accompanied her retelling of Emma's story.

The poor woman. To come all that way only to die a few miles short of her goal was sad indeed, but at least Emma's memories had been happy ones. Seamus had always thought Spanish Point a rather melancholy spot, particularly in light of its history. Emma had obviously seen it differently. If her spirit chose to remain to haunt the beach, God knew she would have plenty of Spanish sailors for company. Perhaps she could cheer them up a bit.

Seamus gave himself a quick mental slap. Not a laughing matter, really. But then, so few things were these days.

The story about the oil producers' involvement was horrific, but it rang truer than any tale he'd ever heard. Unfortunately, bringing those crooks to justice would take more than the efforts of any one person. Even *three* women with the ability to speak with the dearly departed didn't have much chance of success. Small wonder the planet itself had taken a hand in the matter.

Ian had accepted the tale with ease, never questioning Susan's sanity or even asking for proof—not that she could've provided any. Once again, Seamus reminded himself that all he had to do was consult Jillian and Cleona. If they could corroborate Susan's account of the crash and the subsequent events, there could be no disputing Susan's outlandish claims. Susan had their phone numbers. He could call them if he liked, but a face-to-face meeting might be better.

"Have you given any thought to getting together with Jillian and Cleona? Between my house and Mum's we could put them up without any trouble if they want to come to Liscannor."

"You may have to put *me* up soon," she said with a wince. "After tomorrow night, my room at the hotel is spoken for. They said they'd let me know if there was a cancellation, but I can't depend on that."

The thought of Susan staying in his house nearly rendered him speechless, but he managed to recover enough to add, "There'd be room for you as well."

"If that doesn't suit you, there are plenty of holiday rentals hereabouts," Ian said. "Surely they wouldn't all be booked."

"That's a thought," Susan said. "We could share the rent."

"I'd be sending the bill to your airline, meself," Ian said with a snort.

"Don't worry. They've already given us each plenty of money. I can afford to rent a house, even without help."

Seamus would've been happier if she'd been destitute. That way the offer to stay at his place would have been impossible to refuse.

Not that she'd refused it. Ian had simply given her another, perfectly sensible alternative.

Damn him.

"Save your money and stay with me," Seamus said. "I've an extra bedroom." Not that he wanted her to use any bedroom other than his own, but the offer was a bit more gentlemanly when put that way.

"I'll think about it," she said. In the next instant, she let out a startled cry as Ian throttled the engine back and steered toward the rocks.

"Easy, now," Seamus said. "It only looks like we're about to run aground. The entrance to the harbor is pretty narrow."

"That's putting it mildly," she said as the tiny inlet came into view. "I was beginning to think you had a death wish, Ian."

Ian chuckled. "No chance of that. Been sailing this coast for nearly fifty years. If I'd wanted to die, I could've done it long ago."

Ian cruised through the harbor and guided the boat up close to the quay. Seamus grabbed one of the mooring lines and tied it to the bow.

She eyed the concrete wall with misgiving. "I see we'll be climbing another ladder."

"Aye. I think you can handle it," Seamus said. "If not, I'll climb up and haul you ashore with a rope."

"Very funny."

Granted, his attempt at humor hadn't exactly been sidesplitting, but she was at least smiling. When dealing with Susan, making her smile seemed to be his chief goal. For now.

Perhaps that was his role in saving the world: To keep Susan from succumbing to fits of melancholy before her task was complete. Saving the world might take years. He had years and years of making Susan smile to look forward to.

On that cheery note, he tied off the stern, then ushered Susan toward the ladder. "Ladies first."

With a roll of her eyes, she grasped a rung and pulled herself up. "Don't you be staring at my ass."

"Wouldn't dream of it," Seamus said with a careless wave. No, he wouldn't be staring at her bum. He's be gazing at it with speechless admiration.

There was a difference.

* * * *

Susan climbed the ladder to the top of the quay, then stood marveling at the surf-worn rocks and the vast expanse of the sea beyond. Whitecaps dotted the ever-changing surface, and a steady breeze lifted her hair. Gulls rode the wind, their black and white wings in sharp contrast to the blueness of the sky as they took the occasional dive into the sea. As she watched, one of them came up with a fish, gleaming like silver in the sunshine.

If only people's lives were that simple.

Seamus came up behind her, dropping a casual arm around her shoulders. "Worth the trip, wouldn't you say?"

She had to laugh. "Of course it is. But then, every inch of this coastline is breathtaking." She elbowed him in the ribs. "Which you know quite well."

"Aye. Although even incredible scenery loses some of its gloss when you see it on a daily basis." He hesitated. "Haven't been here for a while, though." He nodded to his left. "The path to the beach is this way."

A tremor shook her. "I don't know whether to be anxious or afraid.'"

He chuckled. "Don't be too disappointed if nothing happens."

In a move as natural as breathing, she slipped an arm around his waist. "Yeah. Sometimes a beach is just a beach." Unlike Spanish Point. Seeing it veiled in Emma's memories would be a tough act to follow. Perhaps that was the lone reason for the excursion along the coast. The only surprise was that she hadn't lost more than one soul there. "I've seen the Atlantic from several perspectives, but must admit I like this view best. Dunno why. I felt the same way at the Cliffs of Moher."

"Could be the wind or the currents," he suggested. "Or the fact that you're facing west when you look at it."

"Who knows?" she said with a shrug. "Maybe it's because I'm

in Ireland. I've always liked it here. Maybe this is where I belong—or some of my stowaways do. Either way, the attraction seems stronger now." She waited for Seamus to make the obvious comment that meeting him was the reason for the change.

He didn't. Perhaps he didn't need to.

Perhaps her brush with death was the reason. Ireland was the place where her feet had touched solid ground after the crash, letting her know that she wasn't lost, hadn't died, and actually had a future.

She drew in a deep breath and gave him a decisive nod. "Okay. I'm ready now."

Taking her by the hand, Seamus turned and walked with her along the quay toward the path. As chilly as the breeze was in late May, she could only imagine the biting wind the locals had to endure in winter. Southward, seaside homes were scattered along a road running parallel to the coast. Near the quay, however, there was nothing but an old ruin. Not a castle—the building style appeared to be more recent than that—but the walls of a long, rectangular structure that could have been home to anything from the local lord's family to the county militia.

The rain had moved out, leaving nothing behind but clear blue sky and ocean waves as far as the eye could see. The path was smooth and sandy, the descent to the beach relatively steep. No booming thunder or bolts of lightning tried to frighten her away this time, and she released Seamus's hand to run down to the shore with the exuberance of a child on holiday. Upon reaching the water's edge, she slipped off her shoes and tossed them to Seamus.

The moment her bare feet touched the wet sand, power surged upward through her body, lifting her hair in crackling strands that were tossed about by the northwest wind. Seamus had made several "fierce ginger" comments. Now, they seemed justified. Spreading her arms wide, she let her head fall back as she gazed up at the sky. Moments later, swarms of sparkling motes flowed from her fingertips to swirl around her outstretched arms like a million microscopic fireflies. She stretched her arms out in front of her, staring at her hands while wishing for darkness to make the tiny lights more visible.

And darkness came.

As though the moon had passed between Earth and its sun, day turned into night, and the motes ignited in a rainbow of sparks. The sea crashed against the shore, gaining in height and fury with each successive wave until a wall of water rose before her.

She lowered her arms, turning her palms downward, and the sea quieted. Sounds reached her ears, faint at first, but steadily increasing in volume. She'd heard it somewhere before.

Whale song.

"Hear the music of the deep and know its power and beauty," sang the whales. *"Beauty to restore the soul, and power to instill unity in all of mankind."*

"But there *is* no unity, and there never has been," Susan shouted, almost ashamed to be a member of such a violent species. "Everything we touch, we destroy."

"Where there is beauty, there is love, and there is beauty in all things—the soil of this earth, the life that springs from its mating with the sun and rain, and the beings that had their beginnings as tiny cells. You have only to look closely to see them for what they are."

Susan dug deep into her soul to find the answer. "The beauty of nature?"

"Not all can see it. Your task is to show them."

The impulse to reply with derisive laughter was strong. "What? Paint pictures and share them with the vilest elements of society? You must be joking."

"The images are already there for you to discover. So few have seen them. They must be shared."

Of course… Christina's drawings.

But how on earth could they be shared with everyone on the planet? How could they alter the perspective of everyone who saw them? Susan had seen pictures drawn by children showing the wondrous joys of love and family. But nearly as many had depicted scenes of hatred, bigotry, and domination. If none of those had the power to make a change, what could Christina have possibly drawn that was any different?

"You will know when you see them," came the reply. *"You will know…"*

The sea grew quiet, save for the soft murmur of the surf. Susan looked down at her hands and at the tide swirling about her feet. The tiny fireflies had gone and the sun was shining once again.

She turned to find Seamus standing a few yards behind her, his eyes wide with shock. She was afraid to move, afraid he might run from her as though she were a monster.

Perhaps that was what she was. A terrifying demon conjured up by the angry souls of those who'd been unjustly robbed of their lives and died in misery and torment. The elements were tough enough to overcome. Why did people have to be so hard on one another?

She had no words to describe what had just happened. All she could do was look at him, standing there, his mind clearly in turmoil. What was he thinking? How to escape? Whether he could justify leaving her there to find her own way back to Liscannor?

The wind fell silent and even the sea seemed to hold its breath as he closed the distance between them.

Eyes twinkling, he grasped her hand and raised it to his lips. "Dunno what I expected, luv. But we surely brought you to the right beach."

* * * *

Never having seen such a sight in his life, Seamus opted for comic relief to soothe the seething emotions the event left behind. Event was the only word he could think of to describe what he'd witnessed, and he needed a bit of breathing space to process it.

She can control the sea.

Granted, the effect appeared to have been isolated, but the mere thought of such power shook him to the core.

You can surely pick them, Seamus Quinn.

Mum would be proud. She'd always wanted him to find a woman with a brilliant future, and from what he'd just seen Susan do, futures didn't get much more brilliant than that.

Her uncertain smile surprised him, especially when she should have been feeling confident and regal. "I suppose you did." Her eyes squeezed shut. "How much of that did you hear?"

"Only what you said. I take it there was more?"

She nodded. "I wasn't the one who was supposed to save the world, Seamus. Not me or Jillian or Cleona. Christina was the savior. Maybe not of the planet itself, but of the souls of humankind. And she was killed because of it. Our last best hope and someone pushed her over a cliff." With a shudder, she stepped from the receding surf onto dry sand. "I could use a drink right about now. Don't suppose you have any Jameson on the boat, do you?"

"I can't imagine an Irish vessel without a bottle or two," Seamus replied. He gazed down the length of the beach. "But let's walk for a bit first, and when you're ready, you can fill me in on what I missed." With her nod, he draped an arm around her shoulders and pulled her close. "You're freezing cold."

"Yeah. That's why I wanted the whiskey, but you're right. A walk will do as well to warm me up and clear the cobwebs. Right now, my mind is a little…fuzzy."

Seamus wasn't exactly thinking clearly himself. What were the odds of one man being involved with two saviors? His heart skipped a beat or two as he considered the possibility that he, himself, was an important factor.

No way. Not a simple seaman like Seamus Quinn.

And yet he'd been there to rescue Susan and her fellow survivors—even arriving ahead of the other boats in the area. If he and Ian had been any closer to the crash site, the *Branwyn Eostre* would've sunk and they would've died along with all the other unfortunate victims.

But they'd been in precisely the right spot. Not too close, just close enough. He'd known and loved Christina, accepting her for the genius she had been. He'd been equally accepting of Susan's claims. Perhaps gullibility was all that was required. That and a willingness to offer his support, not to mention being in the right place at the right time.

Even his boat's name was significant: named after Branwyn, the goddess of love, sexuality, and the sea and Eostre, the goddess of spring, rebirth, fertility, and new beginnings. He tried to recall who'd christened the boat. His father hadn't been her first owner, and to his knowledge she hadn't been renamed. At least, he hoped she hadn't. Changing a boat's name was bad luck, and no one who spent the greater part of their life at sea would knowingly take such an unnecessary risk.

They strolled the length of the beach in silence. The sun was dipping low in the sky as they reached the rocks at the end of the strand. "We'd best be getting back." The sea at night didn't frighten him, but Susan needed her dinner, and if there was a pub within walking distance of this beach, he'd yet to hear of it.

With her nod, they turned and headed back the way they'd come. They'd covered about half the distance before she spoke. "Are you playing at the pub tonight?"

He shook his head. "There's another band playing tonight, so I've the whole evening to spend with you." When she failed to comment, he added quickly, "If that's what you'd like."

"Yeah. I'd like that." Her baby-soft voice was barely audible above the murmuring sea. "You didn't miss anything. I think I've told you what you need to know. But"—she paused a moment, frowning as though sifting through her miraculous conversation with the sea—"Mr. McKenna—he's the sexton at Kilmacrehy Church— he told me that Christina could hear voices coming from the beach below the churchyard. I wonder if she heard the same thing I did."

"Which was?"

"Whales. The freakin' *whales* were singing to me, Seamus! And the craziest part was that I understood them." She ran a hand through her hair, skinning it back from her forehead as she shook her head in bewilderment. "Whales. Just think how many of them we've hunted down and killed." She stopped suddenly, and her mouth fell open. "Holy cow. The whales. That reminds me of that 'Save-the-whales' *Star Trek* movie." A moment later, she bowed her head, grimacing. "That must've come from one of my stowaways. As far as I know, I've never seen that one."

"Me either. Enlighten me."

"There was a space probe that was disrupting everything—

power, communications, navigation—and the *Enterprise* crew had to go back in time to pick up a pair of humpback whales to take back to the future so the whales could answer the probe and get it to go away." When she turned to look him in the eyes, he was struck once again by her similarity to Christina. "They're intelligent and wise. And all we've done is hunt them to near extinction."

"We're doing better about that now," Seamus pointed out. "They're protected around the world."

"Not completely," she insisted. "We haven't done enough. Not *nearly* enough. We've polluted their ocean with garbage and chemicals and created so much noise they can barely hear one another." Sighing, she leaned against him. "Let's go back to Liscannor, Seamus. I can't think about this anymore. At least, not right now. This task seems insurmountable, and I'm *so* tired."

Her voice had been hushed before. Now it was positively faint.

"We can tackle that tomorrow," he said. "You'll feel better after a nice dinner and a good night's sleep." Seamus might not be able to make her sleep, but he could certainly see to it that she got a decent meal.

"And a shot of Jameson," she reminded him.

"That too."

Chapter 12

THE SUN HAD SET BY THE TIME THE *BRANWYN EOSTRE* CRUISED INTO the harbor at Liscannor. Having promised Seamus another dinner in exchange for the boat ride—"You'll never make a million that way, Seamus Quinn," she'd said—she soon discovered that a bowl of coddle and a shot of Jameson did almost as much for her as the Guinness and chowder had the night before. However, whether a good night's sleep would be forthcoming remained to be seen.

Even so, she wasn't a bit surprised to find herself yawning into her napkin before she'd eaten half of her meal. "Sorry," she said. "This has been a really long day."

"The most recent in a series of other long days, I'll wager," Seamus said. "That sort of thing takes its toll."

"Yeah. I thought I was doing so much better, but then it hits me all of a sudden." Granted, she didn't plant roses and outrun storms every day, not to mention talking to spirits of the dead and the whales of the sea, but she should've been able to do that and more without conking out over dinner.

An internal snicker caught her slightly off guard. Evidently she hadn't lost all of her stowaways on the excursion to Baile An Tsagart.

"From our standpoint, those things seem like everyday occurrences."

I suppose they would, Susan replied. *But then, you've all done so much more than I have.*

"True. Although none of us ever did what you're doing now. At least not when we were alive."

What? No psychics among you? I'd have thought there would be at least one."

The only reply she received was another snicker.

"Have you given any thought to my offer?"

Momentarily startled at being addressed by a real live person, Susan took a moment to think before she spoke. "You mean staying at your house? No, I haven't, although I need to. Either that or talk to the hotel people about the possibility of staying there longer." Grimacing, she added, "Going home doesn't appear to be an option at this point."

"Probably not." Seamus reached across the table to cover her hand with his. "You're still trembling."

"Am I?" She drew back her hand and held it up. "Definite tremor." Squeezing her eyes shut, she huffed out a breath. "Damn, this is getting old. If I'm supposed to save the feckin' world, you'd think I'd be given the nerve to actually do it."

"Oh, you have the nerve, all right," he declared. "You've just never been tested like this. You're the only one of the survivors who actually lost people you cared about in the crash. You need to acknowledge your grief."

She responded with an inelegant snort. "You sound like my resident shrink. And, yes, you're both right. The trouble is I can't seem to get in the right frame of mind and stay there."

"Hey, nobody ever said saving the world would be easy. If I had to guess, I'd say it was the toughest job in history." He gestured toward her plate. "You need to finish that coddle. Gotta keep up your strength. Or would you prefer another round from the bar?"

Her burst of laughter drew a glance from the couple seated at the next table. "You're a big help," she drawled. "But at least you made me laugh."

"That would seem to be my purpose in all this."

"What? Making me laugh?"

"Of course. It's the best medicine—or so they say."

She leaned forward with her elbow on the table and her cheek cradled in her palm. After studying him for a moment, something about the glint in his eyes and the mischievous nature of his grin raised her spirits a notch or two. She thought back to the moment when she realized that he was as important as any of her stowaways—or even Cleona or Jillian. She'd been relying on him ever since she'd found him again. Perhaps she needed to rely on him a little more. "Maybe it doesn't matter whether you make me laugh. Maybe you're the best medicine, simply by being here."

"Tisn't hard to do. In fact, I can't think of another place I'd rather be." He glanced away for a second before returning his gaze to her eyes. "Stay with me, Susan. I promise to take very good care of you. You can have your own room—even your own bathroom—and I'll serve you breakfast in bed every morning. I'll give you clean sheets and towels every day. Of course, you'll have to change the bed yourself, but—"

Laughing, she put up a hand. "Stop. You had me with breakfast in bed." She searched her memory for a similar occurrence and didn't find one. "Don't believe I've ever had breakfast in bed. Unless you count that pathetic excuse for food they brought me in the hospital."

A slow smile spread across his face, dimpling both cheeks and crinkling the corners of his deep brown eyes. "Oh, I'm sure I can do better than that. My sister isn't the only one in the family who can cook."

"Hmm… Yes, well, play your cards right and I'll be the one bringing you breakfast in bed."

"That's the plan." He waggled his brow in a roguish manner. "Devious, isn't it?"

She slapped her napkin on the table in mock annoyance. "I *knew* there had to be a catch."

"There always is. I only hope you're willing to be caught."

"Do you know, I might be," she said slowly. "Not yet, of course, but someday. Maybe."

"I reckon that'll have to do." He aimed a pointed stare toward her uneaten coddle. "Now, finish your dinner, and I'll walk you home."

"Aye, aye, Captain," she said and picked up her spoon.

* * * *

Seamus couldn't think of anything he'd like more than to look after Susan for the rest of his life. Protecting her. Providing for her. Loving her. Growing old with her. She brought every masculine instinct to the fore like no other, not even Christina. After dinner, he paid the bill and escorted her to the door. He didn't care who saw his hand cupping the small of her back. In fact, he'd have waved a red flag to draw the attention of everyone in the pub if he'd had one handy.

A steady offshore breeze met them as they stepped outside.

"Cold?" he asked as she pulled her cardigan more tightly around herself.

"Not a bit," she replied. "I'm loving this sea air thing. Makes me wonder why I've spent so much of my life in airports. You never feel the fresh air in those places. They're all so enclosed and regulated—cut off from the rest of the world. There may have been freedom in flying at one time, but the terrorists ruined it for everyone. Just one more risk you have to be willing to take in order to travel."

"Do you think your plan to save the world will put an end to terrorism?"

"Probably not. Not until people stop breeding hatred and mistrust and learn to coexist. You'd think it would be simple, wouldn't you? But it isn't. The emotions are too deeply ingrained."

"What if we all had a common enemy?"

She turned toward him and smiled. "Like an alien invasion?"

"Or Earth turning against us?"

"Earth isn't our enemy," she said with a slow wag of her head. "And even if it was, we can't fight it. We can only placate it."

"You say that like the planet has already turned against us."

"Not exactly. It's more like a parental reprimand."

"I dunno. All the earthquakes, floods, and such seem more like punishment to me."

"Except that the people who perish in those disasters usually aren't the ones plundering the planet. They're the simple folks who live in fragile houses and are barely scraping out a living. That's where we come in—Jillian, Cleona, and me. Our job is to go after the ones in the mansions and palaces."

As she turned seaward again, her high, smooth cheekbones, straight nose, and determined chin captured his gaze. Looking at her, standing there with the wind in her hair, he could imagine her doing all manner of great deeds. Perhaps not on the Joan of Arc level, but close. She was brave and inspiring. A leader. A living, breathing heroine. If only the odds she faced didn't seem so insurmountable.

"Those are some pretty powerful people."

"I know. And I still don't know how we're going to do it. Christina's drawings better contain some seriously strong magic." Without another word, she started off down the street toward her hotel as though she could leave the subject behind by doing so. Or perhaps strive toward the answer.

When they reached the hotel, she hesitated, biting her thumbnail as she glanced toward the sea. "I'm not sure I'm ready to call it a day yet."

Despite having admitted to being tired, the prospect of disturbing dreams was enough to discourage anyone from seeking their bed. "Would you care for a walk down to the Lower Quay?"

"Yeah," she replied with an absent nod. "I believe I would."

They continued on, following the road past the row of houses that faced the sea. Set rock-throwing distance from the water's edge, some were freshly painted and neat as a pin, while others showed the inevitable effects of harsh weather and neglect.

"Seems strange that there'd be houses here," she said. "I can't imagine living so close to the water. Must be pretty bleak in winter."

"Aye. But then a good many of these are holiday homes. Generally empty in the winter months."

She acknowledged his explanation with another absent nod. "Where did you say your house was?"

"I didn't. But it's a bit further inland. At a place called Cahilly."

"Cahilly," she repeated, her voice sounding even softer than usual. "I like the sound of that." She made a full turn on the spot as though taking in the panoramic view. "Must mean 'absence of hills' because there certainly aren't any around here."

"Dunno what its meaning is, actually. Cahilly is also a surname, so the area was probably named after someone who lived there at one time." He shrugged. "These places are so old, it's hard to say where the names came from."

"Seems strange to have a history that dates so far back. Never recorded and so long ago as to be completely forgotten."

He nodded. "The change from Gaelic to English didn't help. Any written records would've been in Gaelic, and for a long time, there were few who could read it. The Irish language is making a comeback, but a good bit of the oral history and folklore got lost along the way, possibly forever."

"Sad, isn't it?" She left the road and walked across the narrow strip of lawn separating the street from the low cliff that overlooked the sea. "Earth probably remembers, though. If it even cares about such things." She peered over the edge. "From the street, you'd never guess there was a beach down there."

"At one time, I knew every inch of that shoreline. Spent hours clambering among the rocks searching for treasure."

"Real treasure?"

"Aye," he replied. "Some were things only a boy would find interesting, while others would've been valued by anyone. You see, the North Atlantic Drift comes in here, fetching up everything from coconuts to gold doubloons."

Fortunately, this particular area was well south of the crash site, and the currents would bring no wreckage from the plane. Witnessing the tragedy had been horrifying. The thought of bodies washing up on the beach where he'd played as a child was even more disturbing.

Especially if one of them had been the body of the woman standing beside him.

Thankfully, he hadn't been the one to find Christina after she'd fallen from the cliff. A group of tourists had spotted her body floating among the rocks and her parents had identified her body— surely one of the most devastating tasks any parent could ever face—and the casket had been closed at her funeral. Seamus hadn't had to witness what the fall had done to her, her slender body broken and her once-lovely face probably battered beyond recognition. So many horrors had taken place along that coast, it was a wonder there weren't legions of ghosts lined up to frighten away any hapless visitors.

Nothing remained of those deaths. No echoing screams of those who'd perished. Not even the whispers of their departing souls. Earth had absorbed their life forces the way it did when any creature passed on, be they plant or animal.

Susan gave him a nudge. "You know, for a boy who found treasures here, you don't seem very happy."

"Thinking about the past too much, I suppose," he said with a shrug. "Doesn't do to dwell on those days. Best to chalk them up as fond memories and move on."

"They weren't all fond, though, were they?"

He shook his head. "Not really. But then, as the saying goes, 'this too shall pass,' which applies to the bad as well as the good."

His heart seemed to swell and his mood lightened as she took his hand. Such a simple touch, and yet it conveyed an endless supply of loving support.

"I want the memory of this moment to last longer than that," she said. "Something to restore my soul during trying times."

"It means that much to you?" His own emotions were easily labeled. Hers were less transparent.

"Yes, and we're going to need all the good vibes we can get, and we'll be needing them soon."

He studied her face expecting a troubled frown but saw only quiet determination. "Have you seen something? Had a premonition of some kind?"

"No. Just a feeling."

She gazed out toward a sea gone suddenly quiet, reminding him of her ability to control the waves. She'd seemed more impressed with her ability to hear whales, and while that was a remarkable skill, controlling the sea had far more profound implications. So much, in fact, he'd have liked to watch her do it again.

"Can you really affect the movement of the sea?" he asked. "Change the height of the waves and such?"

"Maybe. I don't really know." A frown flitted across her brow. "Not sure I'd want to waste it on a demonstration. Might not even be able to."

"I understand." He thought he did, actually. Why waste the

magic on something so trivial?

"I'd much rather demonstrate something else."

"Oh? And what would that be?"

"This." Rising up on her tiptoes, she slid a hand behind his head, her fingers in his hair setting off a wave of excitement as she pulled him down. Soft and delightful, the touch of her lips on his shot lightning bolts of scorching heat straight through his heart before spiraling down to his groin. The woman certainly knew how to divert his attention.

She was right, though. The time had come to leave the past behind and move on. Whatever tragedies awaited them, the good times ahead would surely outweigh the bad, and they would endure long after their ordeal ended.

Drawing her into his embrace, he deepened the kiss, intensifying the heady feeling that was already making breathing difficult. He held his breath, praying she wouldn't stop before he was ready.

Ready, hell. He could've kissed her for days on end and not gotten enough. He could make love to her in a thousand different ways and still search for new methods to please her.

You are well and truly smitten, Seamus Quinn.

Not that he was complaining.

* * * *

Of all the men Susan had encountered in her lifetime, Seamus had to be the most comfortable fellow she'd ever met. With no blatant attempts at seduction or domination, save for making sure she looked after herself, he was generally agreeable and eager to help her in any way he could. The fact that he was a damn good kisser was yet another mark in his favor.

Unless this was another of his devious plots. Make her fall madly in love with him and learn to depend on him before pulling the rug from under her feet.

"Nope. Not gonna happen."

Alone in her hotel room, Susan saw no need to refrain from speaking aloud. "Should've known you guys would chime in on that thought."

"He's exactly what he says he is. No lies. No hidden agendas."

"An honest man. Who knew there was such a thing?"

"There are plenty of honest men, and you know it. You've never given them a chance."

"I gave Chuck a chance. And you know how *that* ended."

The hoot of internal laughter startled her. *"You're the one who ended it. Said you couldn't handle all the secrecy."*

Clearly, there was no hiding the truth from her gang of stowaways. "I never understood that part. Why we had to be so damned discreet. Like he was ashamed for anyone to know we were lovers."

"Perhaps he was. Or perhaps he knew that if your affair became known, he wouldn't have been able to continue playing the field the way he did after he married. And if he'd married you, he wouldn't have been able to hide his indiscretions from someone who worked with him."

Susan had to stifle a gasp of dismay. "Boy, you people don't pull any punches, do you?"

"Total honesty," said the stowaways. *"Tough pill to swallow, isn't it?"*

She couldn't argue the point, nor did she see the need, especially when her other reason for ending the affair was that, no matter how much she loved him, she'd never been able to trust him completely. "Point made. Listen, we've got a big day ahead of us tomorrow, and I'd like to get through it without feeling so exhausted. If you guys don't let me get some sleep, I'll tell Seamus you kept me up all night." This was yet another empty threat because about all he could do was chastise her stowaways. He couldn't actually punch one of them in the nose.

"Nighty night, then."

Yawning, Susan was about to close her eyes and snuggle into the sheets when she remembered the phone. "Damn! Why didn't you people remind me about that phone?"

"Guess we were too interested in the romance."

"Yeah, right," she said with a snort of laughter. "You should be focusing on promoting the greater good instead of playing Cupid." Or acting out any voyeuristic fantasies they might have imagined.

"We heard that. No voyeurism. Honest."

"Oh, hush up."

Chapter 13

A DEAFENING CLAP OF THUNDER WOKE SUSAN IN THE NIGHT, AND A glance at the bedside clock proved she'd slept far longer than she'd expected. No dreams good or bad had disturbed her slumber. Only the rain. Lightning struck nearby, its brief illumination revealing no watchful spirits or frightening specters. Perhaps she'd had enough psychic experiences for one day, although by this time, she ought to be getting used to them.

This would be her last night alone in the hotel. Tomorrow night, she would be sleeping in Seamus's guest room. Funny how she had no qualms about accepting a room from a man she barely knew. Then again, he'd already been the consort of one messiah; clearly Earth's spirit considered him trustworthy. Perhaps the whales did too.

Sitting up in bed, she threw back the covers. No eerie sounds accompanied her as she went over to the window and raised the blind. Rain sluiced down the windowpane, highlighted by the streetlights below. Rain. Simple, ordinary rain. Nothing supernatural about it. A typical spring thundershower. At least, she thought such weather was common for the west coast of Ireland in late May. Or maybe it wasn't. Maybe the storms had something to do with her presence.

Or Christina's.

Then she remembered. She'd been in Ireland in the spring before and had only experienced gentle showers—frequent, perhaps, but light, overall. There were bound to be plenty of storms in winter—the North Atlantic was famous for them—but springtime? Probably not.

"Okay," she whispered. "So this *isn't* normal." The locals must've been freaking out, wondering if the end of the world was upon them.

"My, how melodramatic."

Susan chuckled. She was never truly alone, not even as the single occupant of a hotel room. A moment later, she realized whose voice she'd heard.

"Christina?"

"Oh, you're a sharp one, you are. Had me figured out right away, didn't you?"

Her scalp tightened for a split second before releasing a flood of goose bumps. "You spoke to me in a dream before. Am I dreaming now?"

"Does it matter?"

"Probably not. Does this mean you're one of my stowaways now?" Even as she asked the question, Susan knew the sound wasn't coming from inside her mind. The spirit's voice surrounded her, as though it inhabited the entire room.

"Not exactly. I came with the rain tonight, so we haven't much time."

Apparently even the supernatural had rules. "What about Robert? Was I right about him too?"

"Absolutely. He was my insurance. The whales warned me of the danger—and so did Robert. I couldn't stay away from the cliffs, though. They called to me so strongly. The cliffs should've warned me themselves, but they never did." She paused as though considering the possible reasons for their silence. *"I suppose that was asking too much. There are limits, even to Earth's own powers."*

Lightning flashed again. Several seconds passed before the thunder rolled. The storm was passing through quickly.

"You're doing well with Seamus," she went on. *"He's happier than he's been in years. The way you kissed him was quite adorable."* Somehow, her tone managed to convey a smile. *"He thought so too."*

"I–I'm pleased to hear it." A moment's reflection generated another question. "Wait a minute… You can read his thoughts?"

"Only his emotions," Christina replied. *"The stronger ones, mostly—and he feels very strongly about you."*

Susan briefly considered downplaying the notion but saw no point in arguing with a spirit. They might have limits to their abilities—Susan doubted Christina could even open a door—but their sources of information were as far-reaching as they were reliable.

"You seem concerned about Seamus. Shouldn't I be focusing my energy on saving all of mankind rather than one specific person?"

"When you save one, you begin the process of saving them all."

Susan hesitated, giving this some thought before responding. "True," she finally said. "Although you'd think there'd be more of that peace and love stuff going on than there is. Why so much hatred, violence, and greed? I don't understand the need for such things. They seem so pointless."

"Ah, then... We're two of a kind on that subject. My problem was that I focused too sharply on the world as a whole and not enough on individuals. Together, I believe we can make a difference."

A sliver of lightning flickered in the distance as the rain subsided to a light sprinkle. If Christina came with the storm, her time was growing short, and so many questions remained unasked. "Maybe. But I still don't see how—"

"You will. Go and see Robert. He'll show you my drawings. You'll understand then."

If the art of Van Gogh, Da Vinci, and Rembrandt hadn't saved the world, what chance did the works of anyone have? "Those must be some drawings."

Gentle laughter filled the room, slowly swelling in volume before fading to nothingness.

The rain had stopped, and once again, the room was silent, save for the rush of blood pulsing through Susan's ears.

She stared into the distance, watching as lightning struck a long way off. "What do I do now? Go back to sleep?"

As she'd expected, her stowaways were quick to reply. *"You probably should. Too bad Seamus isn't handy. You really should've moved in with him today. He could've kept you company instead of us."*

"Hmm...maybe. What do you make of Christina?"

"Dunno exactly, but we're pretty sure she's a genius."

"Good. I'm glad we have intelligent help because I'm so tired of all this, I could scream."

"Please don't. You'll wake the neighbors."

"Might get myself kicked out of the hotel sooner," Susan mused. "Then Seamus would have to take me in now."

A whispered exchange took place in Susan's mind. *"Nah. Not worth the trouble. Go to sleep. We'll wake you if anything interesting happens."*

"Okay. Will do."

Susan crawled back into her bed, pulled up the covers, and

didn't think another thought until the sun filtering through the blinds woke her the following morning.

Seamus had said something about attending an early mass, which made her wonder what church Robert belonged to. Obviously, the Kilmacrehy site was no longer suitable for use. Still, he'd said to come anytime. Perhaps he would instinctively know when to expect her. Or maybe Christina was keeping him posted on Susan's whereabouts. Too bad she wasn't doing the same for Susan.

After a quick shower, Susan dressed and went down to the pub. She was beginning to look forward to the full Irish breakfast, and though she doubted she truly needed the calories, at least her appetite was back.

After breakfast, she went for a stroll along the Lower Quay where she and Seamus had walked the night before and soon found herself sitting at the lawn's edge, gazing out at the waves.

Seamus had not only offered her a room, he'd promised her breakfast in bed, which was sounding better all the time. She'd have given a lot for that level of care in the days following the crash— someone to look after her when she barely had the energy to get out of bed, let alone cook anything or go to a pub. The first day after leaving the hospital, she hadn't eaten a thing until nearly four in the afternoon, and even then, she'd had no taste for food.

Four o'clock. Teatime.

"Like in The Long, Dark Teatime of the Soul*,"* a male voice whispered in her mind. *"Sunday afternoons when nothing lies ahead but going back to work on Monday morning."* An audible shudder followed.

Susan suspected this attitude was either a male affliction or something that only affected people who worked a regular schedule. As a flight attendant, Susan's Sunday afternoons were no different from any other day. Nevertheless, she understood the sentiment.

"Oh, yeah. That's *exactly* the way I felt. Stagnant. No goal beyond taking the next breath. No reason for doing much of anything, even to take care of myself, and certainly not for moving forward." She was better now, but traces of darkness still lingered, sometimes haunting her more than the actual ghosts.

The stowaway sighed. *"I always wished I could write like Douglas Adams. I was a decent writer, but there was a sort of lyrical quality to his work."*

"I'm surprised you haven't communed with him—oh, wait. I forgot. He's moved on to somewhere and you guys don't know where that is, do you?"

"Nope. Not a clue. Although, apparently, some souls never do move on. We're all hoping to do that when this is all over."

"What if it's a big, fat nothing?"

Her mind reverberated with raucous laughter. *"We're counting on there being some sort of afterlife. Otherwise, Planet Earth wouldn't have a spirit of its own and we wouldn't be here with you."*

"You're making me wish I'd gone to Sunday school more often," Susan grumbled. "All this spiritual stuff is new to me."

"Going to church isn't required. You can be spiritual anywhere. You felt it in the sea and also at the well, didn't you?"

"Yes, but that's a holy well."

"True, but we're guessing the well was a place of spiritual renewal long before any religious connection was established." The voice had changed, becoming female with an edge of wistful dissatisfaction. *"We probably should have stuck with the old ways."*

"You mean human sacrifice and other bloody rituals to ensure a good harvest?"

"None of that," the woman said. *"Only a gentle connection with the rhythms of life, the seasons, the plants, and the animals. Harmony rather than domination."*

"Okay," Susan said firmly. "Who are you and what are you doing in my head? You aren't the shrink, and Emma has already moved on."

"I'm just a woman who never found her purpose in life. Perhaps there isn't one. Maybe all we have to do is live and die and nothing in between really matters."

"A bit fatalistic, don't you think? And isn't that why we're here? To rediscover what matters?"

"For you and others among the living, perhaps. For us, that discovery comes a tad bit late."

Apparently enlightenment didn't matter if you weren't alive. Or maybe it only occurred when a soul moved on. Automatically, as it were. "You'll get there eventually. All we have to do is finish what we've started." A sigh escaped her. "Too bad I still have no idea how."

"How to do what, exactly?"

Susan glanced up to find Robert standing behind her. He was dressed much the same as he'd been the day before, albeit less grass-stained, and the warmth of his smile seemed to shelter her from the sea breeze. "Thought I'd find you here," he said as he sat down beside her. "Spend a lot of time with the sea meself, even though I was never a fisherman."

"I wasn't expecting to see you, though. You're a long way from home, aren't you?"

"Not so far if you follow the shore. You walked it once yourself."

She frowned. "I suppose I did."

"We do quite a bit of walking in this part of the world. Keeps us fit and brings us closer to nature."

"Yeah. Lots of Americans have lost that connection. You leave your air-conditioned home, get in your air-conditioned car, and drive to your air-conditioned workplace." A teacher of hers had once said that about living in Houston. Fourth grade, as she recalled.

Mrs. Barnes.

She closed her eyes and pictured the school and the playground behind it. An older building with character and history and windows that could actually be opened.

With a groan, she shook her head. "That isn't where I went to school." Her school had been one of those rather sterile, climate-controlled, windowless structures that were more like fortresses than neighborhood schools.

"One of your souls trying to confuse you?"

Momentarily stunned by his assumption, she didn't answer him right away. Had she told Robert about the voices? No, she hadn't. He'd been the one to tell her about how Christina had claimed to hear voices from the sea near the cemetery. He knew more than he should have known. "Has Christina been talking to you?"

"Not of late." Sweeping off his cap, he ran a gnarled hand over his head, then donned the cap before he spoke again. "But she has spoken to you, hasn't she?"

She saw no need to deny it. "Yes, she has. I never actually met her when she was alive."

He nodded as though he'd heard similar claims in the past. "Knew she'd come back somehow. Only a matter o' time."

"She knew she was in danger, and she said you were her insurance." Susan turned to face him. "Did you know the whales spoke to her?"

Pursing his lips he appeared to consider this claim. "Is that what they told you, or did you figure it out for yourself?"

"They were singing to me, so I assumed it was whales. Last night, she came to me with the rain and told me the whales had warned her of the danger, so it would seem that my assumption is correct. Makes you wonder what else they know, doesn't it?"

"Aye, that it does," He waved a hand toward the sea. "There's a whole world down there we know almost nothing about. Attached to the Earth, they are. Not walking about on land and breathing air. Truly *inside* the Earth, not standing upon it."

"Never thought about it that way, but I believe you're right."

He nodded up the coast toward Lahinch. "What do you say we go take a look at what Christina left behind? Your young man will know where to find you."

Susan responded with a quiet laugh. "Seems everyone knows everything. Except me, that is. I don't know anything. Every day is a new adventure."

He got to his feet, surprisingly nimble for a man of his age. "We can keep to the road if you prefer."

Susan eyed her shoes with disfavor. "Not sure I'm wearing the right footgear for anything else."

"Then the road it shall be."

He held out a hand to help her up, which she accepted gratefully. "I've been sitting here longer than I thought," she said as she shook the stiffness from her limbs.

"I'd been watching you from the beach," he said. "You've been there nearly as long as it took me to walk down here."

"How come you aren't in church?"

"Went last evening," he replied. "Figured you'd be coming to see me this morning."

"Yet another thing you knew and I didn't." She dusted off the seat of her pants and took his proffered arm. "I'm really the wrong person for this job, you know. Helluva flight attendant, but a bit under-qualified for planet saving."

"Ah, well, that's why you have help." He started off toward the road with a brisk step. "Christina said someone would come for her drawings, and that I would know the right person because of something she did." He shot her a sly grin. "A ginger-haired Yank planting roses on the grave of an Irish lass she'd probably never met? Why you might as well have waved a flag in me face."

"I suppose it was rather obvious." Susan chuckled. "She said she'd give me the link to something if I planted the roses. Never told me who she was or anything."

"Guess you passed the test, then," he said.

"And I guess you're the link."

"I might be, at that," he said as they rounded the bend toward the main road. "Then again, young Seamus might be the one she was referring to."

"What makes you say that?"

He nodded toward the hotel. "He's over there waiting for you."

Chapter 14

SEAMUS HURRIED ACROSS THE STREET TO GREET SUSAN WITH A quick hug and a rather chaste peck on the cheek even though he would have preferred a much more intimate gesture.

"Been waiting long?" she asked.

"Just got here," he replied. "Was about to go round to knock on your door when I spotted you. Timing is everything, as they say." Seamus held out a hand, which Robert shook warmly. "Nice to see you again, Mr. McKenna."

"Best be calling me Robert," McKenna said. "Something tells me I'll be dealing with you young folk enough to be on a first-name basis."

"Possibly." Seamus had gotten on familiar terms with Susan quick enough, although there were other reasons for that, none of which applied to an aging sexton.

"I've been telling Susan about Christina's drawings," Robert went on. "Did you ever see them?"

"A few," Seamus replied. "But enough to know she was even more special than most people ever guessed."

"Special, indeed," Robert said with a nod. "Gifted."

Noting the frown that briefly creased Susan's brow, Seamus was quick to add, "Susan has a few gifts of her own."

"So it would seem." Robert released Susan's arm and motioned for Seamus to take his place.

Seamus didn't take her hand, opting to drop an arm around her shoulders instead. "She can control the sea." The harshness of his whisper scraped Seamus's throat as though some higher power wanted to keep him quiet. He didn't give a damn. Susan's talents went far beyond Christina's imagination. "And hear the whales."

"No one's arguing with you, lad," Robert said. "And no one will think the less of you for falling for Miss Susan now that Christina has been laid to rest. Six years is a long time."

There had been times during those years when Christina's death seemed like it happened only yesterday. Not anymore. Meeting Susan had put that event, however tragic, in its proper perspective. But if he had indeed fallen for her, which he was quite sure he had, did she need to know it so soon? Perhaps she did. Then again, any romance between them paled in comparison to the saving of all mankind.

Or did it?

Interestingly enough, Susan didn't argue the point, only saying, "Funny you should mention that, because it's been six years since I broke up with my last boyfriend. I hadn't realized..." She stopped as they reached the hotel. "Do we walk or drive?"

"Let's drive," Seamus said. "We may find we have need of a car after we've seen what Robert has to show us."

With a slow nod, she turned to Robert. "Unless you'd rather walk." Her tone was hesitant, deferential, as though she was unsure how to proceed.

Robert shook his head. "I'd not turn down a lift. It's a bit uphill from here, you know."

Susan's pensive expression vanished, only to be replaced with a wry grin. "As uphill as anything ever is around here."

"It's all relative," Seamus said. "If you want mountains, we can take a drive over to County Kerry. Plenty of them there."

Susan gave him a withering glance. "That wasn't a complaint. I wouldn't mind an outing at some point, but for now, County Clare suits me perfectly well."

"Glad to hear it."

Seamus ushered them both to his car, and within a few minutes, they'd arrived at Robert's home, which reminded him of his parents' house before they'd updated the fixtures. Same basic design, but with furnishings that spoke of a bygone era and lace-trimmed curtains that had probably seen at least three generations of McKennas come and go.

"Me wife died about fifteen years ago," Robert said as he

gathered up a few stray pillows and a crocheted afghan from the sofa. "When a man lives alone for that long, the feminine touches start to fade."

"I think it's charming." Susan crossed the sitting room to stand before the window that faced the sea. "What a view!"

Seamus joined her at the window. The ruined church and the graveyard lay on the far side of the Liscannor road, where the land sloped down to the beach. On a clearer day, Lahinch would've been visible from across the bay. Today, however, the town was shrouded in mist.

"She knew better than to keep these at her home," Robert said as he pulled a portfolio from behind a large china cabinet. "Said it wasn't safe. Evidently no one ever thought to look for them here. Never been bothered."

"That's odd," Seamus said as a memory surfaced. "I'd almost forgotten... Someone broke into her parents' house during Christina's funeral, and my place had been rifled through as well. Nothing was taken—at least not that any of us could determine. We assumed it was a group of thieves taking advantage of a time when no one would be home, but had to clear out before they found anything of value." He eyed the portfolio with suspicion. "Makes me wonder if that wasn't what they were looking for."

"No doubt you'd be right," Robert said. "Although how Christina knew all that, I've no idea. But here they are, safe and sound."

Susan tilted her head to one side, her puzzlement as plain as the crease between her brows. "If they were kept secret, how would anyone know they existed, let alone see them as a threat? You've seen them, haven't you, Seamus?"

"Some," he replied. "She did a fair number of them while she was in school." He shrugged. "Anyone could've seen them during the local art exhibits. She may have sent some of her more innovative ideas to someone who didn't want to see any of them become reality."

"That'd be my guess," said Robert. "Either way, she knew she was ahead of her time. I only wish she'd been more concerned for her own safety."

Seamus couldn't argue with that. "I remember she wrote to someone in Dublin once and also sent a letter to London. She was so excited when she told me about it, then utterly devastated when she received some rather dismissive replies. I can't recall the names—a couple of politicians, I believe—but that could've been the connection."

The connection that ultimately got her killed.

Susan's expression clouded. "While Jillian and Ranjiv were helping to solve the murder of a London MP who was an advocate for some of the 'greener' policies, they spotted their suspect having lunch with another MP. Who knows? If someone like that ever got wind of what she was doing, it might've been enough to get her on a hit list."

Seamus considered this before shaking his head. "She wouldn't have contacted just anyone. She'd have chosen a champion for the environment—someone who would've taken her seriously."

"But what if he told a few others about it?" Susan countered. "If they pooh-poohed the idea, he might've let it drop, but he also might've told them where the ideas came from. They weren't exactly secret. At least, not then."

"Maybe that's when she decided they'd be safer with me," Robert said. "She never told me why, but whoever she told about the drawings might've said or done something that made her think they needed to be hidden."

"That's possible." Seamus nodded toward the kitchen table. "Let's have a look at them and see what we've got."

* * * *

By the time Robert had laid them out, Susan knew she'd never seen anything even remotely similar to Christina's artwork. Swirling images depicted the planet as a living, breathing entity, while other drawings were of floods, earthquakes, fires, and droughts—each of them illustrating Earth's frantic efforts to decimate the beings that threatened its health. Other pictures offered innovative alternatives that would enable people to live in harmony with their world.

"There are several of these I don't believe I've seen before,"

Seamus remarked as he perused the contents of the portfolio.

"Some of them seem oddly familiar, though," Susan said. "Like I've seen them on some nature program or documentary." Seamus had mentioned several of Christina's ideas, but Susan had never imagined how detailed the artwork would be—almost to the point of being schematics for creating a whole new way of living life on Earth.

"No conspiracy could quash every advance in science and technology," Seamus said reasonably. "Someone else might've made similar discoveries, but lacked the funding for further development. Christina certainly couldn't have done any of those things on her own."

"That's because oil companies are paying politicians to choke off the money supply," Susan snapped. "But if some of these concepts were to be implemented on a global scale..." She paused, shivering as though someone had walked across her grave—or whatever creepy event shivering was supposed to foretell.

"Mother Earth would be much happier, no doubt," Robert said. "As would we all be in the end."

In the end... Would this truly be the end if no progress could be made toward a less exploitative relationship with the planet? The signs were already there, and none were a question of belief but of fact. One had only to watch the daily weather report to know that something was going terribly wrong.

"Earth is dying," she whispered. "Maybe not the rocks and core, but the very air we breathe, the soil that gives life to the plants will soon be gone. Until only the incessant sun will be left, baking away every life form on the planet. Cleona claimed Earth's spirit told her she was the Carrier of Life's Preservation. Jillian connected with Earth's spirit at Stonehenge. The freakin' whales have been singing to me." Closing her eyes, she shook her head before returning her gaze to the drawings. "And now this, this treasure trove of techniques for saving the world. It's unbelievable."

"No, it isn't," Robert said. "It's your turn now, lass. You and your friends. This is what should've happened long ago. Before Christina died, before we came so close to reaching the point of no return."

She locked eyes with the old man. "You're a part of this too. Aren't you?"

"Aye. That I am, lass. That I am." Awe colored his tone as he spoke, but his words also had a prophetic ring to them, similar to the way the whales had sounded. "I've tended the graves of the dead, waiting and watching. I knew you would come. I knew Earth would be saved. It was only a matter of time."

With a firm nod, she gestured toward the pictures scattered on the table. "We need to do this, and do it quickly. Photograph these drawings and post them on every platform we can think of. See to it that they spread like a virus around the world." A short laugh escaped her. "The internet maybe responsible for many of today's ills, but this is one instance where having a global reach is a good thing. I only hope my phone is up to it."

Phone…

The phone Chuck had given her. She'd actually stuck it in her purse. Why? Why was it so important that she'd kept it? That he'd given it to her at all?

Trivial things that seemed unimportant at first glance…

She focused again on Seamus, whose bewildered expression suggested he needed something a bit more tangible to deal with for a while. "Speaking of phones, is there any hope for one that's been through a plane crash at sea?"

He blinked, opening and closing his mouth like a hooked bass. "Excuse me?"

"A phone. Chuck gave me some stranger's phone right before we boarded. Said he'd found it in the restroom and asked me to turn it in to the lost and found. I never got the chance and I figured I'd be able to drop it off on a return flight to Newark. I didn't, of course. I found it in my pocket when I changed clothes in the hotel in Inisheer. It's been in a bag of rice ever since."

"Probably fried," Seamus said. "You might get one working again if it was dunked in fresh water, but seawater is corrosive. The salt crystallizes in the inner workings."

"I'd still like to see what we can do with it. When I spoke with them yesterday, Jillian and Cleona told me that everything has some significance. I have to at least try."

He scratched his head, drawing her attention to his curly brown hair and his thoughtful expression.

What an adorable man. I keep forgetting that.

"Might be able to pull something off the SD card," he finally said. "Provided there is one. I have one in my phone, but not all models have a port for them."

"I don't know if mine does or not." She shrugged. "It may be a total waste of time to even try, but..." The prickling excitement flooding through her system said otherwise. This was as important as anything Christina had left in Robert's keeping.

"No, I get it," Seamus said. "It's worth a look. Don't suppose you have it with you?"

"Sure do. Right here in this fancy Gucci purse." She rolled her eyes. "If the local assassins had any idea what I've been carrying around, they'd have killed me by now."

"What makes you say that?"

"I'm thinking it's a clue—a clue to something highly significant." The vibration in her head was like a buzzing chain saw. She could feel it. Voices chattering. Minds melding. The ebb and flow of the tide. "God only knows whose phone this is. Maybe it's the murderer's or the creeps that told Chuck to crash the plane." He couldn't have been hearing voices in his head telling him to do such a horrible thing. Or could he? She'd certainly been hearing enough of them. Perhaps he'd been possessed as well, but by evil spirits rather than benign souls.

She shook her head in an effort to eliminate that thought. The best she could tell from her own experience, spirits weren't evil. The living seemed to have a monopoly on that trait. But if this was truly a battle of good versus evil, perhaps there were evil souls, manipulating those they possessed to abuse, exploit, and conquer. The war between the two had been waged throughout human history. If that were the case, how could anyone hope to triumph over evil that never died, but kept returning in different forms?

"One thing at a time, Susan."

For once, she was thankful for her onboard psychiatrist. *You are a psychiatrist, aren't you?*

"Yes. Too bad I can't prescribe medications through you. But then, I'd probably have you and everyone in this room medicated for one mental illness or another."

You have a slightly different perspective now, don't you?

"That's putting it mildly."

"Well, then. Let's have a look at it." Seamus's prodding tone pulled her out of her head and back into reality.

"Um, sure." She opened her purse and quickly found the phone, half expecting it to be glowing like some ancient artifact from an Indiana Jones movie. But it was only a phone—and not even one of the newer models.

"We're in luck," Seamus said as she handed it over. "I have one exactly like it. Let's hope there's a card in it."

The prickling at Susan's nape suggested that luck hadn't played even a minor role in that coincidence. Fate, perhaps. Definitely not luck.

"And…yes! There's a card here." His eyes widened as he easily popped out the tiny plastic wafer. "Not even wedged in with salt."

By this time, the prickling sensation on the back of Susan's neck had spread to her entire body. "Will it mess up your phone if you put it in?"

"I doubt it. Chances are, we just won't be able to access the data," he said, sounding more like a computer whiz than a fisherman.

A man of many talents.

"The phone itself doesn't look too bad," he went on. "We could try charging it up, but we'd probably be wasting our time." He pulled out his own phone, removed the SD card, and inserted the new one. "Let's see what we've got here…" His brows knit together as he paged through the photos. "Well…there are plenty of pictures, but unless you know who these kids are—or who this woman is—we'll probably never know who it belongs to." He handed the phone to Susan. "Recognize anyone?"

The jolt of electricity she'd expected earlier finally struck as Susan stared into the face of a smiling dark-haired girl. A face she'd seen before. This very photo, in fact.

Her gasp of dismay nearly choked her. "That's Chuck's daughter."

Chapter 15

"THAT HAD TO BE HIS PHONE," SUSAN WHISPERED. "BUT WHY WOULD he give it to me and tell me to—" Her eyes squeezed shut. "I can't look at this right now. Just can't."

"No worries, luv." Seamus removed the phone from her slack grasp and pocketed it before covering her icy hands with his own. "I understand completely."

Robert patted her shoulder. "You've had a bit of a shock," he said kindly. "Best you sit down while I make you a cup of tea."

"Might want to add a splash of brandy while you're at it," Seamus suggested as Robert headed for the tea kettle. He'd seen Susan in the immediate aftermath of a plane crash and in the midst of several supernatural events, but he'd never seen her quite so pale before. Placing an arm around her shoulders, he led her to the sofa, where she landed in a heap on the cushions.

The moment he took the seat beside her, she leaned against him and raised a trembling hand to her forehead. "I knew that phone was something important. I never dreamed how much."

"Can't depend on those dreams now, can you?" he said in what he hoped was a soothing tone. "Never coming when you need them or telling you what you need to know." He was babbling, of course, but she seemed to take no notice, merely nodding her replies. He didn't see her reaction as a sign of weakness. After all, a person could only take so much before crumbling, no matter how tough they might be.

"Maybe the phone isn't important after all. He knew he wasn't going to reach Heathrow alive, and he probably thought his family might get it eventually. Or—" On the word, she sat bolt upright, grazing his chin with the top of her head. "Do you think he left a message for them?"

"If so, it's probably stored somewhere on the device that we can't access." He hesitated. "Unless he took pictures—"

"Or a video. That would be on the SD card, wouldn't it?"

"Aye. Although mine usually come up at the bottom of the list whenever I transfer them to my computer." Again, he hesitated. "When Chuck gave you the phone, did he seem different in any way? Nervous? Frightened?"

She shook her head. "Not really. But then, he might have assumed he was being watched. He must've thought he could get away with giving me his phone—especially if whoever was watching him was close enough to hear what he told me about finding it in the restroom. Even so, they should've known he would try to communicate with someone."

"Possibly, but I'll wager they knew you were going to be on the same plane." He saw no need to point out that she also should have died in the crash. She was already shaking enough as it was.

She swallowed with obvious difficulty. "But I survived, and so did that phone—sort of."

Seamus took a moment to consider the possibilities. "If you were followed after Chuck gave you his mobile—and that's quite a big if—they would have seen that you didn't drop it off anywhere. After you boarded, whether you'd kept it in your pocket or stuck it in your purse, the odds of it surviving intact were pretty slim."

"And yet it did." Another tremor shook her. "Not too surprising when you consider who else is on our side. Just wish they'd taken action a teensy bit sooner. I still can't imagine why the three of us made it to safety when the people who came up with all of these great ideas died in the crash or were murdered somewhere else."

Seamus gave her a quick hug, thankful that she'd been among the chosen. "Who knows? Maybe this is the way it has to play out."

"But where's the logic in that? Jillian, Cleona, and I should've died instead of people like Christina and Jacob Emhart and whoever else was headed to that energy summit in Paris."

He gave brief, and admittedly selfish, consideration to the path his own life might have taken had Christina not been pushed off a cliff, before ultimately arriving at the same conclusion. "I'm convinced things happened the way they did for a reason."

She arched a skeptical brow. "As in 'Mother Earth knows best'?"

"That works for me." He wasn't kidding. Susan's survival had already made a huge impact on his life. No doubt the men Jillian and Cleona had teamed up with would say the same. Compared with the staggering number of people who died in the crash, his own happiness seemed irrelevant—perhaps even an affront to the hundreds of grieving families. He only hoped the three women could accomplish something remarkable enough to justify allowing such a tragedy to occur. "You know, luv," he said gently. "There are some things you simply have to take on faith. I believe this is one of them."

"Your faith must be a lot stronger than mine," she declared. "Right now, I'm having trouble believing the sun will rise tomorrow."

Robert carried in a tray laden with a plate of biscuits and a formal rose-and-gold tea set that probably hadn't been used since his wife's death. "After all you've been through, I'd have thought there'd be no limits to your faith." He set the tray on a low table near the sofa and began pouring the tea.

"Not really," Susan said. "I wasn't raised to believe God would solve my every problem, prevent them from happening, or even give me strength to endure."

"But you *have* endured," Seamus said. "You lived to fight another day, and you've already enriched our lives. Don't be selling yourself short."

She gave his hand a squeeze. "Okay then. I'll do my best to keep a stiff upper lip and carry on. Let's see those pictures."

Seamus unlocked the screen and handed her his phone. "Scroll through and see if anything catches your eye."

With a nod, she did as he asked. Her hands were steadier now, at least not visibly shaking. "His poor wife," she said as she paged through the photos. "I can't imagine how she must have felt when she got the news. Now she has to raise those kids without him." Sighing, she continued, "They've done so much to make flying safer since nine-eleven. I guess there are some things you can't prevent, no matter how strict—" She froze suddenly, staring at the phone as though it were a cobra coiling up to strike.

"What is it?" He touched her hand, which was no warmer than it had been a few minutes earlier.

"A screenshot of an email," she replied. "*The* email."

* * * *

Susan stared at the words glaring out from the screen, not quite believing they were real. But they had to be. This was what had brought down Flight 2324. The threat to his family. The threat to the city of London itself.

> WE ARE WATCHING YOUR WIFE AND CHILDREN. IF OCEANUS FLIGHT 2324 HAS NOT CRASHED INTO THE SEA BEFORE IT REACHES IRELAND, YOUR FAMILY WILL TORTURED AND BEHEADED, AND WE WILL BRING THE PLANE DOWN OVER LONDON, KILLING MORE INNOCENT PEOPLE THAN YOU CAN POSSIBLY IMAGINE. WE HAVE THE MEANS. THIS IS YOUR CHOICE. CONTACT NO ONE OR YOUR FAMILY WILL SUFFER.

"I don't understand," she whispered. "Why would he believe this?"

"Might've been afraid not to," Seamus said after perusing the text. "There were attachments to the message—possibly those pictures we've been looking at." He shook his head sadly. "Some of them did seem like surveillance photos. Terrifying stuff."

"No kidding." Following a swift mental review of cockpit protocols, she was no closer to believing he'd acted alone than she'd been on the day of the crash. "The same threat must've been sent to the other pilot—and Chuck did say 'we' in the telepathic message I received."

Seamus nodded, pointing to the photo. "Look at the date. That was the day you took off, wasn't it?"

"Yeah. Right before we were due to board."

"That wouldn't have given him time to do much of anything before the flight."

"Except give me his phone." The moment she said the words, she rejected them, shaking her head. "No. He could've forwarded that email to someone. Whoever sent it couldn't possibly have known." Her mind was working furiously, trying to make sense of—

The psychiatrist's voice cut her thought short. *"Hard to make sense out of something so senseless, isn't it?"*

Figured at least one of you guys would be chiming in eventually.

"What about you?" he asked. *"Would you have acted any differently?"*

"I–I don't know what I would've done."

Seamus stared at her for a moment or two before asking, "The stowaways talking to you again?"

"Yeah," she replied. "The psychiatrist wants to know what I would've done in the same situation. I honestly don't know."

"Giving the phone to you was probably the best idea Chuck could come up with at the time. He couldn't have known you'd hang onto it instead of turning it in right away. I know pilots are generally unflappable, but when the right buttons are pushed…"

"Sending an email would've been better," she insisted. "That phone could've sat in the lost and found for years. No one would've claimed it because the owner would've been dead."

"Hey, no one ever said he was the sharpest knife in the drawer," Seamus said with a grin. "After all, he married someone else after dating you. How smart could he be?"

Despite her roiling emotions, Susan couldn't help laughing, albeit a tad ruefully. "I'm not sure he would agree with you. Besides, I'm the one who broke up with him, not the other way around."

Seamus shrugged. "His loss. But regardless of whether he forwarded that email, he gave you the phone, you still have it, and now we can prove he was coerced into crashing the plane."

"There is that," she agreed. "Although I'm sure the email address it was sent from will lead precisely nowhere. Cleona's convinced it's the oil producers, and I agree, but my God, the power they wield over all of us is terrifying."

"Aye," said Robert as he handed Susan a cup of tea. "You'd think they'd be more concerned about what kind of world they'll be leaving behind for their children, wouldn't you?"

"Clearly, they think a fat inheritance is the only requirement for a happy life. They couldn't care less about breathing clean air and eating untainted food." Susan didn't bother to soften the sharp edge to her reply. "I'll be honest; I've never contemplated the future from my current viewpoint. Living through a plane crash and being possessed by those who didn't kind of skews your perspective."

Robert took a seat in a worn leather armchair that sat in the corner of the living room, where he'd undoubtedly been accustomed to sitting for the greater part of his life. "I wouldn't say it was skewed, meself. Seems more conscientious and realistic."

"That's just it. I never gave environmental issues much thought before. I mean, you hear about climate change and such, but we've made tremendous strides in eliminating so many forms of pollution. Not long ago, I saw a picture comparing New York City in the sixties with the way it looks today. The difference was astonishing. But now, even that seems paltry. We haven't done enough. Not nearly enough." She heaved a sigh. "Sorry for getting so preachy when we should be discussing what we need to do next."

"I'd take that phone to the nearest Garda station," Robert advised. "But before you do, you need to make sure it's backed up somewhere in case they decide to ignore it."

"Or are on the take and erase it," Seamus added.

Susan sat up straight, her fists clenched in anger. "They'd damn well better not ignore it. I'll post it on every social media platform I can think of before I'll let them get away with that."

"Good girl," Seamus said with a chuckle. "And the reporter you told me and Ian about? He could spread the word, also."

"You mean Jillian's friend, Ranjiv?" Actually, he was Jillian's fiancé, if that was believable after only knowing one another for a week or two. Normal people probably didn't do that.

"There's nothing normal about the times we've seen lately," the shrink said in a voice infused with sadness. *"You of all people should realize that."*

I keep forgetting you guys are privy to my thoughts. You're right, though. Nothing is normal now.

"Who's this?" Robert asked. "A reporter, you say?"

"For *The London Times*," Susan replied. "He's going to interview the three of us and hopefully get the story published. We just have to figure out how to tell the tale in a way people will believe."

"Amen to that." Seamus peered at his phone. "There's only one problem with this email. It doesn't even hint at the motive for crashing that plane. Granted, we're all leaning toward the delegates to the energy summit being targeted, but—"

"Not everyone will see it that way," Susan said with a nod. "Still, when you put all of these clues together, a war against clean, renewable energy is the obvious conclusion."

"Unless it's an incredibly bizarre string of coincidences," Seamus suggested.

"I'm beginning to believe there's no such thing." Jillian and Cleona certainly seemed to share that belief. No doubt the stowaways would agree.

"And for the most part, you'd be right," Robert said. "Especially in this case. I can feel the magic."

Susan had been "feeling the magic" even prior to the catastrophe that had taken so many lives and added their souls to hers. What she couldn't explain was why she'd believed the telepathic message she'd received from Chuck was genuine, much less acted on it. Perhaps the urgency of his plea, coming from out of nowhere had done the trick. Nothing of the kind had ever happened to her before. That whales had never sung to her—certainly not in a way she could understand—was a given.

"You should've been there at Baile An Tsagart," Seamus said as though he'd read her thoughts. "Even I felt the magic there."

"So… What do we do now?" she asked, knowing the answer and yet at the same time dreading it.

"Take pictures of these drawings and post them on social media," Seamus said promptly. "Maybe even post that email—or at least show it to the guards. We need to do something to attract the attention of the bad guys so we can trip them up and beat them at their own game."

"Oh, great," Susan said with a groan. "I am *so* ready to get pushed off a cliff. How about you?"

Seamus shot her a withering glance. "You know what I mean. You also need to call Jillian and Cleona and tell that reporter fellow to sharpen his pencils. You've a story to tell, and the longer you wait to tell it, the greater the chance that more innocent people will die."

* * * *

Seamus suspected Susan might turn out to be one of the innocents to whom he was referring, although the more he thought about it, the more he wondered if she hadn't already been targeted. She wasn't innocent anymore. She knew just enough to have some assassin drawing a bead on her. The trick would be getting to the truth ahead of whoever had been given the task of stopping her. He and Robert might also become targets, as well as Ian and anyone else in whom the other two women had seen fit to confide.

"You're right, of course," Susan said with an obvious show of reluctance. "I wish we had more time, but we've already wasted almost three weeks."

"I wouldn't say they'd been wasted," Seamus said. "You had to recover and adjust to your situation. Jillian and Cleona had mysteries to solve and lost souls to appease. If I seem anxious to get this matter concluded, it's probably because there's a wee bit of my own personal gain to be considered."

Her eyes narrowed. "Personal gain?"

"Having you all to myself," he replied. "I'm looking forward to that."

A hint of laughter lurked behind her gaze. "What a selfish fellow you are. Here we are trying to save the world and you're thinking about—just what *are* you thinking about?"

"Why, romance, of course. Where would the happy ending be without the boy getting the girl?"

"You actually believe there'll be a happy ending?"

His heart sank a notch at the incredulity in her tone. "If there isn't, then what are we fighting for?"

She shrugged. "I'm not sure. I keep telling myself that my life doesn't matter now because it already should've ended. This is extra time for me. Maybe even borrowed time." Her gaze met his with an impact he could almost feel. "There are no guarantees of a happily-ever-after, Seamus. Not for any of us. For all we know, there were no survivors of that crash. The three of us could have only been resurrected long enough to see this through. And when it's all over, death will return to claim us."

"You're scaring me now, lass," Robert said. "I can't see why you would think that. God wouldn't save you only to sacrifice you later."

"Why not?" she demanded. "What if there isn't a God? What if there is no heaven and no hell? What if the only powers belong to the planet itself?"

"Then Mother Earth is God, and when we die, we'll return to the mother that gave us life." Robert's voice was quiet and assured. "It makes no difference where God is or in what form he—or she—exists. But I believe you'll survive this the same way you survived the plane crash."

"You came back for me," Seamus blurted out, surprised that he was actually able to put his feelings into words. "Christina sent you. Or Earth sent you. But that doesn't matter. What matters is that you're here now. Alive and well. And we're here to help you."

Susan sighed. "If only it were that simple. Just figure all this out—and somehow manage to stay alive—and everything will be hunky-dory for all eternity."

"Got a better plan?"

"Not really. Christina should've lived for this, not me. I'm no genius. I have no fabulous, earth-shaking ideas for the future of humanity, and I'm no heroine either. I'm only a flight attendant who's been carrying a torch for the wrong man for far too long. If I hadn't cared so much about him, I probably wouldn't have been on that damn plane. I'd have been flying to Tahiti or Acapulco, not floundering about in the North Atlantic."

"You were chosen," Seamus said. "I'm sure of it."

Robert nodded. "I believe that as well. Heroism isn't a

conscious decision. It's a matter of doing the right thing, regardless of the cost."

"Keep talking." Susan swept her hair back behind her ears, then leaned forward, hugging her knees to her chest. "Maybe at some point I'll actually believe it. Why do I need these constant pep talks? I feel okay for a while, like I'm even strong enough to see this through, and then I crash again."

Seamus smoothed a hand over her back. "A reminder that you're only human?"

With a sharp exhale, she shook her head. "No human should've survived that crash. We were all supposed to die." Once again, he could see the exhaustion in the lines around her eyes and mouth as she turned toward him. "Take me home, Seamus. I think I'm done for the day." Her short laugh ended on a sob. "And it isn't even noon yet."

"Just going on twelve now," Robert said after a glance toward his watch. "Drink your tea now, lass," he said kindly. "You'll feel better. Me wife used to say tea could cure anything."

"She's probably right about it curing most things," Susan said. "Not sure it can cure what's ailing me."

"And that would be..." Seamus prompted.

She frowned. "Ordinarily, I'd say it was survivor's guilt, but in this case, it's more like survivor's remorse."

He stared at her for a long moment before realizing his mouth was hanging open. "You wish you'd died in the crash? Still?" She'd said something along those lines before, but he thought she'd gotten over it. Apparently the prospect of spending what he hoped would be the rest of her life with him wasn't much of an enticement. "Even after the whales sang to you?"

"You'd think that would've been the clincher, wouldn't you?" She shook her head as though trying to clear it. "I think—" She stopped there, tilting her head slightly as she squeezed her eyes shut. "It's my stowaways," she said when she finally opened her eyes. "I'm feeling their sadness and regrets. Not my own." A moment later, she added, "That explains a lot."

"Did they tell you that?"

"Not in so many words. It's more of a feeling than an actual confession."

Never having communed with spirits before, Seamus couldn't argue with her assessment. "I sure hope you're right. I'd have thought you'd be pleased to be alive."

"I am," she said. "The rest of them aren't a bit happy with their situation."

"Even the psychiatrist?"

"He probably isn't very happy either," she replied. "Right now, he needs to work on cheering up the rest of the gang instead of focusing on me." She frowned again. "For the most part, I seem to be okay."

"Perhaps what you need is a distraction," Seamus said. "Something even the stowaways can enjoy."

"And that would be…?"

He'd already taken her to St. Brigid's Well, had dinner with her at the pub, and even played a few songs for her. The boat ride hadn't exactly been a pleasure cruise. Perhaps what she needed was…

"Ever ridden a horse?"

Chapter 16

SUSAN WASN'T SURE WHERE THE FEELING CAME FROM, BUT SHE HAD a sudden, undeniable urge to go galloping across a broad, sandy beach.

Must be on someone's bucket list.

"That would be my list," a woman's voice replied. *"Say yes. Please."*

Such a plea could scarcely be ignored, especially since Susan was fairly certain a ride would do her and the rest of the stowaways a world of good. "Yes, I have," she said in reply to Seamus's query. "But it's been a while."

"No worries. A cousin of mine owns a riding stable, and she has horses suitable for beginners as well as experienced riders."

"The same cousin who works in the pub?"

He shook his head. "Different branch of the family. Sorcha lives near Lahinch. The beach there is great for a good gallop."

If the collective sigh resonating through Susan's mind was anything to go by, the one voice that had spoken wasn't alone in her wish. No doubt several souls would move on after an outing like that. Trouble was, at this point, she wasn't sure losing any of them was necessarily a good thing. In the coming days, she was going to need all the help she could get.

"Hmm… Sounds lovely, but even if I'd packed my boots and breeches, they wouldn't have made it this far." Not that she had ever possessed either of those things, although adding a riding habit to her wardrobe suddenly struck her as a perfectly marvelous idea.

"No problem," he said with a smile. "Sorcha is used to outfitting the tourists. She has plenty of extras. What say you?"

He hadn't steered her wrong yet, and that grin of his was as addicting as it was charming. "Sounds wonderful."

She only hoped her stowaways didn't all abandon her at once. The ensuing headache would probably knock her right out of the saddle.

* * * *

The way the horseback riding notion had popped into his head made Seamus wonder if he didn't have a few extra souls of his own in there egging him on. "I haven't been doing much riding lately myself." Yet another activity that Christina's death had curtailed. She'd been so natural on a horse—one of those who could almost claim to have been born in the saddle. Even the most difficult horses went better for her than they did for anyone else.

A moment later, Robert echoed his thoughts. "Haven't been riding since Christina died, have you?"

"No, I haven't. Sorcha can vouch for that. Just haven't felt like it."

"But you do now." Robert smiled. "I'm very glad to hear it."

Seamus couldn't imagine why Robert would care one way or the other. "Oh? And why is that?"

"Events are in motion," the old sexton replied. "Moving in the right direction at last."

Susan frowned. "How could you possibly—? Oh, never mind. If you're a part of this, there are things you would know."

Robert nodded. "The flow has been disrupted for many years now. Unfortunately, there was nothing I could do but watch it happen. I tried to set the pattern right once." He shook his head sadly. "Only made things worse."

Despite his acceptance of Susan's role in saving the world, Seamus was having trouble wrapping his head around the concept of Robert as the keeper of the timeline—correct or otherwise. "You're saying you know how history is supposed to play out?"

"Aye, that I do," Robert replied. "But only as an observer. Never as an active participant." His eyes filled with tears. "Broke me heart when Christina was killed. I warned her to stay away from the cliffs, but she wouldn't listen. I believe she understood her role as well as I did. You see, the chain of history is so delicate. Weaken one link and the direction shifts. Break a link, and righting the setbacks takes triple the time—and often triple the pain."

Susan tipped her head to one side as she peered at their host. "Robert...exactly how old *are* you?"

A tiny grin lifted the corner of the old man's mouth. "There are many who would like to know that, but I'll never tell. Can't, actually. Mainly because I don't know meself."

"As old as Father Time?" she suggested.

"Ah, now," said Robert. "That would be telling, wouldn't it?"

Seamus had known the sexton of Kilmacrehy all his life. He'd always been there, tending the graves and the ruined church. He'd always looked the same too—even in Seamus's earliest childhood memories. Of course, through the eyes of a child, most adults appeared ancient. This was different. Why had he never realized it before? Was that part of Robert's power, to forever remain an old man, never aging, never dying, without anyone ever taking any notice?

"Did Christina know who you were?" Susan asked.

"She suspected." The old sexton grinned. "Just as the two of you are suspecting now."

With respect to Seamus's suspicions, Robert was either Father Time himself or he was as mad as a hatter. His money was on the former.

"I'm not alone," Robert went on. "There are more of us. Watchers, we call ourselves."

"And you've lived forever?" Susan's eyes were as round as saucers, although considering what had been happening to her, they shouldn't have been. She should have simply been nodding and smiling.

"Not forever," Robert replied. "There's a large part of Earth's history that I haven't witnessed." He sighed. "Witnessing is really all we can do, which is often more of a curse than a blessing."

Seamus stared at the old man, still not quite believing his own ears.

Robert took a sip of his tea and continued as though they were engaged in perfectly ordinary teatime conversation. "I've seen world wars fought and millions of people born only to die—in the merest blink, it seems."

"But you aren't only witnessing now," Susan said. "You're involved—at least in an advisory capacity."

"Mmm...perhaps," he mused. "More of a protector, actually. From the time she was a child, Christina knew what I was and that I could be trusted. She was special, you see. Just as you are."

Susan reacted with a derisive snort. "Now maybe—although what you said about the curse of being a Watcher certainly applies in my case. I don't know exactly what I am, but I'd much rather go back to being plain ol' me."

"Those who seek power are often the least deserving," Robert said with a sage nod. "But when leadership is thrust upon you...well, now. That's different."

"A leader? Is that what I am?"

"I would say so."

Susan's hand shook as she set her cup on the low table before her. Her voice, however, was steady and clear. "Cleona was told she was the Carrier of Life's Preservation. Not sure whether Jillian has a title or not, but she ought to be the leader, not me."

"Ah, but you are a leader, whether you like it or not. Jillian is the Chosen One—the one Earth speaks to through the stones. But you, Susan...you're the Bringer of Justice. Not a job to be taken lightly."

Susan's eyes widened even further. "I'm not taking it lightly. All I want to know is how to do it."

He shrugged. "Figuring out the method is part of your task."

"But you know how it should happen?"

Smiling, he shook his head.

"You can't tell me. Can you?" Her tone was flat, resigned—a statement rather than a question. "That would be much too easy."

"I only know the correct path when I see it and feel the rightness of it."

"And you're feeling...how?" she prompted.

"I already told you. Events are moving in the right direction at last." He glanced at Seamus. "In more ways than you could possibly imagine."

Seamus knew exactly what the old man meant. In the years since Christina's death, despair had clung to him like a second skin, which was undoubtedly why his family and friends had been so protective. Witnessing a catastrophic plane crash should've made him feel even worse. Instead, although his mood had seemed totally inappropriate at the time, he'd been surprisingly happy, as though the fog left behind by Christina's loss had finally been lifted. Meeting Susan had changed him—improving both his attitude and his outlook. Before that, he hadn't truly been living. Only existing.

"I believe you're right, Robert," Seamus said. "I feel it too."

Susan arched a brow. "Well…that makes two of you. I'm game if you are. Guess the right moves will come to me at the appropriate time." With a nod toward the dinner table, she added, "For now, I believe we should photograph those drawings. We can upload them later."

"And I'll do the same," said Robert.

"Keep up with the times, do you?" Susan's tiny smile betrayed her amusement.

"I've over a thousand friends on Facebook," Robert said with a touch of pride. "And nearly as many followers on Twitter."

"Not content to simply watch this round play out, are you?"

"Couldn't hurt to do me own part," Robert replied.

Seamus frowned. "Once you do that, the drawings might not be safe here."

The old man laughed. "You don't think they've been behind that cabinet all this time, do you? I've a much better hiding place where no one will ever find them."

"Best not tell us where that is," Seamus advised. "In this case, the less we know the better off we'll be." He didn't anticipate being tortured for information, but he saw no reason to take any chances.

"Posting those pictures might still draw out the bad guys, though," Susan warned. "You need to watch your back as well as the timeline."

"We should all be watching our backs, and each other's." Seamus had no objection to watching Susan's back, which was a pleasure in itself. He certainly had no desire to see anyone put a bullet in it.

Susan hesitated, biting her lip in a pensive manner. "Robert, is your timeline monitoring ability local or global?"

"For the most part, it's local." Robert grimaced. "Although that last election you Yanks had resulted in some far-reaching effects."

"Tell me about it." With a groan, she leaned forward, covering her face with her hands. "I still can't believe it actually happened. When I think of the crap we've had to deal with ever since—" She raised her head. "Wait a minute… Are you saying that was a mistake in the timeline?"

"A setback for Earth, to be sure," Robert replied. "But not insurmountable." His smile conveyed warmth and understanding. "We must always have hope—hope that good will triumph over evil in the end."

"If we survive long enough to see it," she said with a snort. "I'm beginning to have my doubts."

"Humankind has only recently progressed beyond its infancy." The inherent wisdom of Robert's pronouncement served as a reminder of how ageless he seemed. Ageless and timeless. "Right now it's like a toddler testing the limits of its powers. There will be mistakes and stumbles, but there will also be growth."

"A toddler?" she echoed. "If that's the case, I'm glad I won't live long enough to see the adolescence. Talk about growing pains."

Robert nodded. "Much of this has been difficult to watch— wars, famines, hatred, and greed. But you must understand that humans are not inherently evil, only a bit selfish."

"More than a bit, I'd say," Seamus remarked. He'd seen that failing in himself—only viewing Christina's death from his personal perspective, not as a loss affecting anyone outside their community, and certainly not the entire world. Like so many things he hadn't fully understood, he was slowly coming to terms with the global impact of her existence.

"I'll admit, I never thought of our species as being children," Susan said. "We've come so far, made so many advances… But you're absolutely right; we're like a bunch of self-centered two-year-olds who must be disciplined before they get completely out of control." She sat up abruptly, slapping her knees before practically leaping to her feet. "Let's do it. Let's take pictures of those drawings and spread the word. Then we'll go riding and try to forget about all this conspiracy stuff for a while."

Seamus rose to stand beside her, ready to undertake any course of action she suggested. In his mind, nothing was quite as inspiring as a fiery, ginger-haired woman on a mission. "And start again with our spirits renewed?"

"Interesting choice of words, but yeah." Her lips twitched with genuine amusement. "With our spirits renewed."

* * * *

Robert's internet connection was more than up to the task of uploading the numerous photographs, after which, Susan and Seamus drove to his cousin's stable in relative silence. She liked that he didn't feel the need to fill the silence with meaningless chatter. Too much was happening for trivialities. Besides, this ride was more for therapy than entertainment.

A ride on the beach...

Long ago, she'd seen a painting with that title hanging in a hospital room where her grandfather had been ill and dying. Whoever decided to put it there had chosen well. The soft colors of the sea and sky combined with horses as elegant as the ladies mounted upon them to soothe as well as distract. Gazing at that painting had transported her to another place and time. A time when her grandmother might have been one of the riders, followed by a gentleman on a gray horse who could have been her grandfather before age and sickness had robbed him of youth and vigor.

That particular memory was Susan's own; no stowaway could lay claim to it. She could only wonder why she'd never pursued the idea of riding on a beach before this. The painting itself wasn't nearby, but there were plenty of horses and beaches. Perhaps she'd never been in quite the same place—at least, not mentally. Not even in the days following her breakup with Chuck.

But she was here now, about to climb aboard a jet black Irish hunter named Zaria. The stable itself was an ancient stone and mortar structure that spoke to Susan in a language buried so deep she didn't understand the actual words, but the meaning was clear.

You belong here.

The smell of horses and leather triggered a wave of nostalgia that flooded her mind with memories that were definitely not her own. Galloping across an open field, jumping fence after fence on a chestnut hunter while the hounds ran on ahead, baying at the top of their voices. A big bay Irish warmblood performing a freestyle dressage routine with an ease that reflected years of training. Mucking out stalls on a chilly morning while the barn's occupants munched their feed. The echoing *clip-clop* of shod hooves on a cobbled stable yard.

Following a quick check of the girth, Susan gathered up the reins and mounted the mare with a smoothness her own muscle memory couldn't possibly have produced. As she settled herself in the saddle, she felt an immediate sense of oneness with a horse she'd never even seen before.

Zaria must've felt it as well. Arching her neck, she stood like a statue until Susan set her in motion with an infinitesimal shift of her weight.

"Everything okay?" Seamus asked as Susan guided the mare around the stable yard.

"We're fine." Surprised she was even able to utter a word, Susan continued around the yard, negotiating a corner with precision as the horse's body curved in response to leg aids that were second nature to her now. Someone else was riding Zaria—someone whose contented sighs echoed through Susan's mind like rustling silk.

Will I still be able to do this after you move on?

"*I hope so,*" came the fervent reply. "*Can't promise anything, because none of us know any more than you do.*"

Please don't leave yet, Susan begged. *I want you here for the entire ride. I can learn to ride on my own someday, but you...you need this.*

"*The next incarnation awaits us,*" a different voice announced. "*There is no end. Only new beginnings. May you be reborn in happier times.*"

Susan closed her eyes, reminded of the "may you live in

interesting times" wish that was reportedly an ancient Chinese curse. The times she'd been living through were certainly interesting. Perhaps she'd been cursed. Perhaps the entire world had been cursed.

"The Chinese don't know everything." The heavily accented English suggested that this particular soul's knowledge had been acquired first-hand. *"If we did, China would be kinder to our Earth. But the exploitation goes on and on. Hunger is a powerful motivator."*

Susan was ashamed that such a simple explanation hadn't occurred to her. Greed wasn't the only reason for Earth's woes. People could only afford to focus their energy on conservation after their basic needs had been met. Inequality was the root of the problem. The haves versus the have-nots. But wasn't inequality caused by greed?

"Ready to head out?" Seamus asked.

With no easy solution to the conundrum she faced, clearing the cobwebs from her mind seemed to be the best approach.

"Absolutely," Susan replied. "Lead on."

Exhilaration coursed through Susan's veins, flushing out doubts and fears as Zaria blew past Seamus's big bay gelding and plunged on through the surf. She'd never ridden so fast before, and she was at a loss to understand how the smaller horse was able to overtake the larger one with such ease.

"That's because you're moving with her, not against her. Stay on the packed sand and she'll go even faster."

A press of Susan's leg shifted Zaria away from the water's edge, and the mare pounded across the beach, her mane whipping in the wind like frothy ink as they left Seamus and his mount behind. No doubt he would go all macho on her and whine at being bested.

"No, he won't. He's the happiest he's ever been. I can feel it."

"Christina?"

Of course. They were galloping straight toward the cemetery where Christina was buried. The ruins of Kilmacrehy church were clearly visible up ahead.

"You certainly know how to pick your moments," Susan

muttered.

"Can't let you two have all the fun." Joyous laughter rippled through Susan's mind. *"This is glorious."*

Susan agreed—that is, until she spotted a lone runner approaching. "Careful now," she warned. "Let's not be trampling the joggers."

"You might consider it in this case." Christina's normally sweet voice hardened with unmistakable fury. *"That's the woman who pushed me off the cliff."*

Chapter 17

SUSAN SLOWED ZARIA TO A TROT. SHE DIDN'T NEED CHRISTINA'S help to identify the woman; she recognized her the moment their eyes met. She hadn't changed much in six years. Still had the same exotic eyes, high cheekbones, and long brown ponytail.

Damn, that was fast. She'd only uploaded Christina's drawings a little over an hour ago, and the bad guys had already sent an assassin after her. Doing her best to appear nonchalant, she simply smiled and waved at the woman as they drew abreast of one another. Not surprisingly, the runner merely nodded.

A glance over her shoulder after the woman ran past revealed Seamus also waving at the assassin as he approached her.

If he only knew.

"Use your powers, Susan," Christina urged. *"Hit her with a really big wave."*

Seriously?

She brought Zaria to a halt and turned her around to wait for Seamus.

"You win," Seamus declared, holding up a hand in surrender as he reached them. No, he wasn't upset and whining about her horse being faster. He was as gracious in defeat as he was—well, every time she'd ever been with him.

"Did you see her?" Susan whispered.

"Who? You mean that runner we passed?"

Susan nodded, leveling a steady glare at the waves breaking on the shore where the assassin ran. The temptation to do as Christina suggested was very strong. But what then? Hit her with a wave and then capture and interrogate her? Accuse her of murder or simply let her drown? No one would have any reason to believe Susan would want her dead, and a rogue wave was, well, a rogue wave. She might be questioned as a witness, but accused of murder? Not very likely.

"Is she—?"

Seamus didn't need to finish his question, nor did Susan need to silence him with a quelling glance. His wide-eyed expression said it all.

He knew. "You don't suppose—?"

"That she's here to take one or both of us out? Possibly. Although she might be here for Robert."

Seamus stared after the runner's retreating form. "Could she kill him? I mean, if he's what he says he is, would it be possible?"

"No telling. He might be really old, but he never said he was immortal." She paused for a moment, collecting her thoughts. "To be perfectly honest, I'm not sure what an assassin could possibly do to stop us now. Christina's artwork has already been posted online. Killing us or Robert won't keep it from going viral."

"Maybe that isn't why she's here," Seamus mused. "I doubt this 'conspiracy' could move that fast. For all we know, she might've been here all along. Maybe she never left, hoping to finish what she started by finding and destroying those drawings."

"For six years? Seems unlikely. I say we follow her."

Seamus chuckled. "We're so inconspicuous. She'd never suspect us."

"We're just two ordinary people out for a ride," Susan insisted. "She couldn't possibly know we recognized her. Probably feels perfectly safe."

"We're the ones who might not be safe. She could be carrying a weapon of some sort."

"She didn't use a weapon to kill Christina. Maybe pushing people off cliffs is her specialty."

"No cliffs around here," Seamus remarked. "And we both know how well you can control the waves." He shrugged. "Race you back down the beach?"

She ruffled Zaria's mane. The mare hadn't completely caught her breath from the previous run. "A little slower this time, I think. That way we can watch her from a distance and see where she goes."

"I'm all for that." His assessing gaze swept over her, leaving warm tingles in its wake. "You're a proper good rider, Miss Susan."

"Apparently several of my stowaways know how to ride. They're, um, coaching me." She tilted her head to one side. If she'd had any pangs signaling their departure, she hadn't noticed them. Then again, she'd also asked everyone to wait until the ride was over before moving on. That is, if they had any control over the process. Hopefully they wouldn't all abandon her the moment they caught up with Christina's killer.

Not the best time for a headache.

"*No worries,*" Christina said suddenly. "*I'm keeping them here.*"

You can do that?

Gentle laughter filled Susan's mind. "*Not really. But everyone is enjoying the ride. Now if you could just catch up with that murdering bitch, we might see some action.*"

Susan pressed Zaria into a trot. "My stowaways also seem anxious to catch that woman—they're a bit bloodthirsty, really. Although I don't know what they think we'll do if we catch her."

"You missed your chance before," Seamus said as his gelding drew abreast of the mare. "Could've drowned her quite easily."

Susan rolled her eyes. "I'm not a killer, Seamus. Don't think I want to start now."

"Might have to, though." He drew in a deep breath and grimaced as though about to divulge something rather distasteful. "I did a bit of research last night. Seems the scientists aboard that plane weren't the first to be targeted for developing alternative energy sources. Some have been killed while others only got their projects defunded and their ideas squashed. There's a ridiculous amount of money still to be made from untapped fossil fuels—in the hundreds of trillions of dollars."

"So what you're saying is that this has been happening for a while."

"So it would seem."

"That fits with what Jillian and Cleona told me. The murders they solved occurred about ten or twelve years ago, and the victims were either involved in climate change or renewable energy research." She shook her head slowly. "Hundreds of trillions... No wonder they're so unwilling to give it up."

"Even if it kills us all."

"Poor Earth. If she wasn't so full of riches, perhaps we could live with her in greater harmony."

Seamus smiled. "Don't be giving the old girl any ideas. She might try to bury them even deeper. Then where would we be?" He peered ahead to where the runner still jogged along the shoreline. "We'd best pick up the pace if we don't want to lose her."

Susan nodded. As though she'd read Susan's mind, Zaria picked up an easy canter. Susan had never dreamed that riding a horse could be accomplished with such subtlety. No kicking, whipping, or screaming. Only tiny shifts in weight and leg pressure that were probably invisible to the casual observer.

I have to remember this. Even if I lose every one of my riders when we reach the stable, I have to remember.

In view of the overwhelming gut feeling, the why wasn't important—and it was indeed her own gut feeling. Not the extra entities for whom she was playing host. She would have thought catching Christina's killer would take priority—no doubt it would come to the fore eventually—but this ride was taking on greater importance than she ever would have guessed.

"Thanks for suggesting the ride," she said abruptly. "It was...important."

"Not only because of who we saw?"

She shook her head. "It's more than that. So much more."

* * * *

The smile curving Susan's lips kept Seamus from any further prodding. She was happy. Actually happy. Not laughing at something he might have said to tease her, but genuinely pleased.

Clearly she liked horses more than boats.

That was fine with him. The *Branwyn Eostre* was his livelihood. Music was his passion. Riding, on the other hand, was exhilarating and fun. If Susan never boarded his boat again or even listened to the band play, this was something they could share. Fun had been elusive since Christina's death. Susan had helped him recapture it.

Assisting her to accomplish whatever tasks she'd been assigned was a small price to pay for the greater reward.

The last thing he wanted was for her to return to the States when her mission was complete. Pulling up roots to live in a different country was a lot to ask of a woman, and although she was understandably upset by the recent crash—many people in her situation would vow never to fly again—would she be willing to give up her career to remain in Liscannor?

In that instant, he realized that she didn't have to live in Ireland. He would follow her wherever she went.

But only if she loved him.

Susan slowed her horse to a walk. "Look. She's heading for the bridge to Lahinch."

Seamus had been so lost in thought he'd momentarily forgotten they were no longer simply riding for pleasure. The arrival of Christina's killer had interrupted their brief holiday in a way that couldn't be ignored.

Christina's killer…

Having been convinced that Christina's death was a suicide, he'd blamed himself for not being there to prevent it rather than harboring vengeful thoughts toward an actual perpetrator. The animosity hadn't festered for years—not the way his own guilt had done. The transition between the two verdicts had been so sudden, he still hadn't gotten around to forgiving himself. He realized he couldn't have been with her all the time, nor had he suspected she was in any danger. He'd actually been out to sea when she died. His worst nightmare had been the possibility that he might have witnessed her death. Now he almost wished he had. That way he would've known she'd been murdered and might even have been able to identify her assailant.

"How can we convince the guards she's the one who killed Christina?"

"That's just it. We can't," Susan said flatly. "Not unless we can get her to confess or—" She stopped there, trapping her lower lip between her teeth.

"Or what?"

She blew out a pent-up breath. "Goad her into coming after one of us."

He didn't have to ask who she thought would be the best person to use as bait. She'd already pegged herself as a probable target. "You aren't serious."

"Oh, but I am," she replied. "Not that I have any intention of allowing her to succeed. But you must see the need to set a trap for her."

Seamus shook his head. "I believe we'd be better off confronting her. Telling her we know she did it might be enough to get her to confess."

"Possibly. Of course, if she's what we think she is, she's undoubtedly committed more than one murder. There might be witnesses to other deaths who might be able to identify her."

He scanned the beach and the road that ran parallel to it, noting the direction their quarry was taking. "Looks like she's heading back toward Liscannor," he said. "You know… the more I think about it, the less likely it is that she never left the area after killing Christina. I'm fairly certain I've never seen that woman before in my life."

"That makes more sense. Still, it's a bit unsettling that she'd show up here on the same day we post Christina's artwork online."

"Which makes the extent of the conspiracy even more terrifying."

She snorted a laugh. "The fact that Earth decided to fight back is proof of just how terrifying this is. I'd be willing to bet this conspiracy has tainted every government on the planet—and most of the corporations. They turn us against each other to keep us distracted while they rape the planet and pick our pockets at the same time. Living in peace and harmony with nature doesn't make anyone rich. And now we have cell phones and video games to keep us occupied while the rest of the world starves to death, becomes mired in unwinnable wars, or chokes on its own filth. People need to open their eyes and take a good, long look at what's really happening."

Susan's righteous anger came through loud and clear, but Seamus heard something else—an echo of sorts. A glance to his right revealed what she'd conjured up. The sea was, for want of a better description, waving at her. A wall of water rose up and curled over to form a tube just offshore, keeping pace with their progress. The only other possible explanation was that a leviathan was following her like a dog on a leash.

The horses they rode should've been snorting and fleeing in terror. Instead, they merely turned their heads seaward for a brief moment before continuing to plod on across the sand. A glance toward the road revealed the alleged assassin stopping dead in her tracks.

Susan let out a snarl and the wave shot out in front of them, forming a long arm of water that reached all the way to the road where the woman stood, her open-mouthed dismay clearly visible despite the distance between them. The wave knocked her flat, then sucked her down to the shore to lay sprawled on the sand before them.

In an instant, Susan vaulted from her horse and ran to the woman's side, her intent obviously not to rescue but to capture and accuse. The woman gasped for breath as Susan hauled her to her feet.

"You murdering bitch." Susan's voice echoed with the power of countless souls trapped amid a raging gale. "You are the handmaiden of evil, and for that, you must pay. You will *all* pay. "

Trembling, the woman collapsed at Susan's feet. "I was paid. Never knew the reasons. Never cared. I had no choice. It was either that or watch my family starve or be killed. You can't know what that's like."

Despite her short, gasping sentences, Seamus could hear the accent that matched her distinctively Eastern European features. He dismounted and gathered up Zaria's reins, although the mare was clearly as spellbound by the scene playing out before her as he was.

"Oh, I believe I do," Susan said harshly. "You aren't the only ones suffering. We will all be suffering soon. The human race is on the brink of extinction because once we've exhausted this planet's resources, there will be nowhere for us to go. We aren't advanced enough to find another world on which to live. Space is too vast and we're kidding ourselves to think that we could ever live on Mars the way we live on Earth. Our existence will end with a whimper and our civilizations will crumble into dust."

"Most people can't think that far ahead," the woman said sadly. "Not when fear and hunger are so real."

"We *must* think that far ahead," Susan insisted. "We must sacrifice in order to survive. We have no choice now. We've left it too late."

"But you have superhuman powers." She gazed up at Susan with the first glimmer of hope Seamus had seen her display. "I've just witnessed it. You could save us. You could save us all."

Susan's eyes narrowed. "That's the plan, but you cannot deny your guilt. I will not shield you from justice."

The wretched woman looked down at the sand, clawing at it with trembling fingers. "No. I cannot deny it." Drawing in an unsteady breath, she raised her head. "But I can tell you what I know. I know who my contacts are and who paid me. Discovering who it was that held power over me gave me strength. I am Nadia Tireskova. I was born in Soviet Russia, and believe me, the KGB is still active. They've simply gone underground. They have controlled me in one way or another since the day I was born. But no longer. I will help you fight."

From Seamus's point of view, Nadia had no alternative but to pledge her allegiance to Susan because, when it came to power, the KGB had nothing on Susan Maxwell. "You're saying the Russians are behind this?" He didn't bother to hide his skepticism. "Seems more far-reaching than that."

"It is," Nadia replied. "The Russians are only part of the conspiracy. The Americans, the British, the Saudis… They all seek to be the greater power, and the most potent weapon they have is oil."

Seamus would have gladly dragged little Miss KGB into the nearest Garda station and left her there to rot. For years he'd blamed himself for Christina's suicide, and now the actual perpetrator was groveling in the sand right there in front of him. This woman had killed someone he loved very dearly. She deserved nothing but contempt. "We shouldn't even be listening to her, Susan. She's naught but a curst assassin."

Susan arched a brow. "Yes, and I don't doubt we could prove it—or get her to confess in front of other witnesses. But you're forgetting who we have on our side. If it weren't for the resulting anarchy, Mother Earth probably would've already toppled every one of those governments—and you can imagine how easily and effectively she could do it. The thing is, most governments aren't as much to blame as the people who keep them in power. They're the ones funding campaigns and manipulating voters. That's where the true evil lies."

Nadia nodded. "The money I've received comes from a bank in Riyadh. I wish I could say my direct contacts were from that part of the world, but they aren't. An Englishman gives me instructions and an American provides me with whatever I need to complete the assignment."

"Assignment?" Seamus echoed. "You kill people for a living and you call it an *assignment*?" His anger flared and he clenched his teeth so tightly, it was a wonder they didn't crack under the strain. "Listen, if you were sent here to kill us, why should we believe a word you say? You're only trying to save your own skin."

"No one sent me here to kill either of you." She gestured toward Susan. "They don't know about her yet. I have a network of my own the KGB knows nothing about. Ever since the crash we've had our eyes on the survivors. No one should have survived that disaster. No one was *meant* to survive, and yet they did. There's something special about them."

Seamus rolled his eyes. First a sexton he'd known all his life turned out to be an ageless keeper of the timeline, and now a KGB double agent had decided there was something miraculous about the survivors. That she was correct was irrelevant, because if she could figure it out, so could someone with a lot more to lose—an idea that shook him to his core. "How would you know that? Or are you still a bit stunned from being captured by a wave?"

Nadia shook her head. "No. I was startled at first, but no more." She looked up at Susan. "You are the one we've been waiting for.

Now that you're here, the revolution will begin."

Seamus took a moment to study Nadia more closely. Assuming she'd at least been in her late teens or early twenties when the Soviet Union broke up—he doubted even the KGB admitted schoolgirls to their ranks—she would now be in her mid-forties, possibly even her early fifties. She looked younger than that. A *lot* younger.

"You aren't a Watcher by any chance? Are you?"

Chapter 18

"I DON'T KNOW WHAT YOU MEAN BY THAT," NADIA REPLIED, AND from her mystified expression, Susan could only assume she was telling the truth.

Seamus seemed unconvinced. "But you said the KGB controlled you, and you're too young—"

"My father was an agent. When he wanted out after the breakup of the Soviet Union, they let him go, for a price. *I* was that price." She brushed a stray lock of dark brown hair from her face and got to her feet. "He doesn't know what I've done. He thinks I'm a sales representative for a textile manufacturer, which, if nothing else, explains the amount of traveling I have to do."

Susan wanted to trust her, but a paid assassin? Really? Did she have a use for someone with such skills, especially the one who'd killed Seamus's former lover? Her head hurt just thinking about it.

No. The pain slicing through her temple was caused by several of the stowaways abandoning ship. Apparently they assumed the ride on the beach had come to a rather abrupt halt. For her part, if she'd been one of those spirits, she'd have stuck around for the grand finale—unless Susan was destined to die soon, at which time her stint as a lifeboat to the others would also come to an end. Perhaps they knew what was in store for her and decided to leave early.

"We don't know anything like that."

The shrink was back. *Haven't heard from you for a while. What do you make of this woman?*

"I believe she's telling the truth, and you could certainly use a group of undercover operatives, even if you don't plan to use them as hit men. See if she'll tell you more about them."

At last, some concrete advice.

"Okay," Susan began. "Suppose you start by telling us more

about this 'network' of yours. How do we know we can trust them? Or you, for that matter?"

"You can't," Nadia replied. "I have no way to prove any of it. But there are about a hundred of us, scattered all over the world." She frowned. "Unfortunately, we haven't been as effective as we'd hoped. We should've been able to prevent that plane crash, but we failed. Oh, we've disrupted several other plots, but that one…" She fell silent, shaking her head slowly. "The organization was too complex."

"Yet you still keep trying?" Susan prompted.

"We have no reason not to. The crimes against humanity and nature are more prevalent than ever. Plus, we have you now. I saw what you did today, and another of us followed you to Baile an Tsagart. I must admit, I found what he says he saw there difficult to believe."

Susan was loath to admit it, but she had similar feelings on the subject. Already, she felt as though her conversation with the whales had either happened to someone else or was nothing more than a dream. "Did he realize who I was talking with?"

"He couldn't tell, but the way the sea responded to you…" Nadia paused, shuddering, which wasn't surprising considering the ambient temperature and the fact that she was soaking wet. "That and what you did to me… I've never been so terrified in my life."

That explained a few things, the most significant being why an assassin would be so rattled. Considering what they did for a living, Susan had always assumed assassins were virtually unflappable. But then, most people freaked out when the tables were turned. "Good. That was my intention."

Seamus took a step toward Nadia, a menacing scowl replacing his normally genial expression. "Mind telling us exactly when you stopped working for the KGB to strike out on your own?"

To her credit, Nadia stood her ground. "I'm still working for them, although I haven't been as"—she hesitated as though searching for the right word—"*successful* as I was in the past."

"Guess most of your assignments weren't as easy as pushing someone off a cliff then, were they?" Not surprisingly, Seamus was seething with anger, his white-knuckled grip on the reins illustrating the tremendous effort required to hold his emotions in check. Considering all the heartbreak he'd endured in the wake of Christina's death, if he'd had a decent weapon handy, he probably would've been tempted to use it.

Nadia met his furious glare with an unflinching gaze. "You were her lover, were you not?"

"Yes, I was," Seamus snapped. "Do you have any idea how much I've suffered—how much her family and this entire county have suffered—believing her death was a suicide? Good God, woman! How can you possibly expect us to trust you after putting us through that?" He was silent for barely a heartbeat before adding, "And don't give me that 'to err is human; to forgive divine' shite, because I'm a long damn way from being divine."

"And I'm not even human, am I?" Nadia said sadly. "You might be right about that. There are times when my claim to humanity seems unjustified. I have been what you accuse me of being—a cold, calculating killer. But only because I had to be. Becoming an assassin was never my choice."

"You have a *choice* every time you pull the trigger." Expelling a long, exasperated breath, he turned to Susan. "What are we going to do with her? Turn her in to the guards or feed her to the bloody whales?"

Susan understood his anger. She'd felt the same impotent fury in the wake of the crash, knowing that a man she loved had been forced to murder hundreds of people in one precipitous dive into the sea. She weighed their options before she spoke.

"Unless she's willing to confess to Christina's murder, we can't turn her in to the police. You can't very well claim to have suddenly remembered seeing her push Christina off the cliff. You were nowhere near the scene at the time and neither was I." She hesitated, tapping a knuckle to her chin. "My testimony that Christina's spirit identified her own killer is more likely to get me locked up than it would Nadia."

Seamus nodded. "Telling the guards you captured her with a wave would be even worse."

Nadia stared first at Susan, then Seamus, and back again. "W–what are you saying?"

"Ghosts," Susan replied. "Spirits of the dead. Souls trapped inside my own mind telling me things only they could know."

If Nadia had been pale before, she was positively ashen now. She traced her blue-tinged lips with a tongue that left behind no trace of moisture. "You've been...possessed?"

"In a manner of speaking. However, unlike the more stereotypical spooks, they're relatively benign. At least they are until we meet up with someone who actually killed one of them. In that case, I have a feeling they'd do something downright terrifying. Lucky for you, you weren't in on the plane crash plot."

Susan had never been face to face with an honest-to-God assassin before, much less one who was shaking in her shoes. She was, although she hated to admit it, enjoying herself just a tad. A glance at Seamus proved he not only understood what she was doing, he approved.

"As for feeding you to the whales," Susan went on, "I'm thinking sharks would be best. Most whales only eat krill." Cocking her head, she bent over and peered into Nadia's downcast eyes. "Are we getting to you yet?"

"You are, indeed," Nadia replied. "I'm surprised I've never been haunted by the ghosts of those I've killed." She raised her head and sighed. "Perhaps I have. Perhaps that's why I chose to rebel."

"You never answered my question," Seamus said. "When did you stop being 'successful'?"

Susan knew precisely which piece of information he was fishing for. He wanted to know whether Christina's death came before or after Nadia's rebellion. His ability to forgive enough to work with Nadia hinged on her reply.

"Some time after pushing your lover off the Cliffs of Moher." Nadia had control of herself now. But was she telling the truth or another lie?

"I should have refused," she went on. "A woman so recently past her childhood? What threat could she possibly have posed to anyone? Unfortunately, my doubts didn't begin to surface until afterward." A thoughtful frown creased her brow. "Perhaps I have been haunted—if not by her ghost, then by my own conscience. But whatever the reason, that was when I decided to seek another path." Her eyes locked with Susan's. "I risked the safety of my family as well as my own life to do so."

"So you're saying you didn't complete any of your *assignments* after killing Christina?" His sarcastic emphasis of "assignments" proved Seamus still wasn't convinced. "Or did you pick and choose who you allowed to escape?"

Susan wasn't ready to accept Nadia's story either. However, she was willing to hear her out.

"Let's just say my aim isn't as sharp as it used to be," Nadia replied. "I've arranged to have someone in place to bump my target enough for me to wound rather than kill." She grimaced. "I have endured a great deal of pain as a result of those failures."

Susan didn't particularly care to hear how that pain had been inflicted. "Are you prepared to stop altogether? Or is this your way of discovering and then protecting whoever your superiors have targeted?"

Nadia shrugged. "I haven't received an assignment in some time. To be honest, I've been expecting to be told to kill you, Susan. The order hasn't come through as yet."

"Well, thank God for that," Seamus exclaimed. "If you kill another woman I love, I'll be sorely tempted to—"

Susan laid a gentle hand on his arm. "No threats, Seamus. Save them for those who are truly deserving—the instigators rather than the pawns."

A smile tugged the corner of her mouth. He loved her, did he? She'd suspected as much. Bless him. She was well on her way to loving him back. Too bad the time wasn't right for romance. Any passionate interludes would probably be cut short, just as this ride on the beach had been.

Still, to have him hold her while she slept would be worth the risk. Jillian and Cleona had found love with their respective cohorts. Susan shouldn't turn it down, especially if it meant she might actually sleep through the night.

"What a crappy reason for taking a man to your bed. He loves you, Susan. He needs your love and you need him. You care for him. I can feel it. Don't cheat yourself or him by denying the attraction."

With those choice words from Seamus's deceased lover, Susan turned to Nadia. "But if your people kill another man I love, the fury of a woman scorned will seem like child's play in comparison."

Seamus covered her hand with his and gave it a quick squeeze.

"Message received," Christina reported.

I knew that.

"Just wanted to be sure."

So what do you make of her? Should we trust her? You of all people should have a say.

A sigh echoed through Susan's mind. *"I hate to admit it, but she's telling the truth. I believe she can be trusted."*

"Okay, Nadia. You'd better get into some dry clothes before you freeze to death." Susan took Zaria's reins from Seamus and mounted with no less ease than she had before. Time would tell whether she'd retained her stowaway's riding ability or whether the riders hadn't all left her yet.

"If I did, it would be no more than I deserved."

"See you later, then," Susan said as she turned the mare back toward the beach. "I'm guessing you know where to find us?"

"Yes, I do," Nadia replied. "And if I know where you're staying, you can bet anyone who means you harm could find you just as easily."

"No worries about that," Seamus said as he swung himself into the gelding's saddle. "She's already checked out of the hotel." With a smile that bordered on smug, he added, "She's moving in with me this afternoon."

Somewhere in the back of her mind, the stowaways cheered.

Instead of making the obvious suggestive remark, Nadia merely acknowledged this information with a brief nod, then turned and jogged off toward the road.

Susan waited until Nadia was out of earshot before she spoke. "You make it sound like we'll be sleeping together."

"We can if you like." Seamus's grin was the picture of

innocence, as was the offhand nature of his shrug. "I certainly wouldn't kick you out of bed."

"Hmm… Yeah, well, we'll cross that bridge when we come to it."

"Might be sooner than you think," Seamus said as they started toward Lahinch. "I mean, I do have a second bedroom, and there is a bed in there. But that's also where I store my extra fishing gear. If you want to sleep in a room that doesn't reek of fish, it'll have to be mine."

Thus far, Seamus had been nothing but honest, helpful, and kind. Strange that he would pick this particular moment to resort to trickery. She stared at him for a long moment, trying to decide whether he was pulling her leg—until she realized she didn't care.

Laughing, she threw up a hand in surrender. "Okay, I give up. If the bad guys are gunning for me, I might as well enjoy myself while I can."

"You'll get no arguments from me," he said. "Although I'm thinking there's more to it than simple enjoyment." Pausing, he glanced downward as he adjusted his grip on the reins. "Look, I know you lost someone special in the crash, but—"

"Chuck and I were over and done with years ago. While it's true I still cared about him and I'm very sorry he's gone, as far as romance is concerned, there's no rebound effect at work here." She nudged Zaria sideways, closing the short distance between the two horses before holding out her hand. "If my heart was broken, it's had more than enough time to heal."

Seamus nodded as he took her outstretched hand in a firm grasp. "So has mine. Time to move on."

* * * *

Who'd have thought it would take meeting up with a Russian assassin-turned-double-agent to convince Susan she was better off sharing a bed with him than sleeping alone?

Not that it had actually happened that way, but the end result was the same. Seamus saw no need to force the issue, or even discuss it any further. She'd said yes, or at least agreed there was a connection between them—a connection that had nothing to do with spirits or souls or her ability to control the sea. Nothing to do with Christina or Robert either. This was between them and them alone.

Until he remembered that she was never truly alone.

"Think you can get the stowaways to take a hike for a while?"

She shook her head. "It doesn't work that way. Wish it did, but—"

"No worries. We'll figure something out. I mean, them bearing witness doesn't really bother me. It's sort of like turning a picture of someone around to keep them from seeing what you're doing—although I can honestly say I've never done that."

"True," she said after a moment or two. "I bet I lose a bunch if we ever actually…"

Seamus was a little surprised she'd be so hesitant to say the words aloud. "Make love?"

"Um, yeah. To hear Jillian and Cleona tell it, some of their spirits stuck around more for the romance than the adventure."

"I can understand that. I prefer romance myself."

"Same here—except that if history is any indication, romance can be every bit as painful."

"Aye. We can both attest to that. But I'm willing to give it a go if you are."

She sighed. "It'd be nice to think that something good could come from this mess. Aside from the greater good, that is."

"We can make that happen," he said. "It's only a matter of breaking the ice and admitting that the possibility exists."

"More like *accepting* the possibility. It's just that romance seems out of place with so much other stuff going on."

He couldn't help but laugh. "Seems like all the great romances occur during a war or some sort of disaster."

"Like in *Casablanca*, you mean?"

"Aye. In this story, that you're Ingrid Bergman's character is a given, but am I Humphrey Bogart or the chap she wound up with—the one whose name I can't recall for the life of me?"

Susan chuckled. "I can't remember his name either." Her expression went blank for a moment. "Hold on… Paul Henreid played Victor Laszlo. Bogart was Rick Blaine, Bergman was Ilsa

Lund."

"That came from your stowaways, didn't it?"

"Sure did."

"Should've guessed one of them would know that."

"Cleona said it was like having a search engine in her head. Not quite as good as Google, but not too shabby."

"Hmm, yes, I suppose it would be useful." With a sidelong glance, he prompted, "So, Ilsa... Which am I? Rick or Victor?"

A slow, enigmatic smile twitched her lips. "A bit of both."

He didn't ask her to explain. As long as he was the one who got the girl, the specific "bits" were irrelevant. "That works for me."

Chapter 19

THE LONG STRETCH OF SAND AHEAD BECKONED TO SUSAN WITH astonishing power—the desire of the stowaway who had urged her to ride combined with her own inner yearning.

"One more gallop along the water's edge. Please."

My thoughts exactly.

Zaria must've felt it as well, for with only the slightest shifting of Susan's weight, the mare launched into a canter from the walk, then quickly stretched into a full gallop.

Exhilaration flooded Susan's soul, lifting it higher with each stride, her heart swelling with a combination of sorrow and joy.

One last ride.

The anchor tethering that lost soul to the living being who'd had carried her up from the depths of the sea began to weaken as the mare splashed through the shallow waves breaking on the shore. A glance at Seamus's face as his mount thundered alongside hers detected no trace of sadness, unencumbered as he was by souls that were not his own. Only Cleona and Jillian could understand how she felt—and perhaps Kevan. They shared a uniqueness that set them apart from every other person on earth.

I'll miss you. I'll miss you all.

"It's for the best," the voice said. *"Thank you, and goodbye."*

A gentle twinge marked the soul's passing, and for a moment, Susan feared she might tumble from the saddle. But nothing changed. She still followed the mare's movements with her own body as naturally and easily as she had before. Unaccustomed to the exercise, she would undoubtedly pay for the ride with sore muscles, but she deemed it worth the pain.

"You lost one, didn't you?" Seamus asked as they slowed to a walk where the sand gave way to rocks.

"Was it that obvious?"

He nodded. "I've seen it happen enough to recognize the signs." His gaze sharpened. "You okay?"

"Yeah. That one hurt less, but I feel the loss more, if that makes any sense. She was grounding me in a way the others hadn't—an earthy, nurturing soul. I didn't realize how much she helped me until she was gone." She smiled. "Guess I'll have to muddle through somehow."

"You'll do more than muddle through," Seamus insisted. "I have faith in you. *They* have faith in you or they wouldn't have stowed away in your mind."

Prior to the crash, Susan had given very little thought to faith. Now she realized it was an integral part of everything she'd ever done. She truly did have faith that the sun would rise and that she would still be breathing when it did. A moment's reflection solidified that belief because in the greater scheme of things little else mattered.

"At least I'm still alive," she said after a bit. "Perhaps that's all it takes."

If he thought her comments were strange, he didn't remark upon them, merely nodding his agreement before glancing at the sky. "Be time for dinner soon. What do you say we head back to the stable?"

"Must be nice to be able to tell time by looking at the sky. I suppose that's a sailor thing."

"Possibly," he replied. "But I have other methods. My stomach for one, and it's telling me it's almost suppertime."

"Should've known you'd have an alternate method. Me, I just look at my watch." The watch that had truly seen her through thick and thin. Many a successful flight and at least one that ended rather badly. "And you're right," she said after consulting her trusty wristwatch. "It's time we headed back. This has been one hell of a day."

If he thought the night would be an improvement, he didn't mention it. He had to be thinking about it, though. She was essentially moving in with him. Moving in when she'd only shared a kiss or two with him. Now she'd be sharing his bed? Seriously?

One look at him proved the sheer rightness of it all. He was part of her life now. In a way, it seemed he always had been. Even though he hadn't been with her in the past, he'd been alive, waiting to become a part of her future.

She laughed inwardly, marveling that what was supposed to have cleared her mind had only succeeded in making her wax philosophic. Was that the correct usage of the phrase? God only knew—or perhaps the stowaways did. Either way, no one was talking. All she heard were the ongoing thoughts from within her own mind. She'd never found the way to turn off those thoughts and make her mind a blank. Perhaps if she had, Earth's spirit would have spoken to her sooner. Was that enlightenment? Hearing the planet speak when every other voice was finally silent?

She looked at Seamus again. "I think I need help getting my brain to shut up."

"I can think of an excellent way to do that."

"Oh, let me guess," she said with a mocking roll of her eyes. "Sex?"

"Of course, but first, you require sustenance." He tapped his chin with a fingertip. "I'm thinking bangers and mash."

"Sounds really good."

He grinned. "It also has the virtue of being relatively easy to make—not to mention quick."

She arched a brow. "Anxious, are you?"

"You could say that," he replied. "Been patient as the day is long up to now, but as we both know, the day is startin' ta wane."

From somewhere deep within, her laughter erupted. Seamus was good for her—good for her soul and every other soul she possessed. "It is at that," she agreed. "You can teach me how to make authentic bangers and mash, and I'll teach you how to—" To be honest, she wasn't sure what she could possibly teach him. He seemed to know so much already.

Mischief danced in his eyes. "How to what? Make love to a gorgeous ginger-haired Yank?"

Chances were he already knew how to do that too. If not, he would figure it out soon enough. "I was going to say 'make an apple pie,' but that'll do."

* * * *

Seamus's house was older than some of the surrounding structures, and as such, was more traditionally Irish than the holiday homes near the shore. History was embedded in the walls—smells evoking memories of peat fires, freshly baked soda bread, and simmering pots of stew. Despite its simple bachelor furnishings with muted browns and greens in quiet contrast with cream-colored walls, the place felt like home. Shelves of books lined one wall of the front room, which contained a sofa, two easy chairs, a scattering of small tables, and the inevitable television.

"Have you lived here long?" she asked as he carried in her bags.

"About five years or so," he replied. He nodded toward an open doorway. "Kitchen is that way. I'll take these into the bedroom."

She started to follow him, but thought better of it. Dinner first, she reminded herself firmly. Oddly enough, being alone with him didn't cause her any anxiety whatsoever. This wasn't a contrived rendezvous between two virtual strangers. Staying in his house was as natural and organic to their situation as any other experience she'd shared with him.

Five years, he'd said, which meant he hadn't shared this particular house with Christina. There would be no ghosts to fuss at Susan for taking on the position of the lady of the manor. At least not in the ordinary sense. Even if Christina had ever lived there, Susan apparently had her blessing.

The stowaways didn't appear to have abandoned ship the moment she crossed the threshold either, although she doubted the sea could speak to her from there. Being situated further inland, the house could only have been reached by a tidal wave of catastrophic proportions.

A cool draft met her as she entered the kitchen, making her rethink the possibility of a resident ghost. Her breasts tingled with the cold, and after dropping her purse on the table, she wrapped her sweater more tightly around herself. The chill dissipated so quickly, she might have imagined it.

Only a few short weeks ago, she wouldn't have spared a thought for ghosts or any other type of spirit. Now, she seemed to expect them wherever she went. Looking back, it was a wonder more voices hadn't spoken to her from the graveyard at Kilmacrehy. Perhaps the others buried there had no need to linger among the stones and had moved on. Either that or, having no interest in saving the planet, Susan wasn't the one to whom they wished to speak.

Most people took their world for granted, with little or no regard for the consequences of their actions while others were too concerned with staying alive to care. A more even distribution of wealth would help to change that. Unfortunately, Susan didn't have the power to fix financial inequality. At least, not without resorting to the sort of revolutionary tactics the French had used to level the playing field in their country. Taxation was the best option, and while it was infinitely preferable to the axes and pitchforks method, someone in power had to propose, implement, and enforce those laws.

I can't think about that right now.

Healing each and every one of the world's woes wasn't her job anyway. She was the Bringer of Justice.

What the hell did that mean? Was she supposed to throw all the corrupt billionaires in jail? Make the sea destroy their oceanfront homes? Become some sort of modern-day Robin Hood, robbing from the rich and giving to the poor?

She pressed her fingertips to her temples in an effort to quiet her incessant thoughts as Seamus returned.

"The stowaways skipping out on you?"

"No," she replied. "My overactive brain is hounding me—again."

Taking her hands, he raised them to his lips, kissing each palm before pulling her closer. With a sigh, he bowed his head and rested his forehead against hers. "Bangers and mash, remember?"

"Gotcha." She attempted a smile. "I'll fry the bangers if you'll make the mash."

"That works for me." Warmth spread from the spot where his lips lightly touched her cheek. "And don't worry. This will all sort itself out eventually."

"Not a lifelong endeavor?"

"I'm thinking it'll be more of a short-term thing. Then you can get back to normal."

"Whatever *that* is. Cleona and Jillian lost their extra souls once they'd completed their specific tasks. Unfortunately, my job seems to be more…vague."

"No more worrying about that," he said briskly. "At least not for now." Releasing her from his embrace, he turned and opened the fridge. He tossed a package of sausages and an onion onto the table. "I like to cook the bangers in with the onions and butter for the gravy. Frying pan is on the stove. Knives are in the top drawer on the right. Think about what you're doing and *only* what you're doing. Got it?"

"Aye, aye, Captain," she said, somehow managing to quash the urge to salute.

A tiny smile touched his lips, but he said no more. After setting a pan of water on the stove, he began washing and peeling the potatoes at the sink.

Susan wasn't sure she could shut her brain down, but he was right. Unwrapping the sausages, chopping the onion, and heating butter in the skillet all provided an excellent distraction from her obsessive thinking.

Live in the moment.

A few minutes later, Seamus scraped the freshly chopped potatoes from his cutting board into the pan of water. After switching on the burner, he paused to scrutinize her efforts. "Looks like one of your stowaways must've been an Irish chef."

She took a step back and fixed him with an indignant glare. "What makes you think I wouldn't know how to cook anything on my own?"

He shrugged. "I didn't think flight attendants spent enough time at home to do much cooking."

"Maybe so," she admitted. "But that doesn't mean I never learned how to chop onions and fry sausages." With a sniff, she added, "I can even boil water."

"I'm glad to hear it." He gave the potatoes a stir and turned down the heat. "Not much fun doing it alone, though, is it?"

"Not really. Might be more fun if I had a kitchen like this one. Mine is pretty tiny and it's kinda empty most of the time." Generally speaking, she ate whatever was easiest and most readily available, which usually wound up being a frozen entrée.

"Ah, well," he said. "You can hang out in my kitchen as much as you like."

"Thanks. I'll keep that in mind."

His offer was more than tempting. Staying in one place long enough to learn where all the pots and pans were located sounded absolutely marvelous. Spices in the pantry, meat and vegetables in the fridge, and a whole world of recipes from which to choose—not to mention the time to actually come up with some of her own— seemed a welcome change from grabbing a sandwich at an airport bistro.

She didn't regret her life as a flight attendant. After all, she'd flown to more places in a few years than even the most avid travelers visited in a lifetime. Of all those places—practically every European country and most American states—Ireland had always held a special place in her heart. She'd never been sure why that was, although someone once pointed out that Ireland's Forty Shades of Green went well with her red hair.

Silly reason.

A far better explanation was standing next to her testing potatoes with a fork.

Had she been expecting to meet the man of her dreams in Ireland? Subconsciously, perhaps. She certainly hadn't planned it that way.

Nor had she planned on the overwhelming urge to put down her spatula and kiss him until the sausages burned and the potatoes boiled dry.

Well, maybe not *that* long, but at least until the sausages had browned enough on one side to need turning.

"Hey, now," he chided. "Thought I told you not to think about anything but what you were doing."

Susan's cheeks prickled with heat that had more to do with

embarrassment than the warmth from the stove. "I *am* thinking about what I'm doing," she insisted. "Sort of."

"At least promise me you aren't thinking about how to save the world."

"I can attest to that with absolute honesty and certainty."

His eyes widened slightly. "Okay. Something tells me I'd best not be pressing you any further. Might get struck by a rogue wave."

Since she'd already decided her effect on the sea probably didn't extend that far, she grinned. "You only have to wait until after dinner."

"I can do that." He cleared his throat with an obvious effort. "Speaking of which, I'll get started on the gravy."

* * * *

Despite the delicious nature of it, dinner had been a rather hurried affair. Susan was attempting to make quick work of the dishes when she turned away from the sink to find Seamus standing so close behind her, it was a wonder she hadn't felt his breath on her neck.

Wrapping his arms around the small of her back, he pulled her closer still. "Dinner with you was lovely, but there's no need to be washin' the dishes right now. They'll keep. This won't." He closed the remaining distance between them, pressing his lips to hers in a way that spoke of hunger, delight, and a touch of relief. Soft at first, he deepened the kiss until Susan's mind truly did fall silent. No thoughts. No sounds. Only blissful, blessed silence.

She dried her hands on the back of his shirt before threading her fingers through the curls at his nape, only then realizing how much she'd longed to do it and how right it felt to be in this man's kitchen, warm in his embrace, expecting to make love with him now and for the rest of her life.

Her heart raced and her breath quickened. She could've said no. Could've insisted they wait, but for what? For another assassin to take Nadia's place and finish what had begun with Christina's demise?

No. No waiting. Not like she'd waited for Chuck.

And she *had* been waiting. She knew that now. Waiting for something to happen between them again. Waiting for something because the ending hadn't turned out the way she'd expected it to.

With Chuck's last desperate plea for her to save herself, that episode had ended, putting the final nail in the coffin of a romance that never truly was. This was what mattered. The here and now with Seamus, the man she wanted, trusted, and loved. The one who was helping her save the world—or at least bring those who would destroy it to justice.

Seamus suited her better. The perfect height. The perfect shape. They fit together like two peas in a pod.

My how trite…

Didn't matter now because she was in his arms, being quite literally swept off her feet by her charming Irish fisherman and carried to his room. He was wrong about that other bedroom. She'd checked it herself while he was cooking, and it didn't smell the least bit fishy. He could believe what he liked, but no coercion had been necessary. She'd have been in his bed anyway. She was, after all, the Bringer of Justice.

And he was about to get what was coming to him.

Chapter 20

SUSAN HADN'T WANTED HIM IN THE BEGINNING. SEAMUS WAS certain of that. Given that she'd nearly drowned or been killed in some other gruesome manner mere minutes before, her lack of interest wasn't too surprising. She'd also lost a man she'd once loved in the crash. Small wonder she'd had little love to spare for him, despite his having been one of her rescuers.

None of this was the sort of thing a man should be thinking about when he was in the process of removing a woman's clothing. He'd wanted to do the same thing to her on the day they met. Granted, his reasoning then was that she was soaking wet and freezing, but he'd come close to stripping off more than his sweater for her.

Then she vanished from his life as abruptly as she'd entered it. He was sure he would never see her again outside the news—a story that had barely begun to die down by the time she'd shown up at the dock. She'd been cleaner and dryer than before, but the fire had gone out of her eyes.

Judging from the way she was looking at him now, however, the blaze had reignited. Fortunately, that fire burned with passion rather than fury, and he was more than willing to feed the flames.

He wasn't a virgin. He'd made love with Christina many times, and while her greatest passion had been for other things—her art, her calling—he'd never doubted her love for him. Filled with all the hormonal lust of a man not long out of his teens, what he'd lacked in experience, he made up for with enthusiasm.

He was wiser now, and he recognized that the years spent alone had been his way of protecting his heart. But that protection came at a price, creating a deep, abiding loneliness that left an empty space deep inside him. A space only Susan could fill.

He'd lit a candle by the bed so he could see what he'd been craving, what he'd tried so hard to protect and nurture. But even without the flame, she would have been dazzling. Her ginger hair caught the late evening light, making even her skin glow like a crimson sunset.

Red sky at night, sailor's delight.

Red sky in the morning, sailors take warning.

He'd been hearing that verse his entire life. His father chanted it anytime the sky turned red. The best he could tell, red skies were a reasonably accurate predictor of the weather. But Susan? She would be a delight at any hour and in any weather.

Closing his eyes, he focused his attention on her fingertips as they skimmed over his back. He leaned into her warmth, alternately tasting and teasing her with his tongue. Her soap or perfume or some scent all her own filled his head and urged him onward. Her softness and warmth lit a fire in his blood, filling his body with need. He didn't care if he got burned. One touch of her hand could quench the flames and then inspire yet another raging inferno.

No passive partner, she met his kisses with a fervor that matched his own, touching him in ways that denied any shyness. She was as bold and beautiful as her flaming hair, tasting him the way he'd tasted her, licking and sucking him until reason fled.

He'd been the one to prepare this scenario, but she was the one who took it to the next level. Protection was accomplished with quick, deft fingers before she climbed atop him, straddling him like a horse. His breath deserted his lungs as she eased down to take him inside.

Did she know how stunning she was as she rose and fell above him? Lighting that candle had been the right choice. The effect was magical, creating a golden aura that radiated from her like a beacon. Like some ancient warrior goddess, her passion and undeniable strength gave her mastery over him and all mankind.

A moment later, she relinquished that power as she leaned sideways, cueing his next move. Rolling her over, he held her close, reluctant to allow even the tiniest space to come between them. Soon, however, the need to see her overwhelmed him, and he pushed himself up with his hands. She lay back on the sheets, her eyes gleaming in the candlelight, the tips of her lashes sparkling like tiny stars.

"Do you know how beautiful you are? How much I want you? How long I've waited for you?"

Smiling, she shook her head. "We're together now. That's all that matters."

Her words surprised him. He'd have thought she would want to hear such things from him. She was right, though. Completely and utterly right.

She pulled him down, searing his lips with her kiss as she wrapped her legs around him. Needing no further encouragement, he plunged into her, over and over until he was once again captivated by the ethereal glow lighting her face. Her element should have been fire, not water. And yet she'd somehow managed to conquer the sea and bend it to her will. Perhaps she was fire *and* water. But how?

He lost himself in her then, his mind going blank until all he could do was feel, leaving nothing beyond the occasional gulp of air to remind him that he hadn't died in her arms.

Without warning, she convulsed around him, wringing every last drop of his essence from his flesh.

Time stopped. Silence fell. The world imploded, taking him with it.

For one brief moment, he abandoned his earthly form to surge outward into the void. Caught up in the current, he drifted on the sea of eternity.

In the next instant, his lungs filled with air and his heart resumed its rhythm, albeit considerably faster than usual. The bed yielded to his weight and movement, assuring him that he still lived.

Susan lay sprawled beneath him, her eyes tightly closed, her body still tangled in the throes of her orgasm. As he drank in the vision of her lovely face, she gazed up at him through heavy-lidded eyes, a smile curving her lips. Light flickered in her eyes, creating fleeting shadows, even though there was no movement to be reflected. Perhaps it was only the light from the candle...

He blinked—somehow knowing what he'd just seen had

nothing to do with candlelight and everything to do with—

Souls.

A multitude of lives stood behind her gaze, waiting for their moment of triumph.

And triumph they would. Over oppression. Over evil. Over greed. She would bring the evildoers down and make them pay. Strip them of wealth and power like an avenging angel.

She ought to have a halo.

No. That would make her one of the dead. Angels weren't living souls. They couldn't possibly feel so vibrant, so undeniably alive.

Her smile widened as she ran a fingertip down the center of his chest. A soft sigh escaped her as yet another hand touched his shoulder, not with love or passion, but in fond farewell.

Christina.

Susan gasped as her hand flew to her temple. "Did you feel that?"

He nodded. "Christina's gone, isn't she?"

"I believe so." She massaged the side of her head with trembling fingertips. "She took several others along with her."

"I don't understand… We may need her. Why would she leave now?"

Susan cupped his cheek in a gentle caress. As he leaned into her touch, he felt her life force pulsing through her palm. "Because saving the world wasn't her only plan. It wasn't even the most important. Nor was solving the mystery of her death. She came back to heal the loss you suffered. From the very beginning, she wanted me to love you, and I do. We can handle the rest on our own."

Until he met Susan, Christina had been his first, best, and only love. The suicide verdict had weighed heavily on his soul. He was absolved of that guilt now. "You're right. Because of Robert, we have her drawings to share with the world. Knowing she didn't take her own life leaves me free to love you as you should be loved." He bent his head and kissed her—a kiss filled with tenderness, promise, and joy. "I'll do my best not to let either of you down."

"I know you will," Susan said. "And I'll try to do the same."

* * * *

Believing him was easy. Susan had never encountered a more inherently honest man—honesty that went all the way down to the cellular level, perhaps even the atomic. After all, atoms couldn't lie or pretend to be something they weren't; they behaved in precisely the same manner at all times. She found that rather comforting.

That was Seamus. As dependable as two hydrogens and one oxygen coming together to make water. She couldn't explain how she knew that with such complete certainty, but she did.

After leaving home, she'd never had anyone she could depend on for much of anything. Sure, she had friends she could call upon if she was ever truly in need, but she rarely required that help. She'd always been independent. Self-reliant. In control of her own destiny. At least as much as anyone could be. She obviously had no power over crashing airplanes or the people who flew them. She could only control herself and her own reactions. She ought to remember that more often and think twice before saying things that couldn't be unsaid.

She certainly had no intention of saying anything that might hurt Seamus. He'd been hurt enough in his life. He'd lost his lover and his father in a relatively short span of time. She never wanted him to regret being the one left alive.

"All I want is for you to be happy," she whispered. "Saving the world comes in a distant second."

A tiny, one-dimpled smile put in an appearance. "Then you'll have to save the world because that's what'll make me the happiest. Watching my beautiful Bringer of Justice fulfill her destiny." He pressed a kiss to her lips. "And making love with you every day for the rest of my life." He rolled off her before adding with a chuckle, "Maybe more than once."

"Promises, promises," she scoffed.

"In fact, I already have some lost time to make up for." He stared upward, frowning. "Let's see now... I've known you for a little over two weeks, so that means—"

She elbowed him gently in the ribs. "No need to make out a schedule. Some things are better when allowed to occur naturally and in their own time."

He laughed again. "If that's the case, you'd best be getting another condom ready. Because unless I miss my guess, the next 'natural occurrence' is arising as we speak."

"Oh, you have *got* to be kidding me."

He shrugged. "See for yourself."

Susan didn't have to look far. When she turned onto her side, the evidence was right there in front of her face. Still, she was skeptical. "That's left over from the last time."

"No m'dear," he said with a grin. "That would be the start of round two."

* * * *

Susan awoke to a golden sunrise and the delightful smells of bacon, eggs, and freshly baked scones. She was about to throw back the covers and get up when she remembered Seamus's promise of breakfast in bed. She rose anyway, and after a quick trip to the loo, she donned a nightie and crawled back beneath the blankets.

Moments later, she was very glad she'd stayed put because Seamus arrived. Looking marvelously rumpled in a gray T-shirt and a pair of plaid flannel pajama bottoms, he carried in a wooden tray laden with a full breakfast and a steaming pot of tea.

"I see you weren't kidding about the breakfast in bed thing."

He arched a brow. "Did you really think I wasn't serious?"

"Well, you know how these things go—promises made in the heat of the moment and all."

"Oh, ye of little faith," he chided. "Although I did promise you a room of your own."

"That's okay. I like this one better." She stacked the pillows behind her and leaned back into their soft warmth, then smoothed out the blankets. "It's nice and cozy."

He sat on the side of the bed with the tray balanced on his knee. "Even without me?"

"You might've left behind a little of the warmth." Noting that there were two cups but only one plate on the tray, she asked, "Have you already eaten or are we sharing?"

"I'll be back with mine in a minute." He set the tray on her lap. "Better eat while it's hot."

True to his word, he returned quickly, his plate and cutlery in hand. "Only had the one tray," he explained as he settled in beside her.

He didn't need to explain why. The clips on the tray's edges marked it as being part of a folding snack table similar to the one Susan had in her own apartment.

"Gotcha." She unfolded her napkin and laid it across her chest. "Ooh, real Irish linen, I presume?"

"Only the best for my best girl," he declared with a nod. "Don't use them that often myself."

"Paper towels for everything?"

"Not everything, perhaps. But most things."

Susan hated to admit it, but she was guilty of the same offense. "Yeah. Buying paper towels is a lot easier than washing the cloth ones." The moment she said it, however, she realized how simple it would be to toss the napkins in with the bath towels. And she would only have to buy them once. Was that the "greener" thing to do? Probably.

"Definitely greener," came the reply. *"I stopped using paper napkins long ago."*

Should've known one of you would have an opinion.

"If you must use disposable napkins," the female voice went on, *"bamboo is best. More sustainable than regular paper."*

Susan's internal eye roll must've been more obvious than she'd intended because Seamus reacted immediately. "What was that for?"

"One of the stowaways has an opinion," she said with a sigh. "Needless to say, she doesn't agree with our wasteful selves. No doubt if I heeded all their advice, I'd be Little Miss Perfect in no time."

"You're already perfect, even if you aren't the sort to insist on using linen instead of paper." He leaned closer to plant a kiss on her cheek. "Besides, even linen wears out eventually."

"Not as fast as paper." She frowned. "Maybe she has a point."

"No worries there. I've a full set of those, plus a matching tablecloth." He took a bite of his scone before adding, "Although I don't use them very much."

"Clearly, we need to mend our ways. Especially since I'm supposed to bring the wicked oil companies to justice. The sea would undoubtedly prefer we didn't use it as a garbage dump, as well."

Seamus chuckled. "Then I'm glad I used the good linens. Wouldn't want to get on the wrong side of the sea."

"It's a wonder the oceans haven't tried to wipe us out before now. Although if the polar ice caps keep melting, that could happen." She shook her head sadly. "We've been so arrogant, thinking that nothing we do will have any consequences and that Earth will always be there for us." She waved a hand at the plate of food in front of her. "You can't blame anyone for wanting the kind of life we have. So many people don't even come close. Of course if we'd all cooperate and learn to coexist with one another, we might have a chance. Dunno what it will take to make that happen. I don't think my Bringer of Justice title will impress anyone, especially if they're currently waging a war or raking in trillions of dollars in the oil business."

"I remember back during the Arab oil embargo in the seventies. We should've turned our backs on fossil fuels just to spite them. But no, all we did was drill for more oil at home. Made me sick then. Makes me even sicker now. Good luck stopping them."

Pain like an electric shock ripped through Susan's temple. She cried out and pressed her fingertips to the spot.

Seamus turned toward her so quickly, tea threatened to slosh from the cups. "You okay?"

"Yeah," she replied as the pain began to subside. "One of my stowaways just spouted off and left in a huff."

"Not thinking positively enough for them?"

"Possibly." She hesitated, frowning. "Maybe the time has come for us to join forces with Cleona and Jillian. I think we need them here."

"Like I said, I've a spare room and so does Ian, come to think of it. Mum does too. Go ahead and give them a call."

On the word, Susan's phone rang. After retrieving it from the nightstand, she glanced at the caller ID, then aimed the screen at

Seamus. "Guess great minds think alike, huh?"

"There's no such thing as a coincidence anymore, is there?"

"Hardly," Susan said as she took the call. "Hey, Jillian. Believe it or not, I was just about to call you."

"I'm not surprised," Jillian said. "At least, not if you've seen the morning papers."

"Why, what's up?"

"They found the black box."

Chapter 21

SUSAN WAITED A MOMENT TO SEE WHETHER ANY OF HER STOWAWAYS took that news as their cue to bow out. Surprisingly enough, none of them did.

"Seriously? Bet they had to dig pretty deep to find it. Unless the sea spit it back up." Her next thought was that if they'd recovered the cockpit recorder, they may also have recovered the bodies of the two pilots. "Have they brought up any more bodies?"

"A few," Jillian replied. "But after two weeks, there may not be anything identifiable left to find."

There'd been very little to recover in the aftermath of nine-eleven either. Granted, fire hadn't been an issue in this case, but the sea was filled with scavengers. The thought that she could easily have been among the dead triggered a shudder.

"But you aren't dead," her resident shrink reminded her. *"You're alive and well, and we're counting on you for justice. Remember that."*

I'll try.

"You're probably right," she said. "Listen, I know this may cause some problems for you, but I think you and Cleona need to be here. Finding a hotel won't be necessary. Seamus has an extra room and so does his mother. Ranjiv and Kevan might not be able to get away, but—"

Jillian chuckled. "You figure a couple of freeloaders like me and Cleona certainly could?"

"Sorry," Susan said. "Didn't mean it to sound that way, but that's about all we are these days." Even falling in love with Seamus and being dubbed the Bringer of Justice couldn't alter the state of limbo she'd been in since the crash. No job, no family nearby, no obligations—at least, nothing beyond watering the roses she'd planted on Christina's grave, and somehow, she suspected Mother Nature and Robert McKenna would see to that. She'd never felt quite so...detached.

"If you feel detached, it's because of us," the shrink told her. *"We're the ones in limbo. Not you."*

I need to remember that too.

"True," Jillian said. "I guess it's time to prove our worth. Cleona can probably get there faster than I can. I'll have to fly to Shannon or take the ferry from Liverpool to Dublin, and then drive on from there."

"You sound like you were already planning a visit."

"Guilty as charged," Jillian said. "I can't speak for Cleona, but I had a feeling we would join forces eventually. The mysteries she and I solved are only two pieces of a much larger puzzle."

"Your extra entities moved on when you did that, right?"

"Almost immediately," Jillian replied.

"Mine must have a different agenda, then. I haven't lost anywhere near all of them."

"You had more than I did to begin with," Jillian said. With a sardonic laugh, she added, "Guess they thought you stood a better chance of surviving."

"Yet another aspect of this we'll never be able to explain." There were so many of those already, her brain hurt just thinking about it. "I'll be glad to have you here. I've had plenty of help from Seamus and a few others, but this is bigger than me. If I'm sure of anything, it's that. What I'm not sure about is whether I can handle this mission alone."

"Don't sell yourself short." After a long pause, Jillian continued in a more sober manner. "You're the reason Cleona and I are still alive. Without you and that raft, we'd have made it to the surface only to drown or die from hypothermia. Even my champion swimmer entity wouldn't have tackled the North Atlantic without a wetsuit and a damn good support team."

Before Susan could even form a comment, the shrink's voice rang through her mind, cutting through the murmurs of the other stowaways. *"She's right, you know. Listen to her."*

"That's what I need," Susan said. "A team. We'll be stronger together."

"Pooling our powers, you mean?" Jillian only *sounded* flippant; Susan knew she was perfectly serious. "We might even need to demonstrate them."

The mention of a demonstration set the wheels of Susan's imagination in motion. A press conference near the sea. Perhaps a memorial ceremony by the cliffs. Waves rearing higher than O'Brien's Tower on her command before sinking to flat calm.

The stowaways all began clamoring at once.

"That's it!" said one. *"Perfect!"* said another. When they quieted, the shrink said gently, *"I'm with you all the way, Susan."*

She took a deep breath and plunged ahead. "I'm thinking we need to break our silence and go public. I don't know about you, but I've avoided talking about the crash with everyone, especially the press. That was wrong of me. I should have been out drumming up support from the moment we were rescued."

"You mean we should talk openly about the magic?"

"Oh, most definitely the magic."

That was the key she'd sought—and simultaneously avoided. The world's population didn't need to hear the calm voices of reason about what was to come if they continued on their current path. They'd been hearing that sort of thing for decades and had largely ignored or denied the warnings. They would only respond to a theatrical—perhaps even frightening—approach.

"We've been going about this the wrong way," Susan continued. "We need to stop worrying whether people will question our sanity if we tell the truth about the crash. Ranjiv needs to write the real, no-holds-barred story, complete with the ghosts and our connections with the spirits of the land and sea. People need to know this isn't coming from the scientific community, but a supernatural force that is greater than all of us. Plenty of folks don't believe in science or mysticism. Our job is to convince them, and we have to do it in an unmistakable, unforgettable way."

"Hmm… Are you suggesting we scare them?"

"Absolutely. Humankind needs to be shaking in their shoes like the errant children they are. Discussing climate change and economic inequality in rational terms only works for a few, and not everyone believes in God, much less fears Him. The masses need to know that global Armageddon is a genuine threat. Only then can this revolution proceed toward its ultimate goal. Halting the exploitation of Earth's resources won't be enough. The exploitation of our fellow human beings must cease as well."

She could see it now. Clean air. Clean food. Clean, renewable energy. The beauty of nature surrounding every living soul to bring about peaceful coexistence. The thirst for power and riches diminishing until egalitarianism and cooperation became the norm.

Jillian chuckled. "Boy, Mother Earth really knew what she was doing when she chose you to be the Bringer of Justice."

"Not really. There've been plenty of other crusaders. Some succeeded in small ways, while others had a much greater impact. But not all lived long enough to fulfill their destiny. Christina's vision of the future was brilliant, and we know what happened to her. Too many of those who envisioned a peaceful, loving society for all were killed for speaking out. Religions were formed around martyrs whose original teachings of love and understanding have been bastardized beyond recognition. Wars have been fought over petty differences between monarchs and governments. All of that has to stop or we will not survive."

Considering the long pause that followed, Susan wondered if she'd gotten too preachy and gone too far. The peculiar ringing tones of prophesy echoed through the air, giving her the sense that someone else had used her mouth to speak.

Jillian cleared her throat. "Right. I'll give Cleona a call, and we'll both be there as quickly as possible." With a sigh of obvious relief, she added, "It'll be so nice to be able to tell the truth for a change."

"Same here. See you soon."

Susan ended the call, only then recalling she wasn't alone in the bed. She stole a peek at Seamus who, as she might have expected, was staring at her with open-mouthed fascination.

"Guess I'd best be cleaning my fishing tackle out of the spare room."

"I should probably help you with that," Susan said. "Especially since I'm the one who brought all this down on you." She smiled. "Remember how simple your life used to be?"

"Downright boring, in fact." Tossing back the covers, he rose from the bed. "I must say I'm enjoying the variety." After gathering up the empty dishes, he balanced the tray on one hand. "Can't wait to see your little demonstration."

She studied him carefully. "You do agree this is the best way, don't you?"

"Aye. If the show you put on is anything like what I've already seen you do, you'll make believers out of every soul on the planet."

"That's the plan."

He leaned over and dropped a swift kiss on her lips, then headed for the door.

* * * *

Seamus had been wondering when Susan would decide to take that route. If he'd been the one to have control of the sea, by this time, he probably would've used that talent to herd fish into his nets. He was halfway to the kitchen before he realized the inherent dishonesty of such a blatant misuse of power.

"No sport in that," he muttered to himself.

What he'd seen Susan do had certainly made a believer out of him, and he knew of at least one reformed assassin who'd been absolutely terrified by her abilities. If Susan could convince enough people and gain a following, she could make a huge difference in energy policies all over the world. The question was would she have to travel around the world to do it? Or was her influence already global rather than local? Only time would tell, but if the prickling sensation on the nape of his neck was any indication, her "demonstration" was going to blow the minds of every person on the planet, himself included.

In the meantime, a bit of housekeeping was in order. He needed to stock up on groceries for one thing. Sheets and towels were another.

If he'd ever had any aspirations to greatness, he dismissed them.

His task was to host the party, not be the guest of honor. Not an earth-shattering role in the greater scheme of things, perhaps, but someone had to see to the creature comforts of Earth's chosen warriors.

Was warrior the right word? Or would emissaries be more apt?

Either way, Susan was going to have to go it alone until that evening because he had a cruise to the Aran Islands booked for the day. He could cancel the reservation—after all, Susan's mission was far more important than a sightseeing tour—but fulfilling his obligations was a matter of pride for him, not to mention a good business practice. The *Branwyn Eostre* tours had a host of excellent online reviews, and he hated to put that star rating at risk. Still, if Susan needed him, he would cancel.

He was about to head back to the bedroom to ask her when Susan strolled into the kitchen. "Can I help?"

Seamus tapped his chin as he contemplated the matter. "I promised you breakfast in bed and clean sheets and towels. Can't recall whether that promise included clean dishes."

"I don't believe it did." She glanced toward the sink. "Don't know where anything goes, but I can at least do the washing." She turned on the hot water and added detergent to the sink as it filled. "What are you up to today?"

"I've a cruise to the Aran Islands. They want to do a bit of fishing as well. Probably won't be back until about six."

She nodded as she set the plates down in the sudsy water. "Susan and Cleona won't be here for a while—maybe not until tomorrow. In the meantime, I guess I should stock up on groceries." She frowned. "I feel like I ought to be doing something else. Something more...relevant."

"Might want to get a bit of practice in for your 'demonstration.'" The moment the words passed his lips, he wanted to take them back. "Although since I'll be out on the boat, I'd appreciate it if you'd avoid creating any tsunamis."

"I'm sure you aren't the only one," she said. "Maybe I should stick to working on my speech. Less dangerous." She shook her head. "I still can't believe this is for real. Me, giving a speech."

"To the entire world, no less."

The look she shot him should've been lethal. Fortunately, he was immune.

"You aren't helping any, Seamus. Here I am, trying to put this whole"—she waved a soapy hand in a rapid version of Queen Elizabeth's classic gesture—"*thing* into perspective, and—"

"Can't be done," he said with a slow wag of his head. "What you're attempting has never even been thought of before. Speaking to everyone in the world from the planet itself—or is it the sea?"

"God only knows," she said wearily. "I don't suppose it matters if the visual is miraculous enough, and I can't imagine any *practice* being necessary—or possible." She waved her hand again. "Misuse of power and all that."

Since this observation echoed his own earlier thoughts, he couldn't disagree. Dropping an arm around her shoulders, he planted a firm kiss on her cheek. "I'm sure whatever you decide will be perfect. But I'd best get going now or Ian will be coming after me with a sharp stick."

"We can't have that."

Snatching up a towel, Susan dried her hands before turning into his embrace. The kiss she gave him was far better than the one he'd just given her, making him wish for weather stormy enough to make putting out to sea too much of a risk, paying tourists or no.

"*Bon voyage, mon capitaine.* I'll be right here when you get back."

She kissed him again, with less ardor, perhaps, but the result was exactly the same. If she kept it up, Seamus wouldn't be able to walk, much less walk away.

"Be back as soon as I can," he promised. "If Cleona or Jillian show up, you know where to put them."

Her deep, throaty chuckle threatened to finish what her kisses had begun. "In the bedroom that smells like fish?" That she'd seen through his feeble ploy came as no surprise. She was a sharp one and no mistake. And he certainly enjoyed hearing her laugh. There was a time when he didn't believe he ever would.

"Ye canna blame a lad for tryin', now. Can you, lass?"

She took a step back, folding her arms over her chest. "Listen, if I'm ever going to learn to talk like a real Irishwoman, you can't be confusing me with different accents."

"But that was me best Scottish accent," he protested. "Won a prize for it once, I did."

"Is that right?" The twinkle in her eyes belied her dry tone. "In a school play, I presume?"

He shook his head. "High school talent contest. Sang "Loch Lomond" like a feckin' native." Taking her hands, he kissed them both in turn before using them to pull her close. "Besides, most Yanks can't tell the difference between a Scot and an Irishman—or a Brit, for that matter."

"You might be surprised." She arched a brow. "You people are no better. Bet you can't tell which part of America I'm from."

"Yes, but that's only because I know you were born in Florida and later moved to the northeast. Newark, was it? Or is that only the airport you fly out of the most?"

Her eyes widened. "I can't believe you remember all that."

"Ye of little faith," he chided. "I've made it my business to learn everything there is to know about Susan Maxwell. Although, if you have a middle name, I've yet to hear it."

"It's Elaine." Her voice had lost its sardonic edge, reverting to the baby-soft timbre that he found so captivating—perhaps because it didn't reflect her personality in any way.

Or did it? She was a puzzle, this Bringer of Justice. A fierce ginger with a face like an angel and a voice like a child.

"What's yours?" She seemed suddenly shy, her eyes downcast and her voice even softer than before.

"Michael," he replied. Placing a knuckle beneath her chin, he lifted her head until her gaze met his. "Seamus Michael Quinn, at your service—today and always." He paused, smiling, before pressing a gentle kiss on her lips. "Miss Susan Elaine Maxwell."

Her frown lasted less than a moment. She peered at him, her eyes darting back and forth as though seeking verification for what he'd just said. An instant later, she glanced away, swallowing hard as a tear escaped the corner of her eye.

"Didn't mean to make you cry." He wiped the moisture from her cheek with his thumb. "Don't *ever* want to do that."

"But you do," she whispered. "You are"—her ragged exhale was somewhere between a sob and a laugh—"simply the best man I've ever met. Ever known. Ever *loved*. And I don't deserve you."

The warmth surging through his heart faltered, but only briefly. "I can agree with everything but that last bit. Love isn't about whether we're deserving or not. There's no rhyme or reason, no justice whatsoever. Nor can it be explained. It's a gift."

"And all we have to do is accept or reject it?"

"That's right." When she didn't continue, he prompted, "So which will it be, Susan Elaine? Yes or no?" He held his breath, waiting for her reply.

Susan wrapped her arms around his waist and leaned closer, resting her head on his chest. Had there been any doubts in his mind, her soft sigh would've banished them completely.

"Most definitely yes."

Chapter 22

"POKE AROUND ALL YOU LIKE AND MAKE YOURSELF AT HOME," Seamus said before he left for the day. "I'll be back as soon as I can."

Taking him at his word, Susan began exploring the house she suspected was to become her home. Not surprisingly, it was a bachelor's domain, albeit with the odd feminine touch undoubtedly bestowed upon it by his mother. Susan had never cared much for frills and lace, so the décor suited her very well. After a thorough exploration of each room, she made herself a cup of tea and was sitting at the kitchen table contemplating her next move when her phone rang.

"I talked to Jillian about coming to Liscannor," Cleona began. "You're sure Seamus has room for both of us?"

"Absolutely. There's a spare bedroom with a double bed and a sofa that's long enough to stretch out on if necessary." Susan gave her the address, then asked, "Any idea when you'll get here?"

"Probably not until later this afternoon," Cleona replied. "Kevan's bringing me, but he needs to look after his sheep, so he won't be staying. Did Jillian say whether Ranjiv would be coming with her?"

"No, but I'm thinking he might, what with the interview and all. He and Jillian could stay at Seamus's mother's house if necessary, although having everyone under the same roof would certainly be more convenient." And possibly more dangerous. Staying in the same house would make them an easier target for an assassin.

I can't think about that right now.

"Sounds good," Cleona said. "Jillian and I also discussed your plan to come clean about what really happened during and after the crash. I hope it doesn't backfire on us."

"You can opt out if you like," Susan said. "But we'll present a more formidable front if we stick together."

Cleona laughed. "I've never been considered *formidable* in my entire life. Not even close."

"I dunno," Susan drawled. "That assassin you dragged across the parking lot with your purse strap probably sees you in an entirely different light."

She laughed again. "That was my righteous anger taking over. Or maybe the Array was giving me strength." Following a brief pause, she continued, "They left me right after that. Their last stand, so to speak."

"How did you feel when they left?"

"Like I'd lost every friend I ever had," Cleona replied. "Thank God Kevan was there with me. If I'd lost him at the same time, I don't know what I would've done."

"I hear you. Several of mine moved on last night, including Seamus's late girlfriend, Christina. She wasn't technically one of my stowaways, and while her innovative ideas were what got her killed, she had a somewhat different agenda."

"Something to do with Seamus, I presume?"

"Yeah. All she wanted was for him to be happy." With a snort of laughter, she added, "So far, he's been the only perk throughout this entire ordeal."

"I feel the same way about Kevan. I don't ever plan to leave him—or Ireland—and I seriously doubt Jillian will go back to Tennessee when this is all over. She and Ranjiv are pretty tight."

"The crash made expats of all three of us. The funny thing is I feel like I belong here. Like I've *always* belonged here."

"I know what you mean," Cleona said. "Although that might be because I'm half Irish and have family living here. They've made me feel very welcome."

"So has Seamus, but if I have a single drop of Irish blood in me, I've never heard about it. The affinity I feel for Ireland might come from my stowaways, although I don't think it matters."

"If you love him, it probably doesn't."

"You're right about that much." Susan blew out a breath.

"Guess I'd better let you get on the road and I'll"—she glanced around the kitchen—"get a room ready for you." She had to laugh. "Something else I've never done before."

"I'm sure you're up to the task," Cleona said. "See you soon."

"Have a safe trip."

Susan ended the call, thinking what an odd thing that was to say to someone who'd already survived one of the worst excursions across the Atlantic since the *Titanic* tangled with that infamous iceberg. To die in a car accident now would be the ultimate irony.

"Not gonna happen," a woman's voice said.

"Hey, gang," Susan said. "How're things with you?"

"Not so bad. There's more room in here now."

She rolled her eyes. "I wouldn't think you'd actually take up any space—or be aware of being crowded."

"It's all relative. Sort of like having more distance between synapses. Not nearly as much noise either."

"So what you're saying is there's science rather than mysticism behind all this?"

"Not really. Just my feeble attempt to put things in perspective."

"I see. Well, unless you can help me clean the house, I probably don't need you right now."

"We can keep you company—or provide entertainment. We've even got an opera singer in here."

"Oh, please..."

"Just kidding. She's actually more of a pop star than an opera singer. Beautiful voice."

Susan tried to recall hearing from this particular entity before and couldn't quite place it. "Who are you and what have you done with my shrink?"

"My name is Agnes, and don't worry about Elliott. He's still here. He figured you needed a different kind of help today. Now, me, I've played hostess for many a house guest, so I can help you with that."

"And your advice is?"

"Guests who have good food, hot water, clean towels, and a fresh bed to sleep in rarely complain about being bored."

"Hmm… Somehow I don't think boredom will be a factor."

"You never know. Saving the world is a lot like police work. Looks exciting on TV, but in reality, it's boring as hell."

"Even with assassins lurking around every corner?"

A derisive snort echoed through Susan's skull. *"Oh, come on now. You've only met the one, and she turned out to be more of an ally than a threat."*

"True. Speaking of which, I should probably try to find her and let her know what we're planning."

"Somehow, I'd think she'd be the one to find you," Agnes said with a touch of sarcasm. *"She probably knows exactly where you are and even what you and Seamus were up to last night."* Following a significant pause, she added, *"Good thing Christina is gone now. Collaborating with an assassin while you're carrying around the soul of one of her victims could be tricky."*

"I hadn't thought of that. Not that we've done any collaborating yet."

"No, but you will. With her contacts, she can help you organize the big event."

"As in providing security?"

"Something like that. You should have lunch at Quinn's and see who shows up."

"Good idea. In the meantime, I need to get started on that bedroom. Can't have it smelling like fish when Cleona gets here." The room hadn't smelled bad to Susan, but perhaps Cleona's nose was more sensitive.

"In my experience, nothing works quite as well as mopping the floor and washing the curtains to freshen up a room—and I'm guessing Seamus hasn't done either of those things for a good, long while."

Susan couldn't help but agree. His house was clean enough overall, but Seamus didn't strike her as the type to engage in floor mopping and curtain washing on a regular basis. Come to think of it, she'd never done much in the way of housework herself. Spring cleaning had never been a priority, especially given how little time she actually spent in her apartment.

With a deep breath, she got to feet. "Curtains and sheets first, then the floor. Right?"

"Righto."

* * * *

By the time Susan had finished with the cleaning, she was more than ready for lunch at Quinn's. The pub offered a hearty fare, which included traditional pub grub along with several contemporary dishes. While her stomach growled its discontent, she perused the menu, eventually deciding on the beef and stout pie. Topped with puff pastry and filled with chunks of beef and vegetables in a rich savory broth, the pie not only smelled heavenly, one bite was enough to banish any concerns over the upcoming "event." At least, temporarily.

Irish cuisine agrees with me.

She'd always enjoyed her layovers in Ireland, but this was different, more meaningful, like coming home. People from ages past had drawn strength from the same comforting food. Now, she was doing the same—although the pint of Guinness she'd been sipping might have had more to do with her change in attitude.

Being surrounded by Seamus's relatives made her a tad uneasy, but his cousin Iris was every bit as friendly as she'd been when he and Susan had eaten dinner there. Enid hadn't ventured out of the kitchen for a confrontation, which meant she was either too busy or not interested. Or perhaps she only worked the dinner shift.

I have a lot to learn.

She'd spotted his mother, Lorna, behind the bar, laughing and chatting with some of her customers on her way in. Seamus must've gotten his looks from his father because he didn't favor his mother in the slightest. A petite woman with short blond hair going gray, she'd only given Susan a quick nod in greeting, but Susan was positive she'd been recognized. If Lorna wanted to speak to the woman who was sharing her son's bed, she knew where to find her. Unless she was content to wait until Susan went up to the till to pay for her lunch.

A surreptitious scan of the crowded pub proved that at least one of Liscannor's visitors hadn't stopped in for a pint or a bite to eat.

Nadia Tireskova was nowhere in sight.

"She's watching you," Agnes whispered.

Susan fought the urge to turn around. *Who? Lorna or Nadia?*

"That would be Lorna," Agnes replied. *"The best I can tell, Nadia isn't here. You don't suppose something happened to her, do you?"*

I certainly hope not. If she's been compromised, so are we.

"Then you'd better watch your back. Next time, take a seat in the corner or at least sit facing the door."

The gunfighter's chair?

"You got it."

Susan smiled to herself. Thus far, Agnes was proving to be one of the more entertaining of her stowaways. *So, tell me, Agnes. What sort of work did you do?*

"I was a romance novelist. You wouldn't believe the sort of things I've researched. I can tell you how to treat a snake bite or kill someone and make it look like natural causes. I even know how to make a bow and arrow using nothing but a knife."

A veritable fountain of useful information. Promise you won't leave me yet.

"Trust me. I'm here for the duration. I want to watch you nail those bastards' asses to the wall."

"Did you enjoy your lunch?"

Susan nearly dropped her fork. A swift, upward glance proved that Lorna hadn't been content to wait for Susan to come to her.

"Oh, hello, Mrs. Quinn. Lunch was fabulous. Thank you."

Lorna beamed with pleasure. "My Enid is one fine cook—er, chef—don't you think?"

"Yes, I do."

Lorna placed a hand on the back of the empty chair at Susan's table. "Mind if I join you for a moment?"

"Not at all."

Lorna sat down and immediately cut to the chase. "I hear you're staying with Seamus now. Planning to be there long?"

She shrugged. "That depends on Seamus."

"I see." Lorna's fingertips drummed the tabletop, drawing

attention to a pair of capable-looking hands with short fingernails and a wedding ring that probably hadn't left her finger in thirty years, despite her widowed state. "Has he told you much? About himself, I mean."

Susan met Lorna's shrewd blue eyes with a steady gaze. "Are you asking if he's told me about Christina?"

"That and other things."

"He's told me quite a bit, actually. About Christina." She paused, wondering just how much she should admit to knowing, until a flick of Lorna's brow warned her not to bother holding back. "And also about his father. I'm very sorry for your loss."

Lorna acknowledged the condolence with a brief nod and a tight-lipped smile. "Seamus has suffered far more than I have. So much grief for such a young man. I hope you'll understand my concern. I don't want him falling for a Yank who'll be back in New York in another month."

"Newark," Susan corrected. "Never lived in New York, although I've spent a lot of time in the airports."

"I suppose you have. Planning to go back to work soon?"

Susan shook her head. "I've been given an indefinite leave of absence. The job will be there when I'm ready."

"And when you *are* ready, what about Seamus? What happens to him then?"

"I hope he'll be waiting for me when my plane lands." Susan aimed a meaningful look at the woman who, if all went well, might one day be her mother-in-law. "Just like I'll be waiting for him when he comes ashore."

For a moment, Lorna's emotions seemed to get the better of her. Turning her head, she dashed a tear from her eyes. "If only I could believe you mean that."

"I love your son, Mrs. Quinn. I know it seems very sudden, but trust me—"

Lorna put up a hand. "That's all I need to know. If you can make him happy, I'll be the first to welcome you into the family. Just don't go jumping off any cliffs."

Susan didn't pretend to misunderstand. "Do you really believe she jumped?"

"No. Never did. Couldn't prove it, of course, but she and Seamus were so happy together, and she loved him so much. She was such a sweet girl and not the least bit selfish. I can't imagine her ever wanting to hurt anyone, let alone herself, and certainly not Seamus. For the first year after she died, I couldn't help thinking she'd have done him a favor to take him with her." A blink sent an errant tear tumbling down her cheek. "I was sure I'd seen him smile for the last time."

"That must've been hard for you."

"It was. *Very* hard. He went on with his life, of course. And for the most part he seemed normal enough, until you looked in his eyes. The light had gone out of them." She pressed her lips together as though trying to hold back words that were too painful to utter. "Oh, you'd spot the old Seamus now and then when he was playing banjo with his mates. But the moment he stepped off the bandstand..." Leaning forward, she clasped her hands on the table in front of her. "He was doing better even before he met you. But now, the light is back, full force. And it's because of you. I'm so afraid—"

Susan reached across the table to cover Lorna's trembling hands with one of her own. "I won't leave him, Mrs. Quinn. Not willingly. You have my word on it."

The older woman's barely audible "Thank you" was followed by a sob that shook her entire body.

Lorna had been kidding herself to believe that Seamus had suffered the most. Any caring parent would feel their child's pain even more acutely than they did. Susan didn't have to be a mother to know that.

She was toying with the idea of telling her the real story behind Christina's death—perhaps even going so far as to explain how she knew the details—when a glance toward the bar convinced her that this was not the best time.

Seamus's mother would learn the truth at some point, but not when Christina's murderer sat perched on a barstool, staring at them over the brim of a foamy pint.

Chapter 23

"TOLD YOU SHE'D FIND YOU." AGNES HAD THE GOOD GRACE NOT TO sound smug. *"She strikes me as being a damn fine spy."*

I'm sure you're right. Need to finish this up before I talk to her, though.

"Righto."

Redirecting her attention to the woman seated across from her, Susan gave Lorna's hand a squeeze. "Everything's going to work out. You'll see. I'll do my very best to make Seamus happy."

"And I'm sure he'll do the same for you." Drawing in a deep breath, Lorna sat up and wiped the remaining tears from her eyes before attempting a tremulous smile. "You'll think I'm naught but a weepy old woman if I keep this up."

Susan smiled back at her. "I'd never think that about you. You've done an admirable job of carrying on after so much heartbreak."

"I don't feel very admirable. I simply did what needed to be done until enough time had passed that I wasn't so"—she glanced upward as though seeking the right word from above—"hollow anymore. You feel that way at first. Like a hollow, empty shell. Then slowly, life creeps back into you, then warmth, then laughter. That's when you know you'll survive—when you can laugh again."

"I'll remember that," Susan said, although she already knew it to be true. The laughter she'd shared with Seamus hadn't erased the past. It had simply marked the point when she'd moved past the horrors she'd witnessed and was ready to work toward preventing future tragedies.

"Seamus is laughing again too," Lorna said with more than a trace of relief. "Ever since he and Ian picked up the three of you, I've seen a change in him. At first, I thought that after witnessing the crash, he finally understood how precious life is, and that he was squandering his own life by refusing to love again."

Susan couldn't find any fault in that assessment, mainly because she'd reached the same conclusion. She'd wasted years on Chuck, and he'd paid her back by letting her board a doomed flight. For the first time since that fateful day, she was truly glad he wasn't among her stowaways.

"But I was wrong about that," Lorna said before Susan could comment. "He was happier simply because he'd met you."

Had Seamus known she would seek him out? Had his faith in destiny been that strong? She smiled to herself, wondering if Robert had been the one to give him hope. Perhaps not recently, but when Christina died, or even before that when Seamus was a child.

"I'm glad to hear it. He's made a huge difference in me as well."

Lorna's smile seemed stronger this time. "Seamus has always been like that. His sunny disposition affects everyone around him—which is probably why he's so good with the tourists. He could earn a fine living doing nothing else. He only goes fishing because he loves it." She paused as a blush stained her cheeks. "And also because we need the fish here at the pub."

Since Susan had already sampled the pub's excellent seafood, she couldn't help but smile. "Sounds like the perfect arrangement for everyone."

"Your career is what worries me." A frown clouded Lorna's features. "You were very nearly killed not long ago. I know flying is likely safer than fishing, but—"

"You know something, Lorna? My safety is one thing you probably don't need to worry about. Something tells me my 'career' is about to undergo a significant change."

"Oh, in what way?"

"Not sure yet." She raised her glass in salute before draining the last of the Guinness. "But I believe you'll get the idea when it happens."

"Well, then, I'll leave you to it." Lorna pushed herself up from the table. "Thank you so much for bearing with me. You've eased my mind considerably." She glanced toward Susan's empty glass.

"Shall I draw you another pint?"

"Nope. I'm good. I think I'll take a walk down to the quay."

"The sea is lovely this time of day. Enjoy your walk." With that, Lorna headed back to the bar, fielding drink requests and trading small talk with her customers as though her conversation with Susan had been no more serious than a casual chat with a stranger.

Susan knew the value of being able to instantly don a smiling, helpful manner in the wake of emotional turmoil. Clearly, Lorna had the technique down pat.

Leave your own concerns behind and focus on the needs of the people you serve.

Moments before, she'd done her best to calm Lorna's fears. Now, as she reached for her purse, her fingers trembled as she fumbled for the strap. A moment's reflection suggested the probable cause: Instead of the limited number of passengers on a plane, she would be serving the entire human population—the prospect of which was enough to give anybody the shakes.

"It's only nerves," Agnes insisted. *"You've just had your first run-in with your future mother-in-law. Your reaction is perfectly natural."*

Yeah, right. Now all I have to do is walk out of here and meet up with a Russian spy. Nothing in my flight attendant training could've prepared me for this.

"Au contraire, mon amie," Agnes countered. *"You've probably served drinks to more assassins and spies than you can shake a stick at. You just didn't know it at the time."*

Ah, well... Ignorance is bliss.

"Maybe so, but the last time you talked to Nadia, you clobbered her with a rogue wave."

True. And I already said I was going for a walk along the quay...

"Exactly. You have the upper hand here. Remember that."

Thanks, Agnes. You've been a big help.

"You are quite welcome. Now, you go, girl!"

Her composure restored, Susan rose from her chair, paid a smiling Lorna Quinn for her meal, and left the pub.

* * * *

Susan walked purposefully down the street to the water's edge, where she'd spoken with Robert only the day before, leaving Nadia no choice but to follow her. Once there, without any conscious thought whatsoever, Susan stretched out her hand and turned her palm downward.

In an instant, the waves crashing against the rocks below quieted, and an area of flat calm spread out across the sea. The longer she held the ocean at bay, the larger the area became until the smooth, glassy surface reached the horizon and the shoreline as far as the eye could see.

With her attention focused on controlling the water, Susan was unaware of Nadia's approach until she spoke.

"Has anyone else seen you do that?"

Susan drew back her hand and glanced both ways along the coast. Strangely enough, the two women were alone. No one else was anywhere near, not even a boat or a seagull. The sea quickly resumed its normal ebb and flow.

"I guess not." She turned to face the Russian woman. "I wasn't even sure I could do it. Nor did I intend to." She frowned. "Maybe no one can see when I'm practicing."

"Except me."

"Yeah. Except you."

"You already have my loyalty, Susan. You have no need to frighten me anymore."

Susan nodded. "I take it you have some news for me."

"I do," Nadia replied. "Word of your purpose has spread, and my network is preparing for action. We stand ready to protect you, but I must warn you, the enemy is also on alert. Your name is on a watch list."

"Why am I not surprised?" Even more surprising was her total lack of fear. She raised a brow. "Why now? What's changed?"

"The photos you posted online have been seen by those who know their origin. They also know who's responsible for circulating them."

"It's a little late to stop that now, isn't it?"

"Possibly, but you don't understand how these people operate. They believe any threats to their dominance must be neutralized."

"Neutralized?" Susan echoed. "As in terminated?"

"Not always," Nadia said cautiously. "They have other methods. Ways to undermine your credibility, even your sanity."

"Hmm… Well, I've got news for them. We're going public with the story. The *real* story—ghosts, Mother Earth, the whales, and all. I also have evidence that at least one of the pilots—and probably both—was blackmailed into ditching the plane." Tipping her head to one side, she studied Nadia from the corner of her eye. "Should I be telling you this?"

"To be informed is to be prepared," Nadia replied.

"She'll give you no trouble, Miss Susan. Everything is as it should be."

Susan hadn't been the least bit shocked when Nadia joined her on the quay. Robert's arrival was an entirely different story. The best Susan could tell, he'd materialized on the spot, almost as if he'd been beamed there by a *Star Trek* transporter.

"Even so, we must be cautious," he continued. "The enemy is moving."

Susan blinked. Hard. In only two sentences, he'd gone from riding a *Star Trek* transporter beam to sounding like Obi Wan Kenobi and Gandalf rolled into one.

"Not a bad ally," Agnes commented. *"I like his style."*

Susan had to press her fingers to her lips to keep from laughing—or screaming. She wasn't sure which.

Her reaction didn't go unnoticed. "I've been waiting a very long time to use those lines," Robert said with a grin. "At last, I can have a bit of fun."

"I guess that means everything is going according to plan. Right?"

He spread his hands and shrugged. "With a few variations, perhaps. But all in all—"

Nadia glared at him with fire in her dark, exotic eyes. "Who *are* you?"

Robert glanced at Nadia as though he'd only just noticed her, then tapped the brim of his cap. "Robert McKenna, sexton of Kilmacrehy Church and cemetery, at your service, miss."

Apparently Nadia didn't consider this an adequate response. She stomped her foot in patent frustration. "I don't care what your name is. What do you know about the enemy?"

"He's the keeper of the timeline or something like that," Susan explained. "I don't know how else—"

"I'm a Watcher," Robert said as he swept the Russian woman with a slow, assessing gaze. "And you, if I'm not mistaken, are the one who killed our dear Christina." Tilting his head, he pursed his lips. "Although, strictly speaking, you only pushed her off the cliff. The rocks and the sea are what actually killed her."

Judging from the way the veins in her neck were bulging, Susan suspected Nadia was about to have stroke.

"Take it easy, you two. We're all on the same side." She glanced at Nadia. "At least, we are now. I think."

Robert actually smiled. "I know that quite well, Miss Susan. I simply couldn't help meself." The look he directed at Nadia was devoid of levity, reminding Susan of Seamus's initial reaction to meeting the former assassin. "You see, Christina was a great favorite of mine. I've no love to spare for her murderer."

"But you must know Nadia's story," Susan said with a touch of desperation. She couldn't possibly pull this off if her own team couldn't be civil to one another. "If it's true, that is."

"As it happens, I do," he said. "And yes, her tale of woe is perfectly true. But we all make choices." Once again, he aimed a piercing glare at Nadia. "Don't we?"

"Yes, we do," Nadia admitted, sounding far more subdued than she had during her previous outbursts. "Many of mine were wrong. I hope to make up for them in some small way by helping Susan."

"A reformed KGB assassin..." He rubbed his chin in a contemplative manner. "Should make for an interesting ally."

Susan held up a hand in protest. "Hold on a minute, Robert. If you know all this, why didn't you come forward when Christina was killed? You could've proved her death wasn't a suicide."

"Because, like you, my information didn't come from direct

observation," Robert said with an apologetic shrug. "I wasn't on the cliff at the time. No one would've believed me."

"I suppose you're right. But you could've at least told Seamus."

"And what good would that have done? He might've taken on her enemies and gotten himself killed as well. No. We Watchers must remain silent when events don't flow as they should." He sighed with palpable regret. "And the flow has gone wrong so many, many times."

"I get that," Susan said. "But that doesn't explain why you're telling us this stuff now."

"I'm telling you because you've decided to take a different approach," he replied. "You have, haven't you?"

Susan nodded. "Yes. I'm going to tell the whole story, holding nothing back. And the sea will help me prove it—even if I have to make it turn cartwheels."

Robert looked past her and actually laughed. "Yes, I believe it will."

After glimpsing Nadia's expression of wide-eyed astonishment, Susan was almost afraid to turn around until the peculiar sounds behind her left her with no alternative.

Roughly a mile offshore, the sea was indeed turning cartwheels. Several enormous waterwheels rotated hundreds of feet in the air, first one direction, and then the other. Experimentally, Susan pointed a finger at one of the wheels and moved it to the north as easily as dragging and dropping an item on a touchscreen computer. After she'd spaced the wheels to her satisfaction, she muttered, "All we need now are a few whales."

On the word, a trio of humpback whales breached, leaping from the water and falling backward, slapping the surface with their fins and tails.

"It's like a freakin' circus," Susan whispered as even more whales joined in, creating a display that eclipsed the choreographed routines of any synchronized swim team she'd ever seen.

A display that was also drawing a crowd.

Along a shoreline that had been conspicuously empty only minutes before, dozens of people had gathered, and more were fleeing nearby homes and businesses as though every fire alarm in town had gone off.

I'm not ready for this yet.

"This is only a preview," sang the whales. *"We'll come back whenever you call."*

Susan waited until she was sure most of the spectators had gotten a good view of the performance. Then she raised her right hand and swept it from side to side, erasing the scene.

The sea resumed its normal appearance so quickly, Susan could almost believe nothing unusual had ever happened.

That is, until she heard the groans of disappointment from the onlookers.

She stared out across the bay, only then realizing her demonstration had more than likely been visible from the opposite shore. Lahinch was more heavily populated than Liscannor, with a beach and golf course and other tourist attractions. God only knew how many witnesses there had actually been. The question was whether any of them noticed she'd been the show's director.

Her query was answered when a small boy with rosy cheeks and unruly brown curls tugged at her sleeve.

"Do it again!" he urged. "I want to watch the whales dance!"

"Another time, perhaps," Susan said. "I think they've done enough for today."

"Jason!" a pretty blond woman wearing bottle green trousers and a flowered blouse called out as she hurried toward them. "Leave the lady alone. She couldn't possibly have anything to do with—" She stopped a few paces away, staring at Susan as though she'd seen a ghost—or worse.

For a moment, Susan thought she'd inadvertently given the woman "The Look"—until she heard the whales.

"Encore," they sang as they breached several yards offshore.

Their routine was more random this time, appearing like perfectly natural whale behavior.

"You see, Jason?" the woman said as she knelt down and clasped the boy's hand. "The whales are only out there having fun, just like they always do."

Jason shook his head vigorously. "But the sea isn't spinning in circles anymore, Mum. Even whales can't make it do that." He looked up at Susan with undisguised admiration. "She did it. I know because I saw her make it stop."

Susan had to hand it to the kid. He wasn't the least bit fooled.

Unfortunately, neither were several of the people standing across the road from them. Judging from the way they held up their cell phones—keeping them steady without tapping the screens—they were recording videos rather than taking still photographs.

"Whoo hoo!" Agnes exclaimed. *"This is gonna go viral."*

Chapter 24

SUSAN GROANED. *IF THOSE VIDEOS DON'T WIND UP GETTING ME killed. I really hadn't planned to do that. It just…happened.*

"Which is why it's so significant," Agnes insisted. *"Sometimes the unexpected has more impact than a carefully orchestrated event. No expectations. No preconceptions."*

"I think it might be best if we, uh, take a hike," Susan said to her companions. "I'd like to avoid any further questions if possible."

"That's right," Robert said with a nod. "Keep 'em guessing."

"I agree." Nadia leaned closer and lowered her voice. "You'll be on a hit list now. Your protection just became a much higher priority."

"I'd better warn Jillian and Cleona to keep a low profile," Susan said, doing her best to tamp down her own fear. "Shouldn't be too hard for Cleona; she and Kevan are driving in from Kenmare in a private car. But Jillian will be on a commercial flight or a public ferry."

"I'm on it." Nadia pulled a cell phone from her pocket and tapped the screen several times before aiming a surreptitious glance at Robert. "You aren't the only one watching out for her. My people are watchers too."

"I never doubted you for a moment," Robert declared.

"Could've fooled me." Nadia pocketed her phone and linked her arm through Susan's. "Let's get you out of here before this crowd gets out of hand."

"You really think it will?" At the moment, the nearest onlookers were milling about in what appeared to be a state of bewilderment, perhaps even shock. They certainly weren't throwing stones, nor was anyone hounding her for an autograph.

"I've seen stranger things happen," Nadia said. "Those who

believe in miracles will be thankful they were here when the event took place. The analytical types will try to figure out how you did it. The smaller minds will go haywire trying to process what they've witnessed, and they'll eventually select one of three options: hatred, ridicule, or obsession. Trust me, you don't want to be here when they finally decide."

Susan was about to go quietly when she spotted Enid, Iris, and Lorna in the crowd. Judging from their stricken expressions, "miracle worker" wasn't on their list of qualifications for Seamus's future wife. "Oh, God. I'm in deep shit now."

"You were in deep shit from the moment you boarded that plane," Nadia said tersely. "Let's go."

Susan gave Lorna a weak smile as Nadia hustled her away from the shore. The half-hearted wave she received in return wasn't terribly encouraging, but it was better than nothing.

"At least it wasn't a rotten tomato," Agnes said. *"Don't worry. They'll come around eventually."*

Susan would've liked to have Seamus's family on board with their plans. Good thing he already knew everything. If she'd been keeping him in the dark, she really *would* be in trouble.

"Where to now?" Susan asked as they reached the main road. "Robert's house?"

Somehow it seemed the safest place. She really didn't want everyone knowing she was staying with Seamus.

Oh, who am I kidding?

Anyone who knew Seamus and his family probably already knew precisely where she'd gone when she left the hotel. And in a tiny community like Liscannor, *anyone* more than likely included *everyone*.

"That's actually not a bad idea," Nadia said. "There's only one problem. He's gone."

"Gone? What do you mean, gone?" Susan stopped and looked around her. Robert was nowhere in sight. "He was right beside me a moment ago."

"Well, he isn't here any longer. Are you sure he isn't a ghost?"

"I don't think so. But he's really old and there *is* something supernatural about him. He claims he isn't Father Time, but he might as well be." He certainly seemed to be able to teleport himself, which was a useful trick for an elderly gentleman.

Nadia glanced over her shoulder. "So far, no one is following us. Since Robert isn't here, we'll head for Seamus's place."

"Sounds good. My car is parked by the pub." Susan was still pondering Robert's abilities—a topic Nadia appeared to have abandoned. "Do you think Robert is keeping the crowd from coming after us?"

"Perhaps." Nadia kept on walking, swiveling her head in a different direction with every step as though expecting a gang of ninja warriors to suddenly materialize the way Robert had.

"You aren't saying much," Susan observed. "Don't tell me you're freaked out by all the whales and waterwheels."

Nadia arched a brow. "Would you blame me if I were?"

"No. Probably not." Especially since Susan was a little freaked out herself. She pointed at the blue hatchback up ahead. "That's my car."

"I know."

"Sorry," Susan said with a tiny chuckle. "Forgot who I was talking to."

As Susan might have predicted, Nadia didn't laugh. "You drive." She nodded toward the motorcycle parked across the street. "I'll follow."

"Ooh, a Triumph Street Triple RS in Phantom Black." Judging from her dreamy sigh, if Agnes had actually been there, alive and in person, she would've been drooling. *"Perfect ride for a Russian spy."*

You would know, I suppose.

"Absolutely. The hero in my last novel rode one just like it. One of the most fun things I've ever researched."

Fun? You mean you actually rode one?

"Oh, yeah. Took it out for a test run on the track. The salesman was very helpful, not to mention attractive. Too rich for my blood, of course. Awesome machine, though."

I'll take your word for it.

Susan unlocked the car and hopped inside. Nadia fired up the Triumph before Susan's trembling fingers managed to insert the key in the ignition. A check of the rearview mirror revealed Nadia's helmet to be every bit as badass as her ride.

"And here I am in a freakin' hatchback," Susan lamented. "I ought to at least be driving an Aston Martin."

"So true, dear," Agnes said sadly. *"So true."*

However, unlike James Bond, Susan and Nadia made the short trip to Seamus's house without the requisite car chase. Neither of them so much as squealed a tire.

"My, how disappointing," Agnes remarked when they arrived. *"Maybe the assassins are already inside. Although they might've simply planted a bomb and skedaddled. It'll probably go off when you turn on the stove."*

"You know if I die, you won't have anywhere to stow away anymore, don't you?"

"Yeah. I know," Agnes replied. *"Just trying to liven things up a bit."*

Susan frowned. "I thought you said you were a romance writer. Sounds more like you should've been writing thrillers."

"Whoever said romance can't be thrilling?"

"Point taken."

Susan got out of the car and waved at Nadia as she parked her motorcycle nearby. "Think you ought to go in first and check for explosives?"

Nadia actually laughed. "I don't think you could've made it onto a hit list in the past twenty minutes. Thirty, maybe. Not twenty."

"And here I was starting to think you KGB types had your shit together."

"Bureaucracy slows everything down," Nadia said with a shrug. "The KGB is no different." However, despite her assurances, she whipped out the sort of professional-grade handgun Susan had never seen outside of an action film and opened the door. Once inside, she glanced around the kitchen, then motioned for Susan to enter. "Wait here while I search the rest of the house."

Although impressed by Nadia's choice of weaponry, the

mundane nature of a manual search left Susan as disappointed as Agnes had been. "Thought you'd at least have some sort of scanner or weapons detector on you."

"You don't need that stuff if you know what you're looking for."

Susan arched a brow. "Takes an assassin to know an assassin's methods?"

"Something like that."

After a thorough check of what had to have been every room, nook, and cranny, Nadia finally returned to the kitchen and gave the all clear. "But only for the inside of the house. I still need to search the perimeter."

"Have at it." Susan glanced at her watch. "Cleona should be here in an hour or so. Wouldn't want the place to explode the moment she knocks on the door."

Nadia's expression of grim determination never wavered. "You probably don't have anything to worry about until Jillian arrives. With all three of you together, the threat level increases exponentially."

Deeming it inappropriate, Susan managed to suppress the chuckle rising in her throat. Even though *she* might've felt like she'd stepped onto the set of a James Bond flick, Nadia appeared to be perfectly serious.

Interestingly, the Russian's clothes didn't exactly scream spy or assassin. Her black leather jacket was as much a nod to her choice of vehicle as it was her occupation. In addition to the jacket, she wore a dark gray, scoop-necked knit top, faded jeans that were fraying at the hem, and black ankle boots—all of which fit her like the proverbial glove. If she was carrying any other concealed weapons they must've been small because Susan couldn't spot any bulges.

"Probably has a knife in her boot," Agnes said. *"Might even have a grenade in her jacket. Lots of pockets in those things, you know."*

"So, Nadia... Are you my bodyguard?"

"For now." Arms folded beneath her breasts, Nadia leaned against the kitchen table, resting her hip on the edge. "Fortunately,

I'm not working alone."

"Who else—?"

"Might be best if you don't know," Nadia said. "Wouldn't want you to inadvertently blow anyone's cover."

Susan gaped at her. "Really?" After the initial squeak, she paused to clear her throat and force her voice back down to a normal pitch. "Well…we can't have that, can we?"

Seeming to ignore Susan's momentary display of nerves, Nadia pushed away from the table and started for the door. "Stay here. I'll be back."

Susan stared at her retreating figure until the door closed behind her. "You know something? I liked her a lot better when she wasn't being so—"

"Competent?" Agnes suggested.

"I was going to say bossy."

"That too. What are you going to do with her when this is all over? Throw her ass in jail?"

"I should, although there's no evidence against her. It would be her word against mine. Like Robert said, he wasn't there on the cliff when it happened, and neither was I. Even after we admit to the supernatural aspects of this crazy story of ours, I can't believe that sort of evidence would be admissible in court. She would have to confess."

"But she has confessed—to you, Seamus, and Robert. You'll have to report her or else you'll be guilty of obstruction of justice."

"I'm probably guilty of that right now." Susan plopped down in the nearest chair, wishing she'd made a pot of tea before she began all this soul-searching.

"I'd make it for you if I could," Agnes said. *"But we both know I can't."*

Susan smiled. "Eavesdropper."

"Hey, it's what we do—about all we can *do at this point. Unlike you. You're going to do great things, Susan. I can feel it. All we have to do is make sure you live long enough to see it through."*

"Even if it means collaborating with a reformed assassin?"

"Unfortunately, yes."

"Then I guess I'd better make that tea." With a sigh, she rose from her chair. "God knows we can't do anything without a cup of tea."

"Prefer coffee myself," Agnes confided. *"But whatever floats your boat."*

* * * *

The minute Seamus tied the *Branwyn Eostre* to the quay, he knew something was up. A strange stillness had fallen over the entire town. Granted, Liscannor was quieter than most as a rule, but this was different.

"What do you suppose is going on?" Seamus mused.

"I dunno," Ian replied. "But I'll take a wild guess and say it has something to do with that ginger-haired Yank you've taken in."

Seamus had already briefed Ian on the latest developments, all of which the older man had accepted without question or surprise. He wondered why believing in Susan was so easy for his crewmate, until he recalled that Ian had also been a witness to the crash. The survival of the three women had been miraculous enough to convince even the most skeptical observer that anything was possible.

"No doubt you're right."

After securing the boat for the night, he and Ian hoisted the fish-filled cooler up onto the dock. He waved farewell to Ian, extended the handle on the cooler, and began wheeling it up the road toward the pub. The befuddled expressions on the faces of those he passed along the way did nothing to allay his suspicions, nor did the furtive glances he received.

The pub was oddly silent as well. The din of conversation with its occasional bursts of raucous laughter was conspicuously absent, the patrons speaking in hushed tones, if they spoke at all. He left the cooler inside the doorway to the kitchen before heading toward the bar. His mother's tight-lipped smile as he approached confirmed his fears.

"Did something weird happen today?"

Lorna didn't say a word at first, merely pulled a pint of Guinness and slid it across the bar. "I had a chat with Susan when she came in for lunch today. I like her. I truly do, and I'm sure she would've made you very happy, but—"

Shards of alarm stabbed his heart, and he immediately began chastising himself for leaving her alone. "What's happened to her?"

"Nothing," Lorna said quickly. "At least, not that I've heard. It's what she did down by the sea that has me somewhat…baffled. Me and everyone else who saw it."

Having witnessed a few of Susan's encounters with the Atlantic, Seamus could only assume this demonstration was the most momentous to date. However, he had no intention of admitting to anything before hearing the whole story. "And what might that be?"

"I didn't see it all, but those who did…" Shuddering, she swallowed with obvious difficulty. "She can control the waves, Seamus." Her voice dropped to a whisper. "And the whales."

Seamus slid onto the nearest barstool and reached for the Guinness. "Dash it all, I thought she was going to wait a bit to do her stuff. Should've guessed she'd get carried away while I was gone."

His mother stared at him as though she didn't quite believe his rather flippant response. "You knew what she could do?"

He took a sip of his beer. "Aye. I've seen it before. And if that didn't make a believer out of me, nothing would."

"I'm still not sure whether I believe what I saw. I've never seen anything like it before in my life." She picked up a glass and began polishing it with a dishcloth as though the mundane task would lend a particle of normalcy to a bizarre turn of events. "There was a woman with her—rather foreign-looking with a high-priced motorcycle—they left town together." Frowning, she cocked her head to the side. "No one realized what she was doing at first. It was when everything stopped that it became obvious that Susan was the cause." She peered up at him with a look on her face Seamus hadn't seen since his father's death—an expression he'd hoped he would never see again. "Who *is* she, Seamus? And how could anyone—any *human*—possibly do what she did?"

"Oh, she's human enough," Seamus replied. "Let's just say she has…connections."

"Connections?" Lorna echoed. "Connections to what?"

"The sea, the whales, perhaps even Mother Earth herself." He leaned forward, closing the distance between them to ensure at least a modicum of privacy. "She's special, you see. She knows things, hears things. She survived that plane crash for a reason, Mum. She's the Bringer of Justice, and she's here to save the feckin' world."

What little color remained in her cheeks drained from Lorna's face completely, and for a moment, he was afraid she might faint. He reached across the bar and grasped her hand—a hand as icy as the North Sea in mid-winter.

"It's okay, Mum. She's here to bring peace and harmony—with our fellow man and with nature. There are people who will pay for their crimes against humanity, against life on Earth, and against the planet as a whole. You, my dear, sweet mum, are not one of them."

Lorna stared at him as though she'd never seen him before in her life. "I can scarcely believe what you're saying. I wouldn't believe any of it if I hadn't seen what she did with my own eyes. It was like witnessing a miracle."

"Not *like* a miracle, Mum. It *was* a miracle."

She was silent for a moment, as though attempting to process what he'd said before immediately abandoning the attempt. "But what about you, Seamus? How do you fit into all of this?"

To be honest, he'd wondered the same thing himself. He'd yet to put his role into words. Perhaps now was the time. "My purpose is to give Susan all the love and support I possibly can. And also to help her connect with the sea."

In that moment, he realized he'd done the same for Christina. Robert might be a Watcher, but he, Seamus Michael Quinn, had been blessed to love and be loved by two of the most remarkable women the world had ever seen. One a true genius, the other a savior.

"I'm also the link between her and Christina. I'm the ground wire that keeps them tethered to Earth's surface so they can remain here to help us rather than flying off into space. Or up to heaven. Maybe that's it. They'd be angels without me to hold them here."

"You couldn't stop Christina from dying."

"No. But I did prevent her from moving on afterward." He

squeezed his mother's hand. "She stayed because she was worried about me. She's finally at peace. And so am I."

A sob shook his mother's frame as she clutched his hand. "I'm so glad to hear you say that. I've been so worried about you." Releasing his hand, she took a step back and wiped away her tears. "I didn't think I had any tears left in me. She made me cry, that one did—*and* eased my mind. But now... You said she was going to bring justice and save the world. Does that mean she's here to judge us for our sins?"

"No. Her goal is to save the planet, not our souls—although she may put the fear of God into a few greedy scoundrels in the process. She's more earthly than heavenly; her connection is to the planet and its oceans rather than the hereafter. She's like a priestess of the old ways, whose purpose is to teach us to live and work in harmony with the seasons, the sun and moon, the weather, the tides, the planting, and the harvest."

Feeling somewhat embarrassed by the preachy turn his explanation had taken, Seamus glanced over his shoulder, hoping he hadn't been overheard. To his surprise, every last person in the pub was staring at him with open-mouthed wonder.

Was this the beginning of Susan's effect on the world and its people? Had the seeds of change already been sown?

Seamus didn't have the answers, but Robert would know.

The question was, would he tell?

Chapter 25

AFTER ASSURING EVERYONE IN THE PUB THAT THE WORLD WAS *NOT* going to end anytime soon, Seamus deemed it best for him to return home as quickly as possible. God only knew what Susan had been up to all afternoon, and he was dying to hear the story from the horse's mouth.

The drive home took mere minutes yet seemed like an eternity. He hadn't seen Susan all day, and the hours of separation made him anxious for her company. Unfortunately, he doubted she would be alone. When he turned into his driveway, the presence of a somewhat battered Volvo confirmed his assumption that their first houseguest had arrived.

The high-priced motorcycle his mother had mentioned, which most likely belonged to Nadia Tireskova, was nowhere in sight. Seamus had no problem with that. The thought of Christina's murderer in his house didn't set well with him at all, even if she had seen the error of her ways.

Assuming Susan was entertaining their guests in the front room, he opted to go in through the kitchen to drop off the fish he'd brought home for dinner. As it turned out, his assumption was incorrect. Susan was seated at the kitchen table along with Cleona Mahoney and a man with curly black hair and a severe burn scar on the left side of his face.

He greeted the petite brunette with a smile. "I almost didn't recognize you, Cleona. You look much better than you did when I saw you last."

"I *feel* much better too," Cleona declared. She jumped up from her chair and wrapped her arms around him in an enthusiastic hug. "It's so good to see you again, Seamus." She nodded toward her companion who had also risen from his chair. "I'd like you to meet my friend, Kevan MacFinnin."

"Nice to meet you, Seamus," Kevan said as the two men shook hands. "I've heard a lot about you."

"Same here." Susan had already told Seamus how the pair had been instrumental in catching the man responsible for a bombing that killed a climatology professor and Kevan's parents and left Kevan permanently scarred. That in itself was significant enough, but like Susan, Earth's spirit had also given Cleona a title. As the Carrier of Life's Preservation, she had discovered the key to a secret formula that promised to revolutionize the field of solar energy and end the world's dependence on fossil fuels.

Or so they hoped. The formula hadn't been made public as yet. Therefore, it hadn't come to the notice of anyone who could recognize it for what it was, much less implement it.

But if Susan's plan to share the true story with the world went well, all that was about to change.

"So, Susan," he began. "What's this I hear about an 'event' earlier this afternoon? Liscannor is abuzz with the story—or should I say stunned into silence?"

"Sorry," Susan said sheepishly. "I never meant to do any of that. I mean, the waves calmed when I held out my hand. But later on, I was talking to Nadia and Robert about going public with the real story and making the sea turn cartwheels to help me prove it, and that's exactly what it did. Then I mumbled something about needing some whales, and a bunch of humpbacks showed up and put on one hell of a show."

"I can show you a video if you like," Cleona said. "It's all over the internet."

"A video?" Seamus echoed. "Seriously?"

Susan groaned. "I didn't realize anyone was recording until *after* I waved a hand to end the performance. I might've gotten away with it if a little boy hadn't come running up, begging me to do it again." With a slow wag of her head, she added, "I'm really not ready for this. Not yet."

"I think it's terrific," Kevan said. "Nothing like a good teaser to get everyone primed for the main event."

"Or get your name on a hit list," Susan said. "Nadia thinks we'll all be in danger now—said it'll 'increase exponentially' once Jillian gets here."

"Hold on a sec," Cleona said. "Have I missed something? Who's Nadia?"

Susan exchanged a speaking glance with Seamus before replying. "She's, um, a KGB assassin."

"*Former* KGB assassin," Seamus corrected. "That is, if we can believe her."

"I think we can," Susan said. "Robert seems to have accepted her, and if anyone would know whether she was on the level, he would. I'll tell you one thing, though; she sure knows her stuff. Hustled me back to my car and followed me here on the coolest motorcycle you've ever seen. Gave the house a thorough search before letting me go any farther than the doorway."

Cleona nodded, but still looked a tad puzzled. "And who is Robert?"

"This is *such* a long story," Susan said with a sigh. "Clearly, I should've been taking notes or keeping a journal."

"I did that already," Cleona said. "Got it right here." Retrieving a thumb drive from her purse, she slapped it on the table. "Took forever to get it right, but I figured it would save some time when Ranjiv gets here."

"You can borrow my laptop if you'd like to start writing yours," Seamus told Susan. "In the meantime, you three might want to head on into the front room—unless you want to watch me clean these fish." He smiled at the other man. "Will you be staying for dinner, Kevan? I've a couple of nice, big cod here. There'd be plenty."

"If I do that, I might as well spend the night," Kevan replied. "But I've a flock to look after, so I'd best be going."

Cleona cleared her throat. "Um, about that...Uncle Fergus said he and Sinead would take care of your sheep if you decided not to come back tonight. We just need to let them know."

"Jillian won't be here until tomorrow," Susan added. "So there'd be plenty of room."

Arching a brow, Kevan peered at Cleona. "Did they make the

offer or did you ask them?"

"They volunteered, I'll have you know," Cleona said primly. "Although I'm sure they would've said yes if I'd asked. They've all been so sweet to me."

"I'll stay, then," Kevan said. "Besides, I'd like to hear more of Susan's story."

"Tell you what, Susan," Cleona began. "I'm pretty good with a keyboard. You tell us the story, and I'll type it up for you." She nodded toward Seamus. "I'm sure we'll need your input as well." She tapped the thumb drive. "Kevan and I collaborated on this one."

"It's quite a job, I can tell you." Kevan ran a hand through his hair as if reliving the tedious nature of the task. "Getting the facts straight is hard enough, but some of the things that happened seem almost silly when you try to write it out." With a nod toward Cleona, he continued, "She had this mystical experience where she became a tree. I was standing right there beside her, and I can assure you she didn't actually grow roots and branches."

Having been present for several of Susan's "mystical experiences," Seamus could attest to their at least having been visible, if not audible. "Speaking of which, I'd like to see that video if you've got it there on your phone."

Cleona giggled. "Even if I didn't, trust me, you wouldn't have to look very hard to find it. Just type in 'Liscannor, Ireland' and it pops right up." She laughed again. "That's how we found it. I was Googling the best route to take between here and Kenmare, and there it was."

Cleona gave her phone a few taps and handed it to him. "This is the best one I found. The first part was taken through a window. The picture gets better when the photographer goes outside."

"I'd like to see that too." Susan got up from the table and came around to where Seamus was standing. Sliding an arm around his waist, she leaned in closer as he tapped the icon to start the playback.

Despite being filmed through the grimy window of what must have been one of the houses in the row facing the sea, Susan was clearly visible as she stood near the edge of the Lower Quay, looking for all the world as though she'd put the ocean to sleep with her calming presence. When Nadia joined her a few minutes later, the sea returned to normal—until Robert arrived. His first thought upon seeing the elderly sexton was that he was real enough to be photographed. Lately, there'd been times when he wasn't too sure about that.

Within moments, giant water wheels erupted from the sea's surface. Suddenly, the picture changed, becoming an erratic blur of walls and furniture followed by a flash of bright light. As the camera refocused, he could see Susan, her back toward the camera as she pointed a finger and actually moved one of the huge swirling masses of water. When she had placed them in an evenly spaced row, the whales joined in. He'd seen her do some remarkable things, but this one had them all beat. It wasn't until the little boy came running up to tug on her hand that Seamus finally found the words to describe his feelings.

"Susan, love," he said slowly. "I've never been more proud of anyone in my entire life." Wrapping her in his embrace, he kissed her soundly on the lips, then drew back to gaze into her brilliant green eyes. "My dear, sweet, *fierce* Bringer of Justice. You truly are going to save the world."

* * * *

Heat flooded Susan's cheeks as Seamus hugged her again. He'd believed in her before even she knew what she was capable of doing. Now, having seen what she'd done through the eyes of a spectator, she had a better understanding of the impact her relationship with the sea would have on people around the world. Another demonstration might not even be necessary. They'd already seen what she could do. Now they needed to understand why.

Of course, there would be naysayers and skeptics who would claim the video was fake, simply the product of some crackpot with a knack for film editing. But the eyewitnesses would not be silenced. As evidenced by the video she'd just seen, the story would spread.

She glanced at the data beneath the picture and her heart began to pound. "Ten million views. Four *million* shares?" she whispered. "It's only been a few hours."

The enormity of one video's reach shook her to the core.

"That shouldn't surprise you," Elliott the Shrink said in his most matter-of-fact tone. *"There are more than seven billion people on this planet. Check the stats in the morning. The views should have reached at least a billion by then."*

"I didn't know there were that many cell phones out there." Overwhelmed by the turn of events, Susan blurted out her response. Fortunately, what she'd said fit in with what she'd said before. Sort of.

"Almost as many as there are people. Social media can be a powerful tool. Remember how the Libyans used it to overthrow Gaddafi?"

Yes, but the last I heard, things were still pretty crazy over there.

"Perhaps, but at least it was a start. You have the opportunity to bring about worldwide change. Make the most of it. Don't leave anyone out. Make it clear that you aren't simply speaking to Western governments, businesses, and religions, but to the planet as a whole. People in the most remote areas need to know you're also speaking for them. That Earth is here for all of us to share. We only have to treat her with the respect she deserves."

You sound like you've been talking to her.

"Perhaps I have. Or perhaps I simply view the world through the eyes of a physician whose practice was based on scientific research. Science doesn't lie. People do."

Susan blinked, only then realizing that while she'd been exchanging thoughts with Elliott, the conversation in Seamus's kitchen had gone on without her.

Cleona was practically bubbling with enthusiasm. "That's the beauty of it. Nothing in that video relates to politics or religion. It's simply a human female interacting with nature."

"Maybe," Susan said, catching the thread of the discussion. "I only wish I hadn't felt like I was making the sea and the whales do circus tricks."

"If you were, they seemed perfectly willing to oblige," Cleona said. "And remember, this was only a demonstration, not an example of how things will go in the future."

"But won't people expect that?" Susan asked. "Will fishermen expect me to tell fish to jump into their nets? Will farmers ask me to make it rain on their crops? Will I be held responsible for every feast or famine?"

Seamus gave her a one-armed squeeze. "Having already given that some thought, I can honestly say I won't ask you to do my fishing for me—not that you would ever consider doing such a thing."

Susan rested her head against his shoulder, drawing strength from his warm, supportive presence. "Not everyone is as honest and reasonable as you. Hunger tends to make people desperate."

"Then it's up to you to see that no one goes hungry," Seamus said. "We have the wherewithal to feed the entire planet. Get people to work together instead of fighting over scraps and the hunger problem will solve itself."

"You make it sound so simple."

"If it were," Seamus countered, "we wouldn't need a Bringer of Justice, would we?"

"Or a Carrier of Life's Preservation," Kevan added. "What's Jillian's title? Not sure I've ever heard it."

Seamus chuckled. "According to Robert, she's the Chosen One. Although I think both of these ladies could also claim that title."

Cleona and Kevan exchanged a significant glance, but Susan was the one who spoke.

"If we're the 'Chosen Ones,' then you guys are too. We couldn't do this without your help. I know I couldn't." Turning toward Seamus, she kissed his cheek, hoping that small gesture was enough to convey the depth of her feelings for him.

From the beginning, Seamus had treated her with kindness and respect. He'd been patient with her when he could have easily dismissed her as a lunatic. She owed him so much.

"Go on with you, now," he chided. "You'll be puttin' me to the blush."

"It's true, though." Cleona reached over to take Kevan's hand. "Each of us teamed up with a very special man."

Kevan leaned closer and raised her Cleona's face to his with a finger beneath her pert cleft chin. "And we teamed up with some very special ladies." The kiss he gave her was brief, but intimate enough to put a bloom in her cheeks.

When the pair had first arrived, Susan had been shocked by the extent of scarring on Kevan's left cheek. Looking at him now with his head turned in such a way that the scars were no longer visible, she couldn't help thinking what a crime it was to mar an otherwise astonishingly handsome face. Dark hair fell just shy of his shoulders in a tangle of unruly curls, and a pair of expressive eyes lurked beneath well-defined brows. His straight, prominent nose gave him an air of nobility, like the aristocratic hero in a historical romance.

He was as different from Seamus as two men could possibly be, except for the curly hair and unmistakable accent. But while she could certainly appreciate Kevan's dramatic good looks, she still preferred Seamus's twinkling brown eyes and smiling brand of Irish charm.

"Have it your way, then," Seamus said, interrupting her reverie. "But if you don't want rotten fish for dinner, I'd best be getting them cleaned and filleted."

Susan sighed. "And my 'story' won't write itself. If you'd log me onto your computer, I'll get started."

Kevan pushed back his chair and stood. "I'll give you a hand with dinner. I make a mean bowl of champ."

"Great," said Seamus. "We'll have that and some fried red cabbage with bacon along with the fish." He shot Susan the full, two-dimpled grin that never failed to make her heart beat a bit faster. "Gotta keep our Chosen Ones well fed." He waved a hand toward the front room. "This way to my computer."

As the two women followed in Seamus's wake, Susan leaned closer to Cleona, whispering, "What the hell is champ?"

"Mashed potatoes with chopped scallions and gobs of butter," Cleona whispered back. "Awesome stuff."

"Gotcha."

Chapter 26

SUSAN WAS GLAD SHE COULD TELL HER STORY TO CLEONA FIRST, because Kevan was absolutely right. Some of her experiences *did* sound silly when put into words. The way the whales sang to her, the way the sea responded to her signals. And if not silly, ridiculously impossible—like carrying around extra souls with whom she could actually converse.

Fortunately, she had an honest-to-goodness writer on board to coach her on what to say.

"Get the story down first," Agnes advised. *"Then go back and edit. As Nora Roberts once said, 'You can't fix a blank page.'"*

Very true. Is that how you write, er, wrote?

"Not really. I was what they call a pantser, as in writing by the seat of my pants." She paused. *"Can't say that around the British, though. To them, the word 'pants' refers to underwear."* She laughed. *"And 'trouserer' just doesn't sound right."*

No kidding.

"Of course, everyone has a rough first draft of some sort, even if they edit each paragraph as soon as it's written, which is what I used to do. I always found better ways of saying certain things when I read through a manuscript after I'd put it aside for a while." She chuckled again before adding, *"Unfortunately, some of those changes didn't occur to me until after the book was published. No going back then."*

The same held true in Susan's case, even though she wasn't actually writing a book. Once she went public, her statement would be out there for the whole world to see. Getting it right the first time was of the utmost importance.

"Imperative, I'd say," Agnes said.

"Good word."

Cleona looked up from the computer screen in surprise. "What word are you talking about?"

A blush prickled Susan's face. "Sorry. That comment should've been internal rather than verbal."

"Ah, yes," Cleona said with a knowing smile. "Conversing with your stowaways, I presume?"

"Yeah. I'm really gonna miss them when they're gone."

Nodding, Cleona resumed her typing. "Maybe you'll get lucky and keep yours. Although it *is* kinda nice having my brain to myself again. Much easier to maintain focus."

"I imagine it would be." After a moment's reflection, she added, "I'm not as lonely as I used to be, that's for sure."

A slow smile curved Cleona's lips. "I'd have thought Seamus would have more to do with that than your stowaways."

"Of course he does, but they're with me all the time. He actually has to go off to work most days."

"Yeah. Kevan has to tend his flock, but at least he doesn't have to go far." She paused as a tiny shiver shook her body. "Must be scary with Seamus out on the boat where anything could happen to him."

Susan sat up straighter, her eyes wide with the shock of sudden insight. "It already has." The blush she'd felt in her cheeks earlier became a full-body tingle. "He told me he'd fallen overboard three times. His father rescued him once, then Ian pulled him out, and the last time he claims to have essentially saved himself. Even with his father and Ian's help, what are the odds he would survive each time?"

"I have no idea," Cleona replied. "Although I doubt he's the only fisherman with a record like that."

Susan chewed at her lip. "He didn't act like it was particularly miraculous. But what if it was? What if the sea has been protecting him all his life?"

Cleona arched a brow. "Makes you feel a little better about him being out on the boat all day, doesn't it?"

"Maybe so."

The sea hadn't saved Christina when Nadia pushed her off the cliff, though. That meant the sea was either highly selective about the people it saved or Seamus's survival was nothing more than a stroke of good fortune. Or coincidence.

Unless the sea considered Christina to be more expendable than Seamus. With her drawings safely in Robert's possession, perhaps she'd already served her purpose. Seamus, on the other hand, still had a role to play.

Fortunately, most people didn't die the moment their goals were achieved. They slid gracefully into old age, living many years beyond what might be considered the high point of their lives.

I really need to remember that.

"I'm done," Cleona announced. "Take a look."

Susan exchanged her perch on the arm of the sofa for the desk chair in which Cleona had been sitting. She scrolled to the top of the document, then laced her fingers together and cracked her knuckles.

Okay, Agnes, time to do your stuff.

"*Oh, no,*" Agnes protested. "*This needs to be written in your voice, not mine. Otherwise it won't ring true. I can help you with the flow, but you need to use the sort of expressions and comparisons you would normally use.*"

Does that mean I can't use "imperative?"

"*Not unless it feels natural for you.*"

Oh, all right…

With an inward grumble, Susan began reading. She was pleased to discover that Cleona had not only done an excellent job of capturing the essence of the story, for the most part, she'd used Susan's own words.

"You weren't kidding when you said you were good at this, Cleona. This reads like a synopsis for a novel."

Cleona shrugged. "Writing mine gave me plenty of practice. Jillian and Ranjiv have probably been working on their version too. I'm sure Ranjiv will have some questions, but the more details we include in our statements, the fewer questions there'll be."

Somehow, Susan doubted that. No matter how good the explanation, there would always be questions. Always.

"Our statements will carry a fair amount of weight, but not

everyone will take the time to read them. Think of all the scientific data that has been ignored or ridiculed because it doesn't mesh with the desires of the rich and powerful. Alarming statistics and documentaries haven't been enough to convince the naysayers."

"Which is why we need a real demonstration," Cleona said. "The bigger and splashier, the better."

"I agree," Susan said. "We need to stir up emotions on a global scale. As long as someone is there to tell you everything's going to be okay, nothing will change. We have to convince people the danger is real and that we must change our ways before we destroy ourselves."

She leaned back in her chair, staring off into space. What were her choices? Show everyone what would happen when sea levels rose? Somehow, she didn't think flooding the world's coastal cities was the best option. But what alternative did she have? A great many people didn't consider melting polar ice caps to be a threat. Not grasping the difference between climate and weather, they believed they only needed to point toward the snow and freezing temperatures outside their windows to prove that global warming was a myth.

Susan and her fellow survivors needed to fight fire with fire. They had to make those threats seem frighteningly real—changes that affected every man, woman, and child on the planet. All the violent storms, earthquakes, and floods hadn't been enough to convince people they had to change their ways. After all, such catastrophes were nothing new; they'd been happening long before humankind came onto the scene.

Susan doubted this was something she had to do alone. She wasn't the only one with supernatural powers. Robert had his fair share, although they were more difficult to display than Susan's. Jillian and Cleona had connected with Earth as well as the souls of those who'd perished when their jumbo jet dove into the sea. Did that connection still exist? For the life of her, she failed to see why it wouldn't. The stowaways were there for information and moral support. Earth and its oceans provided the power.

Had Cleona spoken to Susan using the stone towers even after her "Array" had left her?

She saved her own document, then searched the thumb drive for Cleona's. Opening the file, she scrolled to the bottom. A quick read-through verified the timing. The Array had definitely left her *before* she used the Cahergall stone fort to speak to Susan at O'Brien's Tower.

Conversing between the towers would certainly make for an interesting demonstration, but it was also the sort of thing that could be staged convincingly enough to cast doubt. For this to work there could be no doubts.

Making the sea turn cartwheels might also be deemed a magic trick, despite the inherent expense and difficulty of pulling off such a stunt. Slapping someone with a wave the way she'd taken down Nadia would be more convincing—certainly more random.

No. For their plan to succeed, this had to be a feat of monumental, perhaps even biblical, proportions.

Oh, my God. That's it.

But could she actually do it?

* * * *

To the best of his recollection, Seamus had never cooked dinner for two women with the aid of another man. Unless he were to count cleaning fish with Ian or his father. He'd certainly never done it in his own kitchen.

Kevan made it easy. He struck Seamus as a sensible fellow with a decent sense of humor. Plus, when it came to making champ, he didn't skimp on the butter.

Of course, Kevan scored the most points for already being attached to Cleona, perhaps even engaged. He wasn't privy to their plans, but scars or no scars, Kevan was the sort of man most women found attractive. No doubt Cleona intended to hang onto him. They made a nice couple too—he as dark and brooding as a squall line while she bloomed like a flower in the wake of a storm.

Jillian and Ranjiv were already planning to tie the knot, although the death of Ranjiv's mother would undoubtedly postpone the ceremony for quite some time.

Seamus hadn't asked Susan to marry him, mainly because he thought it best to wait until things settled down a bit, but his intentions were clear. He wanted Susan to be his wife. Whether sooner or later didn't matter. Their happily-ever-after would come in its own good time.

Seamus took the cod from the oven, and after ensuring that it was white and flaky, he transferred it to a platter, then added a squeeze of lemon juice and a sprinkling of parsley.

"Time to call the ladies," he said as he set the platter on the table.

Despite his mother's housewarming gift of enough plates to set a table for six, with a chef in the family, Seamus didn't entertain often. Anytime he'd gotten together with his mates, he'd gone to the pub rather than hosting a private dinner party at home—a pattern that would probably change now that he was contemplating marriage.

As he stood there, surveying the table, the image of friends and family seated around it overrode reality. He could even hear children laughing. *His* children. His and Susan's...

A shake of his head dispelled the vision and returned him to the present.

However, a trace of awe must've remained in his expression because Susan peered at him with concern as she took her seat. "Are you okay?"

"Right as rain," he declared. "Merely pondering the future." Squaring his shoulders, he joined his guests at the table.

"A happy future, I trust," Kevan said.

"I do believe it will be." He smiled at Susan. "Right now, we have good food and good company. What more could anyone ask for?"

Susan returned his smile with a rather vague one of her own, almost as though having been assured of his well-being she'd drifted back into her own thoughts. Knowing how much she had on her mind, he let it pass. Unfortunately, she still seemed detached, even requiring a prompt from Cleona to pass the cabbage.

"Sorry," she said as she handed the bowl to Cleona without taking any for herself. "Going over everything that's happened since the crash has me a little fuzzy-headed." She stared at her empty plate for a long moment, shaking her head slowly. "This has been a really strange day."

Seamus certainly couldn't argue with that, and neither did anyone else. Even though he couldn't force her to eat, he could at least make sure she had food in front of her. "Here, have some fish," he said as he slid a portion of the cod onto her plate. "You'll feel better after you've eaten something."

She nodded absently as he dished out hefty servings of champ and cabbage. He'd seen her like this before. He only hoped eating dinner would have the same beneficial effect it'd had on her in the past.

He drew back, aghast, as she slumped forward, sobbing as she buried her face in her hands. A moment later, her head snapped up and she slammed her hands on the table.

"What if I can't do it? My country has been taken over by greedy corporations, climate-change deniers, and corrupt, power-hungry politicians. Nothing we do will be enough to stop them. They're too convinced of their right to do as they please and damn the consequences. We may have Earth on our side, but we can still fail. What happens then?"

"We won't fail," Cleona said quietly. "Even after Jillian and I accomplished our tasks, we knew we weren't finished. You are no different. You solved the mystery of Christina's death and ensured that her ideas were shared with the world. You discovered proof that at least one of the pilots was blackmailed into crashing the plane. But change won't happen overnight. Ideas require time to grow and develop. You only need to provide irrefutable proof that Mother Earth has powers no one ever dreamed she would have, and that she is infuriated by our careless use of the gifts we've been given."

Seamus gazed at Cleona with awe. She was such a tiny woman, with a face as luminous and serene as the statue of St. Brigid. She possessed the same aura of inner peace, yet she'd taken on a known assassin with courage derived from the firm knowledge that she would not fail.

Susan had the same inherent strength as Cleona, even though it seemed to come and go with her moods—or rather, the moods of her stowaways. Those momentary lapses had always been followed by renewed vigor and purpose. This one would be no different. All he had to do was wait.

With a sigh, Susan picked up her fork and dug into the cod. "You're right. The truth is, I have a terrific idea for my demonstration. I'm just not convinced I can pull it off."

Cleona arched a brow at her fellow survivor. "Come on now, Susan. After what you did this afternoon, do you really think the sea wouldn't—or couldn't—do anything you could dream up?"

Susan shrugged. "I suppose not. So far, all I've had to do is think of something, and it happens."

"The sea also reflects your moods," Seamus put in. "I'll never forget that angry surge when you first saw Nadia and realized who she was." He shuddered. "Enough to put the fear of God into anyone."

"Or the fear of the sea," Susan countered. She took a tiny bite of her fish, taking ample time to chew and swallow before adding, "Although most of us at least have a healthy respect for it."

"Don't forget how the sea saved us," Cleona said. "I'd be dead if it hadn't pulled me out of the wreckage."

"Didn't save everyone, though, did it?" Susan took another bite of the fish. "Certainly not all-powerful or infallible. Couldn't stop the plane from coming down when the pilots were so determined to crash it."

"Those poor men," Cleona whispered. "Having to trade their lives and the lives of their passengers and crew for those of other innocent people. Have you shown that email to the police yet?"

Seamus shook his head. "No, we haven't. But then, they can't know exactly *when* we found it, now, can they?"

"True," Kevan said. "We heard the divers recovered the black box. Don't suppose anything has been made public yet, has it?"

"Not as far as I know," Seamus replied. "Although I doubt there'd be anything on the flight recorder to explain why they crashed the plane. If they were set on protecting their families, they'd have kept quiet."

"Seems like they would've had to say *something*," Kevan

insisted. "Or at least pass notes back and forth."

"That's possible," Susan said. "I've known David McAfee for nearly as long as I've known Chuck. He had a wife and two children. I can't believe he would've risked their lives to save his own. He and Chuck must've worked together to crash the plane." Her expression grew thoughtful. "That's one hell of a choice for anyone to make, although going through it with someone else might've made it a little easier." She sighed. "We'll probably never know the whole story, though. Will we?"

"If anyone would know Chuck's thoughts at the time, you would," Seamus said. "Are you sure there was nothing more?"

Susan shook her head. "The only suggestion they collaborated was his use of 'we.' Not that it matters now. The end result is still the same."

On that melancholy note, they continued with the meal. They were nearly finished when Cleona finally broke the silence. "So, Susan," she began. "Any thoughts as to where you're going to give your 'demonstration'?"

Susan didn't hesitate. "The top of O'Brien's Tower by the Cliffs of Moher."

Cleona smiled. "Your favorite spot for communication?"

"Something like that."

"Any idea when?" Kevan asked. "I don't want to miss it."

"Not yet," Susan replied. "But soon. First, we need to report finding that email and we also need to work on reposting Christina's art."

"Don't forget Jacob Emhart's formula," Cleona cautioned.

Susan nodded. "I really hope someone will recognize it for what it truly is and come forward." She looked down at her plate as though she had no memory of having eaten anything, and yet the food had disappeared. "The lengths people will go to in order to hang onto wealth and power still boggles my mind. Destroying so many lives and the environment just to keep the fossil fuel industry up and running." She clenched her jaw. "Their callous disregard for the future makes me so mad I could spit."

"Take that anger and channel it into your demonstration,"

Seamus advised. "After that, no one will be able to say they haven't been warned." Deeming it time to lighten the mood, he announced, "In the meantime, who wants dessert? I brought along one of Enid's famous apple cakes."

"*Now* you tell us." With a grimace, Kevan leaned back in his chair, placing a hand over his stomach. "Not sure I have room after all that."

Seamus chuckled. "Sorry. I can't share *all* of my secrets."

Judging from Susan's enigmatic expression, she hadn't shared all of her secrets either. No doubt about it, this demonstration of hers was going to be a real eye-opener.

The trick would be keeping her alive long enough to see it through.

Chapter 27

SEAMUS WENT TO FETCH THE CAKE WITH A LOT MORE ON HIS MIND than serving dessert. He didn't like admitting that Susan's life might be in danger, even to himself. Granted, they'd already discussed the possibility, but that was before her interaction with the sea had thrust her into the public eye. Whether intentional or not, the video of her practicing for the big event would bring all sorts of heat down on them.

And I don't even own a gun.

The scariest part was that the one person he knew of who probably *did* own a gun was Christina's killer.

He trusted Nadia. He truly did. He just couldn't quite bring himself to forgive her.

She'd even been in this house. *His* house. Checking for God only knew what—bugs, thugs, or even bombs. Where had she gone after that? Susan hadn't said.

"I really hate to bring this up now," he said as he set the cake on the table. "But where *is* Nadia? Is she keeping you under surveillance? Or are the rest of her cohorts here helping her?"

"I have no idea," Susan replied. "She left right before Cleona and Kevan got here. Almost like she knew precisely when they would arrive."

Seamus served up a slice of the cake and handed it to Cleona. "She probably *did* know. That is, if the house was being watched."

"I'm sure it is now," Susan said. "After that comment about the 'exponential increase' in the threat level, I can't imagine she'd leave us unprotected."

"Me either," Cleona said. "Not if she's who she says she is. I presume you have no reason to doubt her?"

"Oh, there's plenty of evidence to prove she's the enemy—she actually admitted to being a KGB assassin—but there's just as much to make us believe she's on our side now." Susan accepted the cake Seamus offered her in the same distracted manner with which she'd passed around the cabbage. "I really hope she is. It's nice to have *some* people on our side. She may turn out to be the only protection we have."

"You don't think Earth will keep us safe?" Cleona asked. "I know it's probably stretching credibility a bit, but Kevan and I came to the conclusion that we were sort of...invincible. He and I both managed to survive attacks while nearly everyone around us died, so we figured Earth would provide us with some sort of protection until we're actually, you know...finished."

"You have a point." Susan glanced at Seamus. "I'm beginning to think you're just as invincible."

"Oh, you must be joking," Seamus protested as he handed Kevan his dessert. "I'm as mortal as the next man."

Her arched brow suggested otherwise. "The sea spit you back out three times. Right?"

The impact of what she was suggesting caused the knife he held to clatter to the table, and Seamus landed in his chair with a thud. "I wouldn't put it quite like that. I had help, and plenty of it."

"Didn't you say you saved yourself the last time?"

"Yes, but—"

"Should you have been able to?"

He frowned as he recalled that last terrifying episode. "Not really. In fact, I was sure I was dead." He hadn't thought about that day for a long, long time—had tried to put it out of his mind, albeit not very successfully. He'd come within a hairsbreadth of drowning. That he hadn't was still something of a mystery. "Are you saying the *sea* rescued me? For what?"

Susan's sardonic expression quickly melted into an indulgent smile. "Do you really have to ask that?" Her caress of his cheek sparked waves of warmth that reached all the way to his soul. "You were saved for this mission. For Christina. And for me."

Seamus wasn't sure he could even speak, let alone form a coherent reply. After all, Susan was the one destined to bring justice to the world, not him. His was only a supporting role, one that could've been played by any number of men. So why bother to save him from certain death?

"There's nothing special about me," he said when he finally found his voice. "I'm a perfectly ordinary man."

Her smile broadened. "Ordinary, perhaps—actually, I believe we can each claim that dubious distinction—but you were chosen, just the same. And like other ordinary people, you have the opportunity to do extraordinary things. To make a difference and to help others do the same. You see, there are no ordinary people. Everyone is unique, with their own contributions to make, however small and insignificant they may seem."

She grasped his hand, lacing her fingers through his. "The climax of our story is about to unfold. Don't discount your role in the outcome." Raising their joined hands to her lips, she kissed the back of his hand. "From my perspective, you're indispensable."

Seamus didn't need a mirror to see his blush. The prickling heat in his cheeks told the tale. "If I haven't said this before, please forgive me, because I should have. Mother Earth chose her champions well."

"She also did a damn fine job of choosing our cohorts." She released his hand and gave it a pat. "Now, eat some cake and let's get on with it."

* * * *

Considering the number of times Seamus had managed to dispel Susan's doubts, doing the same for him shouldn't have come so late in the game. Granted, they would probably never know the truth behind his survival, but believing in oneself was generally a good thing.

Interestingly enough, in helping him to see his own worth, she'd solidified her belief in her own ability to do exactly as she planned.

"Good girl," Agnes said. *"We're in the homestretch. Nothing can stop us now."*

Susan wasn't quite so optimistic. *As long as no one interferes. There are still plenty of people who would do anything to stop us. I'm putting an awful lot of faith in a KGB assassin.*

"You and your friends are about to become the darlings of the entire world," Agnes insisted. *"Trust me; there are others who will protect you."*

I sure hope you're right.

Susan ate her dessert in silence, scarcely noticing the flavor. Enjoying a treat was difficult when her restlessness grew with each passing moment. They were in a waiting period, a time of preparation while an army they knew nothing about worked behind the scenes to help her bring about change. *Over a hundred*, Nadia had said. At the time, that number had seemed impressive. Now, she wasn't so sure. Even if they were as capable as the Russian woman, would a hundred operatives be enough?

In times like these, throngs of overly enthusiastic supporters could be every bit as dangerous as an angry mob. The fact that she and her friends were able to sit down to a quiet dinner without being disturbed suggested that Nadia and her network really were out there, working in the shadows to keep them all safe.

And Robert... Where was he and what was he doing? Popping here and there to see if the timeline was progressing smoothly? Or was he tending the churchyard, satisfied that all was well? For her part, she hoped he was out watering the roses she'd planted on Christina's grave. Although, if Christina had truly moved on, would she even care about the flowers anymore?

"Tomorrow morning we'll take that SD card and Chuck's phone over to the Garda station in Lisdoonvarna," Seamus said, interrupting her reverie. "Only takes about twenty minutes, but we'll have to leave a bit early because Ian and I have a cruise booked for nine o'clock. I went to school with a couple of the guards there. They'll give it the proper attention."

"Just as long as they don't lose it," Susan said with a shudder. "It's the one piece of concrete evidence we have to prove the pilots were acting under duress. Not sure the telepathic message I received would carry as much weight."

"Maybe not yet," Cleona said. "But at some point, that message may prove to be the most important piece of evidence we have."

Susan frowned. "Really? How so?"

"It's the first indication that some higher power had chosen to intervene," Cleona replied. "The moment when Mother Earth decided she was mad as hell and she wasn't going to take it anymore."

"That line sounds vaguely familiar," Seamus said, frowning. "Like it was in a book or a movie."

"*Network,*" Susan stated firmly. "It was from a movie called *Network.*" For once, she didn't need Agnes or any of her other stowaways to help her recall the title of a movie that was made long before she was born.

That one, she'd seen.

And it didn't end well.

* * * *

As wound up as she was when she went to bed that night, if she hadn't been sleeping with Seamus, Susan doubted she would've slept at all. His kisses and warm, solid presence kept her grounded. Otherwise, her mind would never have settled long enough to allow her to fall asleep. Even the stowaways had been restless, and Agnes wasn't the only one speaking up. Throughout the evening, more voices chimed in to offer encouragement and suggestions. In the end, she had to threaten them with banishment if they didn't quiet down.

She awoke the next morning to weather so foul, Ian called to say he'd already canceled their bookings for the day.

"Can't go out in this weather," Seamus announced when he hung up the phone. "I may be as invincible as you say I am, but no one else onboard will be."

In Susan's opinion, the stormy weather was fortuitous enough to have been contrived by a higher power—someone who knew she and Seamus needed to spend the day doing something other than fishing or taking sightseers to the Aran Islands.

After breakfast, Kevan headed back to his farm while Seamus drove Susan and Cleona to the Garda station in Lisdoonvarna.

"That's Kilmacrehy church up ahead, Cleona," Seamus announced as they approached the turnoff.

"Christina is buried there, isn't she?" she asked.

"Aye," Seamus replied. "And Robert lives just up the road. We can stop in to see him on the way back. No doubt this gale is keeping him indoors as well."

"I look forward to meeting him," Cleona said. "A Watcher of the timeline… Who knew there was such a thing?"

"We're finding out all sorts of things no one knew existed before," Susan said. "Earth spirits, sea spirits, whales that sing in a way I can hear and understand, stone towers acting as communication portals… Unbelievable."

She stared at the church as they drew abreast of the entrance to the grounds. Torrential rain obscured the ruined structure, making it seem more ghostly than ever before. A similar storm had struck on the day she'd planted roses on Christina's grave, rendering the jug of water she'd lugged to the site completely unnecessary. Nor was there any need for Robert to water the roses today. Not with this much rain.

"Robert never said how long he's been here, watching time pass by," Seamus commented, interrupting her thoughts. "Must be a tough job."

"Yeah," Cleona said. "Imagine not being able to change the course of history when you know something has gone wrong. *Very* frustrating."

"He said he'd tried to intervene once before but only made things worse. Didn't say what that was either." Susan gazed back at the church as it faded in the distance. When she lost sight of it as they rounded a bend in the road, she turned to face the front again. The windshield wipers swept back and forth, marking the passage of time like a pair of metronomes. "He's so old… Do you suppose he's the only sexton that crumbling ruin of a church has ever had?"

"Wouldn't surprise me," Seamus replied. He shook his head slowly. "All the things we think we know when we've haven't even begun to scratch the surface."

His wistful tone caught Susan's attention. The offhand remark he'd made earlier about his invincibility notwithstanding, he seemed as preoccupied as she was herself. Perhaps he was trying to come to grips with his indestructible status. Or maybe being saved in that manner was an affront to his self-esteem.

No. That couldn't be it. He wasn't the type of man to refuse help simply to assert his masculinity. Nevertheless, he'd been given enough food for thought to keep anyone's mind in turmoil. Until the day she hired his boat, he probably never imagined his role extended beyond that of a fisherman whose boat just happened to be the first to arrive on the scene. He was so much more than that.

She reached over and took his hand, delighting in its warm, calloused strength. The smiles they exchanged warmed her even further. Growing old with this man would be such a joy; she absolutely refused to be denied the opportunity.

True to his word, Seamus brought the car to a stop at the Lisdoonvarna Garda Station within the specified time. The station was an unassuming tan building wedged between a hotel and a bar. Its only identifying feature was the Garda emblem on a coach-style light fixture perched above the door.

The station was no less Spartan on the inside. Plain wooden desks, worn countertops, stacks of paper, and the ever-present computers. Several men milled about, some in uniform and some not. A quiet day, perhaps. No miscreants to process, no complaints being filed.

This is too easy.

A brief exchange with the woman at the front desk brought Seamus's friend, Garda Sergeant Cian Malone, from the rear of the building. A tall, lanky, and rather homely fellow with short blond hair and blue eyes, he met Seamus with a delighted grin and a hearty handshake.

"Why, if it isn't Seamus Quinn. I would've thought you'd be off to Hollywood, such a dashing hero as you were, picking up the ladies from that plane crash."

"Not yet." Seamus nodded toward Susan. "I've two of those same ladies right here."

"You don't say?" Cian shook each of their hands as Seamus introduced them. "I saw the video of that crash. Can't believe anyone survived. You're a couple o' pretty miracles indeed."

Susan rolled her eyes. "Don't suppose you've seen the latest video, have you?"

He gazed at her with patent surprise. "That was you, then, was it? No one seemed quite sure. Could scarcely believe my own eyes when I watched it. Don't guess you'd care to tell me how you did that, would you?"

"Magic," Susan replied. "But that isn't why we're here." She glanced around the station, noting that their conversation had already drawn a few curious stares. "Is there someplace we can sit down and talk? Privately?"

"Aye. I've an office in the back." Cian turned and motioned for them to follow. "This way."

Susan exchanged a terse look with Seamus, who patted her on the back, his hand lingering long enough to help calm her nerves.

Once inside the office, Cian waved toward a row of chairs lined up against the wall. "Have a seat," he said as he settled himself behind his cluttered desk. "What can I do for you?"

Susan sucked in a shaky breath. "I–I found something we think is important. Or rather, someone gave it to me."

Cian leaned forward. "Oh? And what might that be?"

Reaching into her pocket, Susan pulled out the phone and laid it on the desk. "One of the pilots, Chuck Travers, gave me this right before we boarded the flight to London. He said he'd found it in the restroom and asked if I'd drop it off at the lost and found." A second deep breath steadied her voice considerably. "I got busy and forgot about it until I found it in my pocket when we changed into dry clothes in Inisheer. Being submerged in seawater had ruined it, of course, but I kept it anyway. You see, I once had an affair with Chuck, and he was still very special to me. Knowing he was dead, well, it was the last thing he'd given me, and I was reluctant to part with it."

"Understandable," Cian said with a nod. "Go on."

"I put the phone in a bag of rice, thinking I might be able to get it to work at some point and maybe even figure out who it belonged to. Later on, I mentioned it to Seamus, and he told me that while the phone was probably history, the SD card might be worth a look. Since he had the same type of phone, he switched the cards and was able to access the photographs. I recognized some of the people in the photos as Chuck's daughters. I couldn't understand why he would've given me his phone instead of the one he'd found. That is, until I saw this."

She slid a printed copy of the email they'd found across the desk.

A flush crept up Cian's neck as he studied the page. After a long moment, he cleared his throat. "And you're sure this was his phone?"

"No. Chuck and I weren't that...close anymore. Hadn't been for years. He must've thought the photos would be found eventually— that someone might be curious enough to try to determine who the phone belonged to—and his reasons for crashing the plane would be explained. It was a long shot, of course, but he probably wasn't thinking too clearly at the time."

"And because the phone was still in your possession when the flight took off, it went down with the plane anyway." Cian gave his chin a thoughtful rub. "Strange he didn't warn you."

Although Chuck had indeed warned her, Susan doubted the time was right to admit to everything. "I think he was too afraid his family would suffer." She pointed at the phone. "He must've figured this was the best he could do."

Cian picked up the device. "Is the card in it?"

She nodded. "We switched them back when we realized whose phone it was." Not until after they'd uploaded the images to Seamus's computer, of course. That was one tidbit of information they didn't plan to share with anyone until the email was well-documented and, hopefully, made public.

Cian popped out the memory card. "You know," he said slowly. "There's another possibility. These cards will fit into almost any mobile phone. Your pilot friend may have actually found someone else's mobile and exchanged the cards. That way, anyone watching him would've seen that he wasn't giving you his own phone."

Susan couldn't imagine anyone watching that closely, but that scenario certainly would've given Chuck's strategy a much greater chance of success. "If the phone truly belonged to someone else, that person might've called the terminal or gone there to look for it, and the photos would've been discovered. That is, if I hadn't neglected to turn it in to the lost and found." She shook her head. "That was the one thing I couldn't figure; why he would believe anyone would even bother to look for his phone after he died—especially not in the lost and found."

Staring at the card, the sergeant turned it over in his hand. "Such a tiny little miracle, but a miracle all the same. Almost as if this was why you survived. The truth will out, as they say."

Susan knew there was a great deal more to it than that, but the abrupt release of her own nervous tension made her very glad she was sitting down. Otherwise, she'd have collapsed in the floor.

As if sensing Susan's roiling emotions, Cleona grasped her hand. "The other miracle was him finding a phone to switch cards with."

"Aye," Seamus said. "A much greater power must've taken a hand."

For perhaps the thousandth time, Susan wished that greater power had "taken a hand" a little sooner. But perhaps this was how history had to play out for their ultimate goal to be achieved.

No doubt Robert would say the same.

Chapter 28

UNLIKE THE STORM, WHICH HAD LET UP APPRECIABLY BY THE TIME they left the Garda station, Susan's emotions remained unsettled. Handing over the last thing given to her by her former lover was no easy task, but what bugged her most was having to depend on others to do the right thing. Although Seamus had expressed a great deal of faith in his friend, whether the sergeant's superiors could be trusted was a factor over which they had absolutely no control.

They were almost to Robert's house when her fears finally reached the boiling point. "I swear if that email isn't the top news story by tomorrow morning, I'm posting our copy online."

"Give them time," Seamus advised. "Remember, they need to ensure the pilots' families are safe before releasing a statement to the press."

She expelled an exasperated breath. "You're right. My nerves must be getting the better of me."

Despite having been told pretty much the same thing by her stowaways, hearing it from a real live person rather than a gang of disembodied voices eased her mind considerably.

"Hear that?" Elliott the Shrink, said. *"She's already outgrowing us—which is probably a good thing since we won't be around much longer."*

How do you feel about that?

"Feel?" he echoed. *"I'm not sure we 'feel' anything. That being said, this arrangement of ours isn't what anyone would call normal. No doubt you'll be much better off when we're gone."*

He didn't say how he and the others would like relinquishing the last tenuous hold they had on life. Even though they'd been granted a reprieve of sorts, they existed only as thoughts rather than living, breathing human beings. Perhaps they looked forward to the end of the story as much as Susan did herself.

Not surprisingly, Robert was waiting outside his door when Seamus drove up to the house.

"Ah, Cleona," he said as everyone exited the car. "Nice to see you here in Ireland. It's where you belong, you know." His smile stretched into a broad grin. "And planning a life with your perfect match. A good lad, Kevan is. A very good lad."

"I'm glad you think so," Cleona said. "I'm kinda taken with him myself." In an aside to Susan, she whispered, "I like this guy already."

"Same here." Grasping Cleona's hand, Susan hurried up the walkway toward the porch.

"What's the rush?" Cleona protested. "It's barely raining at all now."

"I'm not worried about getting wet," Susan snapped. "I just don't think it's a good idea to stand out in the open long enough for a hit man to draw a bead on one of us."

"Good point." Cleona quickened her pace.

When they reached the porch, Susan glanced back at Seamus, who seemed bent on surveying the surrounding area before starting toward the house.

"Don't see anyone about." He waved a hand. "Go on inside while I take a look around back." What he would do if he found anyone, he didn't say.

"No worries here," Robert said. "But I know you'll feel better for checking it out."

Susan smiled as her gaze met Robert's twinkling eyes on the way inside. A Watcher would have a better feel for lurking assassins than anyone else, with the possible exception of another assassin. "Don't suppose you've heard anything from Nadia, have you?"

"No," he replied. "But that's as it should be."

In response to Cleona's slight frown, Susan aimed a thumb at Robert. "He says lots of stuff like that."

Cleona giggled. "Cool."

Robert gave Cleona a fatherly pat on the cheek. "Ah, you're a right one, you are, Miss Cleona. You and Kevan took down that nasty man at Ballycarbery good and proper—as we all knew you would."

"Sounds like you Watchers are in cahoots with one another," Susan observed.

"On some matters, yes," he said. "Others aren't quite so…momentous."

Cleona stared at him, clearly fascinated. "How many of you are there?"

"Enough," he replied. "You had one watching you and Kevan. You just didn't know it."

Seamus came inside and closed the door behind him. "Didn't see anything amiss. Have you had any trouble here?"

"None whatsoever," Robert replied. "Miss Christina's drawings are where they should be, all right and tight." With a wicked chuckle, he added, "Posted a few on Twitter again this morning. Gained me a horde of retweets and several new followers. Word is spreading."

"Wouldn't do much good for me to Tweet anything," Cleona grumbled. "I don't have many followers."

"But you *are* connected with a university," Robert reminded her. "Precisely the sort of people we want to contact."

"Hmm… I hadn't thought of that. Better do it before I quit my job or they're liable to be too miffed with me to care *what* I post."

"Put the right hash tags on your tweets and the right people will see them," Robert said wisely. "It's as simple as that."

Susan chuckled. "Robert, you didn't *invent* Twitter by any chance, did you?"

"Ah, no," he replied. "But that doesn't keep me from using it to our advantage." He smiled and waved them toward the kitchen. "Everyone have a seat at the table. The tea should be ready to pour, and"—he put a hand to his ear as a timer began to chime—"the scones are done."

"You knew we were coming," Seamus said flatly. "Didn't you?"

Robert shrugged. "How not?"

The fingers Cleona pressed to her lips failed to stop her peal of laughter. "This is *so* awesome."

Robert shot her a wink as he shuffled toward the stove. "When the timeline progresses as it should, the future is quite easy to predict." Donning an oven mitt, he took a tray of lightly browned scones from the oven and set it on the counter. "Actually, I saw you pass by a while ago. Figured you'd be stopping by on your way home."

Seamus nodded. "And, of course, you knew precisely where we were going and how long we'd be gone."

"There is that," Robert acknowledged. He slid the scones into a napkin-lined basket, then stepped back, tapping his chin as he glanced about the room. "Now where is me pot o' jam? Ah, there it is, already on the table. Right where it should be, along with the clotted cream."

Susan took a seat. Not only were the jam and cream on the table, the same rose-and-gold tea service he'd used on their previous visit was surrounded by matching plates, linen napkins, and cutlery with the unmistakable gleam of real silver. "Are we celebrating something?"

"What makes you think that?" Robert asked as he handed her the basket of scones. "Nothing quite like freshly brewed tea and piping hot scones to warm you up on a rainy day, is there?"

"Come on, Robert," she persisted. "Silver and china?"

"Ah, you caught me. Was hoping to surprise you. Unless, of course, you've checked the data on yesterday's performance."

Totally bewildered, for a long moment, all Susan could do was gape at him. "Should I have?"

He pulled a cell phone from his breast pocket, gave the screen a few taps, and handed her the device. "Take a look."

Susan's heart nearly stopped as she counted the zeros. Twice. "Over a billion views and seventy-five million shares?"

"Aye." Thankfully, Robert took the phone from her trembling hand before she dropped it. Holding it close to his face, he peered at the screen. "It's up some since I last checked. Don't believe any post in existence can claim as many hits. You're a bona fide celebrity, Miss Susan."

"Or a prophet," Agnes chimed in. *"Imagine what the prophets*

back in the old days could've done if they'd had the internet."

"Probably would've screwed up the world even more than it is now," Elliot said. *"Not that I have anything against prophets on the whole, but it's probably best that some of them didn't have a global audience."*

Once again, Susan was glad she'd been sitting down. "I'll never be able to walk unnoticed into a grocery store again."

Robert pursed his lips, appearing to give her assumption careful consideration. "I doubt it'll come to that. Someone else will probably be doing your shopping."

"Predicting the future again, Robert?" The arch of his brow and the twinkle in his eyes added a humorous note to Seamus's question, but Susan wasn't fooled. His stake in her future was nearly as high as her own.

The older man shrugged. "Not with any precision—at least, not along those lines. I'm only guessing the offerings she'll receive will be more edible than monetary."

"I don't *want* people to bring me offerings—of *any* kind," Susan exclaimed. "Besides, they'll be far more likely to take potshots at me for ruining their fun."

"At first, perhaps," Robert conceded. "But once they see how much better the world will be, they'll treat you like a saint."

Susan took a deep breath and squeezed her eyes shut as if that might slow her racing thoughts. "I'm not a saint. I'm a freakin' flight attendant."

Robert shook his head. *"Former* flight attendant. Don't believe you'll be doing that sort of thing anymore." He chuckled. "Not sure anyone would want to be on a flight of yours anyway. They'd probably confess to all manner of sins just to keep you from crashing the plane."

Reflecting her rising panic level, Susan's voice rose a full octave when she spoke. "I didn't crash that plane, and neither did Jillian or Cleona. I—"

"Easy now, lass," Robert said gently. "I'm only teasing you. But the only way you'll be flying from now on is as a passenger. You can take my word on that."

Recognizing the utter futility of arguing with a man who knew how history was supposed to play out, she threw up her hands in surrender. "Okay. If I'm going to be an unemployed saint, I might need those offerings after all." The glowering look she aimed at the old man quickly gave way to a smile. "Starting with one of those scones."

* * * *

Seamus was pleased Susan could find humor in her situation. Not only would laughter help her retain her sanity, it also tended to put events in their proper perspective. People who took themselves too seriously often wound up as—not to put too fine a point on it— pompous assholes. Offhand, he could think of several whose names seemed to have a permanent place in the news that would benefit from being taken down a peg or two.

Before long, Robert had Cleona and Susan both laughing at his witticisms. He had to hand it to the old man; he could certainly charm the ladies—and make a dashed fine scone. He watched as Susan broke open a fluffy scone and then topped it with a dollop of clotted cream and a dab of strawberry jam like a true native of the British Isles.

He and Susan grew silent, enjoying their tea while Robert and Cleona exchanged email addresses and friended each other on the various social media platforms.

"I'll email you the photos of Christina's artwork," Robert was saying to Cleona. "Post them often and at different times of the day and night. If anyone asks what they are, just say they're ideas for alternative, renewable energy. Put hash tags on them where appropriate. Word will spread." He grinned at Susan. "I'd say post Susan's video—and you can do that, of course—but I'm not sure it needs any more help. The hits grow by leaps and bounds every hour."

The old man's phone dinged and he glanced up at the clock on the wall as though verifying the time. "You should be going as soon as you've finished your tea. Jillian and Ranjiv will be arriving soon. Wouldn't want the house to be empty when they get there."

Seamus popped the last bit of scone in his mouth, then drained his teacup. "No point in having a Watcher around if you don't listen to him."

"'S nothing to do with being a Watcher," Robert said, waving his phone. "Got a text from Nadia."

"This just keeps getting weirder and weirder," Seamus remarked. He glanced at the two women. "Whenever you ladies are ready, we'll be off."

"She also said to tell you the way is clear," Robert added. "Which is as it should be."

Susan wiped her fingers as though reluctant to stain the snowy damask napkin. "Is that your new catch phrase?"

Robert smiled. "Define *new*."

* * * *

Seamus had barely had time to park the car in his driveway before Ranjiv and Jillian arrived. Between Robert and Nadia, Susan doubted she would ever miss an appointment again.

Following a cheerful reunion complete with several enthusiastic hugs, she looked around for the little schnauzer Jillian had rescued after the crash. "You didn't bring Katie with you?"

"No," Jillian replied. "We thought it best to leave her with Ranjiv's neighbor, Shalini, in case there was any…trouble. They have an elderly Corgi. She and Katie get along pretty well."

Susan knew precisely the sort of "trouble" to which Jillian was referring. "Speaking of trouble, did you have any problems getting here?"

"Not at all," Jillian replied. "Ranjiv and I might've been invisible for all the attention paid to us. During the drive to Liverpool, I kept looking over my shoulder expecting to see truckloads of bad guys chasing after us. I never saw anything that was even remotely suspicious. The same holds true for the drive from Dublin."

"I'm glad to hear it," Susan said. "After some of the things Nadia said—" She stopped. "I haven't told you about her yet, have I?"

"Nope," Jillian replied. "Nadia, huh? The name sounds sort of…Russian."

Susan winced. "That's because it is." Suddenly, the irony of her situation struck her as hysterically funny. Here she was, trusting a former KGB assassin when she ought to have been pounding on the door of the American embassy, begging some government official to save her.

When her laughter finally subsided enough for her to speak, she waved a hand toward Seamus's laptop. "This stuff is getting harder to explain all the time. How about you two read my statement, and we'll go from there."

Ranjiv moved in behind Jillian as she took a seat at the desk. He was every bit as attractive as Kevan, although in an entirely different way. He was tall and dark with a distinguished air, and his British accent added an interesting flavor to his Indian heritage. He and Jillian made a striking couple, the one dark and exotically handsome while the other was as slender and fair as a daffodil.

Agnes groaned. *"My, how poetic."*

Okay. So I'm not much of a writer. Give me a break.

"Actually, she reminds me of a young Meryl Streep."

Susan focused her gaze on her fellow survivor. *I can see that. Sort of. Do I remind you of anyone?*

"Nobody I can think of," Agnes replied. *"As far as I can tell, you're completely unique."*

Yeah, right.

"No, wait," Agnes said. *"I've got it. You look like Maureen O'Hara. Don't sound anything like her, but you have the same fire."*

Another fierce ginger?

"Of course. Terrific actress. She died not long ago. Used to live in a big white house on the shore of Glengariff Harbor. Lovely woman."

I'll take that as a compliment.

"As it was intended."

"I'll bring in your bags while you're reading," Seamus said, diverting Susan's thoughts from the subject of movie star lookalikes. "They in the boot?"

Ranjiv nodded. "Excuse the mess. My car does double duty as a mobile office."

Jillian glanced up from the computer screen. "A very *cluttered* office."

"Mine's the same way," Cleona said. "Nobody can ever find anything on my desk except me, which is usually a good thing. I don't envy whoever takes over my job."

"Same here," Jillian said.

Susan didn't have the type of job that required an office. However, she *did* have an apartment in Newark. Going back to clean it out was not a task she relished, nor was doing so first and foremost in her mind. No doubt the opportunity would present itself eventually.

"I'll give you a hand," she said as she followed Seamus out to the car. "Too bad Kevan couldn't stay. Although it would've been kinda crowded with all six of us here."

"Aye, we've quite the full house now, haven't we?" Seamus raised the rear hatch of the aging Range Rover. "I'm starting to wish I'd held out for a third bedroom when I went house-hunting."

"You *have* a third bedroom," Susan said dryly. "It's full of junk."

"What? The attic, you mean?" He handed her the smaller of the two suitcases. "I suppose it could be used as a bedroom. Never thought of it that way. Be a bit hot up there under the eaves in the summertime, though."

"Seamus," she said firmly, "it never gets *hot* anywhere in County Clare. Not even in August. I know because I checked the average temps online."

"I suppose it's a question of what you're used to."

"Yeah, well, I'm used to temperatures a lot higher than sixty-five degrees. Fahrenheit, that is. Sounds even worse in Celsius."

He pulled out the second suitcase and closed the hatch. "Is that a problem for you?"

"No, but it's given me a much greater appreciation for wool sweaters than I ever had before. Sure, it gets cold in Newark, but it doesn't stay chilly like this all the time. I may have to go up under the eaves once in a while just to get warm."

Sliding an arm around her waist, he eased her closer. "I can do better than that."

"What? Build a fire, you mean?"

"Maybe. Although I was actually thinking more along these lines." He planted a soft kiss on her cheek before moving on to her lips. "You're staying warm enough at night, aren't you?"

"Mmm... Yeah." She was already considerably warmer than she'd been a few moments before. "Might have to get some of those fingerless gloves to wear during the day, though."

He kissed her again. "Better now?"

"Some," she replied. "Keep going."

Seamus seemed quite willing to oblige, deepening his kisses until Susan could think of nothing beyond the delightful pressure of his lips on hers and the warm strength of his embrace. She hadn't been entirely truthful about her intolerance of County Clare's weather, or even the amount of junk in his attic. Seamus's kisses had a way of clearing disturbing thoughts from her head, a purging she craved more with each passing day.

She shivered as his kisses progressed from her lips to her neck.

"We'd best be getting inside," he whispered against her skin. "Wouldn't want you to catch a chill."

"I'm not cold," she insisted. "You're what's making me shiver."

"If that's the case, I'd best be clearing out the attic so I can set up a bed under the eaves. Have to keep my fierce ginger warm. Even when she's wearing nothing at all."

She sighed. "You'll have me so spoiled."

"Can't imagine anyone I'd rather spoil," he said. "You did that to me, you know—ruined me for anyone else." He cupped her cheeks in his palms as his gaze roved back and forth over her face. "I'm so glad you came back to me." He kissed her again—softer this time, but with no less passion. "I'll do whatever it takes to make you want to stay."

Unfortunately, whether she stayed or left might turn out to be yet another matter over which she had no control. "What if being the Bringer of Justice takes me away from you? What then?"

"You can always come back. I'll be here."

Without another word, he released her, then picked up the two suitcases and carried them into the house.

Chapter 29

SUSAN TOOK THE LARGER OF THE TWO SUITCASES, WHICH SHE assumed was Jillian's, into the bedroom Cleona had shared with Kevan the night before. Cleona probably would've chosen to sleep on the sofa rather than split up Jillian and Ranjiv, but Susan couldn't picture a gentlemanly type like Ranjiv agreeing to such an arrangement.

She dawdled over the task until there was truly nothing more she could do to avoid returning to the living room. She couldn't fathom why having her statement read by Jillian and Ranjiv would make her so antsy. After all, Susan had dictated the entire story to Cleona, and Kevan had read it later.

"You're nervous because he's a reporter," Elliott said. *"He's the one who has to turn it in to his editor who we hope will publish it."*

While this was a perfectly reasonable explanation, Susan still couldn't bring herself to sit down and relax, choosing to perch on the arm of the sofa instead. By the time they'd finished reading and Susan had clarified a few minor points, her palms were as sweaty as her feet were icy. "What about your editor, Ranjiv? Have you spoken to him—or her—about it?"

Ranjiv grinned. "When I warned him the story might be hard to believe, all he said was, 'I saw what Susan Maxwell did in Liscannor. Whatever you write about any of those women will not only have the virtue of being the unvarnished truth, it will also sell a lot of newspapers.' Especially since I promised them exclusive rights. Other outlets can run the story afterward, but they'll have to quote *The London Times* as their source."

Jillian laughed. "You'll probably win a Pulitzer."

"Doesn't matter," Ranjiv said with a shrug. "What matters is the effect the story has on the world." His gaze landed on Susan. "Any thoughts as to what you're going to do or say?"

"She won't tell us," Cleona said before Susan could even draw a breath to reply. "All she'll say is that it's going to be on top of O'Brien's Tower at the Cliffs of Moher."

Ranjiv nodded. "That's right. Keep them guessing. The element of suspense will draw more of a crowd. Jillian's story is already in reasonably good shape, but I'll give them each another read-through and do a bit more polishing. Once I have your approval, I'll turn everything in—probably tomorrow morning." He tilted his head as though considering his options. "If we give the story another day or so to spread, the Cliffs of Moher event will draw the biggest crowd County Clare has ever seen." He peered at Susan. "Something to do with the sea, I presume?"

Figuring she had nothing to lose by confirming the obvious assumption, she nodded. "It might be best to make sure there aren't any boats in the vicinity."

"Hmm... That'll be tough given what we've already seen of your talents. Sightseers will want to view the event from every possible angle. Although I'm guessing most ship owners will have sense enough to steer clear once they've been warned."

"I certainly hope so. The last thing we need is another disaster." No doubt she could move them out of the way like she'd moved the waterwheels, but there were no guarantees. Nor could there be any trial runs.

This event would be one of the most unforgettable and irrefutable episodes in human history—or the biggest fiasco.

"You could include the date and time in the newspaper story," Cleona suggested. "Along with a warning to any boats in the area."

"Post a small craft warning of sorts?" Ranjiv nodded. "That would work." He met Susan's gaze without even the slightest flinch. "How far out would you want the ban?"

Susan winced, then glanced at Seamus. "Would a five mile radius be too much?"

"I don't believe so," Seamus replied. "The only problem would be the ferries running between Doolin and the Aran Islands throughout the day. The earliest leaves Inisheer at eight in the morning and the last leaves Doolin at five thirty."

"Earlier would be best," Susan said. "Six or seven, maybe?"

"Don't want the sun to be in anyone's eyes?" Ranjiv suggested.

"Um, no," Susan replied, slightly rattled by Ranjiv's shrewd interpretation. Would anyone else guess what she planned to do? Would it matter? "I just hope the weather is clear."

"Something tells me it will be," Cleona said. "Although we could ask Robert. He'd probably know better than anyone."

Jillian laughed. "If you pick a date and time, Mother Earth, Poseidon, and the Rain gods—or whoever's in charge of such things—will probably make sure you have the conditions you want."

"Okay, Ranjiv," Susan began. "Today is Tuesday. If you send the story in tomorrow, when does it appear in the paper?"

"Thursday."

"And your editor has been given a heads-up?"

"Absolutely. He's holding the front page for it."

"The front page? Really?" Although Susan understood the importance of sharing their story with the world, she was still amazed that anyone else did.

"Hey, you lead with your strengths," Ranjiv replied. "The front page sells the paper, and ours doesn't exactly have the largest circulation in Britain. We're hoping to change that."

"All right then," Susan said decisively. "Seven o'clock Saturday morning—weather permitting."

"Sure you don't want a nice, howling gale to liven things up a bit?" Seamus's twinkling eyes and mischievous grin said he was joking.

Susan, however, was perfectly serious. "Nope. I want clear skies and calm seas."

"Then I'll do my best to see you get them."

"Controlling the weather now are you, Seamus?" Susan asked in her most lilting Irish brogue imitation.

"No, but I *can* keep the boats away. All I need to do is put the word out on the docks that Saturday morning would be a good time to stay ashore." His grin broadened, crinkling the corners of his eyes in a manner that never failed to make Susan's heart skip a beat or two. "I've already checked the weather forecast."

* * * *

Seamus didn't know if he could stand the suspense for one day, let alone the better part of four. Fortunately, he had a job to occupy his time. Susan would probably lose her mind.

"Speaking of the forecast, the weather should improve by tomorrow. Anyone care to go out with Ian and me?" Truth be told, the current day's weather had been the exact opposite of the actual forecast. The weather service was probably still receiving irate phone calls and scratching their heads over that one. But that was the sort of thing to be expected when Mother Nature took charge.

Despite the importance of staying ashore today, canceling any more cruises wouldn't help his reputation or his wallet. "I've a fishing trip scheduled for the morning and a cruise to the Arans in the afternoon." He winked at Susan. "You might even be able to get in a wee bit of ocean-control practice."

"Or talk to the whales," Cleona suggested. "I'd love to know what they have to say."

"Couldn't hurt for you to do something newsworthy before Saturday," Ranjiv said, nodding in a contemplative manner. "We want to generate as much interest as possible."

Susan exhaled a short, derisive laugh. "Give the hit men more reasons to come after us, you mean?"

"Not at all," Ranjiv said. "I believe we've established that no one is gunning for you."

"*Yet,*" Susan said, clearly unconvinced.

Seamus couldn't blame her for being leery. After all, someone had gone to a great deal of trouble to bring down an airliner filled with hundreds of passengers in order to kill the handful of scientists onboard. Their own presumed invincibility undoubtedly had its limits. However, they couldn't very well hide under a rock until Saturday.

"I wouldn't mind seeing the Aran Islands again," Cleona said. "We didn't get to do much in the way of sightseeing when we were there before."

He smiled at the petite brunette, recalling what a nervous wreck she'd been when they'd docked at Inisheer. As upset as she'd been, he wouldn't have been surprised to hear she'd forgotten she was ever there.

"The islands are definitely worth a look," he said. "The big island, Inishmore, has several interesting attractions—spectacular cliffs, the ruins of an old monastery, and Dún Aenghus, which is a two thousand-year-old Celtic fort perched on the edge of a cliff. You can wander about on foot or tour the island by bicycle, mini-bus, or pony trap."

Susan chuckled. "Forgot about your tour-guide alter ego." With a sigh, she added, "Being a plain ol' tourist would sure be nice for a change."

Seamus nodded. These three ladies had been through hell and back. If nothing else, they deserved some down time. "With so many jobs in these parts related to the tourist trade, we've all got a speech or two we can trot out when needed." He grinned. "I'd be more than happy to let you hear the rest of mine if you're so inclined."

Susan's smile would've prompted him to recite every monologue in his rather extensive repertoire if she hadn't stopped him. "I'll hear them soon enough," she said. "But thank you. I feel a lot better now."

He could see that for himself. The lines of worry around her eyes had vanished and her shoulders had visibly relaxed.

"Well then, if you've no objections, I'll get started on the stew for tonight's dinner." He glanced around the room. "Anyone care to help out? We've a bit of that apple cake left from last night, so dessert is already taken care of."

Cleona raised a hand. "I will. Aunt Ita has been giving me lessons. I've made Irish stew once before, and I'd like to try making soda bread."

"You're on." Seamus headed for the kitchen with Cleona in his wake, hoping Susan would follow along. She, more than anyone, needed something to take her mind off the upcoming event. He'd just taken an armful of ingredients from the fridge when she wandered in.

"Can't let you two have all the fun," she said as she donned an apron.

Soon, he and Susan were chopping up meat and vegetables while Cleona worked on the bread. Having a lively crowd in his house was a welcome change from the echoing loneliness that normally prevailed. He'd become accustomed to the silence, barely noticing its presence until friendly conversation replaced it.

Ranjiv worked on into late afternoon, then switched over to his own computer after copying the files to a thumb drive when he was finished. "The more copies, the better," he explained. "Now, if each of you ladies would read through your account to verify the details, I'll make the necessary corrections."

Susan yawned as she began reading her story, demonstrating how tired she must've been. While the other two women seemed to have fully recovered from their ordeal, continued stress and strain had slowed Susan's recovery. Going fishing in the morning, followed by lunch at the pub and a run to the Arans would do her a world of good—if all that activity didn't wear her out completely.

After all, she needed to save a little strength for Saturday's festivities.

* * * *

Susan never would've guessed she would actually enjoy fishing. Granted, standing around with a fishing pole in hand was comparatively boring, but actually catching something? *That* was exciting.

Susan had to admit, Seamus and Ian had this fishing-with-tourists thing down pat. She and her friends had each caught at least two while some of the other passengers had managed three or four, which Seamus cheerfully tagged and put on ice. Proving that experience won out over beginner's luck, he and Ian caught more than a dozen between them.

"For a nominal fee, the chef at Quinn's Restaurant will cook each angler's catch for lunch or hold it over for dinner," Seamus announced as they cruised into Liscannor's tiny harbor. "And trust me, what my sister Enid can do with a freshly caught fish must be tasted to be believed."

"I'll second that," Susan said. "I've never been a big fan of seafood, but the fish I had for dinner in the pub was incredible."

"I'm having mine for lunch," Jillian said. "Don't know if it's the sea air or what, but even after that huge breakfast we had, I'm starving."

Like dinner the night before, breakfast had been a group effort. The curried scrambled eggs Ranjiv had made were to die for, and Cleona demonstrated a knack for making scones that rivaled Robert's. For her part, Susan couldn't recall having as much fun in her life. The only down side was that it took surviving a disastrous plane crash for them to even meet one another.

"You wouldn't have met us either," Agnes said. *"And I probably wouldn't have gotten to go fishing. What a glorious day this is!"*

Susan agreed. As horrible as the weather had been the day before, this day was perfect. Abundant sunshine and a soft breeze that was cool rather than chilly. Her only complaint was that, with strangers aboard, she hadn't had the opportunity to practice her "skills."

"No worries there," Agnes soothed. *"I have absolute faith in your ability to do exactly as you intend."*

If no one kills me before I get the chance.

"Enough of that nonsense," Agnes scolded. *"Nadia is doing a bang-up job of protecting you—or taking out the bad guys. Not sure which—or how she's doing it. Makes me wonder if she isn't a Watcher after all."*

Maybe she belongs to some other category. A Doer rather than a Watcher.

"Perhaps," Agnes said. *"Although I'd call them Protectors, myself. 'Doer' sounds a bit silly."*

Susan smiled to herself. *I bow to your superior story-telling talent, Agnes.*

"Thank you, dear."

After the boat was secured, everyone headed up the road to the pub. By the time Seamus had dropped the cooler off at the kitchen door, Iris was already taking drink orders.

"I'm impressed," Jillian remarked. "Must be overwhelming to have so many people coming in at once, even if they are bringing along the entrée. I mean, the fish still has to be cleaned and cooked."

Seamus shrugged as he took his seat. "Busloads of tourists show up here often enough. After a while, you learn to take it in stride." He winked. "Not that anyone had better be in a big hurry for their lunch."

Jillian groaned. "Then I at least need some bread and butter to tide me over."

"No worries," Seamus said. "Iris will bring some soda bread out shortly."

"When do we have to be back on the boat?" Susan asked.

"Not until one o'clock," he replied. "We've plenty of time."

She liked that about him. Prompt and efficient, while at the same time genial and unhurried—like Ireland itself. Despite the frenzied life she'd led, dashing through airports to make connecting flights, she was already adapting to the natural rhythm of life in County Clare—not to mention life with Seamus Quinn.

He was so…*perfect*. She leaned back in her chair, smiling as she recalled the night he'd kissed her, right there in the middle of the pub to stop her from raving like a madwoman.

"Something to tell your grandchildren," Agnes said.

If I have any.

"Oh, you will, my dear. I'm sure of it."

I'll take your word for it. Meanwhile, I have a sudden urge to chat with Seamus's mother.

"Think I'll go ask Lorna to pull me a pint," she said, rising from her chair. "Anyone else interested?" She grinned at Jillian. "A pint o' Guinness is like drinking a loaf of bread, you know."

"Count me in," Jillian said. "Although as empty as I am, it'll probably go straight to my head."

Susan was still chuckling as she approached the bar. She hadn't seen Lorna since waving to her as Nadia hustled her away following the most recent display of her connection with the sea.

"You're looking happy," Lorna commented. "Shall I pull you a Guinness?"

Susan nodded. "Two, please." She watched as Lorna filled the first glass with dark, foamy beer. "How've you been since I saw you last?"

Lorna arched a brow. "Trying to come to grips with what I witnessed the other day." She slid the pint across the bar.

Susan shrugged. "Understandable." She took a sip of the beer, hoping to bolster her courage. "I'm having the same problem myself." She glanced over her shoulder. The pub was crowded but subdued. "What I don't understand is why we don't have swarms of photographers and reporters harassing the crap out of us. Seems kind of...spooky."

"Liscannor is a small community. We protect our own," Lorna said with a sniff. "No one, and I do mean no one, has said a bloody thing about who you are, where you're staying, or who might be helping you."

Clearly, Susan had friends she didn't even know about yet—or perhaps she'd gained them by being Seamus's love interest. There was, however, another possible explanation. "Did Robert McKenna say anything to you after the, um, 'incident'?"

"As a group you mean? Aye, he did. Told us this was only the first of the most important events in County Clare's history, perhaps even the world. Swore us all to secrecy, he did."

"But several videos were posted online... What did he say about them?"

"He told us to post them anonymously. And as for you, what with you being new to the area, I doubt if any of the onlookers even realized who you were."

Susan's back had been to the crowd for most of the whale-and-waterwheel event, and the show taking place out in the ocean was far more interesting than she would've been. The only time she'd glanced toward the cameras was when the little boy had begged her to repeat the performance. She'd never admitted to actually being in control.

She was about to drop the entire subject when she recalled what Ranjiv had said about his editor's response to running the story. She tipped her head toward the table where her friends were already buttering slices of soda bread. "Ranjiv over there is a reporter for *The London Times.* His editor knew exactly who was in the video. I don't know how, but he knew."

"Possibly because Ranjiv told him?" Lorna suggested.

Susan shook her head. "That's not how he put it." Mystified, she glanced around the pub again. She and her fellow survivors might as well have been invisible for all the attention anyone paid them. "So our identities and whereabouts are only apparent to those with a need to know, huh? Spookier and spookier."

She shouldn't have been surprised. Evidently Mother Earth wasn't leaving anything to chance anymore. Susan took some comfort in that.

An elderly gentleman shuffled up to the bar and ordered a pint of ale. Lorna filled the glass and passed it over with a smile took the man's money and made change before she spoke again.

"That's possible, I suppose. Nothing seems too peculiar to be true anymore. I can promise you one thing, though. No one in Liscannor will admit to anything, but those paparazzi types can be very diligent—and persistent."

Chapter 30

SEAMUS HAD MADE THE RUN TO THE ARANS COUNTLESS TIMES, BOTH before and after his father's death. He'd done it in the rain, in seas rough enough to warrant never leaving the dock, and on days when the sun flatly refused to shine. Twice they'd been caught by a squall and had to turn back. But he could honestly say he'd never done it with a dolphin escort. A *massive* dolphin escort.

"Don't think we'll get through this trip without attracting attention," he muttered to Ian. "I'm surprised we don't have a feckin' flotilla of reporters following us."

"Aye," Ian said. "More Atlantic white-sides than I've ever seen at one time, even when they were attacking a pod of harbor porpoises. Plenty of those types and a good number of bottlenoses as well. Never seen such a thing in me life."

Harbor porpoises were plentiful in and around the docks, hence the name, but they tended to be chased off by the Atlantic white-sided dolphins and the bottlenose variety. Like Ian, Seamus had never seen the three species actually seem to cooperate before.

If cooperate was the right word. More like they shared a common interest. They were staying clear of the bow and the propeller, but that was all. Leaping and splashing in an enormous circle around the *Branwyn Eostre*, they matched the boat's course and speed with uncanny precision. The children onboard voiced their delight, as did the adults.

The paying passengers, that is. Susan and her friends appeared to have a much different interpretation of the event. They were astonished, yes, but their expressions also conveyed more than a trace of alarm.

Susan sidled up to him, taking his hand. "Do you suppose they'll follow us all the way to the dock?"

"Possibly, but that's not uncommon. They like to interact with boats and hang around the docks. It's the sheer number of them that's unusual." The best he could tell, the pod extended a good twenty meters in every direction. "Hope you've been taking pictures. I doubt you'll ever see the like again."

"Pictures *and* video," she said. "The way things are going, my phone will be dead before we ever get to Inishmore."

He arched a brow. "Shall I take a wild guess and say they're here because of you?"

"Shh," she hissed. "Not so loud. They'll hear you."

"Who? The dolphins or the other passengers?" Laughing, he slid an arm around her waist and pulled her close enough to whisper in her ear. Even out to sea with the wind in her hair, she smelled like heaven. "You could tell them to leave. I'm sure they'd do whatever you ask of them."

"I haven't *asked* them to do anything, and I don't care if they stick around." She clutched the open edges of her cardigan and tugged them together. "I just don't want them to get hurt."

"They seldom do. Oh, now and then one gets too close, but they're used to boats."

She frowned. "Maybe I should ask them to back off a little." Hunching her shoulders, she leaned into him, shivering, although whether from cold or nerves, he couldn't have said. "Just wish I knew how to do it."

Seamus studied the choppy, dolphin-studded seas. "I believe that did it," he said, pointing toward the starboard side. "Take a gander."

"Oh, you must be—" Her jaw dropped as she followed the direction of his gesture. Their "escort" was now maintaining a ten-meter buffer zone on all sides of the boat. "I should've known. I only had to *think* about whales and they started breaching the last time." With a low chuckle, she added, "Guess I'd better be careful what I wish for, huh?"

"I'll not argue with that," he said. "We certainly don't want any whales leaping across the bow."

"Do you really think—? No. Better not go there."

"Exactly. They obviously like being near you, but there's a limit to how well we can coexist in such close quarters."

She nodded somewhat absently as she gazed out over the vast number of seemingly joyous dolphins. "Someday, I'd like to put on a wetsuit and snorkel and go swimming with them."

"The whales or the dolphins?"

"Either one," she replied. "I've always been fascinated by them—or perhaps I'm simply in awe. They're just so…"

"Cool," Cleona supplied as she drew nearer. "I've always thought so too. I'm sorry I missed seeing the whales-and-waterwheels show in person, but this is incredible." She hesitated. "Don't suppose you can hear what they're saying or thinking, can you?"

Susan shrugged. "Not really. The best I can tell, they understand me a lot better than I understand them."

"Perhaps that will improve with time," Cleona suggested. "You could be the link between humans and all intelligent life in the sea."

Susan shuddered. "Thought I was only supposed to bring justice to the environmental baddies of the world."

Cleona's expression grew thoughtful. "Yes, but there's more to this than simply protecting the environment. There've been times when nature had the upper hand, but in fighting back, we've isolated ourselves from it—living indoors to keep warm or cool or dry, never venturing out unless we absolutely have to. I was living like that not long ago myself. Not everyone feels the same way, of course. But so many do, and it's wrong. So wrong."

Seamus had spent a good part of his life on a boat, but as cold as the North Atlantic was, he'd rarely ventured into it on purpose. Even those hardy souls who surfed the waves at Spanish Point wore wetsuits more often than not. He'd been more in tune with the sea when he was a boy, venturing out amid the rocks and waves. Sadly, he'd lost that connection as he grew older.

As if they'd sensed they needed to be part of the conversation, Jillian and Ranjiv came over from the opposite side of the deck to join them.

"What we need is a closer relationship with our world," Cleona went on. "Ancient people knew things about the stars and the seasons that we don't even notice anymore. I've been out with Kevan in his pastures at night. I've never seen stars like that before. Never paid any attention to the phases of the moon either. I'd never even thought to look for it during the daytime—didn't even realize you could see it at certain times during the month. Our lives have become so narrow, so…artificial." She waved toward the dolphins that still swam in formation around the boat. "Even if the whales and dolphins *were* trying to communicate with us, we were too busy killing them to listen."

* * * *

Susan was trying to listen—opening her mind to the possibility. Trying to hear, trying to understand.

Who are you? What do you want?

Too many voices. She'd had to sort out the stowaways. But the dolphins. So many chattering squeaks. She couldn't make sense of any of it.

Until she realized what she was hearing.

The melody came through slowly—only a few notes at first, then swelling to a glorious chorus as the music of the sea filled her ears with its lilting high notes and low-pitched rumbles. Closing her eyes, she sifted through the sounds. She could detect no words, but there was a message in there somewhere. If she'd been in the water, no doubt she could've heard it better—air distorted the tune, and with it, the meaning. She fought to cut through the interference, trying desperately to understand.

Suddenly, the meaning became piercingly clear.

She stood up straighter, opening her eyes as the truth rang through her mind—not like the voices of the stowaways, but in a song even more subtle than that of the whales.

"They saved me," she whispered. "All this time, I didn't know. I thought it must've been the sea."

"What are you saying?" As much as Seamus had already heard of their experiences during and after the crash, nothing should've surprised him. Yet the shock and awe were quite plain—in his words, his tone, and his inflection. She heard nuances she'd never even attempted to focus on before. The dolphin language had already taught her that.

"The dolphins," she replied. "They were the ones who pulled me from the wreck. I'd forgotten—or was too dazed to realize what was happening." She stared at Jillian and Cleona. "They were right there with us, making sure we didn't drown."

Jillian gaped at her with even more disbelief than Seamus had shown. "Are you sure? I don't remember it that way at all."

"Neither do I," Cleona insisted. "The sea saved me, like a huge arm reaching down with grasping fingers to grab hold and pull me up."

"A bubble of air forced me out of the plane," Jillian said. "Then I swam to the surface with coaching from one of my extra entities— the swimmer, Shanda Smythe."

Susan shook her head. "They were there. Maybe you didn't see them, but they were there in case we needed them." She gasped as the rest of the tale surged up to her from the waves. "The raft I released should've surfaced even before we did, but it didn't. It got stuck. The dolphins pulled it free."

She closed her eyes again, sending out notes of gratitude to the dolphins in the language they understood.

Songs of merriment and joy came flowing back—the dolphin equivalent of "You're welcome"—followed by expressions of regret at their inability to save any others. Most of those they'd pulled from the wreck were already dead. The rest were unconscious and drowned before they could be pushed to the surface.

Susan understood their sorrow. Even though she'd been warned, she'd barely had sufficient time to save herself, let alone anyone else.

You did your best, she told them. *The instigators didn't intend for anyone to survive.*

When she reopened her eyes, she found all four of her friends gazing at her in wonder.

"You're talking to dolphins now," Cleona whispered. "I only spoke with Earth when I became a tree." She giggled. "Sounds silly when I say that out loud, doesn't it?"

"No sillier than talking to dolphins," Susan replied. "Most people would think we were nuts." She looked first at Seamus and then at Ranjiv. "You two are truly unique."

"More privileged than unique," Seamus said. "But we had reasons of our own to believe."

Ranjiv nodded. "We not only *wanted* to believe, we simply had no alternative. The supporting evidence was too strong."

She smiled. "That's why Saturday's event has to be seen all over the world."

"We'll make sure it is," Ranjiv said. "After all, that Watcher chap isn't the only one with a Twitter account."

"I've been thinking…" Jillian fretted her lower lip with her teeth. "Maybe we should set up a YouTube channel to post our videos."

"Already done," Ranjiv said. "I've set up accounts on every platform there is."

"Leaving no stones unturned?" Susan said with a wry grin.

"None whatsoever," he replied. "We've got this. You just have to do your thing on Saturday, and for the rest, well, we'll have to wait and see, won't we?"

* * * *

After everything that had happened in the past few weeks, Susan couldn't imagine their scheme *not* going as planned. There was too much at stake and their backing was unprecedented.

The dolphins waved farewell when the *Branwyn Eostre* docked at Inishmore—yet another sight that had to be seen to be believed. As a group—and there must've been at least a thousand of them— they flipped their tails up in the air, waving vigorously before vanishing into the depths.

She understood their concerns quite well. Humankind threatened their undersea world as well as dry land and the air above. Oceanographers had been warning of the damage being done for decades. Improvements had been made, but they weren't enough. Not nearly enough.

The five of them rented bicycles and spent the rest of the afternoon exploring the island. The wind seemed incessant, but the sun was warm on Susan's face as she pedaled along the roads from one attraction to the next. The monastic ruins were certainly interesting, but the land itself interested her far more than anything mankind had done to change it. She'd felt the ancient awesomeness before, but never quite as strongly as she did there.

She glanced at Jillian and Cleona and saw similar expressions on both of their faces. "You feel it too. Don't you?"

"Oh, yeah," Cleona replied, her voice breathy with reverence. "This is like the Black Valley. Earth is chiming all around me, urging me to take root here." A frown flicked her brow before being replaced with smile so enigmatic, it would've made the *Mona Lisa* seem positively jolly. "Sounds silly, but that's what I'm hearing."

Jillian rested her hand on a rocky pile. "This place is so old. Perhaps even older than Stonehenge. These stones have been used many, many times, and they have an infinite number of stories to tell—some tragic, some joyous." She blinked and her eyes widened, her lashes flickering much as Cleona's brow had done.

"What is it?" Susan asked. "What are you seeing?"

"Nothing," Jillian replied, but the inscrutable glance she exchanged with Cleona said otherwise.

"You're keeping secrets from me? Now?" Susan could scarcely believe what was happening. She could understand a bunch of dolphins, but she had no idea what two human women were thinking.

"Ironic, isn't it?" Agnes said. *"But then, you're also keeping your plans secret."*

I hadn't thought of that.

She exhaled sharply. "Touché."

Jillian patted her arm. "Not all secrets are bad, Susan." She winked at Cleona. "We still have a part to play in this saga. You'll understand when the time comes."

Since this was pretty much Susan's take on Saturday's Big Event, she couldn't very well argue the point. "Gotcha." She heaved a sigh. "Guess we'd better go take a gander at that Celtic fort—What did you call it, Seamus?"

"Dún Aenghus," Seamus replied as he and Ranjiv strolled over to where the three women were gathered.

"Yeah, that," Susan said, choosing not to attempt pronunciation. "I want to see it before it really does tumble into the sea."

Seamus laughed. "It's been sitting up there for two thousand years, and the original building on the site dates back another thousand years. Don't believe it's going to all going to fall down anytime soon."

"You never know," Susan said darkly. "This could be the day."

Nevertheless, by the time they'd hiked up to the fort, Susan almost wished she'd chosen this particular spot from which to save the planet. Like the Cliffs of Moher, the hilltop site boasted a spectacular view, but at the fort, portions of which truly had tumbled from the cliff, the feeling was spiritual rather than commanding. The whispering voices of the dead circled the eerily silent structure almost as though, like the stones themselves, they were part of the very bones of the fort.

Susan nudged Jillian. "Do you hear that?"

Jillian nodded. "I thought I was done with whispering voices."

A glance at Cleona confirmed that she too, heard the mournful cries carried on the wind. Susan wasn't about to ask Seamus and Ranjiv if they heard it, although *feeling* spiritual wasn't quite the same as actually being possessed—or in her case, inhabited—by ghosts.

Looking back down the hill they'd climbed to reach the fort, Susan could almost see the throngs of people gathered there to hear what she had to say. The longer she watched, the clearer their shapes became. Dressed in every style of clothing from ancient to contemporary, the ghosts of everyone who'd ever ventured to that site were assembled there. She had no idea how she knew who they were, but they numbered in the thousands, blanketing the hillside with their solemn vigil.

"We are with you," they chorused. *"For if there is no Earth, no sea, and no sky, there can be no life for our descendants."*

Such a simple statement, and so true as to have been obvious to anyone. Yet comparatively few even gave a thought to it.

She didn't have to ask her two companions if they'd heard those words, because they stood on either side of her, joining hands as they gazed out over the vast crowd.

"We will do our best to preserve life on Earth, for your sake and the sake of your descendants." Susan's voice sounded much stronger than she'd expected. But then, she'd been talking to ghosts for weeks now. A few thousand more shouldn't faze her.

She glanced toward Jillian, who said, "I, The Chosen One to whom Earth speaks through the stones, give you my promise."

Cleona took a step forward. "I am the Carrier of Life's Preservation. Together, we will ensure that life on Earth does not end, but continues until our sun goes dark."

"And I am the Bringer of Justice," Susan announced. "Together, we will prevail against those whose mindless greed would destroy our world and all its natural beauty."

"We hear you and offer our aid," the ghosts said with a collective nod. *"The time of reckoning has come."*

The scene before them wavered, then slowly dissipated, feathering away like smoke.

Once again the green windswept hillside lay empty, save for a few tourists who continued their trek to the fort as though they hadn't been surrounded by a multitude of spirits only moments before.

Chapter 31

"THE FORT IS BELIEVED TO HAVE BEEN MORE OF A SPIRITUAL SITE than a military one," Seamus was saying as he and Ranjiv returned from the cliff's edge. "Granted, you can see for miles, but because most enemies would probably approach from the other direction, it isn't much use as a lookout tower." He stopped short when his gaze connected with Susan's. "Don't tell me I've gone and missed another one?"

"Um, yeah," Susan replied. "Although I'm not sure you guys would've seen anything if you'd been here."

"Kevan might have," Cleona said wistfully. "Sure wish he was here. That's the trouble with raising animals. They tend to tie you down."

"He'll be back Friday night, right?" Susan asked.

Cleona nodded. "He said he'd leave as soon as he finished his evening chores. Might be pretty late by the time he gets here."

Seamus was still technically on the job himself. "Speaking of 'late,' we'd best be heading back to the dock. Don't want my other passengers to get their knickers in a twist. You can tell us all about it on the way. We've plenty of time."

He slid his arm around Susan's waist, and she leaned into him, returning his gesture with a one-armed hug of her own.

"That's a tough one," she said. "I'm not real sure I know how to explain it."

"Another of those stories that sounds ridiculous when you start paraphrasing?" Ranjiv suggested as he offered Jillian his arm.

"Yeah," Jillian replied. "Basically, a bunch of ghosts offered to help us out." She hesitated, her eyes widening slightly. "And I do mean a *lot* of ghosts."

"They're concerned their descendants won't have anywhere to

live," Susan said. "Which is precisely what everyone *should* be worried about. There are plenty of people who are too busy taking care of themselves to give much thought to future generations, but the people who *do* have the wherewithal to make a difference are too wrapped up in things like mansions, swimming pools, and supercars that aren't even street-legal." She huffed out a breath that was quickly followed with an apologetic shrug. "Sorry. I saw something about this sheik and his ridiculously expensive car online this morning. The stuff that spools me up is getting easier to find every day."

"You're more sensitive to it now," Seamus said. "I know because I'm having the same trouble."

Before he met Susan, he hadn't given much thought to the fate of his own descendants, mainly because the way his life had been headed, he hadn't expected to have any. He felt differently now. The possibility of marriage and children had suddenly become very real, and the last thing he wanted for his offspring was for them to grow up in a polluted, post-apocalyptic world.

He couldn't claim to have been ignorant of the problems facing the inhabitants of Earth, and he'd always striven to be part of the solution rather than the problem. His life in Liscannor was as environmentally friendly as he could make it. He recycled, reused, and repaired everything he possibly could. Unfortunately, he also knew that a large part of what routinely fell into the sea, whether accidentally or on purpose, wasn't biodegradable. The islands of floating trash in the Pacific might've been more myth than fact, but the congregation of micro-particles of plastic still threatened marine life from the bottom to the very top of the food chain. He'd done his best to avoid adding to the mess, but he was only one man with one boat.

For now, he had to take it on faith that solutions for change hadn't been left too late. No doubt Mother Earth knew where the point of no return was, and given her current intervention, that point hasn't been reached as yet.

During the return trip, he viewed the ruins they passed from a different perspective. Would aliens visiting Earth in the distant future find nothing but the relics of a civilization that had essentially poisoned itself? Or would they discover a world filled with intelligent beings who lived in harmony with their planet? The deplorable events in recent years suggested they would be more likely to discover the former rather than the latter.

Susan and her friends could mean the difference between those two outcomes.

He didn't care to think about what would happen should they fail.

* * * *

Despite the breaking news on Thursday morning, no hordes of curiosity seekers had as yet descended upon County Clare. Videos of the *Branwyn Eostre*'s dolphin escort to Inishmore surfaced online and garnered millions of views, but the video with the whales remained in the lead. Ranjiv's interview with the three survivors of Oceanus Flight 2324 was published in a morning edition, along with an article about the recovery of the black box. As Susan had suspected, the flight recorder's data had yielded no clues regarding the cause of the crash. The email Chuck had received seemed to be the bigger news story, partly because it wasn't exclusive to Ranjiv's paper, but mainly due to its shocking message.

However, by Friday morning, every news broadcast and newspaper—whether available online or at the corner market—had jumped on Ranjiv's story like a duck on a june bug.

The three women each received several calls, mainly from their families. Unfortunately, the call Susan received from her parents was nearly as upsetting as the crash itself.

"They think I've lost my marbles," she reported after switching off her phone. "Said I should take the first plane back to the States and check myself into a mental hospital." With a bitter chuckle, she added, "They didn't seem to think that carrying around a psychiatrist's spirit qualified as therapy."

Given that her own parents didn't believe her, Susan had begun to doubt if anyone would even bother to show up on Saturday.

However, a call from Kevan on his way from Kenmare that evening put those fears to rest. "I'm having the devil of a time getting there," he said. "I've never seen traffic like this in my life. Nearly at a standstill in some places. Looks like you ladies will be drawing quite a crowd."

Now that they were assured that people were indeed gathering for the event, Susan worried that they might be attracting the wrong sort. With that in mind, Seamus called the Garda station in Lisdoonvarna, and they promised to send several guards out to help with security. Susan hadn't heard a peep from Nadia, who was either too busy deploying her operatives or deemed it best to remain invisible.

Ranjiv had arranged for various support services to be on hand, but Susan's internal support system had gone silent. Although she hadn't felt the pangs of their departure, their cheering banter was conspicuously absent. Perhaps they were as nervous about the outcome as Susan was herself.

Kevan arrived late Friday evening, and they all headed over to Quinn's for Seamus and his band's usual Friday night gig. After the first set, Ranjiv left to interview some of the people who were camped out near the cliffs. Robert dropped by briefly, his cheerful demeanor suggesting that the timeline was progressing as it should. Susan took some comfort in that, although his private exchange with Seamus at the bandstand between songs seemed more somber than jovial.

Ranjiv returned just before the end of the last set. "The people out there are nothing like a crowd waiting for a rock concert or even a political rally. Everyone I spoke with seemed subdued but cautiously hopeful—vacillating between expecting the greatest event of their lifetime or the greatest hoax."

"A hoax?" With a groan, Susan put her head down on her folded arms, fighting the urge to bang it against the table. "Obviously I should've been drinking Jameson all evening instead of sticking with tea. I figured I ought to stay sober in case some drunk started hassling me for making the whales dance."

"Has anyone spoken to you?" Ranjiv asked.

"Nope. Not so much as a pat on the shoulder for encouragement. Although Seamus's sister did bring me a piece of cake a while ago.

Guess she thought I needed cheering up."

"You have seemed rather funereal," Kevan remarked. "Hope Seamus and the band don't take it as a commentary on their playing."

"Are you kidding? I'd be a total basket case if I didn't have their music to distract me. My stowaways aren't even talking to me anymore."

"Is that right?" he said with mock surprise. "Perhaps they think you need to keep your wits about you."

"As in not sitting here talking to myself?"

He grinned and took a sip of his beer. "Something like that."

"What about your extra entities, Kevan?" Jillian asked. "Did they all leave when you and Cleona caught that assassin?"

He nodded. "Seems that way. They weren't in the picture Jack Halloran took of us afterward."

Susan gasped. "They show up in pictures? Really? I had no idea."

"Oh, yes," Cleona said. "Sinead took my picture while we were on top of the sentry tower on Garnish Island. You could see them standing all around me."

"Don't suppose you have that with you," Ranjiv said. "I believe I'd like to see that."

"Sure. I've got it right here." Cleona reached into her purse and pulled out her phone. She paged through the photos and then stopped, her mouth agape as she stared at the screen. "They're gone," she whispered. "I never thought to check it again. But they were there. Honestly. Sinead saw them too."

Susan leaned sideways to peer at Cleona's phone. All she saw in the photo was Cleona standing alone on the tower with a breathtaking view of the sea and the surrounding hills stretched out behind her. "Boy, when they move on, they really move on, don't they?"

"I suppose so," Cleona said, her tone laced with regret. "Jacob Emhart was standing right there beside me. And now he's gone."

Kevan gave her a consoling hug. "You shared his formula with the world. Wherever he is now, I'm sure he's very pleased."

Ranjiv glanced over his shoulder, then leaned forward as though he didn't care to be overheard. "Speaking of Emhart... The scientific community is up in arms over his death and the deaths of the other scientists. And from what I can gather, you were right about that formula of his."

"Where did you hear all that?" Cleona asked.

"Twitter," Ranjiv replied. "They're all going crazy over his formula, saying it will revolutionize solar power."

"Maybe that's enough," Susan said slowly. "Maybe I don't have to do this thing after all."

"Oh, no you don't," Jillian snapped. "No backing out now. Not when we're this close to the end."

"She's right," Ranjiv said. "Making the formula available isn't enough. The energy companies have to *want* to use it—rather than sticking with fossil fuels. I mean, let's face it, the oil industry is huge, employing millions of workers while earning a ridiculous amount of money for their shareholders. You have to give them a bloody good reason for giving it up to build solar panels."

Susan slumped back in her chair. "Then I guess we're still on, huh?"

"You're damn straight we are," Jillian said. "Bright and early tomorrow morning."

* * * *

By the time she and Seamus climbed into bed that night, Susan had no idea how she'd made it through the day. "I know I've made it through worse days, but this one really wore me out."

Seamus chuckled. "In case you've forgotten, your current track record for getting through bad days is feckin' perfect."

"That's one way of looking at it." She snuggled closer to him, craving his warmth and his solid presence. So much of what she'd dealt with in recent weeks had taken place exclusively in her mind. He was the most tangible reminder that she was indeed still alive. "Don't know how I'll ever get to sleep tonight. I've got a caffeine buzz that just won't quit. Drinking tea rather than whiskey was obviously a mistake."

He kissed her, deep and lovingly. "Did you think getting totally pissed would be better than what I can do to help you sleep?"

"Not really. In fact, I was sort of counting on that. If you're not too tired, that is."

"If I'm ever too tired for that," he declared, "you may as well stash me in a coffin, because I'll be no good to anyone ever again."

She ran a fingertip from his forehead down the bridge of his nose, over the fullness of his lips, ending with the firm curve of his chin. "You'll always be good for me, Seamus Quinn. Even when you're too old and senile to remember my name. You're the best thing that's ever happened to me."

"What? Better than surviving a plane crash? That must make me quite special indeed."

As always, his lilting brogue made her smile, especially when she knew she was being teased. Despite acknowledging the gravity of her situation, he had a knack for supporting her without allowing her to take herself too seriously. This Bringer of Justice gig was stressful enough as it was. "Hmm... Since the one followed the other, I'm not sure they need to be considered separate."

"Very true." He pulled her close, gliding a calloused hand over the rise of her hip. "There are a couple of other things that should never be considered separate."

"Oh, and what are they?"

"You and me, m'dear," he replied. "You and me."

She sighed. "I couldn't agree more." Closing her eyes, she melted into his embrace, delighting in the feel of his hands on her skin and his lips on her neck. She longed to forget about the future and simply enmesh herself in the joyous task of learning everything about him there was to know—an undertaking that would undoubtedly take a lifetime to accomplish. This was time she wouldn't have had, a love she never would've found, but he was here, warm and strong in her arms, not dominating or tearing her down, but building her up and allowing her to be everything, anything, she chose.

"I love you, Seamus Quinn," she whispered. "Now and forever."

He replied with a kiss that sent tendrils of desire curling throughout her already aroused body. She reached up, threading her fingers through his hair before letting her hand drift down the slope of his shoulder, drinking in the feel of him through her palm.

"Whatever sorrow shakes from your heart, far better things will take their place."

She frowned, not certain whether the words were in her head or if Seamus had spoken aloud. "Sounds like a quote of some sort."

He nodded. "Something Ranjiv told me when we were at Dún Aenghus. There was more to it than that, but it feels appropriate now. We've had our fair share of sorrow, you and I. This is our time to find better things. Better things at long last. I didn't think I would ever love again, but I have, I do, and I will love you. Always."

She pulled him down, kissing him with a fervor beyond any she'd ever felt or even believed herself capable of expressing. Opening herself to him, she took him in—the heat, the passion, and the love—all of that and more. He slid inside her, rocking gently at first, then becoming stronger as she urged him on.

As on every night they'd spent together, he'd set a match to the candle by the bed. She'd been a little embarrassed by it at first, but now she reveled in that light, unable to imagine making love with this wonderful man while denying herself the sheer joy of being able to look at him. The soft glow burnished his tousled curls and highlighted the line of his jaw, the arch of his brow, and the fullness of his lips. His eyes gleamed beneath generous lashes, the low light intensifying her enjoyment of their rich, brown depths.

Time slowed. Even the ticks from the clock on the wall above them sounded with less frequency. The dull thud of his body against hers matched the clock's rhythm, allowing the pleasure to grow at an exquisitely languid pace. She was fully aware of every rung she climbed until at last, she reached the highest level of all. Her eyes squeezed shut as she focused on the minute element of bliss at the center of her being.

Seamus groaned with pleasure. Never once faltering, he continued to wield his own brand of magic until, like a seed responding to water, the tiny particle inside her expanded, filling her with an ecstasy so complete, only one word existed to describe it.

Perfection. Soaring, elevating perfection.

At long last, sorrow had been shaken from her heart, and she welcomed the joy that took its place.

* * * *

Susan had two dreams that night.

In the first, everything went according to plan, resulting in a rosy future. In the other, Earth rained her wrath down upon humankind until there wasn't a soul left alive and every human achievement had crumbled into dust.

She could only hope that the first dream would be the one to come true. The outcome hinged on some minor detail she hadn't seen. No doubt Robert knew what that detail was.

But as always, he probably wouldn't say.

Chapter 32

THE SUN HADN'T EVEN BEGUN TO LIGHTEN THE EASTERN SKY WHEN Susan awoke to the heavenly aroma of baking scones. Seamus was pouring boiling water from the kettle as she entered the kitchen. Jillian and Ranjiv were at the stove, her frying bacon while he scrambled the eggs. As Susan might have predicted, she caught a whiff of curry as she passed behind them.

"I'm not sure I can eat anything," she said meekly. "My stomach feels sort of rebellious this morning."

"Nonsense." Seamus put the lid on the teapot and waved her toward the table where Cleona and Kevan were laying out plates and cutlery. "You just have a seat there. If nothing else, you need your tea."

She attempted a smile. "I drank enough tea last night to float a battleship. Barely slept a wink." Nevertheless, she did as he asked, plopping down in a chair as though she had jelly for bones.

"Hair of the dog, then," he said with a grin. "I'll not have you passing out from hunger in the middle of your speech."

"Speaking of which, do you have it written down somewhere?" Jillian asked.

"Nope. That's part of what kept me awake. I mean, I have a general idea, but it needs to be organic to the situation."

"Organic?" Cleona echoed.

"You know... arising spontaneously from the nature of the moment."

Susan had Agnes to thank for that definition. Like her favorite stowaway did with her novels, she was making everything up as she went along.

"That's right, dear," Agnes said. *"You'll do fine. I have the utmost faith in you—as do we all."*

Susan nearly went limp with relief. *Oh, Agnes, you've no idea how much I've missed you guys.*

"*You were busy,*" Agnes explained. "*Besides, there are some things you simply have to discover and do for yourself.*"

You'll be with me up there on the tower?

"*Absolutely. Wouldn't miss it for the world.*"

Jillian was nearly finished plating up the bacon when the oven timer dinged.

"That'll be the scones," Cleona announced. Snatching up an oven mitt, she pulled the tray from the oven and took a long sniff. "Ah, perfect!" She transferred the hot bread into a basket, which she then waved under Susan's nose. "Sure you don't want one?"

"Okay, okay, *okay*," Susan grumbled. "I'm feeling kinda hungry after all."

"That's better," Seamus said. "Glad we didn't have to twist your arm."

Ranjiv brought over a bowlful of fragrant curried eggs and Jillian followed with the bacon. They all sat down and passed around the bowls and platters.

Like one big, happy family.

Cleona took a bite of scrambled eggs and hummed with pleasure. "Oh, wow. These are even better than yesterday."

Ranjiv grinned. "Made a bit of ghee to cook them in. Makes a difference, doesn't it?"

"Heavens, yes." She took another bite. "I'm going to have to write down some of your recipes. I've never eaten much Indian food before, but you've about got me hooked."

"I can do better in my own kitchen," he said. "Curry powder was about the only Indian spice mix Seamus had in his pantry. You'll have to come over to London sometime."

Cleona laughed. "That sounds so odd, like it's as easy as making a run to Houston. But I guess it is now."

Susan had worked the Newark to London flight so many times, a stopover in London should've seemed commonplace—and in a way it was—but Cleona was right. Susan wouldn't even have to get on a plane to go to London anymore. "I really hope we can keep in touch when this is all over. People tend to go their separate ways after something like this. I mean, if ours had been an ordinary plane crash, we might never have seen each other again. But this? This is different."

"True," Jillian said. "Plane crash survivors are a comparatively small group, but survivors who've experienced what we have..." She shrugged. "We're like astronauts who've actually set foot on the moon. There aren't many others with whom we share common ground."

Cleona nodded. "After the interviews we gave, more people know what's been happening, but yeah, not a shared experience."

For her part, Susan would probably remember this moment anytime she smelled bacon or scones—or walked into an Indian restaurant. She had other memories associated with seawater and jet fuel.

She doubted she would forget those either.

* * * *

Susan had just finished dumping the breakfast dishes in the sink when a loud, revving engine drew her attention.

"Sounds like our escort has arrived," Ranjiv said.

Susan looked out the window, but didn't see anyone. "Nadia, I presume?"

He nodded. "I ran into her last night while I was out conducting interviews. She and her crew were working the crowd, looking for 'unfriendly agitators.' The way she talked, they hadn't found any as yet."

"That's good to hear," Cleona said. "We really don't want any trouble."

"We have guards and medics in place," Ranjiv said. "You can't have a gathering of this size without expecting the worst."

Susan already expected the worst, as in not living to see another sunrise.

"We won't see another sunrise either way," Agnes said. *"Better enjoy this one while I still can."*

I'm so sorry, Agnes. You can't know how much I'll miss you.

"Actually, I do know," she said. *"You've meant a great deal to*

us, but the time for us to move on is nearly here. Which is as it should be."

You sound like Robert.

"I'm okay with that. He's certainly an interesting soul. No telling what'll happen with him next. He might even get to move on himself."

He's certainly earned it, but I'd much rather he stayed.

"We don't always have that choice, do we?"

No, I guess we don't.

* * * *

With Nadia leading the way on her intimidating Triumph, the drive to O'Brien's Tower was accomplished without interference. Seamus and Susan rode with Jillian and Ranjiv in the Range Rover, with Cleona and Kevan following in Kevan's car. Several other motorcycles flanked the vehicles—more like a biker gang escort than the sort provided by the local police.

Susan peered out the window at the road ahead. The way was clear, but she could barely see the ground on either side for all the people milling about.

"Everyone in Ireland must be out there on the cliffs," Jillian remarked, echoing her thoughts.

"Not all of them are Irish," Ranjiv said. "You'd expect plenty of Brits and a few French since they're the closest. But I spoke with people from all over the world—and just about every religion you've ever heard of."

He was right. While most of the crowd wore western-style clothing, Susan caught the occasional glimpse of colorful saris, as well as Middle Eastern and African attire. Religious garb could also be seen scattered throughout the teeming mass of humanity, including the characteristic orange robes of Buddhist monks.

Susan felt a stab of anxiety. "You don't suppose the Dalai Lama is here, do you?"

"Didn't see him," Ranjiv replied. "But it wouldn't surprise me if he were to show up. He's been quoted as saying that the world would be saved by Western women."

"The Pope is a rather progressive fellow as well," Jillian said.

"Do you think he might…"

"Oh, God." Susan leaned forward cupping her forehead in her hands. "Somebody wake me when it's over."

Seamus patted her on the back. "I doubt either of them will come. It's too much of a security risk. This is a big enough risk for you. Good thing we've got Nadia's gang looking out for your safety."

Susan groaned. "One of the great ironies of our time. Being protected by a team of assassins while we're trying to save the world."

Jillian chuckled. "Takes one assassin to spot another."

* * * *

Seamus might've expected a few catcalls, hoots, and whistles when they arrived at the tower, but the crowd was eerily silent as they got out of their cars. The background noise the motorcycles had provided was gone now. The only sounds he heard were the crash of waves on the rocks below and the occasional cry of the gulls.

The weather forecast had been correct this time—clear skies, relatively calm seas, and—strangely—very little wind. Almost as though Earth herself was holding her breath in anticipation.

Like most people living near a major tourist attraction, Seamus had seldom visited the cliffs, and he hadn't climbed to the top of O'Brien's Tower since childhood. The barren loneliness the cliffs evoked had been something to avoid in the years since Christina's death. He didn't enjoy viewing them from the sea either. They were a breathtaking sight, to be sure, but the aura of sadness and regret he felt whenever he looked at them overwhelmed their majestic natural beauty.

Perhaps he could see them differently now, tied as they were not only to this event but to the rescue of the woman at his side. Ahead, Kevan and Ranjiv escorted Cleona and Jillian up the stone steps of the tower. What seemed the strangest when they reached the top was that there was no commentator or master of ceremonies waiting for them. The winner's circle at the Irish Derby would've been teeming with video cameras and microphones, but the tower was completely empty, save for the attendant at the entrance who'd taken their admission fee, just as he would have done on any given Saturday.

Susan had often vacillated between determination and reluctance, and she'd held his arm during the climb to the top as though in need of his support. But now, she walked to the eastern edge with her head held high, the light breeze feathering her ginger hair. He'd laughed earlier when she'd wondered what she should wear. "What *does* one wear when they're trying to save the world?" she'd asked.

He'd left it to her discretion, but he doubted anyone could've chosen better. She wore the clothes she'd been given in Inisheer on the day of the crash—a gray woolen skirt and an emerald-green Aran sweater. Cleona and Jillian had done the same, seemingly without consulting one another.

A glance at his watch proved their timing had been excellent.

The time is now, Susan.

"I'm surprised to see so many of you here today," Susan began in a strong, clear voice. "I can only assume that, like me, you're concerned with the path humankind has been following for so long. Like me, you hope for change. And not just any change, but a change for the better.

"Earth has been trying to warn us of the consequences of our callous disregard for her and the life she supports. The scarred land quakes beneath our feet, and storms wreak havoc from the sky above us. Our brethren in the sea have also felt the pain of our arrogance, but they have been powerless to stop us."

Seamus dragged his gaze from Susan's slim form to scan the crowd gathered around the tower. Robert had warned him to keep a sharp eye out for trouble, but looking out over the sea of humanity, he felt like an astronomer searching for the one planet with intelligent life amid the billions of stars in the night sky.

That is, until movement caught his eye, and he spotted Nadia threading her way through the crowd with a desperate urgency that instantly sharpened his senses. Following the direction of her progress, he zeroed in on her target: A rather innocuous-looking man dressed in a gray suit who was in the process of drawing a handgun from his jacket.

Time slowed to a crawl, distorting Susan's voice like a recording played on the lowest speed. As though his eyes had the power of a zoom lens, distance shortened. He could see the gun being leveled, the finger squeezing the trigger, the eye squinting as the shooter took aim. Nadia was getting close, but not close enough to stop him in time.

Without another thought, Seamus lunged at Susan, not caring if he knocked her down as long as she was safe.

Her startled cry coincided with a searing pain on the top of his head.

He staggered forward, a red haze clouding his vision as he fell.

* * * *

Susan's reaction was swift and merciless. As others scurried to Seamus's aid, the barrel of the gun flashed again, and she swept her hand toward the assailant. The long arm of the sea followed her movements, capturing the assassin even before Nadia could force her way through the crowd to reach him. Closing her fist, Susan raised her hand and the column of water followed suit, the evil man dangling helplessly from the ring of water that held him aloft. His weapon fell to the ground, and Nadia retrieved it. Two Garda officers seemed to materialize from nowhere, handcuffs at the ready, yet gaping at the spectacle above them as though afraid to intervene.

"Make no further attempts to stop the flow of events," Susan shouted. "Gaia grows weary of the assault humankind has perpetrated against her and those who would champion her cause."

Unclenching her fist, she allowed the terrified man to fall, screaming, to the ground. As the tube of water receded back into the sea, the guards quickly handcuffed the cowering criminal, although they seemed reluctant to haul him away.

"Stay then, and let him listen," Susan said. "For he is among those who most need to hear Mother Earth's message."

Susan looked about her. Seamus was clearly conscious, although blood stained his brown hair until it rivaled the color of her own. No one else appeared to be injured.

One of the medics Ranjiv had stationed on the tower pressed a pad of gauze to the wound. The man was clearly shaken by the violent turn of events, but he gave her a quick thumbs-up as she knelt down beside Seamus.

"I'm okay, luv," Seamus whispered. "'Twas naught but a graze."

She cupped his cheek, wiping away the trickle of blood that ran down the side of his face. "If he'd killed you, I—"

"Don't waste any thoughts on that," he said. "You've got bigger fish to fry."

She leaned closer and kissed him as a hero should be kissed, then rose slowly to her feet. As she walked back toward the eastern rim of the tower, she suddenly realized the one thing they'd neglected to consider when addressing a crowd of this magnitude.

"Damn," she whispered to Jillian, who hovered by her side. "I should at least have a bullhorn or a microphone. Why didn't we think of that?"

"Not a problem," Jillian said with a nod. "Cleona and I, we got this."

She grasped Cleona's hand, and together they moved in behind Susan, placing their free hands on each of her shoulders. When Susan spoke again, her voice boomed out over the astonished people assembled there, amplified a hundredfold.

"Listen to me now," she said. "Your lives and the lives of your children depend upon your actions. For there will come a time when money will not buy your safety. Guns will not protect you. Prayers and promises will not appease Mother Earth's righteous anger toward you. The retribution will be unlike any catastrophe our kind has ever seen before. The human race will perish, opening the way for the rise of a new dominant species, one that will hopefully be more intelligent than our own. Our evolution took millions of years, yet our civilization only began some fifty thousand years ago. Earth is four and a half billion years old. We are but a tiny blip in her history. She will not miss us when we are gone. We will go the way of the dinosaurs, and Earth will not look back on our reign with favor. We have exploited and abused her when we should have been living with her in harmony. Now, she is giving us one last chance to prove our worthiness to survive."

Turning seaward, she held her hands above her head with her palms pressed together. "Behold, the power of Gaia, our Water Planet." She lowered her hands slowly, slicing downward through the air.

She didn't even have to look over the cliff to see her effect upon the sea beyond the cliffs. The startled gasps and muted cries of the onlookers were proof enough. Some even screamed as the ocean parted like an enormous block of gelatin.

As she spread her hands apart, the rift in the water widened, extending further from the rocky shore until it reached the wreckage of the doomed airliner. The broken, twisted fuselage and the mangled remnants of the wings that had been torn from it during the dive to the ocean floor were now exposed for all to see.

"Look now at what greed has done. Then look at what our Earth has given us. Our blessed Mother Earth. The planet that gave us life"—she glanced at Seamus—"and love. If we continue along our present path, our destruction is certain. We have the tools and the knowledge to make our Earth into the paradise it should have been from the very beginning. Why haven't we used it? The only motives are greed, which is perhaps the worst reason of all, and hatred for those whose only crime is to be different from ourselves.

"Go now and cast aside your hatred and your greed. Remember the power of Gaia, for there is enough here for all. Our ancestors are crying out to us, their descendants, to make the right choice. To rescue and protect our beloved Earth so that future generations can benefit from her beauty and her bounty."

Susan brought her palms together, and the ocean waters slid noiselessly back into place. Waves crashed against the base of the cliffs as they had always done, and a pair of seagulls circled briefly overhead, crying out as they flew westward over the Atlantic, taking Susan's stowaways with them.

In the waters above the final resting place of those who died aboard Oceanus Flight 2324, a solitary humpback whale breached, its white underside catching the sunlight in a blinding flash before disappearing once more into the depths of the sea.

Chapter 33

SUSAN STAGGERED WITH THE PAIN OF THE STOWAWAYS' DEPARTURE. Gripping the edge of the stone balustrade, she gazed out over the sparkling sea. "Good bye," she whispered. "Wherever you've gone, I hope you find peace and happiness waiting for you."

"They've left you, have they?" Seamus asked as he came up close beside her.

She replied with an absent nod, then spun around to face him, her hands planted firmly on her hips. "You shouldn't be up walking around with a bullet wound in your head," she snapped. "What am I going to do with you?"

He responded with a contrite shrug. "Marry me, I suppose. After all, I've taken a bullet for you." A broad grin replaced his sheepish expression. "You'll *have* to marry me now."

"Don't be ridiculous," she scolded. "I'd have married you anyway, and you know it. And I'd have been much happier if no bullets were involved."

"I'm glad to hear it." He planted a firm kiss on her cheek. "Wouldn't want to make a habit of catching them for you. But just so you know, I'd do it again in a heartbeat."

"I hope you never have to." She reached up and touched his bandage with a gentle fingertip. "It really messes up your hair."

"Aye. I'll have a permanent part, courtesy of that gun-toting lummox. No doubt the guards will have him locked up all right and tight soon enough. Although the look on poor Cian's face just now is one I'll cherish for the rest of my life."

She frowned. "Cian?"

"Me mate from the station in Lisdoonvarna. You remember him, don't you?"

"I...yeah," she said. "I remember him." *Vaguely.* For the life of her, she couldn't recall how long ago they'd visited the station. That and other recent events had already begun to merge into one jumbled-up, barely believable mass, making her very glad she'd written everything down up to this point. No doubt the mild disorientation she felt was due to the loss of her stowaways. At least, she hoped that was all it was. She'd have to ask Cleona and Jillian to be sure. No one else could have possibly known, and Elliott the Shrink was gone.

"Cian's the one who cuffed that curst eejit after you dropped him on his arse. Wish I'd seen that," he added wistfully. "Surely *someone* was taking photos. Happen they'll show up on the telly before long."

Seamus's brogue seemed thicker than usual. While this might have simply been due to high spirits, he had also just been shot in the head. "Are you *sure* that was only a graze? Maybe we should get you to a hospital."

"The medic said the bullet barely scraped the top of my head— got more hair than scalp—but that scalp wounds tend to bleed more than most. I'll go for x-rays later if you like, but right now, I'm more for heading off to the pub. Helping save the world has given me the devil of an appetite."

"It hasn't been that long since we had breakfast." She glanced at her watch. "I mean, it's not even eight o'clock yet."

"Time for second breakfast, then," he said, taking her by the arm. "Come on, m'dear. I do believe a bit of celebration is in order."

* * * *

Seamus reckoned without the sea of humanity awaiting them at the bottom of the tower steps. "Blimey," he exclaimed. "I doubt we'll get a seat in a pub anywhere between here and Dublin."

"Not even in Quinn's?" Susan asked.

"We'd have to hurry to beat the rush, although, as you said, it's only just going on eight. Even so, I should think I'd get preferred seating, what with being the proprietor's son and getting shot and all."

Susan threaded her arm through his. "I'm more worried about getting to the car."

"Keep walking," Nadia said from behind them. "I believe everyone will move out of the way. If not, I will go ahead and clear your path. I failed you before," she added grimly. "I will not fail you now."

Seamus turned to face her. "You didn't fail us. If I hadn't seen you going after that bloke, I'd never have seen him in time."

Nadia shook her head. "Your lives should never have been at risk. We were here to prevent such an occurrence. But the message was delivered, so I must be content with that." She hesitated, frowning. "No. I am *not* content. I have done good works in recent years, but they cannot atone for what I have done in the past."

"Which means?" Seamus was fairly certain he knew the answer; nevertheless, he felt the question had to be asked.

The Russian woman stood ramrod straight, the set of her jaw illustrating her resolve. "I will confess to the murders I have committed."

"I was afraid of that," Susan said sadly. "We'd be happy to put in a good word for you if you think it would help."

"No," Nadia said. "I cannot go on living free when so many lives were cut short because I lacked the courage to resist. I have found that courage now. Never again will I take a life."

"But your family?" Susan's voice broke with emotion as her eyes filled with tears. "What about them?"

"I think—that is, I *know*—the tide has turned. There will be changes within my country's government. I do not believe my family will be at risk any longer. My superiors have nothing to gain if I have already been imprisoned for my crimes."

"Got a lot to lose, though," Seamus reminded her.

Nadia smiled. "They have already lost." With a nod, she moved on ahead to clear the way, but her intervention probably wasn't necessary. No one pressed forward attempting to shake Susan's hand or grovel at her feet—kissing the hem of her robes, as it were. Rather, they stood back in awe and allowed her to pass unhindered.

"The way things are going, we might get a seat at the pub after all," Seamus said when they reached Ranjiv's car.

"I suspect anyone in the pub would be more than willing to give up their table for the Bringer of Justice," Ranjiv said as he and Jillian approached.

Although he was obviously joking, Susan replied as though he'd been perfectly serious. "None of that crap," she insisted. "My part has been played. No one has anything to gain by doing favors for me. I have nothing to give them. From now on, I'm just plain old me."

"You're sure about that?" Jillian asked. "No residual power or conversations with the whales?"

"Nothing at the moment," Susan replied. "Besides, I don't think we'll need those powers anymore. The message was pretty clear, although I'm not sure how far-reaching the effects will be. I guess we'll just have to wait and see." She heaved a sigh. "Dunno about you guys, but I could really use a cup of tea—an entire pot, actually."

"If we can't find room at the pub, we'll go on home," Seamus said. "Seems a bit anti-climactic, though—wouldn't you say?" Seamus was all for tuning up his banjo and playing until his fingers bled. He'd had the same feeling each time he'd narrowly escaped a watery North Atlantic grave. Unlike those who'd survived while others perished, no trace of guilt existed to detract from the simple joy of being alive and in one piece. This time was even more joyous because he could share that feeling with the woman he loved.

Even if he did have a bit of a headache.

Susan was about to climb into the Range Rover when she drew back and glanced around her. "Has anyone seen Robert this morning? I assumed he would be here, but I haven't seen him."

"I haven't left you yet," Robert said, popping up behind her like a feckin' leprechaun. Seamus had been staring right at Susan when she'd questioned the old man's whereabouts, and unless Robert had been crouched behind the car, he truly had materialized out of thin air.

Susan let out a startled yelp and spun around to face the old man. "Don't do that! You almost gave me a coronary."

Robert chuckled. "Dying of a heart attack now would be the ultimate irony, don't you think?" He glanced at the milling crowd, which was already beginning to thin slightly, then touched his cap as he acknowledged each of the women in turn. "Well done, ladies— and quite a good turnout too. Here and everywhere."

Cleona frowned. "What on earth do you mean by that?"

"Ah, that would be telling," he said with an enigmatic smile. "You'll see soon enough." He turned away again, gazing off toward the southeast, then gave a short nod as though he'd made a decision. "Believe I'll stop in at St. Brigid's Well on me way home and talk over old times. She was always a right one, was Brigid." He smiled at the group. "You lot take care now." With a tip of his cap and a wave of farewell, he started off down the road toward Liscannor.

Cleona stared after him until the elderly sexton was out of earshot. "He's old enough to have known St. Brigid?" She looked at Seamus, her eyes wide with bewilderment. "How old does that make him?"

"I have absolutely no idea," Seamus replied. He scratched gingerly at the site of his wound, which had already begun to itch. "Let's have that tea, shall we? I'm feeling fair parched."

* * * *

Quinn's Pub was more crowded than Susan had ever seen it, but she didn't care. She was among her new friends and neighbors, people she would grow to know and love as time went on.

A cheer went up when they entered. Lorna and Enid came rushing up to Seamus, fussing over him and shooing a young couple from their table so he could sit down.

Placing her hands on his shoulders, Lorna forced her son into a chair. "Seamus, Seamus," she muttered as she studied the bandage on his head. "You nearly lost your feckin' brains." She drew back, squeezing her eyes shut. "Can't think about that now." She opened her eyes, bent down, and hugged him. "Such a hero you were!"

Seamus's face was nearly as red as the blood in his hair. "You saw that? How the devil did you get back here ahead of us?"

"Live video stream," Enid said, holding up her phone. "Did you really think something like that wouldn't be shared?"

"I guess not."

Enid turned toward Susan, her brown eyes sparkling with

excitement. "Even without the video, we could hear every word you were saying. Just as clearly as if we'd been up there by the cliffs."

Susan smiled. "We have Jillian and Cleona to thank for that. Freaked me out a little at first. I should've expected it, though—especially after those 'stone tower' conversations Cleona and I used to have." She aimed "The Look" at her two friends. "You might've warned me."

"We couldn't let you have all the fun," Jillian said with a chuckle. "Although I wish I could've seen your expression when you started talking. Might have to check out one of the videos after while."

"You can see it now," Ranjiv said. He stood a little apart from the others, peering at his phone. "The news wires are lit up like you wouldn't believe. CEOs, military leaders, and corrupt politicians all over the world are confessing to some of the worst atrocities you can imagine—including your plane crash and the university bombing that killed Kevan's parents."

Susan gaped at him. "How could all that happen so soon?"

"Partly because of your speech and partly because they're scared out of their wits." Ranjiv paused, shaking his head. "I had to wonder how all those ghosts you ladies saw at the fort on Inishmore would help, but they seem to have taken to haunting the bad guys."

"You're not serious!" Jillian exclaimed.

"Oh, but I am," he insisted. "And another thing…" He pulled Jillian into his embrace for a congratulatory kiss—at least, Susan *assumed* it was congratulatory—then nodded toward Cleona. "These ladies have a pretty amazing connection with Mother Earth. Seems that when they amplified your voice, it was heard all over the world, literally ringing out from towers and mountaintops. Not only that, it was translated. People who didn't speak a word of English understood you perfectly."

Susan was glad she'd been sitting down. "All over the world?" Even without amplification, her voice came out an octave or two higher than usual. She clapped a hand to her mouth, taking several deep breaths before attempting to speak again. "We did it," she whispered. "We really and truly did it."

"Guess I should be getting back to my sheep, then," Kevan said. "Can't expect Cleona's uncle to look after them forever."

"By the way, Kevan," Ranjiv began. "I've been meaning to tell you...I've heard from my editor, and apparently the climatology community is showing considerable interest in your idea to use mirrors to reflect the sun's rays to help reduce global warming."

"Wasn't my idea," Kevan insisted. "I'm no scientist. The idea just popped into my head, and I'm pretty sure it was put there by the professor who died in the bombing along with my parents. Cleona only included it in her statement because of the way we shared the souls in the Array."

"Doesn't matter," Ranjiv said. "Whoever had the idea to begin with never published his theory. So it looks as if you'll be the one to get the credit. Not sure it's all that practical, but the idea may still be useful in some form or another. Better we try everything than leave it until it's too late."

Kevan still seemed unconvinced. "Do you really think correcting our climate will require such drastic measures?"

Ranjiv shrugged. "Who knows? It'll probably take a combination of approaches to make much of a difference. But what matters most is the willingness to even acknowledge the existence of the problem." He looked at Susan. "What you did out there today was incontrovertible evidence that our opinions aren't the only ones that matter."

Cleona nodded. "Gaia is angry with us. We must work together to regain her trust. It may take years, but what choice do we have?"

"None, if we want our species to survive," Jillian said. "If we destroy the environment until we can no longer live here, Earth will recover. We won't. She'll still be here, orbiting the sun long after we're gone."

"Unless we're very, very careful from here on out," Susan said. "We've done our best to set humankind on the right path. Hopefully, the lessons learned today won't be forgotten. But if they ever are, perhaps Earth will choose others to deliver the message again someday." She sighed. "And humankind will ignore that message at their peril."

Seamus took her hand and kissed it, reminding her of the one of the greatest joys of being human. "For myself, I don't believe there'll be another message. This was our final warning, our last and only chance for survival."

"I hope it's enough."

"Only time will tell," he said. "And now that you've done your part to save mankind from its own folly, what would you like to do now?"

She squeezed his hand. From beginning to end, he was the common thread, the tie that bound her to a fate she'd never asked for and certainly never expected. He was also her reward. "I just want to go home."

"And would that home be in Newark or Cahilly?"

"Doesn't matter," she replied. "As long as you're with me, I can live anywhere."

Seamus smiled. "Well, what do you know? The world is looking better already."

About the Author

A native of Louisville, Kentucky, Cheryl Brooks is a former critical care nurse who resides in rural Indiana with her husband, two sons, two horses, three cats, and one dog. Her **Cat Star Chronicles** series was first published by Sourcebooks Casablanca in 2008, and includes *Slave, Warrior, Rogue, Outcast, Fugitive, Hero, Virgin, Stud, Wildcat*, and *Rebel*. Her **Cowboy Heaven** series, also published by Sourcebooks Casablanca, includes *Cowboy Delight* (a novella), *Cowboy Heaven*, and *Must Love Cowboys*. Look for her new **Cat Star Legacy** series from Sourcebooks beginning in 2018. In addition to the **Soul Survivors** trilogy, *Echoes From the Deep, Dreams From the Deep*, and *Justice From the Deep*, she has one self-published erotic romance, *Sex, Love, and a Purple Bikini*, and two erotic short stories, *Midnight in Reno*, and *Pontoon*. Her **Unlikely Lovers** series includes *Unbridled, Uninhibited, Undeniable*, and *Unrivaled*. She has also published *If You Could Read My Mind* writing as Samantha R. Michaels. As a member of *The Sextet*, she has written several erotic novellas published by Siren/Bookstrand. Her other interests include cooking, gardening, singing, and guitar playing. Cheryl is a member of RWA and IRWA. You can visit her online at www.cherylbrooksonline.com or email her at cheryl.brooks52@yahoo.com

www.ingramcontent.com/pod-product-compliance
Lightning Source LLC
Chambersburg PA
CBHW071246170626
46809CB00001B/97